Praise for *Sc*

"With brilliant sexual ch[...] riveting action, and flawle[...] mann's latest quickly draws readers back into her high-stakes Troubleshooters world. . . . Beautifully written and as heart-gripping as it is satisfying."
—*Library Journal* (starred review)

"Well worth the wait. Jam-packed with adrenaline-fueled action and sizzling sexual tension, this is grade-A romantic suspense that will delight RITA award-winning Brockmann's dedicated core of fans as well, and lure new readers." —*Booklist* (starred review)

"Brockmann brings her typical storytelling virtuosity to this new setting and also delves into the dark history of the Japanese internment during World War II and subtly comments on domestic abuse as well as society's continuing racial prejudices through the characters' experiences. A thought-provoking, deeply satisfying romance from a master of the genre."
—*Kirkus Reviews* (starred review)

"Brockmann's reliably sexy Troubleshooters contemporary romantic thriller series continues with this fun, vivid seventeenth installment. . . . As always, Brockmann excels at depicting both lusty lovemaking and the genuine camaraderie of friendship." —*Publishers Weekly*

By Suzanne Brockmann

TROUBLESHOOTERS SERIES

FIGHTING DESTINY SERIES

SUNRISE KEY SERIES

OTHER BOOKS

SOME KIND OF HERO

SUZANNE BROCKMANN

SOME KIND OF HERO

A TROUBLESHOOTERS NOVEL

BALLANTINE BOOKS • NEW YORK

2018 Ballantine Books Mass Market Edition

Copyright © 2017 by Suzanne Brockmann

All rights reserved.

Published in the United States by Ballantine Books, an imprint of
Random House, a division of Random House LLC,
a Penguin Random House Company, New York.

BALLANTINE and the HOUSE colophon are
registered trademarks of Random House LLC.

Originally published in hardcover in the United States by
Ballantine Books, an imprint of Random House, a division of
Random House LLC, in 2017.

ISBN 978-0-345-54384-4
eBook ISBN 978-0-345-54383-7

Cover images: © Claudio Marinesco (SEAL photo); Steve Skinner
Photography/Moment/Getty Images (background)

Printed in the United States of America

randomhousebooks.com

2   4   6   8   9   7   5   3   1
Ballantine Books mass market edition: February 2018

For the die-hard fans—readers and writers alike—of my beloved romance genre. Your relentless belief in the power of love makes this crazy world a kinder, more hopeful place.

SOME KIND OF HERO

CHAPTER ONE

Wednesday

Wait, wasn't that the Navy SEAL?

Yes, the man who was frantically waving his arms at the side of the road, trying to flag down one of the swiftly passing cars in the rapidly deepening twilight, was—absolutely—Shayla's new neighbor.

She recognized him immediately, even here, several miles from their semi-suburban neighborhood, mostly from his impossibly fit physique.

Oh, really . . . ?

Yeah, okay, all right, in truth she recognized the SEAL specifically by his amazing ass. And sue her for being human, but when a man had a pair of shoulders *that* wide and a butt that was almost ridiculously proportionately *not*-that-wide . . . one's eyes tended to be drawn instinctively down toward that seemingly miraculous not-wideness.

Truly though, it was the combo of what was covering that noteworthy derrière—a pair of very nicely fitting camo cargo shorts—plus his trademark flip-flops with a snug olive drab T-shirt that had brought about her initial surge of recognition. She confirmed it—yup, that was definitely her local Navy SEAL—when he turned a head that was covered with regulation-defyingly shaggy, sun-streaked golden-brown hair to reveal his too-handsome face.

Those eyes *had* to be blue.

Even though he'd moved into Shayla's neighborhood nearly two months ago, she still hadn't gotten close enough to the man to be absolutely certain, but really, she knew. Neon blue. Had to be. And they probably twinkled and sparkled, too.

Still, even from a sparkle-obscuring distance, the man was hard to miss. And Shay's curiosity had pinged when he'd pulled a U-Haul in front of the sweet little bungalow-for-rent across the street and her elderly and possibly omnipotent neighbor Mrs. Quinn had muttered, "Just what we need, as if it weren't already too noisy here," before darkly IDing him as a Navy SEAL.

Navy SEAL, hmm? So yes, Shayla had looked at him and his perfect butt a tad more thoroughly than she otherwise might've.

Tonight however, the man was hard to miss for another reason. He'd practically leapt full out into the middle of the oncoming traffic—and there was a lot more of it than usual for a Wednesday evening near the high school.

Shayla hit her brakes and leaned forward slightly to peer at him through her windshield, wondering if he'd been attempting to stop that one specific car in front of her, or if any old car and driver would do.

Bow chicka bow bow! Harry Parker's irreverent voice-in-her-head now sang a riff that was supposed to imitate the porn-worthy wah-wah of an electric guitar.

Shut it, she told him silently since he was a fictional character and therefore invisible, and she wasn't *quite* crazy enough to start talking to herself out loud. At least not yet.

And apparently, the SEAL wasn't picky, because he didn't

wait for her to stop completely before he tried to open her passenger side door.

"I'm sorry, can you help me, I'm not dangerous, I promise," he called to her through the closed window, but she was already hitting the button that popped the lock.

It was pretty clear he didn't recognize her—probably because she'd never gotten around to bringing over a pie to welcome him, his sullen teenaged daughter, and their obvious lack of a Mrs. Navy SEAL to the neighborhood.

That was what Harry, in his infinite-yet-fictional wisdom, had recommended Shayla do. Wear a top with a neckline that plunged and bring her hot new Navy SEAL neighbor a homemade pie. It was a brilliant plan, except nearly all of her tops were crew-necked Ts. And then there was that tiny, pesky fact that she'd never baked a pie before in her life.

"I'm a SEAL, an officer." It was the first thing the man said as he opened her car door and climbed in. He obviously understood the clout of that, particularly here in U.S.-NavyLand, or as civilians called it, San Diego. "Lieutenant Peter Greene. Thank you for stopping."

"You're welcome," Shayla said, oddly tongue-tied at their sudden proximity. Her small car seemed smaller than usual because those shoulders were *broad*. And his movie-star handsomeness stood up to this closer view. In fact, his evenly featured face could've gone into the dictionary next to *perfectly symmetrical*. Or maybe just plain *perfect*. Also, he smelled good. Like sunblock and fresh air and a scent she assumed was pure Navy SEAL hotness.

Even Harry was uncharacteristically silent.

And alas, even though she'd spent her career writing books where this kind of impromptu meet-cute would end with them having screaming animal-sex before the clock struck midnight, Shayla wasn't as bold as her romance novel heroines. She didn't look all that much like them, either. In fact, she was lucky that she'd showered and put on real pants before she'd crawled away from her computer in order to drive-and-drop Frankie at his high school debate club practice. Most of the time she just climbed into her car from the safety of the shuttlebay—aka their closed garage—wearing her plaid PJs beneath her jacket.

She cleared her throat and managed, "What's, um, going on? Are you okay?"

But he was already talking. Explaining. "My daughter is missing, and I think I just saw her getting into a car heading north." He gestured to the busy road in front of them.

Missing.

With two kids of her own, that was a word to chill her to the very depths of her soul. Shayla could still work herself into a cold sweat by remembering that horrible day Tevin had gone on a class day-trip into Boston, but hadn't been on the bus when it returned to the middle school parking lot. That was when they were still living back in Massachusetts, and it turned out that he'd run into his father near the State House. Tevin had stayed in the city to have dinner—and both he and Carter, now her ex, had wrongly assumed the other would call to tell her. Neither had.

Before Shayla had located the teacher who knew what was going on, it had been a *very* frightening few minutes—the likes of which she hoped she'd never again experience.

Now she immediately jammed her car into gear and surged back into the traffic amidst the blaring horns of the drivers she'd cut off.

"Whoa," the SEAL said, quickly fastening his seat belt. "Wow. Thank you."

"This *is* what you wanted, right? *Follow that car?*" she asked as she jockeyed her way into the faster-moving left lane. Funny how that horrible word, *missing,* had magically turned him from too-hot-to-talk-to Navy SEAL to far more accessible worried dad. *Hot* worried dad, sure, but he needed both her help and immediate action, and accordingly her brain had unlocked. "Don't worry, I'm a good driver."

She really is. Great. Harry, too, had gotten his voice back.

Of course, the SEAL couldn't hear him, thank God. "Glad to hear it," he said as he grabbed for the oh-shit bar, which, yes, made his muscular arm do some very interesting and attractive things to his barbed-wire tattoo. Maybe it would help if she imagined those strong arms holding a baby, except . . .

Noooo, that doesn't help at all, Harry said.

Harry was married. *Very* married, to the man of his dreams, she thought pointedly.

He laughed. *True, but I'm also* very *not dead, so . . .*

Shayla hip-checked him out of her head and focused on the task at hand. "Which car are we following?" she asked the SEAL crisply, eyes on the road ahead of her. "Make, model, color . . . ?"

"Maroon sedan. Buick, maybe?" said the real, nonfictional man sitting beside her. His voice had the vowel sounds and musical phrasing of a California surfer. In fact, he sounded a little bit like Luke or Owen Wilson, as if maybe they'd all attended the same SoCal high school. "Older model. Extra large. POS with a peeling soft-top. Don't stop don't stop *don't stop!*"

As she watched, the very stale yellow traffic light in front of her turned red, but she jammed down the gas pedal and blasted through it. *Missing.* If they got pulled over, hopefully the cop would be the parent of a teenager, too.

"How long has your daughter been, you know?" She couldn't say that awful word, as if it were a snake that might bite her if she acknowledged it.

"Missing?" The SEAL said it in unison with Harry.

"Last time I saw Maddie was yesterday morning," the SEAL added, "when I dropped her at school. She didn't come home last night, and when I called the school to check today, apparently she didn't make it to homeroom yesterday either, so . . . Yeah. It's been about thirty-six hours. Jesus."

"They didn't call you yesterday when she didn't show?" Shayla was surprised. She glanced over to find him looking back at her just as the headlights from a passing car lit his face. Eyes, neon blue. Check. But not so much with the twinkle, considering his current case of teenaged-daughter-induced grim.

"They said they did, but no," the SEAL reported as they both continued to search the traffic for the car in question. "There wasn't a message on the home line *or* my cell."

Yikes. That was pretty extreme incompetence for the high school administration—a dedicated team that Shayla knew and trusted.

Or, Harry said, *Maddie hacked the system and changed her parental contact number.*

"She good with computers?" Shayla asked the SEAL.

"I don't think so," he said.

If she had hacking skills, he'd definitely know, Harry stated. *But really all she'd need is a hacker for a friend. Or boyfriend.*

"How old is she?" Shayla asked. The petite, ghostlike, dark-haired, baggy-clothes-wearing girl she'd seen drifting mournfully from the house to her father's truck early each school day could've been anywhere from twelve to eighteen.

"Fifteen," he reported.

"Mine are seventeen and fourteen," she told him. "Both boys."

"Boys," the SEAL said almost wistfully. "I could probably handle a boy. I understand boys."

"Girls really aren't that much different," Shayla pointed out as Harry said, *Nope, nope, nope, too early in this relationship for a feminist diatribe!*

What relationship? She was helping out a neighbor. And how was *that* a diatribe? Still, all Shayla wanted was to help this man find his missing child, so as she continued to push ahead in the still-thick traffic, she asked the SEAL, "Have you tried tracking her phone? Does she *have* a smartphone?"

"Yes to both but she turned off her GPS."

"Or her battery's run out," she suggested.

"Nah, she took her charger." The SEAL seemed certain of that. But then he acquiesced. "At least it wasn't where she normally keeps it in her room. As far as her phone goes, I texted and called her nonstop last night when she didn't come home—right up until she blocked me. I thought about shutting her down, you know, canceling her number, killing her service completely, but . . . I'm afraid without her phone she'll be even less safe, so . . ."

Ooh, he's a deep thinker. No angry knee-jerking. I like that in a man who can probably kill you with just his pinkie finger, Harry said.

"Also," the SEAL continued as he glanced at Shayla again with those ocean-colored eyes, "this way I can still use someone else's phone to text her. Although she's already blocked Zanella—a teammate of mine, *and* Eden, his wife. But I figure Maddie can't block everyone I know, right? *There!*"

He'd spotted the maroon car. "Where?" Shayla searched the traffic but she couldn't see it.

"Five cars ahead, right lane," the SEAL told her. "Damn it, they're turning!"

And she was still in the left lane. "Hold on!" Luckily there was no one directly behind her so she hit the brakes hard and waited for the line of traffic in the right lane to open up before stomping on the gas and taking that same right turn with squealing tires.

"Nice," he said. "Thanks. You *are* good."

"If your daughter's in that car, then we *are* going to find her." It was the kind of dramatic but heartfelt line that Shayla usually let Harry say in one of her books. It felt a little weird coming out of her mouth since, unlike Harry, she was neither courageous nor daring nor a highly skilled FBI agent. But she meant it. Sincerely.

She could now see the car in question. It *was* indeed a piece of shit, or POS, as the lieutenant had said—a barge-like relic from the 1970s. There were two cars and a van between them, but this was a smaller road with a single lane in each direction. And there was a lot of oncoming traffic. Although maybe if she timed it right . . .

"Don't even think about it," the SEAL murmured. "No one's that good of a driver. Also, I don't want to get too close in case she sees me and tries to bolt. All I need is some inexperienced kid wrapping that car—and Maddie—around a tree."

Smart, Harry murmured as Shay nodded. *Have I mentioned I like him?*

"Have you tried calling the parents of her friends?" she asked as they continued their now under-the-speed-limit car chase through this rather charming little neighborhood of tiny homes that had been converted into doctors' and dentists' offices, nearly all dark and shuttered at this evening hour. They were relatively close to the hospital and . . . the mall? She touched the screen of her GPS to see that . . . Yes, there was a mall not far from here—open until nine at this time of year. If she were a fifteen-year-old rebel, mad at the world, where would *she* go at 7:10 on a Wednesday night . . . ?

She glanced up at the SEAL, because he hadn't answered and her question hadn't been a hard one.

He was looking at her again with those blue, blue eyes, and he finally shook his head. "I'm embarrassed because . . .

Well, I don't even know the *first* names of any of her friends, let alone their last names."

Shayla couldn't keep her massively heavy judgment out of the disbelieving look she shot him.

"I know, right?" he said with a heavy sigh. "It's shameful. But, she just moved in with me so she's the new kid at school, and she's in classes with kids way younger than she is because her mom *half-home-schooled her*—Maddie's words. I think that means her mother let her cut as the mood struck. Anyway, whenever I push, all Maddie tells me is *Everyone hates me, I'll be in my room.* And every time I picked her up at school, she was alone, so . . . When she said she didn't have any friends yet, I believed her."

"Except, if she's really in that car up there, she knows *some*one," Shay stated the obvious.

"Yeah, that's currently pretty damn clear. Jesus, I'm over-matched." And now his pretty eyes *were* twinkly, but with bemused disgust and disbelief as he glanced at Shay before turning his attention back to the maroon POS, and a yellow traffic light that was glowing in the distance.

Congestion at that upcoming intersection was what was keeping their current speed down.

The yellow turned to red and Shay braked to a stop behind the long line of cars as she again checked her GPS. There was a gas station on the closest corner of the inter-section and some kind of fast food place across the street. That could be the car's destination. Although, if they were going to the mall instead, they would have to take a right at the light. But they were still well back from it.

The SEAL, meanwhile, was eyeing their distance to the maroon sedan, and she knew he was calculating the time it would take for him to approach it on foot, and deciding whether he could get there before traffic started moving again.

"Have you checked her social media?" Shay asked as up

ahead the light turned green. But seconds ticked by and the traffic still didn't move and the SEAL swore softly, no doubt thinking he could've reached the other car by now. "As a potential source of her friends' names? Maybe Facebook . . . ?"

He shook his head. "Maddie hates Facebook. She says she doesn't even have a page. . . ." He laughed his disgust. "And yeah, that was probably an intentional misdirect so that I wouldn't keep tabs on her," he realized. "Wow, I'm really going for Father of the Year here, aren't I?"

Shayla glanced at him again as they finally rolled forward, but slowly, since the light ahead was already red again. She chose her words carefully. "I'm guessing your stints of solo custody are still new, Lieutenant." Subtext: the divorce was recent.

He laughed again at that and said, "Oh, yeah." And now the maroon sedan was in range of a side street to the left that it could use to escape, so again he stayed in the car. But his frustration was palpable. "*Very* new. And it's Peter."

She realized she hadn't introduced herself yet. "I'm Shayla Whitman. We're neighbors." She kept both hands tightly on the steering wheel because a handshake at this point would've been awkward and weird. "My boys and I live right across the street from you and Maddie."

The SEAL was embarrassed again. "You do? Ah, Jesus, I'm so sorry—"

"Please, it's more than okay. You've obviously been a little preoccupied since you've moved in." She cleared her throat. "At the risk of overstepping my neighborly role, have you . . . called her mother yet?"

Just like that, he shut down, hard and fast. "No."

Oh, dear. "If it were me," Shayla said carefully, "I'd want to know. I'd want to help, I'd want to—"

"Maddie's mother can't help," he said tersely.

"I know it might feel that way," Shayla started as the cars up ahead began moving. But again the light cycled back to red while the maroon sedan was still on their side of the intersection. It was now signaling to make a right—toward the mall, for the win! But it was blocked from doing so by one car in front of it.

The SEAL—Peter—was sitting forward slightly, watching.

"We're okay," Shayla told him.

"No, we're not," he said as that first car in line started signaling and then made a right on red. "God *damn* it."

And just like that, the maroon sedan turned, too.

The two cars and the van directly in front of Shay's car pulled forward but then sat there, essentially locking them in place just a few short yards from the driveway to that corner gas station.

"Shit!" She hit her horn, but of course no one moved.

Do it. Harry's voice was back in her head, absolute in his conviction. *Come on, Shay. Go! Trust me, you don't want to have to watch while a Navy SEAL weeps. They're known both for acting rashly and for crying like babies, you know, at the least little thing—*

"Don't be an idiot." Oops, she'd said that aloud, and now said Navy SEAL was looking at her questioningly. "Don't," she repeated, saving her crazy, talking-to-invisible-friends ass by returning to their previous conversation. "You really need to let Maddie's mother know what's going on."

Meanwhile, Harry was talking over her. *Do it,* he said again. *There're no pedestrians. Do it, Shay, or you'll lose them!*

"All right, all right, I'm doing this!" There *were* no pedestrians in sight, so Shay wrenched her steering wheel toward the sidewalk and hit the gas. Her little car was unhappy about the curb but it was rounded and worn so she finally humped up it and then carefully squeezed between a telephone pole and a row of hedges as the SEAL exhaled his appreciation and surprise.

But how well would it go, she wondered, when she informed the police officer who pulled her over that she only drove on the sidewalk because a fictional FBI agent had insisted that she should?

Not well, Harry agreed, even as the SEAL said, "You've got it! Go! *Go!*"

Her unorthodox move had brought them to the gas station's entrance, and she now quickly zipped past the pumps to cut the corner and make the right turn to once again *Follow that car.*

It was in the left lane, and she quickly caught up with its ancient taillights. And then, sure enough, they both slowed as the maroon sedan signaled to turn left into the shopping mall's main parking garage.

Don't lose them now, Harry said, again in near unison with the SEAL's "You got this!"

And Shayla did have it. She practically piggybacked the sedan as she also took that left with a squeal of tires. Again, the SEAL chuckled at the blaring horn from the oncoming car that she'd deftly cut off. His hands were up over his face, pressing his forehead as if he had a bad headache. But Shay knew he was hiding in case her noisy turn had caught the attention of the maroon car's occupants.

Stay with them, Harry ordered—a far easier task now, since the speed bumps in the garage kept the ancient sedan well under the posted limit. She followed it past the first LEVEL FULL sign and down a ramp.

The parking places in this garage were tight, as was the case in most city malls in coastal California. Tight and hard to come by. If this were the Natick Mall back in her beloved Massachusetts, the maroon sedan would've already found a spot. But the next level was also full, so they just kept slowly going downward.

Which was exactly where she didn't want to be in earthquake-prone California. In the sub-sub-subbasement of a six-story building. Yay! Still, a missing teenaged daughter trumped her earthquake fears, hands down.

Courage doesn't mean you're not afraid—it's acting in spite of your fear.

Thanks, Hare. "So, how are we doing this, Lieutenant?" Shayla asked briskly. "They park, I block them in? You get out and knock on the window? *Hello, is my daughter in there?*"

"Peter," the SEAL said as they went down yet another freaking level. Finally there was no FULL sign, but there were still no nearby spots. "Wow, I don't know. And, yeah, that's smart, but . . . This could get ugly. You know. Loud? Maybe you should just drop me and go."

Shay's heart sank as she looked at him, trying to figure out if he really was merely attempting to spare her the drama—or if there was something going on that he didn't want her to see.

Everyone was hiding *some*thing, but some secrets were darker than others. Shay had learned *that* lesson a little too well.

Still, she kept her voice light. "And later find out that you're really a serial killer whom I've helped stalk his latest victims?" She followed the maroon sedan slowly past the bank of elevators, where there were still no empty spaces. "I don't think so."

The SEAL gave her a look that screamed *Are you freaking kidding me?* It was pretty clear that this was an officer-to-enlisted look—and no doubt one that had served him well in the past. She, however, was not, nor had she ever been, in the U.S. Navy.

So it bounced off her as she gazed back at him. "I'm a writer, and I've written a lot of serial killer books." It was a good excuse. Easier to use than the truth, which was that she'd seen just how shitty some people could be—even to those they professed to love. Yeah, he seemed like a nice guy. But monsters often hid beneath *nice*. And she'd known him what, now? All of twenty minutes?

"I'm not just going to drop you," she continued. "I've come this far, I might as well drive you and Maddie home. Especially since we're all going in the same direction."

"I'm not going to hit her or hurt her or do whatever other kind of violence you might be imagining," the SEAL said, seeing through her words to the reality of why she wasn't going to just leave him there.

I like him even more now, Harry declared. *He could've played along, but he didn't. That's impressive. You have my permission to have sex with him.*

"Well, that's good to hear," Shay told the SEAL as the maroon sedan kept searching for a parking spot. "But I'm going through a severely mistrustful phase, and it would be irresponsible of me to not verify that you are, in fact, as great of a guy as you appear to be. I have to admit, I'm still struggling with *Why on earth haven't you called her mother?*"

"Maddie's mom is dead," the SEAL told her. "She was killed in a car accident, three months ago."

* * *

Peter knew that he'd screwed up, the moment the too-blunt words left his mouth.

"Oh, no." Shayla-his-neighbor's soft brown eyes widened with shock as she gazed at him from behind the wheel of her progressive-mom-mobile. "Oh my God, Peter, I'm *so* sorry!"

At least she'd finally called him *Peter* instead of *Lieutenant,* but she'd definitely gotten the wrong idea.

He sat there in the front seat of her functional, fuel-efficient little car and realized that he was going to have to explain. And Jesus, he'd already told her so much—things he would never have discussed with a stranger under any other circumstances. He hadn't even told his closest teammates more than a small fraction of the shit that was going down these days with Maddie.

Most of them were still agog at the fact that he had a daughter in the first place.

But this woman—Shayla Whitman, his across-the-street neighbor—had taken a risk not just by stopping for him but by chasing the car he was certain he'd seen Maddie climb into. She deserved honest answers, regardless of how hard it was to talk about this.

"No, *I'm* sorry, I really should've said that earlier," Pete started, "but—"

"Oh my God," Shayla cut him off. "No, Lieutenant, please, I'm the one . . . I didn't even consider . . . I didn't mean to be so freaking insensitive." She was really upset, and he was back to *Lieutenant*. Damn it.

"It's okay, really, you didn't know. I should've said something when you first asked if I'd called her but . . ." He tried to explain. "It just . . . it defines us, you know. Maddie and me. It's exhausting, and I was trying not to let that into the car—if that makes any sense at all."

She reached for his hand, nodding as if she actually understood what he meant. It was weird, because as a general rule, people didn't dare touch him. Well, women sometimes did, but only when he was hanging out in a bar, clearly welcoming an intimate connection.

But Shayla didn't squeeze his hand for very long—there was definitely no sexual subtext in her comfort-from-mommy contact. She even patted him a little as she let him go, saying, "I'm so, *so* sorry for your loss." Her sincerity was off the charts and he found himself not just needing to explain, but actually *wanting* to.

What was up with that?

It was probably because he found her mindblowingly refreshing. When was the last time he'd met a woman who was so honest and real—and not already engaged or married to one of his teammates?

Shayla didn't just *drive* a mom-mobile, she actually *was* a mom, with her curly black hair worn naturally and super-short in—what was it called?—a pixie cut, and a sweet face that was almost completely devoid of makeup. Probably because she was too busy with her crazy mom-life to take the time to put it on.

Not that she wasn't pretty enough without it. She was—in a very G-rated, Disney-movie way. She was wearing jeans and a yellow T-shirt that were meant neither to feature nor conceal her curves. But she hadn't simply dressed for comfort. With her gorgeously rich brown skin, bold colors looked good on her and she obviously knew it—no one wore something in that bright of a hue by accident.

She had lively dark brown eyes and a quick, warm smile in an expressive heart-shaped face. It was the kind of face that gave away everything she was feeling, even when she tried to hide it.

In fact, earlier, she'd shot him one powerful look of vaguely comical disapproval that had amused the crap out of him, mostly due to the fact that in his job not just as a SEAL officer but as a BUD/S instructor, he rarely received that kind of judgment and attitude from anyone.

But he dished it out, all the time.

So yes, even though they'd just met, he already liked her—and that was saying something, since it usually took him years of acquaintanceship before he even considered calling someone a friend.

But right now she was imagining he was recently widowed, and that was far from the case.

"It's really Maddie's loss," Pete told her as the car they were following finally signaled its intention to park.

He scrunched down in his seat, again using his hands to shield his face, because the driver was clearly intending to back into the narrow spot. "I came to terms with mine a long time ago," he said. "Lisa—Maddie's mom—and I split up for good when Maddie was about a year old. Thirteen months and four days and . . ." He'd been at sea for most of those months, and home on leave for less than a week when Lisa had packed the car and left before breakfast, but Shayla really didn't need to know that much detail. "Anyway, it's not like my wife just died. I mean, she's not even my ex-wife, because I could never get her to marry me."

And *that* was TMI.

He peeked out at her from behind his hand-shield, but instead of looking like she wanted to jump out of the car, Shayla was nodding as if she appreciated what he'd shared. "You both must've been young when you had Maddie."

"Yeah," Pete said. "Very." He cleared his throat. "Anyway, they moved out of state and lived, well, pretty much anywhere that wasn't San Diego because Lisa grew up here and hated it. That plus my deployments made it hard for Maddie and me to have any kind of real relationship, so here we are. Suddenly Lisa's gone, and I have full custody of my kid, but we're strangers. I'm clueless and Maddie's miserable—apparently enough to run away."

"She's still grieving," Shayla said as the enormous car continued its ponderous twenty-thousand-point turn. "And of course, you are, too. I mean, it's only natural, regardless of how long it's been since you and Lisa broke up. Is Maddie going to counseling?"

"We both are," he said. "Separately and together."

"Wow," she said. She was genuinely impressed. "That's great."

"It'd be a lot more great if it was actually helping," Pete told her.

"It takes time," she said. "Okay, there are two boys in the front seat of the car, and they've definitely noticed that we're just sitting here, not parking. I'm pulling in front of them so they can't leave. What's your Plan B if Maddie runs?"

Jesus, he hadn't thought about that. He hadn't imagined Maddie would literally run away from him, but now that Shayla had brought it up . . . "Um . . ." he said.

"Okay. Maybe she won't try to run," the woman pointed out, "if you start the conversation with something like *Look, I'm not mad at you; you're not in trouble. I just want to go someplace where we can sit down and talk.*"

Pete made a noise that was almost a laugh. "Except I *am* mad at her and she *is* in trouble."

"Then you better come up with something more productive than *um*," Shayla said tartly. "FYI, grabbing her and throwing her into my trunk is *not* an option."

"I would never do that," he said, and this time his laughter was more real.

"Just making sure. The Navy SEAL seems strong in you," she said as the maroon sedan came to a final stop. "Rumor has it SEALs act rashly and cry a lot."

"What?" Pete laughed as he opened the door to climb out. "Where did you hear that?"

"I have my sources," she said with a smile. She leaned forward to look up at him through the open car door, her brown eyes encouraging in her pretty face. "You can do this. Just don't forget to breathe."

CHAPTER TWO

Shay watched as the Navy SEAL squared his very broad shoulders, took a deep breath, and started for the maroon sedan.

Teenagers could be bewildering and infuriating—even to parents who'd been-there-done-that starting with the terrible twos and surviving every awful phase in between.

As the primary caregiver of a grieving fifteen-year-old girl, this man was facing the biggest challenge of his life.

The good news was that he was smart and that he seemed, truly, to care.

Although if he'd cared a tad more over the past decade-plus, and had taken the extra effort to forge a relationship with his daughter, he wouldn't be in this predicament right now.

Judgment on heavy stun! Harry's familiar voice rang in her head.

"Shh!" Shayla attempted to silence him. But okay, yeah. Harry was right. She *was* judging. Again.

To be fair, the subset of divorced-fathers-who-don't-spend-time-with-their-kids is a giant button for you, Harry allowed. *Although, hello? You don't have to give Lieuten-*

ant Hot SEAL your parenting stamp of approval before you play a few rounds of naked Scrabble with him.

She'd never played naked Scrabble, not even with Carter. Maybe especially not with Carter. Her musical ex-husband hadn't been all that into the written word. In fact, she couldn't remember the last time she'd played regular, non-naked Scrabble. And now the boys were more into games like Settlers of Catan and Carcassonne, which, frankly, was one of her current favorites, too.

Harry snapped his fingers to get her attention back as he said, *Well, maybe you should start playing naked Carcassonne. Because, damn. With your Navy SEAL, naked Watching C-SPAN would rate five shiny stars on the international enjoyment index.*

Ha ha ha, Harry was so funny. *His name is Peter and he's not my Navy SEAL,* she thought at him.

Maybe not yet, Harry said. *But if you play your Carcassonne tiles right—*

"Shh," Shay hissed again, pushing him out of her mind as she put down her window. She wanted to hear the conversation—

And police it. Harry refused to leave.

Damn straight she was going to police Peter-the-SEAL's conversation with his wayward fifteen-year-old daughter. She dug through her handbag for her cellphone, because her own Plan B involved calling 9-1-1 if there was trouble. She hoped that wouldn't be the case, but she hoped if it *was,* the lieutenant wouldn't take it personally. She knew, completely, that if Maddie did try to fend him off with a loudly proclaimed *This man is not my father!* or *Bad touch!* that the girl was probably just being a dickish teen. But since Shay didn't know either of them, she wasn't going to risk that the girl might be telling the truth. If she was, and no one believed her . . . That would be terrible.

Shay's Plan B, should she need to use it, was to let the authorities sort it all out.

Excellent. Harry approved. But then again, he would, considering he worked for the FBI. *Oh, and jot down the license plate number while you still remember it.*

The maroon car had backed in, and didn't have a plate on the front. If it had, she simply would've taken a photo with her phone.

As Shay quickly typed the letters and numbers she'd memorized into her phone's notepad app, she watched Peter approach the sedan.

He motioned for the passenger in the front seat to open the door as he said, "I'm looking for my daughter, Maddie Nakamura . . . ?" He leaned down a bit to see into the back of the car. "Long black hair, brown eyes, petite, about five-two . . . ?"

The SEAL stepped back as both the passenger and the driver climbed out. They weren't high school boys as Shay had first thought. They were young men, really—both in their late teens or early twenties.

Both were white. They were dressed in jeans, T-shirts, and unzipped hoodies, and both had facial hair. The driver had a chin-strengthening goatee, while the passenger had a full, bushy hipster beard. He also had long, limp, straight hair that he wore down around his face. Maybe Peter had seen him getting into the maroon sedan and somehow thought he was Maddie . . . ? That seemed so unlikely.

Twilight plus wishful thinking might've created the illusion, Harry murmured. *Damn it, the girl's not in the car.*

Shay could tell from Peter's body language that the backseat was empty as the long-haired, bearded man shook his head. "I don't know any Maggies, do you, Ding?" He looked over at the driver, who had a deer-in-the-headlights blankness on his slack face.

Ding, Harry said as the driver managed to shake his

head, no. *Wimpy McGee's nickname is Ding. Sweet baby Jesus, save us all.*

"It's Maddie," Peter repeated with better enunciation. "With a D." He'd expanded to full, menacing Navy SEAL alpha-male size as he held out his cellphone, where presumably he showed them a photo of his daughter. Ding shuffled a little closer so he could peer at it, too. "Have you seen her? Maddie Nakamura."

He was looking directly at Ding, who needed to clear his throat extensively before he managed to speak. "Don't know any Maddies, either. Sorry, mate. Can't help you." He had a weird Australian-ish accent.

Ding attempted to shuffle away, but Big Beard asked Peter, "Is your last name really Nakamura, man?"

"Maddie took her mother's name. Mine's Greene." The SEAL somehow got even bigger. More dangerous. "Lieutenant Peter Greene."

Oh, that was so James Bond, Harry murmured. *How are you not melting into a puddle?*

"Shh."

"If you see her," Peter continued, "or hear from her, you can reach me at the naval base on Coronado. I'm a BUD/S instructor. A Navy SEAL." He looked hard at Ding. *"Mate."*

Ding quaked, even as Big Beard said, "Wow. Thanks for your service, bro. Seriously, that Navy SEAL shit is *intense.* Sorry we can't help. But good luck finding her. C'mon, Dingo. The mall is calling."

Dingo! Harry was elated. *Of course. Because he's an "Aussie."* He made air quotes.

Shayla agreed. That accent was faux.

Mofo-faux, Harry said. *Your SEAL knows it, too.*

He was *not.* Her. SEAL.

Dingo and his buddy headed toward the elevator, and even though Peter made like he was heading back to Shay's car, he stopped suddenly and called after them, "Oh, one more thing. I'm pretty sure Maddie tells people she's older, but she's only fifteen."

Dingo tripped—no doubt over his giant, hulking guilt.

And, scene! Harry said. He began to slow-clap. *Well done, Greene, Lieutenant Greene! That was a perfectly executed Columbo. Take their picture, Shay. We're going to want to ID 'em as we follow up their tremendously stanky box o' bullshit.*

Shay used her phone and snapped photos of the pair as Dingo's friend covered for him deftly. "Dude, your shoe's untied. I swear to God, I can't take you anywhere." He pushed Dingo down to fumble with his shoelace as he raised his voice. "Sorry, man, I get that you're pissed, but we still don't know her."

"I'm not mad," Peter tried. "Not at her, not at you. She's not in trouble."

Ooh, a man who listens and learns, Harry noted. *That's a new one for you, Shay.*

"Shh."

"I just want to talk," Peter implored the two young men. "Please. Ask Maddie to call me. I just want to know that she's okay."

"*Still* haven't managed to meet her in the past three seconds," Big Beard said as he now hustled Dingo toward the other end of the garage.

Meanwhile, Peter went back to the maroon sedan for one more long look into the backseat. He tried the door, but it was locked. He tried the front door—also locked—then looked around, up at the ceiling where . . .

Yup, Harry said. *Security cameras. A full array. Will he or won't he B&E . . . ? My money says no.*

The SEAL chose not to break and enter. Instead, he climbed back into Shay's car. He still smelled great, despite the disappointment that practically dripped from him.

Shay focused on putting her window back up as she briskly told him, "I made a note of the license plate number. I also got photos of Dingo and Dumber. I figured we might need that to help us ID 'em." She showed him her phone.

"Wow, thanks. Good thinking," Peter said. "Will you text them to me?"

"Of course," she said as he used a finger to flip through her collection, all the way back to, whoops, a selfie she'd taken before her latest ultra-short haircut—of what she'd called her *crazy writer hair* for the readers on her Facebook page. Although, seriously, if she was willing to post that on her public page, she really shouldn't care if her Navy SEAL neighbor saw it. "Just go ahead and send them to your phone."

Peter did just that as she found the signs leading upward to the parking garage's exit. She could move much faster now that she wasn't following the barge-sized maroon car, so she pushed it, wanting to get out of the garage's certain-death-in-an-earthquake zone ASAP.

She'd almost reached aboveground level when he finally spoke. "So . . . I'm not alone in thinking that they know Maddie?"

"Dingo definitely does," Shay said. "He's a terrible liar."

He nodded. "Yeah, Dingo. Jesus. He's probably from exotic, faraway Burbank." At her blank look, he added, "The Valley, the burbs north of LA . . . ?"

"I'm still learning California geography," Shay admitted. "I'm from New York, with a long post-college stop in Boston." She pulled out of the garage and onto the open street. Thank God. She poked at her GPS, but it was still confused, and Harry had, for once, gracefully vanished when the SEAL climbed back into the car. Not that *he* was particularly good with directions, either, considering he was a figment of her imagination. "Right now, for example, I have no idea where I am."

"Bang a right up here," Peter ordered with authority. "And then left at the light. If you don't mind, I want to backtrack all the way to where you picked me up, because . . ." He exhaled hard. "Look, I know this is going to sound crazy, but I *saw* Maddie get into that car."

"It's okay," Shay said. "I'm happy to help." Tevin had borrowed his father's car and was on schedule to pick up his little brother when the debate club practice ended at nine. And because these days her "writing" time consisted mainly of gnashing her teeth as she deleted the paltry few paragraphs she'd written over the past day, it was nice to have something constructive and purposeful to do that had an actual chance of successful completion.

So she banged the right, enjoying the colorful verb even without Harry around to provide comment. While it certainly wasn't the first time she'd heard that expression, it took a certain something-something for someone who wasn't a fictional action-slash-romance hero to use it authentically. But whatever that *je ne sais quoi* was, this Navy SEAL had it in spades.

"At the risk of annoying you," Shay added, "I'd like to suggest that maybe you only *thought* you saw Maddie get into that car."

Peter laughed as she pulled into the designated left-turn lane and waited behind a long line of hopefully signaling cars. "What? You think I saw Long-Hair get in and I mistook him for Maddie? With that beard? No." He shook his head. "He's nearly a foot taller than she is."

"It *was* twilight," Shayla pointed out.

"No," he said again.

"All those shadows, plus the glare from the car's headlights . . ."

"Sorry. I saw her."

"Wishful thinking can do some crazy things to—"

"I know that, but no." He was definite.

"Okay," Shay surrendered. "You saw your daughter get into that car. I think it's safe to assume then, that somewhere between where you saw her get in and the parking garage, she got out. But we had eyes on that car for nearly the entire last eighty percent of the trip."

And even though the maroon car had been out of sight while Shay had done her little sidewalk excursion, when they'd finally caught back up, the car had been in the left lane.

The SEAL knew what she was thinking, and agreed. "Yeah, there's no way they dropped Maddie off after they took the right turn to head to the mall. They were moving too fast. No, it had to've happened closer to the school, before we first caught up to them."

"Maybe . . ." She said it at the same time he did, only she asked it as a question. "The In-N-Out Burger?"

Thank God Harry wasn't here to laugh like a sixth-grader at the weirdly suggestive name of the West Coast burger chain. No, instead she was the one who had to clench her teeth to keep from snickering.

"The one by the school," Peter said absolutely. "Yes."

Shay risked a glance at him, but he was clearly more mature and wasn't even thinking about giggling. "Okay, then. Answer this for me. Why would they pick her up only to drop her off a few hundred yards away?" As a writer, these were the kinds of questions she needed to resolve to make her stories believable.

The SEAL didn't have to think long or hard for his response. "Because she knew I saw her get into that car."

"Okay. But . . . you were on foot at the time," Shayla argued. "Wouldn't she assume that Dingo, with his obvious brilliance as a driver and a human being, would be able to get away from a man on foot?"

This one took him slightly longer. "Maybe she saw *me* get into *your* car, too."

Shay shook her head. "That's pretty weak," she told him. "The timing, you know? And the distance. She gets into Dingo's car. *Go, go!* So he goes, probably pretty fast, and yeah, she's looking out the back window at you, but . . . it took you a while to flag me down. How good is her eyesight? It was already pretty dark, and she must've lost visual contact just a few seconds after Dingo hit the gas. Unless she was like, *Wait, pull over so we can see if someone stops for him,* and sorry, I just don't buy that."

The expression of surprise on the SEAL's face made her wish she'd kept her phone handy so she could take a picture. Instead, she'd have to trust her rather accurate memory.

"I really don't," she repeated. "Sorry."

"No," he said, "I'm impressed. That was a logical breakdown of . . . Are you law enforcement? You said you write about serial killers, but you drive like you've had training." He was aiming those romance-hero-blue eyes at her again as he added, "Please tell me you work for the San Diego police. Because up to now, all I've gotten from them is *Kids who run away nearly always come back of their own accord.*"

Shayla winced. "That's not very helpful."

"No, it's not."

"Welp, sorry to disappoint, I'm just a writer."

"What do you write?" the SEAL asked.

It was a horribly loaded question, but of course he had no way of knowing that. So she kept her answer on the surface, instead of diving into the murky depths of *Nothing, because I've been seriously blocked for close to two years now, to the point that even my most popular characters are on strike.*

Harry, of course, popped back in. *I'm not on strike,* he said. *But you gave me my HEA, and frankly, I'm not going to let you fuck things up between me and Thom. I'm in love and I'm happy. Leave me alone.*

Leave *him* alone . . . ? Harry vanished as Shay started to laugh, but the SEAL was looking at her oddly again, so she told him, "Romantic suspense." It was clear he didn't know quite what that meant, so she clarified. "Fiction. Thrillers with a steamy love story . . . ? I write about a team of FBI agents."

"Are you . . . published?" he asked.

"Yup," she said briskly. "Not easy to do, but I managed—mostly because my characters act with believable intention. If I were writing Maddie, she would *not* have gotten out of Dingo's car at the In-N-Out Burger without a damn good reason. And since there's literally no way she saw you getting into my car . . ."

"Maybe she didn't have to see that. Maybe she just knew it would happen," Peter countered. "If she's learned anything about me at all over the past few months, it's that I don't quit."

Shay made a face. "Yeah, that's still not the strongest motivation. But . . . maybe she *didn't* see you when she got into Dingo's car," she posited. "And maybe she was like, *Where you going?* And they're like, *The mall,* and she's like, *Aagh, nah, I'm sick of the mall. I'm hungry. Just drop me at the burger place.*"

"With what money is she buying herself a burger?" Peter asked. "At most, she had five bucks I gave her for lunch, the morning before she disappeared. And, okay, even if she borrowed some cash from Dingo, where's she gonna go after that? Unless she's got other friends to call and say *Come pick me up.*"

"See, now you're thinking like a writer," Shayla told him.

"I still think she saw me," he said, "so I'm going with *She knew I would follow even if she didn't see it happen.*"

"Fair enough." Shay nodded, although she couldn't help

but think they were missing something here. Still, she not only had two teenagers of her own, but she could also remember being one. Maddie had to know that getting caught by her father after going AWOL for two days would only be worse if he caught her while in the company of two twenty-year-old men, one of whom was probably her boyfriend, God help his fake-Australian soul.

"Let's assume, for now, that Dingo and Big Beard lent her a few dollars and dropped her at the burger place." She embraced Peter's theory. "Next question: What are the odds she'd stick around, waiting for you to figure that out and show up?"

"Slim to none," Peter told her grimly. "I don't expect that she did. But with any luck, someone who works the counter saw her while she was in there. With any luck, she *did* call another friend, who came to pick her up, and someone saw that, too. I have a teammate whose wife has connections with the SDPD. That's been useless so far, but . . . *if* I can confirm that someone picked up Maddie from the In-N-Out Burger, maybe the police'll finally be able to help me track her down by accessing their security cam footage."

"Well, *that* would be a very lucky break," Shay said.

"I could use a little luck right about now," the Navy SEAL said.

She reached over and patted his knee, again channeling Harry's confidence as she said, "You said it yourself, Lieutenant. You don't quit. We'll find her. With or without luck."

CHAPTER THREE

Maddie Nakamura held both her phone and her nose as she lay on her side, curled up in the dark trunk of Dingo's car. It smelled like a mix of oil and old feet in there so she breathed through her mouth, which really didn't help, because *God*.

It was uncomfortably warm, too, but since she could see glimpses of the parking garage's grimy concrete floor through several rusting holes in the chassis, at least she knew she wasn't going to suffocate.

And seriously, even if death was a possibility, she *still* wasn't going to move until she got Dingo's *all-clear* text.

No way was she going to risk her father finding her. Not now. Not yet. Not until she figured a way out of this shit-storm she was in. And frankly, if she never did manage to find Fiona and return Nelson's cash, well, Maddie would just have to vanish off the face of the planet, never to be heard from again.

Not like anyone would miss her.

But seriously, how stupid was it that her father had spotted her over at the school, right at the moment she'd been climbing into Dingo's car? The spring weather was erratic and the past few days had gotten cold at night, and her coat had been in her locker. It seemed safer to sneak into the school to grab it than to attempt to get something from her closet at home. She'd purposely waited until the evening, figuring she'd have less of a chance of getting caught than if she walked in during the school day.

But "Dad"—she only called him that with air quotes and irony—had seen her and there'd been a lot of shouting in Dingo's car until they'd figured out what to do. And thank God Dingo's friend Daryl had been riding shotgun, because if it was up to Dingo, he might've just pulled over, gotten out of the car, and laid down on the sidewalk in total surrender.

Dingo was funny, and kind, and stupidly sweet, but he didn't seem to have that much of a backbone. But with Daryl's help, Maddie managed to convince him that if he let her father follow them into the garage at the mall, they could bluff their way out of this.

And their bluffing was really only possible because Dingo had rigged his ancient, giant car for boondocking, which was another word for urban camping, which was another way of saying he lived in his car like the pathetic homeless loser that he was. But the worn-out cushions of the backseat were easily removed, which opened up the entire back of the car, trunk included, into one large space. Dingo had a foam mattress, and he slept back there, albeit at a creative angle.

And because those seat backs easily pulled out, Maddie could—and did—crawl into the trunk from the backseat while the car was in motion. Daryl then replaced the seat backs. Which meant when they parked here in the mall garage, when "Dad" had looked in Dingo's car windows, Maddie had been in the trunk, safely hidden from view.

Her fate, however, was then in the hands of Dingo and Daryl's ability to lie to her father's grim face.

Her phone finally vibrated. *All clear.*

But she still hesitated. *Are you sure?* she quickly typed with her thumbs.

There gone. Dingo didn't have the greatest grasp of spelling and grammar, but he was proving himself to be a good friend. Although it didn't take much for him to be a better friend than his stupid, stupid ex—evil Fiona—who'd intentionally and malevolently gotten Maddie into this shitty, shitty mess.

It had started day before yesterday, on Monday, after "Dad" dropped her off at school. As was her father's usual total Stormtrooper MO, they'd arrived a half hour early, so she'd wandered over to the parking lot to wait for Fiona. The older girl—Fee was a senior—had left school somewhat mysteriously last Friday morning, after which she'd completely stopped answering her phone.

On that Monday morning, Maddie had tried calling Fee again, but she'd gotten a weird *This number is invalid* message. Which wasn't all *that* strange. In the few months since Maddie first met Fee, the girl had changed her number twice. Once because some weird guy was stalking her, and once because the old number was getting "stale."

Whatever that meant.

So Maddie had hovered near student parking, expecting Fiona to show up in her aunt Susan's shiny little Fiat, with a brand-new phone in hand. Instead, Fee was nowhere to be seen, and Maddie had gotten pointed at and beckoned to by a man in a black truck—one of those giant ones, with a back passenger seat—that was idling just outside of the school grounds.

She recognized him immediately. His name was Nelson and he traveled with a posse of creepy minions. He was older than his boyz by several decades—older even than Maddie's stupid father.

She'd gone with Fee once, a few weeks earlier, to pick

something up from Nelson's auto shop—drugs probably, but Fiona didn't tell and Maddie didn't ask. Still, while they were there, the way Nelson looked at Maddie had grossed her out. But later, in the car, Fee just laughed and said, "He stared because he thinks you're pretty, spaz. Lots of guys are super into Asian girls—in fact you should use makeup so you look more like your mother and less like your father—and you know what else? You actually *would* be pretty if you didn't dress like an eighty-year-old homeless man."

Monday morning, though, Maddie had backed up, fast, and run for the safety of the school. By the time classes were over, she'd come up with a rational explanation for why Nelson might've gestured to her—he was probably looking for Fiona, too.

So when she started her walk home, she wasn't all that concerned at first when that big black truck pulled up alongside her and Nelson's ugly face appeared as he lowered the window in the cab.

But she jumped as two men—bigger, older, shaved-headed men—materialized on either side of her and roughly grabbed her by the arms.

"Hey!" she said, ready to fight, but then Fee's boyfriend, Ricky Dingler, whose nickname was Dingo because he was from Australia, appeared, too.

"It's okay, Mads," Dingo said in his lilting accent as he took her heavy backpack off her shoulder. She tried to hold on to it, but he gently pried her fingers free. "I won't let anyone hurt you."

The skinhead with the intricate neck tattoo said, "Mr. Nelson would like the pleasure of your company."

Maddie wasn't an idiot. She knew that the dead last thing she should do was get into that big black truck—talking to Nelson while standing outside of it was one thing—but somehow before she could open her mouth to scream, the man with the neck tattoo and his buddy with the nose ring had hustled her over there, with Dingo trailing behind, still holding her pack.

Nelson had gotten out so that when they pushed her up into the cab she was sandwiched between him and the XXL driver, a man she recognized because his younger clone was some big deal football-playing asshole at the high school.

As soon as Nelson slammed the door shut, the big driver jammed his truck into gear, and they were zooming away from the school.

The skinhead twins and Dingo were riding in the bed of the truck, so at least they were going wherever she was, but that didn't make it any better. Especially when she turned to look through the back window, and realized Neck-Tattoo was rifling through her backpack.

"Hey!" she said, but then Nelson got her full attention when he put his fat-fingered hand on her knee and let it slip down to the inside of her thigh. She was wearing jeans, but still it was disgusting.

She jerked her leg away. "Don't touch me, Grandpa! Stupid, back there, who apparently isn't above stealing my lunch money, said you wanted to talk? So talk already."

Fiona had told Maddie that Nelson imagined himself to be San Diego's version of Walter White, like from *Breaking Bad,* but he wasn't even close. He had graying hair and a mustache that didn't do much for his too-fleshy face. He had a beer belly and bad breath, and he wheezed when he laughed. And he laughed now at her words.

"Feisty," he said. He leaned across her to tell the football player's older clone, "I like her."

"I'd like her better naked, with my dick in her mouth," the clone said as he looked down at her with his weirdly dead-seeming pale gray eyes. "I bet she's good at that."

That coldly appraising look he gave her actually scared her, but she covered her fear with an enormous disgusted eye roll. "I hope you also like vomit," she said before turn-ing to address Nelson directly. "I have a math test to study for. Is this bullshit going to take long?"

"Won't take long at all," Nelson assured her, "if you've got Fee's money, honey." He wheezed at his stupid rhyme, as if it was some kind of world-class joke.

"Fee's money? What money?" Maddie asked, and Nel-son made *tsk*ing sounds as again he spoke over her to tell Dead-Eyes, "I told you she was going to say that, that she was going to be all *what-the-fuck*." He fluttered his hands in the air, as if imitating her, except she hadn't moved her hands at all.

"You did, boss," Dead-Eyes said.

"I seriously don't know what you're talking about," Maddie said. "I don't even know you. All I know is you're some kind of friend of Fiona's—"

"Fiona's business associate," Nelson corrected her. "Fee had to leave town unexpectedly. She said she gave you the money she owes me."

"What? No!" Maddie shook her head. "I mean, maybe she meant to leave it with me if she told you she was gonna—" she didn't want to get Fee into trouble "—but something must've happened, and . . . she didn't. I haven't seen her since Friday. Seriously."

"She's serious," Nelson told Dead-Eyes. He turned to Maddie. "You *are* Maddie Nakamura."

"Yeah," Maddie said. "But I don't—"

"Fiona said she gave it to you on Friday," Nelson said. "In cash."

Dingo was now holding on to Maddie's backpack in the bed of the truck, and she glanced back at it and him as she tried to remember how much money she'd brought to school. She was pretty sure she only had four dollars left in her wallet after the tragedy that was today's lunch—assuming the skin-heads hadn't stolen it—but she had another forty-seven hidden in the pages of *The Wind in the Willows* on the bookshelf in the bedroom of the bungalow. The last thing she wanted to spend it on was paying off stupid Fiona's stupid debts to her stupid drug dealer, but if she had to . . . "How much does she owe you?" she asked on a heavy sigh.

"Ten thousand dollars."

Maddie nearly choked. "Ten *thousand* . . . ?"

"She said her aunt kicked her out and was sending her home to her mother. She said she stopped at your house and dropped off the cash on her way to the airport," Nelson told her.

"But she didn't," Maddie insisted. "Or, if she did, she dropped it when I wasn't there—"

"She said you were."

"You must've misunderstood or . . . or . . . somehow gotten the message wrong or—"

"I'll play it for you—her message—so you can tell me exactly how I got it wrong." Nelson had his phone hooked into the Bluetooth in the truck, and as he thumbed through his voicemails and hit play, the speakers clicked on.

And yes, that was Fiona's voice coming through with crystal clarity. "So my fucking bitch aunt kicked me out for good. She's shipping me home tonight, and there's not enough time to come over to say goodbye. In fact, I'm on my way to the airport right now. I managed to stop at Maddie's house. Maddie Nakamura? Remember, I told you about her, you met her, and you said she was cute? Well, I left what I owe you with her—I had to, I didn't have another option. But I put it into her cute little hand and she promised me she'd give it to you on Monday morning, but heads up, she's wily and a pathological liar and you might have to chase her. Tell Dingo *sorry*. Oh, wait—" she laughed "—I'm *not* sorry. Tell him I hope he eats shit and dies. Have a nice life!"

"She was lying," Maddie said, her head spinning. *Wily*

and a pathological liar . . . ? She no longer felt the need to protect Fiona. "*She's* the liar—"

"She's never lied to me before," Nelson said.

"Well, she's lying now," Maddie insisted. She turned in her seat to look again into the truck bed where Dingo was sitting. "Dingo knows her even better than I do. Why would she leave that much money with me instead of her own boyfriend?"

"Because Dingler was otherwise occupied all day on Friday," Nelson told her. "She tried, but she couldn't reach him. And since you've been working with her for a while now—"

"*Working* with her?" Maddie was starting to feel like a parrot. "With Fiona? No! That's not true!" She took her phone from the pocket of her cargo pants and unlocked the screen. "Look, check my history! No calls from Fiona, no texts either! Just a lot of me calling and her not picking up! She didn't reach *me* on Friday, either, and she certainly didn't stop by while my father was home!" Fiona knew better than that.

But Nelson wheezed with laughter again. "You expect me to believe you don't have a separate burner phone for business? Fee told me about your arrangement, weeks ago. She said you were one of her best sales associates, but she also said you were devious. And, yes, deceitful. That she had to watch you closely."

Maddie looked at him, and in that moment, she knew. This wasn't a mistake or a mixup or a misunderstanding. Fiona had taken his ten thousand dollars, left town, and framed Maddie. Not only that, but she'd planned to do it, weeks ago. She'd intentionally brought Maddie to Nelson's garage so he'd know both her name and her face.

"You have forty-eight hours to 'find' the money she gave you, and return it to me," Nelson informed her. "And that's me being generous, and giving you a little extra time. After that, the interest rate kicks in, and it's another thousand dollars for each additional day you withhold."

"So, you, like, *want* me to go to the police?" The words were out of Maddie's mouth before she'd thought them through.

Nelson moved fast—faster than she'd dreamed an old, out-of-shape creeper could move—grabbing her by the throat with hot-dog fingers that were shockingly strong.

"You even think of doing that," he said as she tried to breathe but couldn't, so she started to flail, "and you're dead."

Dead-Eyes was still driving, but he moved his arm over to hold her in place, his elbow across her chest as he planted his hand directly between her legs, right on her crotch, and now she was struggling against that, too. But she couldn't move and she couldn't breathe.

"And I know what you're thinking," Nelson continued, his breath hot against her ear as she started to see stars, as his fingers dug even harder into her throat. "You'll be safe, the police will protect you. But they won't. In fact, they won't believe you, especially when drugs are found in your locker, when 'friends' come forward and say you've been selling on campus. No one will believe you. And you'll go to jail and while you're there, I'll have you killed. That's if I don't have you killed before that."

With that, he let her go. As she sucked in air, she attempted to push Dead-Eyes's still-groping hand away from her.

Forty-eight hours had passed *extremely* fast.

Maddie had gone home on Monday, after getting jettisoned from Nelson's truck. She didn't really know what else to do, except to keep trying to reach Fiona. And to start calling Dingo, too. But he wouldn't answer, not at first. She hadn't connected with him until halfway through the day on Tuesday. She'd cut school to look for him, and had finally found him at the 7-Eleven where he sometimes hung out to sell weed. *That* hadn't gone all that well either, but she'd finally guilted him into helping her.

Now, hidden in the trunk of Dingo's car, Maddie rubbed the bruises on her throat as she sent him a second text: *Check-again.*

Please, she added, because there weren't a lot of people in Dingo's life who treated him with respect, including Nelson. Especially Nelson. And she knew, absolutely, that Dingo was risking more than she could imagine to help her like this, behind Nelson's fugly back.

But instead of texting his reply, Dingo unlocked and opened the door of his car and said, "I walked down a level *and* up a level to check. He's gone. You can come out."

As Maddie pushed out the backseat cushion and wiggled through the opening into the body of the car, Dingo added, "You didn't mention that your father was a Navy SEAL. You know, love, he might actually be able to help you."

She climbed over into the front passenger seat as he started the behemoth of a car. "Where's Daryl?"

"I'll take that as a *no comment,*" he muttered. "I s'pose you've got as much to say for the shocker that you're only fifteen."

"Why should that bother you?" Maddie asked. "We're friends. It's not like we're having sex or anything."

"Yeah, but we've been sleeping in the same car," Dingo said, maneuvering his giant vehicle out of the parking space. "And FYI, Daryl thinks we're friends with, you know, those kind of benefits? He told me he preferred to walk home than risk death via angry Navy SEAL."

"Daryl's an idiot," she pointed out. "And I'm not asking my father for anything. He's an idiot, too. Plus he doesn't give a flying shit."

"I'm not sure I picked up *doesn't give a flying shit* when he was all *Where's Maddie* in my face," Dingo countered.

"In fact, it felt an awful lot like *majorly gives a major flying shit*."

"Yeah, well, he's a good little soldier," Maddie said, "and he thinks he's supposed to take care of me."

Dingo glanced at her. "You sure, Mads? He looked pretty cool. I mean, the way you talked about him, I wasn't expecting—"

"The whole California-surfer-dude affect is an intentional mind-fuck," Maddie told him. "He's a BUD/S instructor." At Dingo's blank look, she explained. "He's like a drill sergeant in the world's hardest boot camp. He teaches the idiots who want to be SEALs by trying to make them quit. And yeah, with his cool nickname—Grunge, if you can believe that, even though he doesn't own a single CD and I've never heard him listen to music, not even once—he looks like the kind of dad who'd share his doobie with you after Sunday brunch, but trust me. Not even close."

"Dad" was a Nazi when it came to schedules and curfews and keeping their new house "shipshape." God. He'd even made lists of household chores, like she was a five-year-old, eager to earn a sticky star on her chart.

To be kept on such a short leash after her free-range childhood was maddening. And yeah, to be fair, his punctuality had been a good thing back when Maddie had used what she'd thought of as his monthly blackmail payments to pay Lisa's bills.

Still, she understood—completely—why her free-spirited mother had kept her distance from him for all those years. In fact, her parents were such stark opposites, the very concept that they'd been together long enough to have sex and create Maddie was almost completely unbelievable. They must not have talked. That was Maddie's best guess. It had been pure physical attraction and lust, after which Lisa had immediately fled.

God, she missed her mother far more than she missed

her freedom. Lisa may have been a crappy caregiver—in addition to paying the bills, Maddie was also the one who cooked and cleaned and made sure her mom got to work on time. But her mother had loved her. Of that she had no doubt.

Not so the strict and scary Navy SEAL sperm donor.

"You okay, love?" Dingo asked softly. "Missing your mum again, I bet." Despite his many flaws, he always knew what she was thinking, and he was always kind. "It'll get easier, I promise. And this thing with Nelson? We'll figure it out."

Maddie nodded. Fiona had kept Nelson's ten thousand dollars. That was a given. They just had to find her, so they could get it and give it back. "Let's go see if Fee's aunt Susan is home."

Dingo didn't look happy. Maddie had never met Fiona's aunt, but apparently the woman had hated Dingo with the passion of a blazing supernova. "She always works ridiculously late," he said weakly. "I doubt she's home yet."

Fee's aunt Susan was a divorce lawyer, and she'd recently opened her own practice.

"We can park on the street and wait for her," Maddie decided, and even though Dingo sighed heavily, he nodded and drove.

* * *

No one at the In-N-Out Burger had seen Maddie.

Pete had showed his daughter's photo to everyone working the kitchen and some of the customers, too, but he came up empty.

It didn't mean she hadn't been there, it just made the search that much harder. It was one thing to ask to review the security cam footage if someone *had* seen Maddie, another entirely if the request appeared to be based purely on—how had Shayla put it? Wishful thinking.

Pete's burger tasted like ashes. He'd gotten himself one to go, only because Shayla asked him when he'd eaten last, and he couldn't remember. Dinner, last night? Maybe.

And as much as he didn't want to take the time, he knew he needed to refuel. He'd only get stupider without it.

"How worried should I be?" he asked his incredibly patient neighbor as she pulled out of the parking lot. "Assuming Maddie really is hanging out with Dingo and Dumber . . . ?"

As she drove, Shayla made the face—lips pressed temporarily together, slightly furrowed brow—that told him she was giving careful thought to her coming word choice. "If Maddie's . . . involved with one of them—and my guess would be that it's Dingo—she certainly wouldn't be the first fifteen-year-old girl in the history of the world to be sexually active. She also wouldn't be the first girl to tell her twenty-year-old boyfriend that she's eighteen even though she's not. Or, you know, maybe it just didn't come up. When you were his age, did you ask the hot girls who wanted to sleep with you for *their* ID, with their proof of age?"

"So. DefCon One," he said around his bite of burger.

Shayla's eyes danced as she laughed. "DefCon Four," she corrected him. "Back it down, Lieutenant. You shook the jailbait tree. Let's give Dingo time to have the *Are you freaking kidding me* conversation with Maddie. Although if it's okay with you, I'd like to swing past the mall again. Go back into the parking garage, see if the car's still there. I keep thinking we missed something."

He wiped his mouth and chin with the ridiculously small napkin that had been thrown into his bag. "Personally, I wouldn't mind another conversation with *good old Dingo*." He went into a fake Aussie accent as he crumpled his trash. "Maybe with my hand around his throat this time."

"Yeah, because *that* always works," she said, giving him

that now-familiar hard look that he'd quickly IDed as massive attitude-filled judgment.

Pete smiled at it—at her—despite the bad mix of burger, uneasiness, and ire that was churning in his gut. "Yeah, I know, I was just . . . being a jerk. Frankly, I'm trying really hard not to freak out."

"You're doing great," she told him. She had a switch that she could flip in a heartbeat—from disapproval to 200 percent reassurance. It was fun to watch her do it, because she was also 200 percent sincere.

And smart. Man, the way her brain clicked along at a million miles an hour was a thing of beauty to behold.

And then there were her eyes. . . .

Pete cleared his throat. "Betsy—the counselor—told me that kids who are grieving sometimes use sex for comfort," he told her. "As a way to cope, kind of like drugs or alcohol or Jesus, I don't know. I'm not saying it right, it's more complicated than that. Problem is, I stopped listening because Maddie dresses like she's twelve, in baggy clothes, like her body embarrasses her, so I didn't think I had to worry about her having a fucking twenty-something-year-old lover named fucking Dingo." He heard those f-bombs coming out of his mouth, but he couldn't stop himself so he shook his head. "Sorry."

"It's okay," she said.

"In my head, she's still only a year old," he found himself telling her. "Lisa got the good stuff—the toddler and the six-year-old, you know? I get the teen pregnancy years. Gee, maybe if I'm lucky, we'll have us a good ol' shotgun marriage and Dingo'll move into my house."

Shayla laughed, but her eyes held sympathy. "You can go there, but I'm gonna live in *this* world, where women still have choices, and smart girls—and their inappropriately older boyfriends—know *all* about contraception. Yay!" She laughed again, and then made a *shhh* sound. It was something that she did now and then, almost as if she were shushing her own overactive imagination.

"So . . . what exactly happened to set this off?" she asked. "Did you and Maddie have a fight, or . . . ? If you don't mind my asking."

"No," Pete said. "It's okay. And no fight. No blow-up, nothing big, nothing . . . I mean, yeah, I've had to lay down some rules. Set a curfew. Without it, she just wandered home whenever she felt like it—sometimes past midnight. And I know she wasn't happy when I finally put my foot down. But . . . we've barely had any conversations at all. Getting her to talk is like pulling freaking teeth." He sighed again. "The counselor says to give her space, so that's what I've been trying to do. Me, I've been taking a crash course in Living with a Teenager 101, talking to teammates who have kids, trying to figure out WTF. But most of the men I know have toddlers, so they're clueless, too. You should see the pile of books on my bedside table."

"Shh," she said again, but it was so soft, maybe he'd imagined it.

"How to Talk to Your Teen," Pete continued, and it was weird, like now that he'd finally started talking about this, he couldn't shut the fuck up, "and it's well written, but there's an assumption that you and your kid aren't total strangers. I need a way more basic care-and-feeding manual."

"Don't we all," Shayla murmured.

"I have this one friend," he continued, completely unable to stop himself from babbling on and on. "A teammate. Zanella. Good man. His wife's little brother lives with them. So I thought, damn, good resource, right? But it turns out the kid—Ben—he's the most well-adjusted teenager in the universe. Apparently, he talks to them. Like full sentences. Nouns, verbs, even the occasional adjective."

She laughed at that. "I think it just looks like that from

the outside. Ben's probably had his bad days, with plenty more to come. It's pretty universal—the silent phases. My boys go through them, too. You really just have to be patient. Don't give up."

Pete nodded. "The longest talk I had with Maddie is when she tried to convince me to demand a paternity test, but then send in someone else's DNA so it would come back negative."

"Whaaaat?" Shayla looked at him.

"Yeah. She said, that way I'd be off the hook. She said, that way I could get my life back."

"But then where would *she* be?" Shayla glanced at him again. "Lieutenant, where did Maddie live before she moved out here, to be with you?"

"Palm Springs," Pete said. "Not that Lisa had bothered to tell me, but about a year ago, they moved back to California to be near Lisa's grandmother, Kiyo. Lisa's mother died years ago, but her grandmother's still, well . . . Kiyo's in a nursing home, she's not . . . any kind of option for Maddie." He shook his head. "I actually drove out there this morning, but no one at the facility had seen Maddie since our last visit." He'd tried to call, but they kept putting him on hold, so he'd finally just got into his truck and gone there—wasted six solid hours on the road.

Shayla nodded. "Okay, but is it possible that there's someone else in Palm Springs, not necessarily a blood relative—maybe a good friend of Lisa's—that Maddie might prefer to live with?"

"If that's the case," Pete asked, "then why wouldn't she say something?" But then he laughed and answered his own question. "Maybe because she's not saying much of anything."

"Teenagers are complicated," she reminded him. "Maybe Maddie doesn't think she has a choice. Or maybe she's just not thinking at all. I mean, her mom just died. She's probably still completely overwhelmed."

"So . . . how do I broach that topic?" Pete asked. *"Hey, Maddie, is there anyone else out there, instead of me, that you'd rather live with?"* He shook his head. "I don't want her to think that I don't want her."

"But you just told me that she already believes that," Shayla pointed out. "Was there anyone you saw at the funeral—"

"I wasn't there," he said. "I didn't get called until, well, it was a week and a half after Lisa was buried."

"Seriously?"

"Maddie didn't mention me to anyone," he confessed. "I gotta assume she was in shock. And Kiyo has Alzheimer's, plus a bunch of other health issues. Maddie was already placed in temporary foster care when one of the longtime staff at the nursing home thought to ask about *the Navy SEAL father.* Thank God. That's when social services finally tracked me down."

"Wow. Forgive me for asking this, but it sounds like, well, do you have a sense of how Lisa . . ." Shayla stopped and then started again. "It occurs to me that Lisa may not have painted the, um, most flattering portrait. Of you." As she glanced at him again, it was clear that she knew he wasn't quite following, so she went point-blank. "Is it possible that Lisa trash-talked you to the point that Maddie would've rather risked going into foster care than live with, you know, her horrible monster of a father?"

"Jesus," he said.

She attempted to soften her words. "Even the nicest exes can be shitty when under duress. And if you ever had any trouble, say, making child support payments, Lisa may have—"

"I didn't," Pete cut her off. "No. Not ever." But then he corrected himself. "At first, because they moved around so much, the checks sometimes came back as undeliverable. But about twelve years ago, we set up a direct deposit account, so . . . Problem solved. Of course, that kept me from knowing where they were." He sighed, because Lisa *had* been pretty crazy. "With that said, I really don't know what Lisa told Maddie about me. All I know is that every time I tried to set up a visit, there was some 'emergency' and Lisa canceled." He looked at her again. "And you're right. It's definitely weird that Maddie didn't mention me to any of the social workers."

"That's another really awkward question to ask Maddie," Shayla said. "You don't want to put her on the spot with *Please repeat to me all the nasty crap your mother ever said about me, so I can attempt to refute it in the face of her permanent absence.* If I were you? I'd put on my amateur PI hat and sleuth it out. There are questions you *can* ask Maddie, things like *Where exactly did you live?* and *Where did your mom work?* And *Did your mom have any good friends?* Then you and Maddie can make another road trip to Palm Springs, let her visit her Great-Grandmother Kiyo while you go and round up some of Lisa's neighbors, coworkers, and friends, and ask *them* the hard questions." Her smile was filled with encouragement. "A bonus is that Maddie might really appreciate the chance to talk about her mother. And to hear about Lisa from you—you know, the fun stories, from before things went south."

He nodded again. "That's . . . good advice. Assuming I find Maddie."

"We'll find her," Shay said. "But if we don't—and I mean *don't find her right away* because we'll find her eventually . . . Well, another thing we could do is get a list of everyone who was at Lisa's funeral or memorial service, go talk to them."

She'd said *we.* Four times.

She'd noticed, too, and was instantly embarrassed. "Sorry," she said quickly.

Pete was used to being *we*-ed by the women he encountered. *It's noisy here tonight. We could go to your place* . . . This whole bizarre evening started to feel significantly more familiar—aside from his odd flare of disappointment that Shayla was no different from the rest.

But she had more to say. "It's a mom thing," she explained. "Even when it's someone else's kid that's in trouble, there's this . . . well, it feels like a biological urge to help. So if you need any help—finding Maddie, or even just, you know, a *friend* to talk to—I'm here."

Okay, she'd definitely added extra emphasis to the word *friend,* and now Pete was oddly disappointed by *that.*

"I appreciate it," he managed.

Earlier, Shayla had both squeezed his hand and patted him on the knee, like she was some kind of mom-to-the-universe. It had bugged him, because she wasn't *his* mom—not even close. Yes, she was older than he was, but not by more than a few years. And she was smart, funny, and cute.

Although moms usually came with dads, and he'd expected her to be full-family equipped and filed under *taken.* But it didn't take him long to note that she wasn't wearing a wedding band, which had kind of made his head explode.

Not that Pete was actively looking for a date or a hookup or any variation of the two. Because, really, all he ever had to do to find a little no-strings fun was go to the LadyBug Lounge. The Bug was well known as a SEAL hangout, and he could almost always find an enthusiastic young tourist-type ready to *we* him for a few hours, because she wanted to add *Navy SEAL* to her *Things I Did on My California Vacation* list.

Except, he hadn't been to the Bug in a long time. And not just because he now had a fifteen-year-old for a housemate. Over the past few years or so, even the several hours' investment into a no-strings bar hookup had seemed too labor-intensive.

And even though there was no way in hell that he was going to have any kind of a thing with a woman who lived across the street—complications and repercussions would abound, and breaking up would involve having to move house—he was suddenly curious about Shayla's lack of ring. Maybe she was allergic to metals. Was anyone allergic to gold? He didn't think so. It just seemed so freaking unlikely that she was divorced. Widowed, maybe, but then wouldn't she have kept wearing her wedding band?

He got some answers with an easy fishing expedition. "You, uh, talk about, um, shitty exes like you have direct experience. Or is that just, you know, research for your books . . . ?"

She glanced at him as she slowed to make the left turn into the mall parking garage, again whispering a small *shh* before she answered. "My ex is actually a friend. At least he is *now*. Okay, maybe he's more of a frenemy, but we definitely get along. We have to. The boys need us to."

And now Pete was curious about what kind of fool would fuck up his marriage to this woman.

Shayla was still explaining. "And FYI, it's never going to end. I'm going to be eighty and attending Tevin's as-of-yet-unborn son's *son's* wedding, and Carter is going to be sitting right there, too. With whatever number child-bride he's up to by then—*Ding! That's* the kind of snark I make sure I leave out when I'm talking about him to the boys." She laughed as she glanced at Pete again. "I'm going to blame you for that. I think there's something about you being so honest with me that makes me a little too honest in return. I just . . . Well, silly me, I thought forever actually meant *forever,* so I was . . . blindsided when he told me it didn't."

"Lisa completely vaporized my heart," Pete found himself saying. It was weird. He hadn't meant to say that. He'd just opened his mouth and the words had fallen out. He was almost too shocked to be embarrassed. "Whoa. Sorry. I'm . . ."

Shay glanced at him again as she continued down another level. "Vaporized," she whispered back. "That is a *fantastic* word. It's called a broken heart, but it feels more like a complete Alderaan than . . . Well, it feels like it's just gone, with this weird empty hole in its place. But Carter didn't do that to me. It was my best friend, Kate, who vaporized not just my heart, but, really, *all* my internal organs. And part of my brain, I think."

Jesus. "Your ex cheated with your best friend . . . ?"

"What? No! God!" Shayla laughed. "Noooo. No, no, no, no, no! Two completely separate incidents! Sorry, sorry, sorry, I *so* didn't mean to imply that! Wow, and I'm supposed to be a professional communicator!"

But then there they were. At the spot where the maroon sedan had parked, and she fell immediately silent.

Because the car was gone.

"*Fuck.*" Pete quickly added, "Sorry."

"The word *is* in my vocabulary, Lieutenant, and it seems entirely appropriate. I mean, *phooey! Fudge!*" She shook her head. "Nope. *Not* the same."

He found himself laughing again, and she was smiling, too, but her smile was tinged with her concern. "We probably could've guessed that Dingo's car wouldn't still be here," she continued. "I'm sorry if I wasted time and . . . somehow made it worse."

"No," Pete said. "It was worth the shot. And you definitely . . . aren't . . . making any of it worse. Not even close. I appreciate your . . . friendship. Sincerely. But, I'm the one who's taking up too much of *your* time. We should get you home."

CHAPTER FOUR

Petty Officer First Class Izzy Zanella looked around the tidy little living room of the bungalow that he'd helped his buddy Grunge—AKA Lieutenant Peter Greene—move into just a few short months ago.

It was surreal. Not just the fact that Grunge finally lived off-base in a real house with a yard and everything, but that he lived there *with his teenaged daughter.*

That had been the shocker—the fact that the SEAL officer had a fifteen-year-old daughter that he'd never so much as mentioned to Izzy. Or to anyone else, apparently.

At least not until that day, two months ago, when Grunge had asked Izzy out for lunch, which was as eyebrow-raisingly unusual as if Grunge had told Izzy he'd pick him up in a limo and give him a wrist corsage, too.

Still, Izzy'd gone and they'd sat outside at everyone's favorite little Greek restaurant in downtown Coronado where Grunge had exploded his informational mortar round. "Lisa, my ex—well, we were never married, but . . . Anyway, she was killed in a car accident and now I'm getting custody of our daughter, Maddie."

Whaaaa . . . ?!

The first Izzy had heard of Grunge's ex, Lisa, had been a few months earlier, in a passing conversation. The SEAL officer had referred to her only as a former girlfriend who'd been into musical theater. He'd definitely skipped the whole got-busy-and-had-a-baby-with-her part.

But Izzy managed to push away his indignant hurt—how do you not tell a close friend about something as enormous as the fact that you've got a daughter? You don't, ergo he and Grunge were not *close,* and probably far less *friends* than Izzy had thought, as well. But boo-hoo, he'd been mistaken. His poor widdle hurt feelings were nothing compared to Grunge's—someone the lieutenant had once cared about, deeply enough to make a baby with, had been *killed in a car accident.*

So Izzy'd said, "Oh, man, Pete, I'm so sorry. How can I help?"

Turns out Grunge had wanted to borrow Ben, Izzy's wife Eden's teenaged brother—who was living with them full-time these days. Grunge wanted help in picking out a teenager-appropriate rental house.

He'd also hoped that Ben could become Maddie's insta-friend, but as Ben had pointed out over the past months of trying, these things just couldn't be forced. Apparently Maddie hadn't warmed to Ben—or vice versa. And although Ben had gone above and beyond with his attempts to befriend the girl, she continued to shut him out.

Which brought them to here-and-now, with Maddie AWOL, and Grunge getting more silent and tight-lipped as each hour passed, until he'd announced that he was hiking over to the high school because he couldn't just sit still any longer.

Izzy had volunteered to go with, but Grunge had asked him to stay and try to break the password on the shiny new laptop computer he'd bought for Maddie—to see if she'd left any clues behind. Clues like what, Izzy didn't know, but he was pretty certain she hadn't left behind a Word doc called *Itinerary of Where I'll Stay When I Run Away*. Still, he'd done as Grunge asked by calling all of the various gearheads and hackers that he knew, both in the SEAL Teams and out.

No one was picking up, and he was about to go hands-on himself when his wife, Eden, showed up with two of her besties, Adam Wyndham and Lindsey Jenkins, in tow.

Izzy was pretty sure Eden's intention had been to make a hostage trade—Adam and Lindsey for him—since she was on the verge of leaving town on a long-planned family trip and this was their last night together for a full week. She'd wanted him to come home with her. But once here, she got caught up in helping.

"Eden figured out the laptop's password," Adam now announced with his usual dramatic flamboyance—dude was an actor—as he danced into the living room from the little hallway that led to the bedrooms in the back of the house. "It's *FuckYou123*, in something she calls camel-case. I don't know how she knew that." He spun to look at Eden. "How did you know to even guess that?"

She was right behind him, moving more staidly as she carried Maddie's still-new laptop. Grunge had taken his daughter shopping because the desktop computer she'd shared with her mom back in Palm Springs had been packed up and put into storage with the rest of Lisa's things, and they still hadn't found the right box.

"Because she's brilliant," Izzy said, grinning at his wife.

"It wasn't that hard." Eden shrugged it off even as she smiled back at him. "It's one of the most used passwords, right behind *Password123*. But the best part is that Maddie left Facebook open, so now we've got access to her account."

"Way to go, Eed!" Lindsey Jenkins spoke up from her

place on the sofa, which she'd reclined so she could sit with her feet up. She looked like a beach ball with a head.

An adorable beach ball. She'd recently gotten her thick dark hair cut in a shorter style that she called "baby ready," which added to the whole cute-little-pregnant-girl illusion.

Married to Izzy's SEAL buddy Jenk, Lindsey was, in fact, a strong, kickass woman. She was a former police detective and a current top operative at Troubleshooters Incorporated, Southern California's most elite personal security firm.

Eden worked there, too, but since she didn't come from a law enforcement or military background, her role was less about ass-kicking and more about administrative support. She assisted the office manager and ran the group's in-house daycare.

"This is great. Now we can use Facebook to make a list of Maddie's local friends, and start calling their parents," Lindsey said. "If we strike out there, we'll make a list of her friends' friends, and start calling *their*—"

"I don't think that's going to work," Eden interrupted her. "Maddie doesn't have any local friends, at least not on Facebook. There're only fortysomething people on her friends list, and most are from her school back in Palm Springs. There're a few other Nakamuras—probably family members, but only one's here in San Diego. Hiroko. She's in her late eighties and seems pretty Zen."

"Literally Zen," Adam interjected. "Her profile's all about meditation and painting and her garden. I seriously doubt she's helping Maddie hide from her father."

"Maybe not knowingly," Lindsey pointed out as she made gimme-hands at the computer. "But someone should call her tomorrow."

Izzy already had his phone out. "Why not now?" he asked as, instead of handing Lindsey the laptop, Eden sat down next to her. Which made sense, because Eden had a lap and Lindsey currently didn't.

"It's after eight and elderly people sometimes go to bed super-early," Lindsey said, scrolling down Maddie's Facebook profile as Eden held the computer for her.

"Oh, man, is it really after eight? I have to be on set and coherent at five. I should go." But despite that announcement, Adam plopped himself down on Eden's other side, so he could look at the laptop's screen, too. But then he looked at the sofa they were sitting on. "Is *all* of this furniture brand-new?"

"I was wondering the same thing," Eden said. "Everything in the house is pristine—even the stuff in Grunge's bedroom."

"I noticed that, too," Adam said. "That, plus he sleeps in a twin bed. And yeah, it's one of those extra long ones, but . . . Is it just me, or is that weird?"

"It's weird," Lindsey said, her attention on Maddie's photo albums.

"What were you doing in *Grunge's* bedroom?" Izzy asked, and all three of them looked up at him in surprise.

Eden answered. "You said he asked you to look for clues."

"Yeah. In Maddie's room," Izzy said.

"Well, we had to figure out which room was hers," Eden told him, then turned to Adam. "And it's not *that* weird. There's no way he could fit anything bigger than a twin in there. The room's tiny."

"But the bed in Maddie's room is new, too," Adam said.

"The bed in Maddie's *giant* room," Lindsey pointed out. "Which I now covet . . ."

"Yeah, I know, right? You've got to love a man who gives the master bedroom to his daughter," Eden said. "That attached bath is amazing."

Adam leaned across Eden to ask Lindsey, "Did you see that shower?"

"Mmm-hmm. And tonight I'm gonna dream about that bathtub."

"I feel you, sister," Adam said, "but the burning question remains. Did Grunge really just throw away all of his old furniture when he moved in here?"

Again, they all looked up at Izzy, as if he knew the answer. And, actually, this time, he did.

"He didn't have any furniture," Izzy said. "He lived on base. In the officers' barracks."

"But . . . he didn't even have anything in storage?" Lindsey asked.

"Apparently not," Izzy said. "I mean, he asked me and Danny to help him move in, and we went with him to rent a truck, but then we drove over to that furniture store—that big one, you know, off the Five? When we got there, everything was ready for us to pick up."

"And you didn't think that was odd?" Eden asked.

"Sweetheart," Izzy told his wife. "Think about the furniture *I* had back before we got married."

Relentlessly frugal, Eden had repurposed some of it, but most of it had been Dumpster-bound. "Good point," she said.

Izzy said, "So, no, it's not that weird that he didn't have anything in storage. Not for a guy who's career Navy."

"But what did Grunge do before this, when his daughter came to visit him?" Adam was puzzled. "If he was living in the officers' barracks on base, did they . . . stay in a hotel?"

Eden turned to ask Lindsey, "You didn't tell him?"

"Tell me what?" Adam looked from Lindsey to Eden and back.

The baby must've been kicking again, because Lindsey rubbed her belly as she said, "Nobody knows what he did, or even *if* she visited, because no one knew Grunge even had a daughter."

"Really?" Adam asked. "Not even Izzy?"

And yup, they again all looked up at him, expectantly.

"I thought you knew Grunge from way back," Adam continued. "Like, before you were SEALs."

Izzy nodded. "Grunge and I did our first WestPac together as E-3s. In fact, we hot-bunked on a tiny, low-tech, about-to-be-decommissioned destroyer—this was back before he followed the shining light over to Officers' Territory and before either of us did BUD/S."

"I think I got some of that," Lindsey said, still rubbing her giant baby bump. "E-3's the rank—or is it rating—of someone who's still pretty newly enlisted?"

"If you're talking enlisted, it's called rating," Eden said.

"Yeah, I got very little of it," Adam said. "BUD/S. I know BUD/S—but everyone knows BUD/S is where Navy SEAL wannabes audition to get into the Teams."

"It's a wee bit tougher than an audition," Izzy said.

"*You've* never tried out for a Broadway show," Adam shot back. "That shit is cutthroat. Anyway, I'm massively discouraged, because Tony's been teaching me to speak Navy, and I thought I was doing at least moderately well." Like Lindsey, Adam's life partner was also a SEAL in Izzy's Team. "*Argh, matey, lower the mains'l.* Fuck, I just realized—he's been teaching me to talk like a pirate!" As they all laughed, he added, "But seriously, someone please translate what Izzy just said."

"Back when they first enlisted in the Navy," Eden told him, "they shipped out on something called a WestPac—you float around in the Western Pacific for six solid months. In Izzy and Grunge's case, they were on a really old destroyer that was so crowded they had to share the same bed. They had different shifts, so they slept at different times."

"It's called hot-bunking," Izzy said, "because he'd roll out and I'd roll in, and the mattress would still be warm from his body heat."

"So you're, like, one of his oldest Navy friends," Adam

surmised. "And he never mentioned that he had a daughter, not even while you were hot-bunking—and oh, the things I'm not saying about *that*."

"So . . . not even any baby pictures taped to the bunk?" Lindsey asked.

"Nope." Izzy shrugged. "But we weren't exactly friends back then. More like partners in mutual misery."

"But you're friends now," Eden pointed out. "*I* think of him as a friend. I mean, he's quiet, sure, but . . ."

"Yeah, I dunno," Izzy said. In the foggy and fun-filled years since the USS *Bergeron,* he and Grunge had both become SEALs. And in the past year or so in particular, despite the officer/enlisted divide, they'd gone from respectful teammates to real friends.

Or so Izzy had thought.

"Did *he* even know he had a daughter back then?" Lindsey asked. "There's a trope in romance novels called *secret baby,* and—"

Izzy laughed. "I'm sorry. Secret *what*?"

"Baby," Eden said. "The hero gets someone pregnant, but she doesn't tell him about it, and then anywhere from one to twenty years later, *surprise!* The secret baby needs a kidney, and the hero and heroine reconnect to save her life and they fall in love and everyone lives happily ever after."

"Well, that's intense," Izzy said.

"But the *female* character's not surprised, right?" Adam interjected. "Because that's the story *I'd* want to read."

"Whoa, me, too," Izzy said. "*Hey, what's that stuck between the cushions of the sofa? Holy crap, I must've had a secret baby last night when I fell asleep watching Netflix!*"

Adam laughed.

"Don't mock it, boys," Lindsey told them sternly. "It's a popular theme in a very popular genre."

"I can see how it would be," Izzy said. Eden was a huge romance fan—blazing through several books a week. "With lots of complications and entanglements and angst. But I'm pretty sure Grunge knew he had a daughter from the start. He just didn't tell *me* about her." He gasped. "Which suddenly makes sense if *I'm* the hero of this secret-baby story, and it's not a romance, but instead a tale of deep friendship. Are there secret-baby buddy movies?"

Lindsey had already returned her focus to Maddie's laptop. Eden, however, was smiling broadly at him, except then she frowned, put the laptop on the coffee table, took her phone from her pocket, and then gasped. But unlike his, her drama was not feigned.

"Maddie just texted me!" she said, her own thumbs flying over the tiny keyboard. "She must've unblocked me, but—*No!* She's already blocked me again!"

"What'd she say?" Lindsey asked as Adam chimed in with, "Read it! Read it!"

"Tell my stupid father that I'm OK," Eden read Maddie's text aloud. *"I'm safe, I'm with a friend. I need some space to figure some ship out.* Thank you, autocorrect. *Respect my needs*—ooh, this girl's learned the power of therapy-speak—*and I'll come back when I'm ready. Don't, and I'm gone for good."*

"Dahn dahn dahhhhhn!" Izzy sang an appropriately dire soundtrack, but then said, "Except, if I know Grunge, he's not gonna be moved by a threat from a fifteen-year-old."

"Except, you *don't* know Grunge," Lindsey pointed out. "Apparently no one knows Grunge, so we really can't predict what he's going to do."

"I'm texting him with a screenshot of Maddie's message," Eden said, even as headlights shone in through the front window because a car had pulled into the bungalow's narrow driveway.

"Is that him?" Adam asked.

Eden stood up. "Maybe Maddie's *friend* had a moment of clarity and brought her home. Please, God."

Izzy looked out the window. "Nah, it's Grunge. And . . . a woman." Yes, that was definitely a female human who'd driven the lieutenant home. She got out, and stretched as if they'd been in her little car for a while. She was decidedly not unattractive, if a lot less fancy-clothes-big-hair-and-mondo-makeup than the women G usually hooked up with when he went to the LadyBug. She was older than his typical "date" type, too.

Her body language was friendly and comfortable—maybe a tad overattentive, but Grunge had that effect on just about everyone. His charisma was through the roof—and most people couldn't look away.

He was standing as if he wanted something, though. And maybe that urgency came from his burning need to find his daughter, but it seemed like there was something more to it from the way he was leaning—just a little—toward the woman.

Eden came to look, too, as the woman and Grunge continued whatever conversation they were having over the top of the car. The window was closed, so they couldn't hear more than the murmur of their two voices. But whatever Eden saw made her ask, "Does Grunge have a grown-up lady-friend that we don't know about?"

Izzy looked at his wife. "Babydoll, your guess is as good as mine."

"I've always thought he must have," Eden said. "You know, at least a friends-with-bennies booty-call recipient."

"I've heard the opposite," Adam said. "That he's into the transient, you know, one-and-done?"

"Yep. He's a SEAL groupie-doer," Lindsey put it bluntly.

"Ew, really?" Eden said.

"Don't judge," Adam chided.

"Heads up!" Eden pulled Izzy back, away from the window. "She's coming inside with him, whoever she is. Act normally, everyone."

Act normally? Izzy started to laugh, because this *was* normal. Ergo, the upcoming was going to be interesting.

* * *

When Shayla walked into the Navy SEAL's house to find his living room filled with beautiful people, she knew with a certainty that she was merely the witty neighbor in this story.

Wait, what? Harry, in her head, had been psyched that she was actually going inside Lieutenant Greene's house, even if only "to see if Maddie had left her Facebook account up and open on her new laptop computer, *chicka-chick-bow-bow*," but now he was confused. *The witty what . . . ?*

The witty neighbor was always the sidekick; the friend. As in *not* the romance-novel-type heroine.

In truth, Shay hadn't *really* thought that she'd take on that type of leading role in the SEAL's ongoing drama, but part of her—a small part, egged on by Harry's rampant optimism—had foolishly started to hope. After all, the man *was* lovely to look at with his pretty eyes and all those muscles—and he really seemed genuinely nice. And yes, okay, *nice* was the kiss of death when it came to romance novel heroes, so really what she meant was that he was smart, he was funny, he was thoughtful and kind, *and* he was clearly responsible and reliable, along with intensely, highly skilled. Although, here in the harsh reality of the non-romance-novel world, his incredibly dangerous job was more of a liability than an asset, but still . . . He really was quite perfect for something short-term, like a fling.

You're seriously considering having just a fling. Harry was flatly disbelieving. *Since when do you do short-term flings?*

Well, she had been considering it, but not anymore—not as she looked at the two beautiful young women in the room.

So, what? You're just going to quit? Now Harry was disgusted.

There was nothing here to quit. *Look, you've won,* she thought back at him. Meeting Peter Greene had made Shayla realize that Harry'd been right for quite some time. She *absolutely* needed to get out more, and at the very least she was now convinced that she could, in particular, use a good happy ending—in the crassest, most sexual-innuendo-ish way—to finally and fully exorcise both Carter and all of the other angst and emotional pain from her life.

But that wasn't going to happen any time soon—not with this SEAL. He wasn't Shay's Mr. Right or even her Mr. Right Now, because *she* was his friendly, slightly older neighbor—a variation of the "big sister slash mentor" role. Her job was to dispense wit and wisdom to the man—hold the steamy kisses—and collect his mail while he went galloping off on some crazy, romantic adventure with someone else.

What? Why? Harry still didn't get it.

Look around the room, Shay silently told him. Because, yeah, she'd written this type of book enough times to recognize that one of the two gorgeous and far more age-appropriate women gathered in Lieutenant Peter Greene's remarkably neat living room had to be the heroine to his Navy SEAL hero. And whoops, make that *three* gorgeous and far more age-appropriate *people,* Shay mentally corrected herself before Harry could yowl, because there was also a very adorable and probably gay young man sitting on the sofa.

Harry actually gasped. *Holy shit, that's not just some random adorable gay man, that's Hollywood film actor Adam Wyndham!*

Holy shit, it was. And the actor was clearly a regular in this house, because Peter greeted him with a casual, "Hey, Adam. Lindsey." The second name was aimed with a nod at a delicately pretty dark-haired woman sitting on the other end of the sofa.

But then all three of the beautiful people spoke at once.

"Any luck?" asked Lindsey, who was Asian American and—whoa!

Yeah, I didn't see that *coming,* Harry agreed. *But she's not leaping to her feet to greet him, so she's probably just a friend.*

Lindsey wasn't leaping to her feet because she was hugely pregnant.

Or that. But the SEAL did greet her like he didn't expect to see her in his house, Harry observed.

"Did you find her?" asked the literal movie star as the second woman—slim and ridiculously young, like barely-out-of-college young—chimed in with, "Any sign of her?"

"No," Peter answered them all at once. "I thought I saw Maddie getting into a car, but . . ." He shook his head.

"Did you get my text?" demanded the college student. She was as strikingly beautiful as the pregnant woman, with long, shiny, straight brown hair and dark brown eyes in a face that was quite possibly perfect. "I just sent you a screenshot. Maddie texted me."

"What?" Peter dug for his phone. "She did? When?"

"Just a minute ago."

"That's great news," Shayla exclaimed.

"She says she's okay, she's with a friend and basically, you know, *Leave me alone.* She blocked me again, right after she sent it, so I couldn't respond." The young woman turned to Shayla. "I'm Eden Zanella. My husband, Izzy, is one of Grunge's teammates."

"Grunge?" Shayla repeated, even as she looked over Peter's shoulder to read the text that Maddie had sent. And okay, so the gorgeous young woman was the Eden of Zanella-and-Eden that Peter had mentioned earlier, and obviously not his present-or-future soulmate. Not that Shay, as the witty neighbor, should care.

I don't know why you concluded you're only the neighbor, Harry complained. *And by the way . . . Yowl? Really?*

"Shh," Shay whispered, but then smiled weakly when Peter glanced over at her. Yup, he'd definitely noticed that she regularly hushed her invisible friend. Although, in her defense, big sisters and witty neighbors were allowed to have a larger amount of quirkiness in their personalities, so he was just going to have to deal with it.

Meanwhile, Maddie's text to Eden had been brief and to the point. "She was definitely in that car tonight," Peter concluded after he read it. "She knows I'm looking for her."

"Either that, or Dingo and Dumber called her," Shay said. "Grunge?"

The SEAL glanced up again and twinkled his eyes at her as he smiled tightly. Well, he didn't twinkle them intentionally. It just happened automatically whenever he smiled— and she was just going to have to deal with *that.* "Nickname. Don't ask. Everyone, this is Shayla. She lives across the street, and oddly enough, knows me as *Peter.*"

"Nice to meet you, Shayla. I'm Izzy." There was another man in the room, lurking over near the front window, but Shay hadn't noticed him until he spoke—and then she couldn't believe that she'd missed him. He was even broader and taller than Peter, and darkly, interestingly handsome, with midnight-colored eyes that gleamed with intelligence and amusement as he added, "And yeah, it's a nickname, too. Izzy for I Z—my initials—Irving Zanella. Nicknames are rampant in the Teams."

"I'm Adam," the actor said as if she didn't recognize him, then gestured to the pregnant woman, "and this is Lindsey Jenkins, with her soon-to-emerge plus one. So you live across the street, hmm?"

Lindsey's got a different last name and a wedding band, and FYI, your SEAL isn't gay, Harry noted.

Okay, but maybe Lindsey'd kept her own name upon marriage. Shayla had.

Maybe. Harry wasn't convinced. *But think about that question, with its* hmm *that's loaded with subtext. Adam's really asking "How long have you been shagging our friend Grunge?"*

"Ohmigod, no!" Shay blurted. "I mean, yes, I live across the street. I do. But I just happened to see Lieutenant Greene when I was dropping my son off at the high school, and, um . . ."

Oh, good. Now you sound weirdly defensive, so Adam's gotta think you've been sleeping with the SEAL nonstop for the past two months. And look at Grunge and Lindsey. Do they look even remotely *married to each other?*

They didn't.

"Can you get your friend at the SDPD to run a license plate for me?" Peter was asking Lindsey. He hadn't sat down on the couch next to her—instead he'd merely moved closer and stood there as he rattled off the combination of letters and numbers from Dingo's maroon POS.

"Back in the day, Lindsey was a police detective up in LA," Adam murmured to Shayla as Peter explained how he'd thought he'd seen Maddie getting into that car, and how Shay'd helped him follow it to the mall, where they'd met Dingo and his bearded friend.

"The timing of Maddie's text to Eden could be a coincidence," the SEAL named Izzy pointed out. He'd sat down in one of two easy chairs positioned on either side of a gorgeous old river rock fireplace, and pulled his beautiful wife onto his lap.

"But we don't *really* think that, do we?" Shayla argued. "Peter got *way* up in Dingo and Dumber's faces—" he'd left that little detail out "—and an hour later, Maddie sends *that* text to Eden?"

"Yeah, I'm with Shayla," Lindsey agreed with a smile in Shay's direction. "Finding Maddie might be as simple as running Dingo's plates and getting his home address."

"Assuming he keeps his registration current," Peter said. "Which I seriously doubt. I got a heavy whiff of couch-surfer off of him."

"Still, it's a good place to start," Shay said. "We should also see if we can access Maddie's Facebook page—"

"We can." Eden pointed to a laptop that was open and running a screen saver on a gorgeous oak coffee table. "That's Maddie's. But we already looked through her Facebook friends and hardly anyone's local. Her most recent messages are to someone named Fiona, from Sacramento."

"Oh, good!" Shay sat on the sofa between Lindsey and Adam, pulling the laptop closer so she could look at the screen.

Ahem, Harry said, and she looked up to find everyone looking at her, as Eden said, "That didn't seem like all that much to inspire an *Oh, good.*"

"No no, Sacramento's definitely not good," Shayla explained, "but access to Maddie's page *is* . . . I'm going to scan through her photos, see if I can find Dingo or his long-haired friend."

If it's okay with you, Harry prompted.

Shay cleared her throat and aimed the words at Peter. "If that's okay with you . . . ?"

"Hell, yeah," he said. "It's brilliant. Move over, Adam, I wanna look, too."

CHAPTER FIVE

Maddie stared as Dingo said, "Holy shite."

The condo where Fiona had lived with her aunt Susan had burned.

Badly.

It hadn't burned literally to the ground because it was on the second floor, but the place was clearly uninhabitable. It was hard for Maddie to see the full extent of the damage in the darkness, but it looked as if most of the kitchen roof was gone. And the beige stucco walls surrounding the shattered and now-empty windows were charred and streaked with soot.

"Holy. Shite." Dingo whispered the words again. But he laughed a little, too. "I guess Fiona finally lost it. Big time."

Maddie turned to look at him in disbelief. "You think *Fee* did this . . . ?"

"You think she didn't?" He was already on his phone, accessing the internet. "Looks like it burned . . . Yep, the fire happened on Friday morning. Neighbor saw the smoke and called nine-one-one around nine. No one was injured. That's good, at least."

If Fiona *had* started the fire, that certainly explained why she'd been pulled out of class on Friday, never to return.

"She's psycho," Dingo reminded Maddie as they walked down the street, back to where he'd parked his car. "It's psycho what she's done—framing you like that. Nelson is fuckin' dangerous, and Fee knows it. She wants him to hurt you. Or worse."

"So where's her aunt Susan living now?" Maddie asked.

"Your guess is as good as mine," he said. "Although where does someone horrible who probably doesn't have many friends go when their house burns down? A hotel, probably."

After stopping for donuts and talking Maddie into sending that text to "Dad's" friend Eden, Dingo had finally stopped stalling and driven them out here. Maddie had hoped to find out from Susan if Fee had gone home to her mother's or her father's house in Sacramento—and to get a phone number so they could call her. Although now it was entirely possible, despite what Fiona had said in her message to Nelson, that instead of Susan sending Fee home, the girl had gotten herself locked up.

"Did the article you read say anything about arson?" Maddie asked. "Was anyone arrested?"

"As in Fee?" Dingo countered. "No. It didn't say. But if Fee *is* in jail, that's a win for us. It'll be a quick and easy way to show Nelson that she's lying." He paused as they got back into his car. "On the other hand, she was always talking about how loaded her da was, and how much he was paying Susan each month so that Fee could live here in San Diego. Kinda hard to imagine a scenario in which he lets his only child rot in the slammer."

She shot him a disbelieving look. "Rot in the slammer? Really?"

"Sorry, love, have I got it wrong? It's hard to keep up with your American slang."

"It's perfect—if you're a doofus."

Dingo laughed. "Well, I've never denied that, have I?" He started his car. "Lookit, it's getting late. Shall we call it a night—find a campsite, perhaps get slightly baked before bedtime? Is *baked* acceptable slang for you?"

"It's great," she said, "but it's not late—it's only eight-thirty, Grandpa. Fee told me Susan didn't usually get home from work until after eleven. If we have any shot at all of finding out where she's staying, we need to find her law office. I wonder if she's got a website . . . Will you Google her?"

"Google what?" Dingo asked. *"Auntie Susan's Law Practice?"* He was grinning at his cleverness—and getting back at her for that *doofus* comment.

"Attorney Susan Fiera, San Diego, California," Maddie said.

"Nope, her last name's different from Fee's," Dingo said. "She and Fee's da had different das. Hers was named Smith."

Susan Smith. Great. There were probably dozens of lawyers in SoCal with that impossibly common name.

"But guess what," Dingo said cheerfully as he drove down the street and signaled a left turn that would take them to the Five. "Dread Auntie Sue left a file at home once, and Fee and I brought it over to her office, so I already know where she works. No Googling required."

"So why didn't you just say that already?" Maddie complained.

"I do believe the correct comment from you should be, *Oh, Dingo, you're amazing*—" he overdid the flat American vowels *"—Thank you so much. I don't know where I'd be without you, and I promise never to call you Grandpa again."*

Maddie laughed. "Yeah, that's not gonna happen, but . . . thank you. Really."

Dingo smiled back at her, but then sobered as he said in his real voice, "Even if Fee didn't burn her condo down, Susan won't be happy to see me."

"You can stay in the car," Maddie said.

"And let you face her alone?" Dingo said. "Not a chance in hell, love."

* * *

Pete ran his hands down his face as Shayla scrolled through countless pictures of the many friends of friends on Maddie's Facebook profile. Maddie herself didn't have that many contacts, but most of her contacts had hundreds and some had thousands. And nearly everyone had thousands of photos in their "albums." Photos of teenagers at parties, at the mall, in cars, at school, in their yards, in their bedrooms, in their rec rooms. It was all starting to blur.

"I think maybe I have Dingo-madness," Pete said.

His house had cleared out about a half hour ago. Zanella had been all but waving semaphore flags and tap-dancing Morse code to remind Pete that Eden was leaving in the morning on a trip that would keep her out of town for more than a week. His desperation to spend the rest of the evening alone with his wife was palpable. And it wasn't long after the Zanellas departed that Adam and Lindsey had packed it in, too.

Lindsey was clearly exhausted. She hadn't yet reached her SDPD buddy who could potentially provide an address for Dingo's license plate number, but she'd left the woman a message. As Adam had gently pulled her out the door, she'd promised to call Pete the moment she had any information at all.

Shayla'd glanced at him then—they were only about halfway through, and they'd yet to find either Dingo or Dumber in the myriad of photos. He couldn't tell if she was looking for permission to leave, too, so he said, "I'm sorry, yeah, it's getting late," right as she said, "So do you always hang out with movie stars?"

It took him a second to realize what she was talking about, and he said, "Oh, you mean Adam?" as she said, "It's not late—it's barely nine. And it's not like I have a long drive home."

"He's a member of the Community," Pete told her, and at her blank look, he added, "The SpecOps Community. Adam's fiancé is a SEAL. And nine is late when you get up at oh-three-thirty for training exercises."

"Oh, of course. I'm sorry." She quickly backpedaled and started to stand up. "I'm a night owl and . . . I'm actually an oblivious night owl, so please, in the future don't hesitate to simply tell me when it's time for me to go."

"No," he said. "Wait. Please. I'm mostly a night owl, too. I'm usually BUD/S OIC—officer in charge of SEAL candidate training. Phase One. Hell Week's 24/5, and I like to work at night, so I'm there. All night. But we're between classes, plus I took emergency leave when Maddie didn't come home last night, so . . ." He took a deep breath and went with full honesty. "Frankly, I'd love it if you could stay. If you don't mind. Your help has been . . . Well, I've gone from hopeless to hope . . . *ful*'s not the right word, because I'm not exactly full of hope, but I've got at least a little now. Hope. That maybe I'll be able to figure out what Maddie needs, and how I can make this dad thing work."

Shayla's face and eyes had shifted fully into that warm, soft, caring expression that he already loved the shit out of. "Heartened," she said. "Is that the word you're looking for?"

"Heartened," Pete echoed. "Yeah. I'm heartened. Thank you for heartening me."

She smiled at that, and he couldn't help himself. He looked at her mouth and he even shifted slightly toward her, like his body, on autopilot, was getting ready to kiss her.

Whoa.

That would not be okay. Not after she'd friend-bombed him the way she had, back in the car.

Except now that he'd thought about kissing her, it was hard to think about anything besides where a kiss might go. And now he couldn't stop thinking about the best way to undress her so that she could wrap her long legs around him and—*missing daughter, missing daughter, missing daughter.*

That worked to regain his focus.

Meanwhile Shayla didn't seem to notice—she'd had no problem bringing her full attention back to the computer.

And despite this one little autopilot accident—which would *not* happen again—the fact that she stayed to help didn't feel weird or awkward or inappropriate as the night ticked on.

It felt . . .

Nice. Like he wasn't going through this alone.

"Dingo-madness," Shayla repeated now as she continued scrolling through the zillions of photos.

Pete sighed and sat back. "At this point, every twenty-something idiot I see on Facebook looks like Dingo to me, so . . ."

"Ah," she said. "It sounds like it's kind of a cross between face blindness and whatever it was that the starving guy had in that Charlie Chaplin movie, you know, where he looks at Charlie and sees, what was it? A giant chicken drumstick?"

Pete laughed his appreciation. "Yeah, that's definitely what I've got."

"Aided by sleep deprivation, I bet." Shayla glanced at him. "Why don't you let me handle this for a bit," she suggested, "while you close your eyes. Just for a few minutes. I mean, you might as well, since everyone looks like Dingo to you, right? You actually might be a liability if you start shrieking, *There he is!* every time I flip to a new photo."

She had him there.

"I promise I'll wake you if I find anything—or even if I need a second opinion," she added.

So Pete put his feet up on the coffee table. With his head back against the couch cushions, he gave in and closed his eyes and the world hummed and buzzed and faded slightly. He could feel Shayla's presence beside him and hear the sound of her quiet breathing as she used the touchpad to scroll. It was sleep but not-sleep, but then, to his surprise, darkness descended and he went with it—and checked fully out.

He woke himself up—his internal clock telling him it had been fifteen glorious minutes—suddenly aware that he'd shifted slightly toward Shayla in sleep, and that his leg was now pressed against the warmth of her thigh. *Shit.* He pulled back. Opened his eyes to check his dive watch. Fifteen minutes on the nose. Not bad. He cleared his throat. "Find anything?"

Shayla was hunched over the computer and she didn't look up. "Nope, and I swear to every god out there that I'll wake you if I do."

"I'm good for now." Fifteen minutes was more than enough to clear his head. Pete pulled himself up off the couch and beelined it to the kitchen's coffeemaker. "You want coffee?" he asked. "Water? Tea? Scotch?"

She laughed. "Coffee," she called back. "Please. I'm getting a little bleary from all the pouty-lipped selfies."

"Yeah, what is up with that face everyone makes?" he called back to her as he filled the coffeemaker and turned it on.

"It's a *come do me* face," she said. "Which is disconcerting when thirteen-year-olds make it."

"Jesus," he said.

"Sorry," she called back. "If it's any consolation, Maddie hasn't taken any selfies with that expression. She tends to go for the grim glare."

"Thank God," he said as he opened the fridge. He tried to keep it stocked with fresh veggies and fruit—none of which Maddie had touched. "Hey, can you bring that thing and sit in here? I'm suddenly starving. I'm gonna scramble some eggs."

As he put the egg carton on the counter near the stove, Shayla appeared in the doorway with Maddie's laptop in her hands. He was struck again by how effortlessly pretty she was—like a rock garden filled with wildflowers—and Jesus, *wildflowers* in a *rock garden*? He obviously wasn't suffering from mere Dingo-madness. Maybe he was more fatigued than he'd thought. It was one thing to want to get naked and lose himself in an attractive woman—another entirely to start waxing poetic about *wildflowers*.

Pete grabbed a pan and turned on the heat for the stove's front burner. Protein would help.

"Want some?" he asked, efficiently cracking eggs and tossing the shells into the sink as his neighbor carried the computer toward the center island.

"No, thanks," she said. "Coffee'll do."

He purposely turned to watch her walk—to prove to himself that he could do that without looking at her ass.

Shit. He'd dropped an egg.

He wiped it up with the sponge as she perched that ass that he was not looking at on one of the stools he'd bought specifically for this counter in this little house. In which he'd hoped to live happily ever after with his daughter. Hah.

It was then that she gasped. "Found him!"

"Dingo?" Pete came to look, grabbing the towel to wipe egg from his fingers.

"Nope. But a close second. It's Dumber."

Pete looked over her shoulder, and yes. That was definitely Dingo's long-haired, large-bearded friend from the mall garage. Shayla had those photos she'd taken displayed in a second window on the computer screen, for comparison. It was a solid match.

"His name is Daryl Middleton," she said. "His profile is pretty sparse, not a lot of photos posted—certainly none of Dingo, at least not that I've found yet, but—whoa! Says here he works at the Irish Pub." She smiled up at Pete, excitement dancing in her dark brown eyes. "That's not far from here. It's over near Burgers Plus."

"Oh, I know where it is," Pete said, going back to the stove to turn off the heat under his eggs. His food could wait.

"Except, oh no!" Shayla said. "There's a post from last week where he says he got fired. Apparently, he wasn't there long—and God, it's like he's proud he lasted less than a day. I'm gonna Google him . . ."

"Even if he worked for just one hour, someone at the Irish knows him. I'm still going over."

"Eat first," she said. "And think twice. Even if the owner is there at this time of night, he or she isn't just going to hand over a former employee's personal information to someone who's not a cop. Let's give this to Lindsey, because the only Daryl Middletons I'm finding off-Facebook are in their sixties—and none of them live in San Diego."

Pete wasn't convinced, and somehow she knew that. "What if you go over there," Shayla continued. "And not only do you not get any info, but whoever you talk to calls Daryl and warns him that you're looking for him, so if Maddie and Dingo actually *are* at his place, they immediately adios. Plus, if they have any brains at all, they'll figure out you tracked Daryl to the Irish Pub through Maddie's Facebook, so they change her password and lock us out of her account. And while it's not exactly a gold mine of info, it's better than nothing."

Shit. "Yeah, you're right. That would not be good." Pete turned the burner back on. "So tell me this: Which one of Maddie's friends is Middleton connected to?"

"A girl named Fiona Effable, and oh. Yeah. As I said her last name, well, that's clearly not real, is it?"

Effable. F-able. Right. Pete tried not to twitch too perceptively as he absorbed the fact that Maddie had a friend who publicly referred to herself as *fuckable*.

"Fiona's profile says she lives in Sacramento," Shayla reported, "which is weird, because she and Maddie seem to post to each other a lot. Not lately, but right up until this past Friday. Then, over the weekend and past few days, there's a lot of Maddie solo-posting to Fiona's page—messaging her, too, but no response. It's weird, Maddie keeps asking *Can you Macarena?* Maybe it's some kind of inside joke. But she posted it, let's see, one, two, three . . . five different times. Last time in all caps."

"Macarena, like the dance?" Pete asked.

Shayla shrugged. "I guess. Do people actually still Macarena?"

"I prefer the Mashed Potato," he said, and did a few steps, right there in front of the stove.

Shayla's laughter was musical as it rang through the room. "Oh, my God, that was really good. Where did you learn to dance like that?"

"Lisa," he admitted. He could feel his face heating. Jesus, when was the last time he'd blushed? "She was really into musical theater so I know a lot of basic steps. Including the Macarena." He did a bit of the arms, making her laugh with delight again. "Which, yeah, could be an inside joke. Or maybe it's code."

"Could be either," Shayla said. "Or both. They're teenaged girls."

"How long have they been friends?" Pete wondered. "Can you tell?"

"Hmm." She focused again on the computer. "I can't tell for sure, but . . . Okay. Yeah. It looks like Fiona and Maddie only started posting to each other about . . . two months ago." She looked up at him.

Pete said the obvious. "When Maddie moved to San Diego."

"Maybe Fiona saying she lives in Sacramento's an intentional misdirect," Shayla suggested as the coffeemaker burbled its last and went silent. "Kind of like *Effable*'s not her real name . . . ?"

"*Fiona* might not be her real name either," Pete said, grabbing a pair of mugs from the cabinet and pouring them each a hefty serving. "So what do we do?" Oops, now he was using the word *we*.

Shayla didn't seem to notice—or care—as she shook off his offer of milk and sugar. She, too, drank her coffee black.

"Take a screenshot of Fiona's picture and bring it over to the school tomorrow?" Pete continued.

"Oh, absolutely. Good plan. If she's local, someone in the front office knows her," she agreed. "I'll go over with you in the morning—they know me there. Really well. Mrs. Sullivan—she essentially runs the school—she probably won't be able to give us Fiona's info, but I know she'll be willing to contact her parents for us. In the meantime . . . I'm texting Fiona's picture to Tevin and Frank." She glanced up at him again. "My sons. I'm sending the pix of Dingo and Daryl Middleton, too. And a photo of Maddie, while I'm at it. Might as well see if they know anything."

Pete scraped his perfectly crisp scrambled eggs into a bowl, grabbed a fork, and joined her at the counter. "Thank you. So much. Can I ask you to text the photos to Ben Gillman while you're at it? That's Eden Zanella's little brother.

He's a junior at the high school. He might know something, too. He should be in Maddie's contacts."

"Yup, got him," she said. "No problem. I'm gonna include you and Eden in a group text, though, so Ben's not just suddenly getting pictures from some weird stranger-lady."

She was always thinking. "You'd make a great SEAL," he told her.

Shayla snorted. "Yeah, except for the part where I can't run very fast, my swimming is limited to the dog paddle, I hate the cold, and oh, yeah, I'm afraid of literally everything."

"Everything," he repeated.

"Oh, yeah," she said. "Tornados—although I've never been in one—spiders, earthquakes . . . I *was* in the San Francisco quake, in 1989. I had nightmares for years."

"And yet you moved to California, home of the earthquake," Pete pointed out. "Relatively recently, wasn't it?"

She nodded. "Carter, my ex, got a steady gig in San Diego. It was either move out here and continue to share custody of the boys, or force them to choose which parent they wanted to live with for the school year. I didn't want them to have that pressure. And since I can write—or not-write—anywhere . . ." She shrugged. "Everywhere I go, I make note of the sturdiest-looking door frames and furniture. So if a big truck rumbles past and I suddenly dive under the table, it's not merely because I want to admire your flip-flops."

Pete laughed. "You know, it's not about not being afraid—it's about taking action despite the fear," he pointed out. "That's called courage."

She made that little *shh* sound before smiling and saying, "Yes, well, lucky for you my fear of being mocked trumps my fear of earthquakes, otherwise I'd be sitting here, courageously wearing my earthquake helmet, and you'd be sitting here trying hard not to laugh at me."

He laughed again as he carried his empty bowl to the sink. "Hey, I danced for you. If anyone deserves to be laughed at—"

She made a giant raspberry sound. "Oh, please, if you expect me to believe that a man as smart as you—an officer and a gentleman—doesn't know that the majority of women rate straight-men-who-dare-to-dance as an automatic eleven on the hotness scale . . ." Her voice trailed off and it was her turn to blush—although her gorgeous complexion helped to hide it—because, yes, she'd just called him *hot*.

Of course it was then that Pete's cellphone rang. He'd left it on the counter and he could see the screen. He answered it. "Lindsey, thanks for calling. Shayla's still here—I'm putting you on speaker. What'd you find?"

"I'm afraid I've got nothing yet," Lindsey said apologetically. "I wanted to let you know that I heard back from my contact, and she's not gonna be near a computer until tomorrow morning. She guesses it'll be around oh-eight-hundred at the earliest."

Pete reined in his frustration, concentrating on breathing as Shayla let Lindsey know that they'd come up with Daryl Middleton's name. Lindsey in turn volunteered to ask her friend to run him through the system, too.

"Regardless, we won't get any info until tomorrow," Lindsey repeated. "Try to get some sleep, Grunge," she added and cut the connection.

And then, there they were. Sitting and standing in Pete's kitchen as the realization that he wasn't going to find Maddie tonight sank down around him. It was night two of her little escapade—night two in which he'd get little to no sleep.

Shayla must've been thinking the same thing, because she said, "There's really not a whole lot more we can do tonight.

I mean, yes, tomorrow morning, first thing, we can go to the school. And I'll check in with Tevin, see if he knows anyone in the pictures I sent him. Frank's already texted me. He's clueless, but I expected that. Ben texted back, too—he's gonna check with some friends, but he sounded dubious."

"What time does the school open?" Pete asked. "I mean the office. I know what time school starts, but how early—"

"Mrs. S usually unlocks the door around six-thirty," she told him. "We could leave here as early as six—be there waiting when she arrives—if you could drive me there and back. That way I can leave my car for the boys—I'm pretty sure Carter took his back tonight and . . . Talking them into going to school at six A.M. will be a hard sell."

He nodded. "Yeah, thanks, I'll take you up on that. That would be great."

"And after *that,* depending on whether we find out where Fiona really lives and if we can go and talk to her or her parents, we could take Lindsey's suggestion and drop in on Maddie's great-aunt Hiroko since she lives here in San Diego—see if Maddie's been in touch. Give her a heads-up, in case Maddie reaches out to her."

Hiroko. Right. That was going to be awkward. But Pete kept nodding. "I also want to rent a truck and move everything that's in the storage space in Palm Springs back here. There's room in the garage for it—all of the boxes from Lisa and Maddie's apartment. Having it close'll make it easier to sift through. I'd like to find their old computer. Maddie said they had a desktop that had tons of photos on it. Maybe Daryl and Dingo are friends from Palm Springs."

"I can help you do that," Shayla said. "And remember, after eight, when Lindsey's police contact gets access to the computer . . . Well, it might be as easy as finding out Dingo's address. We drive over there, we find them . . ."

Pete nodded. "To be honest, that's . . . terrifying, too."

Shayla did the warm-eyes-and-face thing. "I'll lend you my earthquake helmet."

He laughed at that—it was impossible not to.

She smiled, but then she cleared her throat. "Seriously, though, since I suspect you're going to have trouble sleeping, may I suggest you do something that might sound . . ." She was doing her careful-word-choice thing again, and she paused before finishing with ". . . a little unusual?"

Pete leaned back against the counter, completely unable to guess where she was going with this. If she'd been anyone else, he might've let his imagination run wild, trying to figure out what she was going to suggest from a variety of options including downing a whole bottle of Scotch, to doing yoga or coloring in a meditation coloring book, to having a rousing round of exhaustive and athletic sex—all to help him sleep.

But she hadn't disappointed him yet—well, the friend-bombing had disappointed, but in a completely unexpected manner.

"Suggest away," he said. "As my parent-of-a-teenager sherpa, my mentor, if you will, I am open to whatever wisdom you're willing to share."

Shayla winced—which was weird, because his words were meant to be complimentary—but she covered it quickly with a smile. "I was thinking about how you said Lisa taught you to dance, and I was wondering if you'd told Maddie anything about that."

He shook his head.

"I think that you should," Shayla said. "In fact, I said this before, but it's worth repeating. I really do think it would help if you told Maddie where she came from. I mean, I can tell—just from the little you've told me—that you truly loved her mother. Maddie needs to know that. She'd probably appreciate hearing the whole story—how you and Lisa met—the good stuff, when the relationship was shiny and new. Not to throw shade at a woman who can no longer defend herself, but Maddie's probably heard plenty about the shitty stuff—the breakup."

Pete nodded. "That's a good idea, but . . ."

Shayla waited, watching him with those eyes.

"Assuming I ever find her, I can talk but I can't make her listen," he said. "Short of tying her up and going all *Clockwork Orange* with her eyelids . . ."

She smiled. "I wasn't thinking so much about talking as writing it down and sending it to her. In an email, maybe. That way we don't have to find her first—which we will—but she can also read it when she's ready. And? It'll be something proactive for you to do tonight, if you can't sleep."

Now it was Pete's turn to wince. "I'm not much of a writer."

Shayla smiled again and said the words he'd hoped she'd say: "I'm happy to help."

CHAPTER SIX

"There she is! There she is! Get ready to follow her!" Maddie hissed, scrunching down in the front seat of Dingo's car as they sat parked at the edge of the strip mall where Fiona's aunt Susan rented a small office. She peeked out over the top of the dashboard, adding with far less certainty, "That *is* her, isn't it?"

Dingo nodded. Yes, the woman tapping her way across the nearly empty parking lot on her ridiculously high heels was indeed Fiona's aunt Susan. Whose condo Fiona had apparently set fire to Friday last.

Fee'd been living with her father's stepsister since last summer—which was when Dingo'd first met the girl at a rave in Santa Monica. They'd hooked up that same night, and then suddenly she was his girlfriend—which had freaked him out a bit. Fiona was gorgeous, true—if you liked blond girls with big breasts and crazy eyes.

The breasts had been nice. The crazy eyes, not so much.

But back when they'd met, she was only visiting for a two-week vacay. So that worked for him, majorly. Except then, suddenly, it was permanent, with Fee moving in with

Auntie Susan and enrolling in the local high school for her senior year.

To be fair, even then, Dingo had been pretty much okay with it. The sex was relatively regular and decent enough despite all the weeping and teeth-gnashing that Fee carried around with her 24/7. But then, a few months ago, she'd introduced him to her new friend Maddie, and . . .

For Dingo, it had been love at first conversation. Maddie was not only significantly better read than Fee, but her favorite movies and music didn't give him a headache from suppressed eye-rolling. Bottom line, though, was her sense of humor. Fee's idea of funny had a heavy mean streak. Maddie's, while sometimes dormant due to her mom's recent tragic death, was delightfully deep and even dark, but never cruel.

"You don't need to hide, love," he told her now as he opened his door. "Susan's already seen my car and she's coming over here to—" What? Spit at him? Dingo chose "—chat." Assuming one could chat at a screamingly high volume. He also suspected Susan was charging over here to grind his face in the fact that Fiona was gone for good. She'd never liked him, but after last month's incident with the hidden camera, her hatred had gone nuclear and she forbade him from seeing Fee.

A rule that Fiona had broken repeatedly, since Susan was never home.

Still, this was gonna suck. Dingo would've preferred Maddie stay in the car, but she got out, too—the better to see his impending humiliation.

Susan opened with a snarling, "What part of *Stay the fuck away from me* do you not understand, you pervert?"

"That camera wasn't mine," he said for the five thousandth time, even as he realized that if she hadn't believed it before, she probably wasn't going to believe it now. Still, he couldn't stop himself, because Maddie was listening. "I've never even owned a digital camera."

Susan •turned to Maddie. "Make sure you check the shower fan or the air vent in your bathroom—or in your bedroom if you let this creepy fucker in there. He hides cameras that he's connected to the internet, so be ready to share your diarrhea face with the entire universe."

God. The look Maddie shot him was filled with disgust and horror, but Dingo couldn't tell if it was aimed at him or Susan. "Yeah, I'm pretty certain, at this point, that it was Fiona's camera," he said weakly.

Susan looked at him as if he were walking, talking dogshit. "Some of those pictures were of *her*. Even she's not *that* screwed up." She'd argued that point before, although, for the first time, as she said the words, she didn't look convinced.

"Lookit, love, we just want to know where Fee's at," Dingo said, leaning extra hard on the accent because it made him sound easygoing and gentle and just other enough, but crap, that *love* was definitely a mistake because the woman bristled. So he talked faster. "Maddie, here, needs to get in touch with her. We're really sorry to bother you like this, but it's kind of urgent."

"Yeah, well, good luck with that," Susan said flatly. "She's back in Sacramento."

Maddie spoke up. "Did she really set fire to your condo?"

Susan sniffed. "It was an accident. One of us—probably me—left a pot on the stove. A pile of mail was nearby. . . . It was an accident."

"I'll take that as a *yes,* and assume Fiona's father is paying to clean it all up," Maddie said.

Susan started to huff and puff in protest, but Dingo interrupted. "Where exactly is she?" he asked. "At her mum's? Or her dad's?" Both of her parents were strict, but according to Fee, her mother was a freak-show who screened all of her phone calls.

"I don't know," Susan said. "And frankly, I don't care."

"Do you have their phone numbers?" Maddie asked. "Or maybe an address?"

Susan looked from Maddie to Dingo. "Chuck and Maisy are divorced—both remarried. So it's Charles and Donna Fiera, and Douglas and Maisy Clark. They all live in Sacramento. Get a phone book and look 'em up." And with that she tippy-tapped away.

"A phone book," Maddie fumed as she got back into Dingo's car. "What, is she seventy? Who even *has* a phone book anymore?"

"That camera really wasn't mine," Dingo felt compelled to say.

"I know that." Maddie aimed some of her ire at him as she dug in the hard plastic pocket on the door and came up with a scrap of paper and pen. She scribbled down the names Susan had rattled off. "Don't be stupid. That whole thing reeks of Fee." She jammed both paper and pen into the cupholder and fastened her seat belt. "Will you drive already?"

"Oh," he said, clearing his throat. "Um. I don't have enough gas to get to Los Angeles, let alone Sacra—"

"We don't need to go to Sacramento," Maddie interrupted. "At least not yet. We just need to get to wherever you can hack into someone's wi-fi so we can look up those stupid phone numbers."

Dingo nodded. That he could do. They were trying not to use Maddie's phone, for fear her dad would somehow be able to track her. And he saved his own limited data usage for emergencies. But there were nonsecure wi-fi hotspots in virtually every neighborhood—and he'd found and used them all as he'd boondocked his way through the Greater San Diego area. He pulled out of the parking lot, and headed for one of his favorite camping spots—a dead-end street near an upscale apartment complex. They could overnight there, too. It was far enough off the main road with no easy turnaround, which meant the police wouldn't drive by and hassle them.

Still, the lack of proximity to a bathroom would make it way less comfortable than last night's stay in a truck stop parking lot—and, of course, just because Dingo hadn't been hassled in the past didn't mean it wouldn't happen tonight. Two people exhaling all night long made his car windows steam up twice as quickly. Someone out walking their dog could see that and call in a complaint which would *make* the police drive past and . . .

It was entirely possible he wanted to park there because he longed to get caught—to get Maddie back into the safety of her father's more-capable hands.

Because she was only freaking fifteen years old, and Nelson was a freaking lunatic.

"Were there any of me?" Maddie asked, startling him out of his reverie. "Probably not, because Susan would've recognized me." She laughed her disgust. "Of course, that doesn't mean Fiona doesn't have 'em."

At Dingo's obvious confusion, she explained, "Photos. From the camera in the bathroom. I've been there. Before it burned down. Susan's condo. Never when Fee's aunt was home, though. But I took a shower there once—after Fee dumped a pot of tomato sauce on me. In hindsight, I'm sure that she did it on purpose—it was totally in my hair so I had to take a shower, so she'd then have naked photos of me. *Shit*." She looked over at him, her eyes worried in the light from the dashboard. "If she was trying to get *you* into serious trouble . . ."

Yup. If naked pix of Maddie showed up on Dingo's computer or phone, well, wouldn't that be some kind of extra-awful felony, since the girl was underage? Forget the impending wrath of her Navy SEAL daddy. . . .

"We'll find them," Maddie decided. "And delete them. And then we'll find and call Fiona."

"If she's at her mum's we won't get through."

"Then we'll find the money we need for the gas to get to Sacramento."

"Find?" Dingo asked. "Like, just lying there on the street? Or find, like, in the cold, dark, locked house of someone who's out for the evening."

"We are *not* thieves," Maddie told him sternly.

"That's all well and good, love, but it's five hundred miles to Sacramento from here. Gas'll cost a small fortune—this creature guzzles the stuff—and that's just one way. We'll also have to get back. And I feel compelled to point out that even if we do drive all the way there and actually find Fee—which is questionable—she's just gonna tell us she's already spent the cash and then laugh in our faces," Dingo said.

"Good," Maddie said. "Because we're gonna record it. The whole conversation. We'll get her to admit to everything—the camera, the photos, the money she stole from Nelson—even starting the fire in Susan's condo."

"And then what?" Dingo asked. "We'll have a blackmail video, but you can't blackmail someone who doesn't give a shit."

"*Some*one will give a shit," Maddie said. "Fee's father gives a shit. And even if he doesn't, at the very least, we can use the video to protect you."

Dingo glanced at her again, but she was serious—gazing back at him with what he'd come to think of as her warrior's face, filled with courage and resolve.

"I'm 'sposed to be taking care of you, love," he whispered.

Maddie nodded. "But that doesn't mean I shouldn't also try to take care of you. You're all I've got, Ding."

And just like that, he was done.

She was still talking. "I think I know where we can get some money—not a lot, but enough for the gas to Sacramento. I have this crazy great-aunt who was always trying to give Lisa these stupid family heirlooms. We can go visit her in the morning, and maybe walk out with an armload of stuff that we can pawn. It won't be worth a whole lot, but . . ." She shrugged.

"That sounds like a bloody brilliant plan," Dingo said, and she smiled back at him.

He'd been goners long before she'd said that—*You're all I've got*—but now?

He was toast.

* * *

I didn't know the city all that well, so I was just driving around trying to find the ocean. See, I'd just spent two years on a really remote island in Indonesia, and the ocean was in my blood.

I was sixteen. I was the new kid at the high school, which sucked as much back then as it probably still sucks today. I'd spent a lot of time alone over those past few years, and the crowds and the noise of the city were intense. So, yeah, I was in my father's car and looking for the beach—while doing some heavy hating on San Diego in general.

I headed west—and traffic was thick, partly because a car had broken down on the shoulder. Trunk's open, hood's up, flashers are on. Someone had attached a white handkerchief to the radio antenna—like the situation's so bad, they've surrendered. And as I was approaching, I could see this little old Asian lady—she was literally tiny—maybe five feet tall and probably in her sixties. At the time that seemed ancient to me. She was wrestling the spare tire out of the trunk of her car. As I got closer, I could see she'd gotten the jack out, too.

And I was watching all these other people—most of them adults—in all these cars in front of me just drive past her, like she was invisible. That was weird to me, coming from a place where if you didn't stop and help someone in trouble, there was a chance that they'd die.

So I pulled over, just behind her, and yup, her back right tire was flat. It was shredded—it's lucky she didn't lose control and crash when it blew.

I climbed out of the car and I said, "May I give you a hand with that, ma'am?"

That was when I realized that she'd picked up the cross wrench and was holding it defensively. My first thought was maybe she's scared because she doesn't speak English. I was pretty sure she was Japanese—there was a Japanese family that owned a ferryboat on our island, and I'd learned a bit of the language—not much, though. We mostly spoke in Malay or Indonesian. Anyway, I held out my hands to show that I wasn't dangerous and I said something like "Good day, Grandmother" in Japanese. I didn't have the vocabulary to tell her that I'd change her tire, so I pointed to the tire and the jack and to myself, and I said, "Help you, I will."

I remember that clearly, because she laughed and lowered the wrench and said—in English that was better than mine—"Thank you, Yoda. Very kind, you are. I'm so glad of that. People who look like you aren't always friendly to people who look like me."

I gaped at her honesty, and I think I blurted something like, "That's terrible!"

She just smiled and said, "I think the spare's flat, but if I can wrestle it onto the car, at least it'll let me limp to a gas station."

We chatted while I got the jack into place. She asked where I'd learned to speak Japanese. I told her about the island and my parents moving back here, and how I missed living so close to the ocean. I'm sure my homesickness was radiating off of me in waves.

She told me she lived about a block from the beach, and if I wanted to, I could park in her driveway when I visited my old friend, the Pacific.

Her name was Hiroko Nakamura, and maybe it's weird that a sixteen-year-old boy was best friends with a sixty-year-old Nisei woman. (Nisei means that Hiroko was born in America. Her parents were Issei—they were born in Japan and immigrated here.)

And maybe it's not weird. I was safe in the quiet of her garden. And I quickly established a routine of stopping in for an early morning—

"Wait," Peter said.

Shayla looked up from the computer screen and into the man's disconcertingly blue eyes. They were still sitting at the breakfast counter in the SEAL's kitchen, and she was reading aloud what they'd already written—the story of how Peter had come to meet Maddie's mother, Lisa, back when they both were in high school.

Those eyes narrowed slightly. "Did I really say that?" he asked.

She knew exactly the *that* to which he was referring.

Harry was hovering and he repeated it: "*I was safe in the quiet of her garden.*"

"I paraphrased," Shayla explained. "You talked in circles around it for about ten paragraphs, so rather than make this an epic tome, I boiled it down to the essence. Isn't it true? You felt safe there."

"Yeah," he admitted. "But . . ."

"Too touchy-feely," she guessed. "For you, maybe, but your audience is a fifteen-year-old girl. She's dealing with some of the very same things that *you* were back then—new city, new school, a loss—"

"My loss wasn't even close to hers," he quickly pointed out.

"But acknowledging it still makes you—sixteen-year-old you—more relatable to Maddie," Shayla countered.

"Okay, but that bit about the garden just feels like I'm, I don't know . . ." He laughed. "Sharing an embarrassing secret."

"What's embarrassing?" Shayla asked. "About wanting to feel safe?"

Seriously? Harry said. *You just seriously asked a Navy SEAL alpha male . . . ?*

It was, indeed, a serious question, and she held Peter's gaze as he silently looked back into her eyes for a moment. A long moment. She tried to ignore that inappropriate feeling of warmth and connection as she stared back at him, determined not to look away.

Peter blinked first. And nodded. "You're right," he said. "Also, the point of this story is . . . to share. I have to get used to the fact that if I'm uncomfortable, that means we're probably doing this right." He met her eyes again. "Right?"

"Yes. Right," Shayla said as Harry laughed and whispered *Oh my God is this guy real? I need you to have sex with him, immediately.* "Shhhh—sure! Absolutely!" She cleared her throat and focused on the computer. "Where were we . . . ? Ah."

I was safe in the quiet of her garden. And I quickly established a routine of stopping in for an early-morning swim, before heading off to the pain in my ass that was school.

Anyway, that long introduction—how I met Hiroko—brings us to a foggy San Diego morning, several weeks later.

I'm sure you can guess what's coming, since you already

know that Hiroko was Lisa's great-aunt. She's Lisa's grand-father's youngest sister, and was childhood friends with Kiyo, Lisa's grandmother.

But back then, I didn't know about that connection and I was caught off-guard.

I'd seen Lisa at school. It would've been hard to miss her. She was a senior and one of the popular kids. She had the lead in the school play, she was dating the school basket-ball star, she was the prom queen. . . . I stayed far away. I had no time for any of that. But Lisa had this charisma. When she walked down the hall, it was impossible to look away.

So. Foggy morning. I drove over, parked in the driveway, and went for my swim.

Hiroko had an outside shower—a small, wooden, open-aired stall attached to the side of her little cottage. I used it to rinse the salt from my skin before I changed and went to class.

Sometimes she was awake and in her kitchen. On those days she always shared her breakfast with me.

But sometimes, probably when she hadn't slept much the night before—insomnia was her mortal enemy—her kitchen door was tightly closed, and the windows were dark.

This was one of those shuttered mornings.

I was quiet as I came, barefoot, up from the beach. I si-lently unlatched the gate to the garden, and went around to the back of the house.

I was running late, so I went for the efficiency of pulling off my trunks and hanging them over the clothesline on my way to the shower. I swung open the door, turned on the water, and was underneath the spray before I realized I was not alone in there.

Lisa was sitting on the bench where I'd left my clothes for school.

That was as far as they'd gotten. "So yeah, *that* was awkward" was how Peter had concluded the story when he'd first recounted it. "We talked, she made sure I wasn't taking advantage of her aunt, and, well, that was that."

Except for the part where he'd been naked in front of a girl he couldn't keep himself from watching when she walked down the high school corridor.

"We're gonna need a few more details," Shayla said briskly now.

"Like what?" he asked.

"Like, what exactly happened. Did you dive for your towel?"

"Nope," Peter said. "She handed it to me. Eventually."

"Eventually? So you're just standing there, hanging out, everything just kind of . . . lazily blowing in the breeze . . . ?"

He smiled at that. "Yeah, but no breeze. I think Lisa was as surprised as I was—maybe more, because my family was unconventional. So I was comfortable with nudity. I turned off the water, and I think I might've said *What the hell,* or the equivalent. She was trying to play it cool, but she blushed, which pretty much gave her away."

Shayla's fingers were flying as she typed his words, even as she asked, "So what did she say when you said *What the hell*?"

"She goes, *Of course Auntie's new pool boy is you, Goldilocks. I should've known.* And I now know what she meant—but then I didn't get the cultural reference, having lived on an island for two years, and also having never seen any porn at that point, so I said something like, *Hiroko's your aunt?* And then, *She doesn't have a pool.*"

"Wait," Shayla said. "Rewind. She called you *Goldilocks*? Like, *And the Three Bears*?"

Pete laughed. "Yeah. Here's another of those shameful secrets. At that time, I had really long blond dreadlocks. One of my friends from the island was a Rastafarian."

"A Rastafarian?" Shay repeated.

"He was from Jamaica and was best friends with a Tibetan monk who'd taken a vow of silence. I'm pretty sure they communicated via interpretive dance. We also had a curmudgeonly eighty-year-old former rock drummer who used the beach as a giant Zen garden, these incredibly jacked German women who were into blacksmithing, and a constantly rotating group of Americans looking for inspiration, which I'm pretty sure was code for getting high and sleeping with someone else's spouse." He laughed again. "It was an artists' colony."

Shayla nodded—suddenly it all made sense. But as fascinating as this was, and as much as she hated reining in this backstory tangent, these were details for another chapter. It was nearly ten-thirty. Her boys had been home for a while—she could see the shifting glow from the TV through her living room window—and she wanted to get back there before they went to bed.

Still, her detail-loving heart broke a bit as she forced herself to ask, "What did Lisa say after you pointed out that Hiroko didn't have a pool?"

Peter smiled. "She said, *Are you seriously tan all over?* And I think I said, *Yes?* And then she kind of shook her head and made a *Harold and Maude* reference, which I also didn't get at the time. That's that cult classic movie—"

"About the suicidal kid who gets into an intimate relationship with an eighty-year-old woman," Shay finished for him. She knew. "Lisa seriously thought . . . ?"

"That I was banging her aunt H," Pete, in turn, finished for her.

And there was another creative use of that verb *to bang*, also used with authenticity.

Was he? Harry wondered.

Shhh, Shay murmured silently.

"At the time, I was clueless," Peter was continuing with a

rueful shrug. "Lisa told me later, you know, that that was what she'd thought. She and her family lived just a few blocks over and a neighbor told her about some kid with really long hair visiting Hiroko at odd hours. So Lisa came swooping in to protect and defend."

"That's really sweet," Shayla said.

"Yeah, I'm not sure about that," he said. "Yes, it's what she said, but in truth, it was more complicated. Hiroko and Lisa didn't always get along. It's possible Lisa was looking for leverage or even blackmail material—more about power and self-defense. But that's not for Maddie to hear. Anyway, I'm standing there, with literally nothing to hide as Lisa grills me as to how I met Hiroko, and where I'm from, and what I'm doing there. I told her, and I guess she believed me.

"She finally stood up and handed me my towel, probably because she'd also figured out that she was way more embarrassed than I was about the full frontal nudity. But then she said, *Hurry up and get dressed, Goldie. We're already late for school. I'll wait for you in your car.*" Pete smiled at the memory. "So I drove her to school, and I'm thinking, *Okay, that was interesting*, but now it was over. You know, it felt kind of like an alien encounter—I was pretty sure it wasn't gonna happen again. Except the next day, after my shower, I head for my car, and she's sitting in the front seat. She hated riding the bus, so it became a regular thing. She called me her *carpool buddy*—when she wasn't calling me *Goldie* or *Goldilocks*. She was funny and smart and blindingly attractive, and she gave me her full attention for twenty minutes every day. I'd get in the car and she'd announce a topic of discussion. *Kirk or Picard? The Beatles: Yes or No? Who'd Win a Wrestling Match: George Bernard Shaw or Shakespeare? Was Filming* Flipper *Animal Abuse?*

"A few days in, I remember thinking, *Huh, I kinda don't hate it here anymore.* A week later, I'm all *Yup, I love San*

Diego. And a few days after that, I knew I was doomed, because I recognized that what I really loved—*who* I really loved—was Lisa Nakamura."

Shayla was typing as fast as her fingers could move, but she just had to glance up, because his tone—his voice—had changed. He sounded softer—dreamy—and yeah, his face and body language had softened perceptibly, too. His eyes were distant and warm—he'd time traveled. And she knew she was looking at the ghost of teenaged Peter Greene, and she wished Maddie could see just how powerful and pure his love for her mother had once been.

He wasn't done. "I was smart enough to recognize that when a girl—especially a senior who was already dating the school's star athlete—used words like *buddy* and nicknames like *Goldilocks*," he continued, "Well, the chances that she'd fall in love with me were a snowball's in hell."

Shayla nodded as she transcribed his words. This was good. With just a few minor tweaks, it would be ready to send.

Still, she wondered if Maddie would recognize what she did—that the melting-in-hell snowball really represented Lisa's chances of *not falling* for Peter. There was no way on earth that that boy could have successfully hidden his feelings from anyone, let alone the object of his affection. And that much adoration would've been hard for anyone to resist.

Also? Harry pointed out, *Lisa had seen him naked, in his all-over golden-tan glory.*

Yup. Game. Over.

CHAPTER SEVEN

Thursday

Tevin was in the kitchen, doing his preworkout morning zombie shuffle, when Shayla was ready to leave.

It wasn't quite six A.M., but she'd glanced out the window to see Peter already waiting for her, standing in his driveway beside his truck, checking his phone.

He was wearing . . . "Oh, dear God."

"Everything all right?" Tevin asked. He looked out the window, too, and saw the SEAL, who was wearing his Naval Officer uniform—the short-sleeved sleek white version, rows upon rows of colorful ribbons on his broad chest. "*That's* the neighbor you're helping? Go, Moms."

"It's not like that," Shay said. "Not even remotely."

"Well, why not?" Tevin looked so much like his father, it was sometimes startling. That quicksilver smile, those adorable dimples and laughing brown eyes, that same warm umber tone to his perfect skin . . . But when he walked and talked, Tevin was absolutely his own sweet self. Dynamic, creative, original, sensitive, caring . . . Her baby boy, in a nearly grown man's body.

"Well, he's younger than I am, for one thing," Shay said.

T looked out the window again. "Not by *that* much," he countered. "Tiffany's, like, fifteen years younger than Dad. Nobody's got problems with that."

He had a point. Even Shayla liked Carter's latest live-in girlfriend. Tiffany might have been young, but she was smart, funny, open, and she genuinely cared about the boys.

Tevin grinned. "What's that old movie you like to watch whenever you get the flu?"

Shayla knew exactly the movie to which her cinema-loving son was referring, but she pretended not to. "*The Bodyguard*? Whitney Houston? *I-eee-I! Will always love—*"

"Yeah, nah-no, come on, you know what I mean—the other one, with what's-his-name from *Pretty Woman*."

"Richard Gere," she said. "Oh, you mean *An Officer and a Gentleman*."

"That's the one. Where Richard Gere literally carries Debra Winger away from her humdrum factory-worker life and she wears his hat at a jaunty and triumphant angle." Only Tevin would know Debra Winger by name. He aimed his broad grin at Shayla and wiggled his eyebrows for emphasis. "Maybe, if you play it right, he'll let you try on his hat."

"It's called a *cover*," Shay told him as she dug her car keys out of her purse and put them on the kitchen counter. "And really, we're just friends."

"Well, you have my permission to—"

She interrupted him. "Wake your brother up soon. Don't be late for school."

"And your subtext, there, is *ignoring you*," Tevin sang the last words.

"I gotta go," Shayla said. "And really, Tev. I'm just trying to help the nice man find his daughter. So ask around at school. See what you can find out about this Fiona girl, too, okay? And don't forget to wake up Frank. He's been sleeping through his alarm lately—"

"I'm awake, I'm awake." Frank emerged from his bedroom, still sleepy-eyed, his hair bed-headed into an impressive faux-hawk. Her second baby, still in a skinny child's body—but probably not for long. "Whoa, you're dressed! I mean, in real clothes."

He hugged her and his head still fit beneath her chin, so Shay took a moment to enjoy that. "As opposed to those fake clothes I wear the rest of the time?" she asked in mock indignation as he slipped back out of her arms.

But Frank was right. She, too, had dressed for this meeting in something other than her usual sweats or jeans. She'd even put on a little makeup. Still, she'd be invisible walking in with the gleaming lieutenant. And that was fine. Her job here was to help him get the info he needed to find Maddie—not to be noticed.

"Mom's going over to the school this morning with the neighborhood Navy SEAL," Tevin told his little brother, whose eyes widened, too, as he caught sight of Peter in his uniform. "The one whose daughter ran away."

"Maggie?" Frank asked as he stood on his toes to get a box of cornflakes out of the cabinet in the kitchen.

"Maddie. Brah, you said she's in your English class. How do you not know her name?"

"She never says anything," Frank protested. "And that's when she bothers to show up. Why should I learn her name when she doesn't—"

"You learn her name, because she's a human being who lives across the street, and is in your English class," Tevin lectured his brother for Shayla.

"She hangs out with that nasty girl," Frank argued as he poured himself a large bowl. "I keep my head down and don't go near *that*."

"The nasty girl—Fiona—is a person, too," Shay pointed out. "Not a *that*."

Frank was quick on his already-size-thirteen feet. "The *that* I was referring to was the cosmic disturbance, not the crazy person creating it."

"Still, it sounds disrespectful, so spell it all the way out," Shayla said. *"I keep my head down and don't go near that cosmic disturbance."*

"Yes, Mother," Frank droned. He glanced at his brother. "Morning's complete when Moms gives me a line-reading of my own dialogue."

"Good communication is the key to *every*thing," Shayla pointed out.

"And *scene*," Tevin teased before turning back to Frank. "You wouldn't happen to know Fiona McNasty's last name? Something Italian American . . . ? I keep thinking Fiona Fiona, but that couldn't be it."

"Nope," Frank said. "Sorry."

Last night, Tevin had told Shayla that Maddie definitely hung out at school with a girl named Fiona. He didn't know her last name, but he called her "a psycho freak-show," which was alarming since Tev tended to get along with everyone. Frank's *nasty* was expected from a child who'd been badly bullied in middle school. He was far more discerning when it came to choosing friends.

Shay's phone vibrated and chirped its text alert. She pulled it out of her pocket, expecting it to be a nudge from Peter. But it wasn't. It was . . .

Maddie!

still safe

Before Shayla had left last night, she'd emailed Maddie a copy of what she called "The Peter/Lisa Meet-Cute." Then she'd texted the girl, letting her know about the sent email while backpedaling furiously with a *Please don't block me, I'm a friend of your father's, I won't text you unless it's important, please just let me know that you're currently safe so he can try to sleep tonight* message. And sure enough, Maddie had texted back a terse *still safe* then, too.

Somehow the girl managed to sound surly in her text—maybe it was her lack of capital letters or punctuation. Still, this morning's message had come unprompted, which was huge.

TY, Shayla texted back—a short and simple *thank you*. And as tempted as she might be to remind Maddie that she was here if the girl needed help of any kind, she knew not to push, so she ended it there.

"Ask your friends about Maddie," she reminded the boys as she headed for the door. "And about Fiona, too." And then she said what she always said, whenever they went their separate ways. "Be safe out there in that crazy world. Don't be a hashtag. I love you."

"Love you, love you, love you, too!" They sang their response to her in perfect harmony—one of the many little melodies their father had taught them back when they were hardly more than babies—which left her smiling as she went out into the cool morning air.

* * *

"Maddie just texted me!" Shayla called to Pete as she came out of her house and down the path to the street. "Only two words: *still safe.* But still, that's great."

As she crossed the street, Pete realized this was the first time he'd seen her in the daylight—which was strange, because it felt as if he'd known her for far longer than a mere half a day.

Shayla looked . . . really good in the morning light.

And okay, just as he'd done, she'd clearly dressed up a bit for this meeting with the high school's office staff—neatly crisp khaki pants with a blue-and-green-patterned sleeveless blouse that followed and flattered her curves as it buttoned down the front. The bright colors were a striking contrast to the warm, rich tones of her skin.

She was wearing makeup, too—not a lot, but more than the close-to-none that she'd had on last night. It sharpened her features, accenting the fullness of her smiling lips, and drawing his attention both to the elegance of her cheekbones and the beauty of her midnight-brown eyes.

Eyes that sparkled as she told him, "I'm certain this means Maddie read your story. I mean, *she* reached out. This was not in response to any kind of nudging. I think it's safe to say that it's working—a connection is being made."

Shayla held up her hand for a high five, so Pete gave her one. She was right—this *was* great. Still, he was feeling . . . weirdly disappointed that she hadn't seemed to notice he was wearing his uniform, with its many rows of ribbons.

Female eyes tended to widen at the sight—just a little bit. But she was completely blasé.

"Did you sleep at all?" she asked.

"Not much," he admitted. "I tried, but . . ." Pete shrugged as he opened the passenger-side door for her. "I actually drove past Hiroko's—looks like she still lives there—you know, near the beach."

"Alone?" Shayla asked as she climbed in. "She must be close to eighty now."

"I don't know," he admitted. "I haven't seen her since, well, I guess the last time was right after Maddie was born. She didn't approve of our failure to get married before having a child. Anyway, it occurred to me that she might be awake, but she wasn't—not at oh-three-hundred, anyway. The place was dark, so I didn't stop."

Instead he'd come back home, and downloaded one of Shayla's books. She'd written well over a dozen. Novels. It had blown his mind. He couldn't imagine writing one book, but she'd written what looked like an ongoing series. Most seemed to center on an FBI team led by an agent named Harry Parker, so he'd randomly picked a book called *Harry's War,* based solely on the title.

It opened with an action-packed scene of a bank robbery escalating into a hostage situation, and he found himself drawn in. The characters sprang instantly to life, and he could see Shayla's ability to think outside of the box not just in the gritty realism of the scenario, but also in Harry's attempt to control the situation. But she also clearly understood Murphy's Law—whatever can go wrong, *will* go wrong—and she used it to go, believably, from bad to worse.

Pete liked it—enough to go back online to figure out which was the very first book in the series, so that he could start reading at the beginning. He found a list easily enough on Shayla's website, but then got caught up surfing through a series of blog interviews in which she talked about her writing process. From the way she described it, writing a book was not unlike going through BUD/S. Yeah, the challenges were *vastly* different, but the single-minded drive and willpower needed to succeed—to finish a seemingly endlessly and insurmountable long-term task—was something he well understood.

It had been nearly dawn by the time he'd IDed and downloaded the first book—*Outside of the Lines*—but he'd already been hooked and many chapters in when his alarm had gone off.

As Pete held the car door, Shayla smiled her thanks at him and she set her handbag—leather and briefcase-sized—at her feet. Nice toes. She'd traded her sneakers for a pair of leather sandals.

"Ooh, here's my other news," she told him. "My boys both recognized her—Maddie's friend Fiona. That's definitely her first name, although they didn't know her last. But they've both seen her at school with Maddie, so yay? The bad news is, Fiona's apparently not the nicest person on the planet. Still, with a little help from Mrs. Sullivan, we'll be talking to her parents—and to Fiona herself—within the next few hours. It's a good bet that she knows exactly where Maddie is."

"God, I really hope it's that easy."

"If it's not, we'll get Dingo's address from his license plate number, or from tracking down his friend Daryl. It's really just a matter of time, Lieutenant," she said as he closed the door behind her.

Jesus, was he really back to being *Lieutenant*? He'd been hoping . . . Well, obviously, first he was hoping that with Shayla's help he'd find Maddie quickly and easily. It was nice to hear her conviction that it was going to happen soon.

Pete crossed around the front of his truck, and as he glanced in through the windshield, he saw that she was smiling and maybe even laughing . . . ? Yeah, she was definitely chuckling as he climbed behind the wheel. "What's funny?"

"I'm so sorry," she said as he pulled out of the driveway and headed for the high school. "It's nothing, really. Well, I'm . . . See, your uniform is so . . . well, very shiny—even more so up close, and . . . you look very nice."

"Thanks." It was what he'd been looking for, except weirdly now it wasn't. "You do, too."

As the words left his lips, he sensed Shayla taking a step back—which was strange since she was sitting down and she didn't move an inch. But she withdrew even further into—yeah, it was her mommy-mode—as she gave him a smile that could only be described as patient and kind, and said, "Thanks."

Okay, that had been stupid of him—an auto-response from years of bar hookups. *You look nice—You do, too. You're looking hot—You are, too. Wanna have sex—Why the hell not? I guess you'll do. . . .*

"Those colors look great on you," he tried. "And . . . I mean, you have . . . really . . . nice arms." *What?* Had he really just said that? Out loud? *Nice arms . . . ? Fuuuhhhck.*

Of course now she was looking at him as if he were one of those serial killers she often wrote about. But, "Thanks?" she said again as she reached in her handbag, pulled out a file folder, and opened it.

"I printed several copies of those photos," she continued, briskly getting down to business, "of Fiona. *And* of Dingo and Daryl Middleton—I figured they might've been high school students in the not-too-distant past. This way we can leave the photos behind—not just flash them on our phones. If we're lucky, Mrs. Sullivan will show them around in the teachers' lounge."

That got him focused—fast. "Wow, that's good thinking, thanks," he said.

"I'm not sure you're going to want me with you in the school office, though," Shayla said. "I think I'll just lurk in the hall."

"What?" Pete said, alarmed as he passed the In-N-Out Burger. "Why? No! Please, I need you in there with me. I need your brilliant writer's brain to come up with all the questions that I know I'll miss."

Now the smile she gave him was full power and beautiful. "Okay, but how about if you go in first. That way you get to wow Mrs. S with—" she made a circular motion in his direction "—that magic, without me there to confuse the issue."

"This *magic*?" he repeated with a laugh, although in truth, he relaxed a little. This was more like it. She was not immune.

Still, she gave him her now-familiar chiding look. "Lieutenant. The Navy definitely designed these uniforms for a very obvious reason."

"Yeah, to keep us from being too hot." As he approached

the turnoff to the high school parking lot, he heard the words he'd said and winced.

Shayla was laughing again, her pretty eyes dancing. "Well, that's a giant fail on the part of the Navy if the goal of these uniforms is to *keep* sailors from *being too hot*."

"Yeah, that came out wrong. I meant, to keep us from *getting* too hot. In the, you know, heat from the summer sun . . . ? On the deck of a ship, in the middle of the ocean . . . ? Not a lot of shade when you're crossing the equator."

"That must be amazing," she said, doing that soft-eyed thing that he loved. "To look around and not see land in any direction . . ."

"Yeah, it's amazing for about an hour," he said as he waited for a break in the traffic to make his turn. "But when you're out there, away from home for six months, it gets way less amazing, really fast."

"But isn't it kind of common, for a sailor, to be *out there,* on a ship, for months at a time?" she asked. "You could've joined the Army."

"Nah, I wanted to be a SEAL," he told her. "But that's how they get you. You can't be a SEAL until you've been in for a set amount of time, and you can't be in the Navy for more than a nanosecond without going out on a WestPac— that's six months in the Western Pacific. It's not as bad as it sounds, because you almost always start from Hawaii, which has its perks. But you definitely don't just join the Navy and show up at BUD/S—that's what we call SEAL training. It stands for Basic Underwater Demolition slash SEAL."

"And that's where you work?" she asked. "As a teacher."

"Instructor," he said, as he pulled into an empty space right by the school's front door. The lights were already on in the front office. "Yeah, that's what I do."

She nodded as she opened the door and picked up her handbag.

As they met on the sidewalk in front of his truck, she handed him the file with the photos and said, "I'll linger in the lobby for just a few minutes, looking at the school art display."

They went inside, and it smelled exactly the same as his old high school, a few miles down the coast.

"Don't linger too long," he said.

* * *

Maddie saw that Great-Aunt Hiroko was awake and already working in her garden as Dingo slowly drove past in the early-morning light.

"Is that her?" he asked.

"Absolutely," Maddie said.

Dingo was amused. "How on earth can you tell?"

The old woman was wearing long sleeves, gloves, and a giant sun hat—and with her head down, her face was obscured. Still it was Hiroko, without a doubt.

"Japanese women—at least in my family—can be kinda insane about staying out of the sun," Maddie told him as he used an empty driveway to turn around, so they could troll slowly back and see the yard from a different perspective. "It used to really piss off Lisa, back in Palm Springs, when someone new at the nursing home took my great-grandmother out into the garden without an umbrella, or even a hat. They'd be all *Doesn't the warm sun feel nice against your skin?* and not understand why Gram'd get so upset."

Gram didn't remember much, but her insistence on staying in the shade had been one of the very last things to go—even long after she'd lost her ability to form words. Maddie still remembered the look on her mother's face when they'd come to visit and found Gram sitting peacefully in the sun.

"She's just an empty shell now," Lisa had said at the time, but Gram's shell lived on, while both her own daughter and now Lisa, her granddaughter, were dead and gone.

It was no fucking fair.

"There, lookit, love, that's the shower thingy where your parents first met," Dingo said.

And God, yes, there it was—a brightly painted white stall made of wooden fencing, attached to the back of the little house. Maddie could see the showerhead and part of the piping—both ancient gray metal—over the top of the scalloped wood.

Last night, she'd read aloud that stupid story that "Dad" had sent via his girlfriend, Shayla. God, she'd felt stupid—two months in, and she hadn't realized he *had* a girlfriend, although why he'd thought he had to hide that fact from her, she couldn't even begin to guess.

At first Maddie had mocked it—this stupid story of how he'd met Great-Aunt Hiroko and Lisa in San Diego, after living on some dumbass island in the middle of nowhere—even though she'd been secretly moved. Not only had her mother sprung vividly to life again on those pages and pages and *pages* that he'd written, but this was a story that Maddie had never heard. Still, after the first few paragraphs, she'd turned her head to ask Dingo, "Can you imagine my stupid father with dreadlocks?"

They'd been lying together in the back of the car, parked at one of Dingo's favorite boondocking sites as she'd read the story on the glowing screen of her phone. He had built a little wall between them with some of his camping gear—her being fifteen really freaked him out.

But he wasn't scornful in the least. "I'd look like a dolt in dreadlocks," he said wistfully. "Takes a certain kind of cool to do it right, and yeah, actually, I *can* imagine him. He could pull it off. Keep going—this is good."

So Maddie'd read him the entire long thing. And later, after Dingo had fallen asleep, she'd lain awake, staring up at the car's stained and drooping cloth ceiling, thinking about Lisa and her father as teenagers, and hungering—which was stupid—to know more.

She'd finally fallen asleep, but had woken up way too soon.

One of the worst parts of boondocking, at least in Maddie's opinion, was the lack of shades to cover the car windows. Not only was that weird when it came to privacy, but when the sun came up, the sun came *up*. Combine that with having to drive to find a bathroom, and the end result was to be wide awake—even if bleary-eyed—at oh-my-god-it's-too-early o'clock.

Every morning.

But Dingo was as congenial as ever, even if he was starting to take on a definite too-many-days-without-a-shower funk, and he'd immediately agreed to drive by the beach, to see if GAH—Great-Aunt Hiroko—was awake.

"It's a little weird that we were planning to come out here today," he said now, as instead of passing the house again, he stopped at the side of the road, "and then, boom, your da sends that story. We should be ready to bounce—I mean, since he knows her, he might've told her you've gone walkabout. . . . That is, if you still even want to stop."

Maddie nodded. "Yeah, I do. But we'll take precautions."

Before reading the story, she hadn't realized that "Dad" knew GAH. It *was* entirely possible he'd called the old lady and asked her to keep an eye out for Maddie. Now, she took out her phone and scrolled through her contacts to Dingo's cell number.

"You can do a pretty good American accent," she said as she backspaced over everything but the D, and then added an A and a D. "If she says anything about you sounding different, tell her you have a cold. And if she asks you anything that you can't answer, sign off fast. Pretend that you've got another call coming in from your whatchamacallit. CO or XO or whatever."

Dingo wasn't happy. "Aaah, love, you're asking for trouble. What if they talk regularly?"

"If they're still that close, then why haven't we visited her since I've moved out here?" Maddie argued as she hit the button that would call Dingo's phone. The old woman in the garden had noticed the stopped car and had pulled herself up to her feet, holding up a hand to further shade her eyes as she looked out at them. "I'm going in, pretending that I'm already on the phone with 'Dad.' I'll put you on speaker so you can say hi—and that'll distort your voice even more. Remember, he's a Navy SEAL. He talks in short sentences, with lots of stupid Navy code: *SpecGrooFifty-Eight. XO, CO, SEAL Team Four Hundred. NavPacOpIntel, DefConFifteen.* Channel Tom Clancy."

Dingo looked both worried and skeptical as his pants pocket started to ring, but Maddie got out of the car, closing the door with a slam, her own phone to her ear.

"Hello, this is your father," Dingo said into her ear, his vowels ridiculously flat as she waved gaily to GAH.

"Yes, Dad," she said loud enough to be overheard as she walked up the path. "Yup, we're here, the address you had was right—and she's home." She raised her voice even more. "Aunt Hiroko? I'm Maddie. Your great-niece. Lisa's daughter?"

"I know who you are." The elderly woman had already taken off her work gloves and now she unlatched the gate. "I was sorry to hear about your mother. I wish someone had called me."

For once, Maddie didn't try to hide the rush of tears that sprang to her eyes. Still, she forced what she hoped was a brave smile. "I'm sorry—it was . . . It's been hard," she admitted. "And Dad and I are still feeling our way—working on figuring things out. Right, Dad?" She spoke into the phone, directly over Dingo, who was muttering, "Self-help book much?"

"Ten-four roger that!" he said, again with the flat vowels.

"I'm going to put you on speaker in a minute, *Dad*," she told him, "after I explain why we're here." Shit, she'd said *we* and Hiroko's gaze flickered over to Dingo's car, where his shadowy shape was sitting behind the steering wheel. But he was watching, and he hunkered down a bit so the old lady wouldn't be able to see that he, too, was talking on his phone.

Hiroko, meanwhile, had returned her impatient gaze to Maddie. In books and movies, old people's eyes were always filled with patience and wisdom and warmth, but Hiroko's were both cool and broadcasting a very clear *tick tock*.

"We're doing a project in school," Maddie lied, "in history class, on the way Japanese people were put in camps here in California during World War Two." Lisa had told her that Hiroko had been obsessed with that historical era.

And sure enough, the old woman took the bait. Her chin came up. "They weren't camps, they were prisons," she said. "It was mass internment of an entire group of people—and many of us weren't Japanese, we were Americans. Japanese Americans, yes, but *Americans*. I was born here. I should have been a citizen—but until 1952 there were laws that restricted Americans like me from doing things like owning property."

"Seriously?" Maddie couldn't help herself. "I mean, yeah, wow, that's great information. Thanks. Dad thought you'd be a good source, since you know so much about it." She spoke into the phone. "Good call, Dad."

"I don't just know it—I lived it, in Manzanar, a prison

camp about four hundred miles north of here," Hiroko said with a fierceness that would've been fascinating to explore—if Maddie had had the time to hang out without worrying that the idiot-asshole drug dealer who was actively hunting her down wasn't about to find and end her.

"You were right," Maddie said into her phone. "I think Aunt Hiroko can help me with this project." She smiled at GAH. "We're supposed to find primary source material, particularly artifacts. I don't have a lot of time right now—school starts soon—but I'd love for my group to interview you and—" She cut herself off as if she'd been interrupted on the phone, then added, "Yeah, yeah, Dad, I know, I know." Back to GAH as she punched the speaker button and held out the phone. The screen clearly read *Dad*. "He has to get going to work—you know, over at the Navy base—but he wanted to say hello. Dad, you're on speaker! Say hello!"

"Hello!" Dingo's voice came out of the phone distorted but definitely male. "Thank you so much for helping my little Maddie-kins!"

Oh, ugh, Dingo, really?

"I haven't yet said that I would," Hiroko pointed out, and everyone froze. Well, everyone being Maddie and Dingo. Hiroko calmly bent down and picked up a glove that she'd dropped.

"Oh, well," Dingo started to say, and Maddie quickly turned off the speaker before he could start stammering and blow this worse than she'd already apparently blown it.

"Thanks, Dad," she said, "I know you need to go. I'll talk to you later. Love you, *mwah*." She cut the connection and slipped her phone into her back pocket, and then met GAH's unwavering cool gaze. Clearly, she'd done this wrong, coming in all happy and shit. Now, she tried to match the old woman's quiet dignity. "I apologize for assuming—"

Hiroko cut her off. "Who's your friend in the car?"

"Oh," Maddie said. "He's just, um . . . a friend. Who sometimes gives me a ride when I need one."

"I'm making breakfast. Scrambled eggs. Call him—use your phone—and invite him in," the old woman said.

If she did that, he'd come up as a very visible *Dad* on her screen. "Oh," Maddie said. "No, I'll just . . ." She shouted. "Dingo! Hey, Ding! Want breakfast?"

Hiroko shook her head in disapproval, then started for the kitchen door as Dingo came galloping eagerly up the path from the car. "Hurry up," the old woman said dourly, "or you'll be late for *school*."

That emphasis on *school* was not accidental. It was obvious that Hiroko wasn't even remotely fooled by any of this. Maddie knew she shouldn't go inside. She should grab Dingo and pull him back into the car and make him drive away.

Still, *scrambled eggs*! She and Dingo had just a few dollars left between them, and the idea of *free* scrambled eggs was too mouthwatering to turn down.

Besides, if GAH called "Dad"—even if she excused herself and went into the bathroom to secretly use the phone—Maddie would know it, and there'd be plenty of time to get away.

* * *

When Shayla opened the door, Mrs. Sullivan was using the phone back in the high school vice principal's inner office. Peter stood waiting, his hat tucked up under his arm, file folder open on the long, room-dividing counter in front of him.

Nice arms.

Trust Harry to pop into her head and mention that.

Yeah, because it was weird, Harry pointed out. *Nice arms?*

She had no idea why Peter had said that, but he was talking to her, so *shh*.

"She knew Fiona immediately, from the photo," the SEAL reported as Shay closed the door behind her.

They were alone in the room—aside from Mrs. S, who'd left that inner office door open a crack, and Harry, who was invisible to all of the uncrazy nonwriters in the room.

"Apparently there's been some drama this past week," Peter continued. "Fiona was living here in San Diego with her aunt, but there was a fire at her condo, and . . . apparently, she was shipped back home to her parents."

"To Sacramento?" Shayla asked. That was where the girl had said she was from on her Facebook profile.

"I don't know." He couldn't hide the worry in his eyes. "Mrs. Sullivan didn't say it in so many words, but I could tell from her attitude that Fiona had been a problem for the school."

"I'm pretty sure every child in this school is a problem for Mrs. S," Shayla whispered reassuringly, reaching out to pat his arm—*nice arms*—which made him smile even as she shushed Harry and snatched her hand back, fast.

"Yeah, maybe," he said. "But still, a *fire* . . . ?"

"Fires happen," Shay told him.

"After which Fiona was shipped home."

"That doesn't mean she's a budding arsonist," she argued. "If her aunt's condo burned, where's she going to live? She may have gone home simply because she no longer has a place to stay."

"Okay. You're right." Peter nodded. "But bottom line, Fiona's gone. I find it hard to believe it's a coincidence that Maddie's gone missing at the same time that her only friend left town."

"That's probably *not* a coincidence," Shayla agreed. "Even if it was simply the straw that broke the camel's back. Because remember, Fiona's not Maddie's only friend.

There's also Dingo. It's possible that the emotional distress of Fiona leaving combined with Maddie knowing that if you found out about Dingo, you'd forbid her from dating him—as any parent would . . ."

"Well, *that's* a first!" Mrs. Sullivan interrupted them as she came huffing out toward the front desk, looking irritated. Of course, the default expression on her Scandinavian-featured, long-suffering, ruddy-cheeked pioneer-woman face was supreme annoyance—she accessorized it with her relentless Margaret Thatcher–inspired wardrobe and the fading blond hair that she wore twisted up into a bun. "The father refused to speak to you," she told Peter indignantly.

And okay. *That* was worth getting irritated about. Unless Shay'd misunderstood. "Fiona's father," she clarified, and Mrs. S looked hard at her.

"Can I help you, Mrs. DeSoto?"

"It's Shayla Whitman," Shay corrected her for the seven millionth time, reminding her, "The boys have their father's name, which I don't share."

"Shayla's helping me find Maddie," Peter said, whereupon Mrs. S gave Shay a different kind of look. A knowing look—like the help she was providing was the naked, orgasmic kind.

Shayla swiftly brought the woman's attention back to the problem at hand. "Fiona's father actually *refused* . . . ?"

"Flatly," Mrs. S said. "He barely let me speak. No, he would not talk to anyone. As far as he was concerned, Fiona was done here, and that was that. So I told him you knew Fiona's last name, of course. Fiona Fiera, and that I couldn't stop you from calling him—Charles Fiera of Sacramento—if you looked him up." She exhaled her disdain. "Some people! I think he thought you were Susan what's-her-name's—the aunt's—downstairs neighbor. Calling about additional damages from the fire."

"What exactly happened?" Shayla asked. "This fire. Was anyone hurt?"

"I don't think so," Mrs. S said. "A cat. Who lived downstairs. But not badly. She needed oxygen from one of the firefighters. The photo of that's gone viral." She smiled and her face transformed so completely that her pale blue eyes even sparkled. "*So* adorable."

"Oh, my God, I think I saw that on Instagram," Shay said. "But I can't remember exactly when, was it . . . ?"

"Friday," Mrs. Sullivan reported as the cat lover retreated and the warrior woman's battle mask slipped back into place. "Fiona was pulled out of class by the police."

"Because they thought she'd set it . . . ?" Shay glanced at Peter, who was quite possibly grinding his teeth into nubs at that news, no doubt from imagining that his daughter's best friend was, indeed, an arsonist.

"The aunt seemed to think so on Friday," Mrs. S reported. "There was quite a bit of screaming and accusations. Right in this office."

"That must've been awful," Shay said. "Was Maddie there?"

"Absolutely not."

"Maybe lurking out in the hall?"

"Well, I don't know that for sure," the woman admitted, moving to the computer and accessing its keyboard. "But I'll check her schedule. It was in the middle of third period and . . . No, she was in English with Ms. Reinberg. That's on the other end of the building, so it's very unlikely, even if she left to go to the bathroom, that she would've come all the way down here."

"But it's not impossible," Peter pointed out.

"Frank's in Maddie's English class," Shayla told him. "I can check to see if he remembers if she left the room on Friday."

"Thanks," he said.

"Actually," Shay said, "it may have been more traumatic for Maddie if she didn't know what happened—if her friend just vanished. If Fiona just stopped answering her phone, and didn't respond to Facebook messages."

Shayla didn't know the details of Lisa's accident, but it didn't take much to imagine the news of her death reaching Maddie in a similar way, with initial silence, and a growing sense of dread.

Peter met her gaze, his blue eyes sharp. She knew that he was thinking, too, about all of those seemingly coded Facebook messages from Maddie to Fiona, the final one in all caps.

Where are you? Are you dead, too? Harry said, hitting the subtext on the head.

"Fiona's aunt," Peter said, turning back to Mrs. Sullivan. "She's local—or at least she was, before the fire. Do you still have—"

Mrs. S was already tapping on the computer keyboard, and she interrupted before he could ask. "She was cut from the same unpleasant cloth as the father. I mean, yes. I have her work and various home phone numbers right here—" she pointed at the screen "—but I wouldn't be shocked if, when I called her, she also refused to talk to you." She looked from Peter to Shayla, widening her eyes substantially. "Oh! But if you'll excuse me for just a few minutes, I realize I forgot to start the pot of coffee in the back room. I must do that immediately." And with that, she turned abruptly on her sensible heels and disappeared through the door to the back, this time closing it firmly behind her.

Shay looked at Peter. "Was that the invitation to break the rules that I thought it was?"

"Yeah." Peter nodded.

She smiled. "Go, Mrs. S!"

But the little half-door built into the room-long counter

was securely locked—and it was designed so that students couldn't simply reach over from this side and unlock it.

Peter put his hat down and was about to push himself up and over the barrier so he could look at the contact info Mrs. S had left up on the computer monitor for them to see, but Shay stopped him.

"Let me," she said. "I'm a civilian. Let's not get you into trouble."

"I don't mind trouble," he said.

"Yeah, yeah." She waved him off, kicking off her sandals. "Navy SEAL. Middle name's *trouble,* I got it. Still. Let's not tempt fate. Give me a boost." She made a classic foothold by interlocking her fingers as example, and when he did the same, she stepped into his hands and he lifted her effortlessly up so that her butt was on the counter. She swung her legs over and slipped down, and . . . There was the info they needed, right on the screen. "Susan Smith—oh, God, yes, with that name, she'd've been hard to track—Mrs. S, you are an angel." She rattled off the phone numbers—home, work plus extension, and cell—as Peter put them right into his phone. "Ooh, as long as we're here . . ." A simple downward scroll revealed info—separate no doubt because of divorce—for both Fiona's father and mother, and Shayla read that to Peter, too. Phone numbers and addresses in—bingo!—Sacramento.

It was easier to get back over the counter from this end, since there was a desk-level surface that she could climb onto with her knees before squatting and getting her bottom up onto the counter. She swung her legs back over.

And then Peter was there to catch her—not that she needed or expected him to do that. In fact, he made her dismount awkward, because she ended up doing a full-length slide down the entire front of his body. His extremely solid uniform-clad body.

Like *that* wasn't distracting.

She landed with her toes on the ground, with her hands braced on his shoulders. His hands were on her hips as he still held her tightly, his face mere centimeters from hers.

Up close, those eyes were crazy beautiful—the blue was streaked with white and black and even gold.

Up close, the lines on his golden-tanned face—from wisdom and laughter and spending too much time unprotected in the sun—were even more attractive.

He's not as young as you pretend that he is.

Yeah, she could see that from this proximity.

Shayla knew that this was a moment. They were having a moment, or maybe *she* was having a moment, and he was having something else entirely—something weird and embarrassing and awkward. Whatever it was, time suspended and hung as he didn't let her go and she, likewise, didn't pull away. But he also didn't lower his head to do something like, oh, say, kiss her. In fact, he didn't freaking move.

So kiss him!

Peter's pretty eyes flickered down to her mouth and then back, because, God, she'd obviously just looked hard at *his* mouth. And now *she* was the one who was flashing hot and cold with weirdness and awkward embarrassment, but she still couldn't pull away.

It's up to you. He's too much of an officer and a gentleman.

Or maybe not. Maybe Peter just didn't want to kiss her. She was, after all, the neighbor—they were friends. Help-him-write-deeply-personal-stories-about-his-teenaged-love-affair-with-his-daughter's-mother kind of friends. Not touch-the-roof-of-his-mouth-with-her-tongue friends.

KISS HIM!

"No," Shayla said forcefully in response to Harry's head-filling demand—except, whoops, she'd just shouted in Peter's startled face.

He, of course, immediately let her go with a quick "Jesus, sorry, I'm so sorry!"

"No, no! I didn't mean you! I wasn't talking to—*shit!*" she countered quickly, but in scrambling away from him, she stepped on her sandal exactly the wrong way. "Oh, *God!*" It was reminiscent of a Lego to the bare arch in the dark of night—a full ten on the parental agony WTF scale. This was compounded by the fact that she'd just released the crazy krakens in a verbal geyser that couldn't be easily explained. *That* no *I just shouted in your face was in response to my invisible friend.* Yeah, that was going to go over well.

She completed her current circus act by tripping on her other sandal, and would've gone down to the floor if Peter hadn't lunged to catch her again. She grabbed for him, too, her hands now on the warmth of his skin—deliciously smooth over the hard steel of those insane muscles—as she tightly held on to him just above his elbows and below his shirtsleeves.

And then, because she was an idiot, she opened her mouth and blurted out the words he'd said to her in the truck: "Nice arms."

It was supposed to be funny or clever or maybe both funny *and* clever, but nope. And yes, now they were *definitely* both sharing the exact same type of moment—the weird, embarrassed, awkward kind.

"Yeah, wow, um," Peter said as he made sure she was steady before he let her go.

Shay's mind was blank—solidly, stupidly blank—save for the sounds of Harry's deep sigh and eye roll.

Say something, Harry then urged.

"Did you know that some people can actually taste words?" Shay asked Peter.

Not that. Harry started to laugh his despair.

"No, seriously," she said, straightening her clothes—her

shirt had pulled up a bit, kind of the way Captain Kirk's did in his classic *Trek* uniform. The actor, William Shatner, had learned to compensate for the low-budget design by grabbing the bottom hem and giving an authoritative tug downward, and it had become an iconic gesture of decisiveness and command. She now did the same. See? Totally in control. Except for the sound of Harry's laughter echoing madly inside of her head.

Peter, meanwhile, was looking a tad confused.

"One of my characters had really bad migraines," she told him, "but I don't get 'em, I'm lucky, right? Anyway, I went onto one of those medical symptom–checker websites to do a little research and while I was surfing around, I saw that one of the things on their general symptoms list was *Can you taste words?* And ever since then, I've used that as a personal benchmark. How'm I doing? Great, because you know what? Things might be bad, but I'm still not tasting words."

Peter laughed as Harry finally stopped.

But before Shayla could segue into an explanation of how she wasn't crazy, she was just a writer, and sometimes writers talked to the fictional character who resided in their heads, Mrs. Sullivan chose that moment to re-emerge from the back room.

"Sorry about that," the woman announced. She eyed Peter's cover, which he'd set on the counter next to the folder, and Shay knew that she, too—like all women of a certain age—itched to embrace her inner Debra Winger and try it on. "Is there anything else I can help you with today?"

Peter moved the picture of Fiona to reveal the photo of the two young men from the parking garage. "Do you know either of these men?" He pointed. "This one's Daryl Middleton; the other we only know by his nickname. Dingo."

Shay cleared her throat to ask, "Is it possible they were former students?"

Mrs. S took the photo and looked closely. "Daryl Middleton, no. That's a family name I would've remembered." She glanced up. "I'm a bit of an Anglophile."

"I know that that probably wasn't a non sequitur," Peter said. "But . . ."

"Prince William's wife's name is Kate Middleton," Shay murmured.

"Ah. What about Dingo?" he asked.

"I don't think so," Mrs. S said, but she didn't sound convinced. "I'm sorry, it's hard to tell. Add a few years, plus the facial hair . . . That boy-to-man change can be extreme. But if you can leave the photo, I'll ask around the teachers' lounge."

CHAPTER EIGHT

Izzy was sad.

He'd pretended not to be as he'd dropped Eden and their giant extended family off at the airport. He'd actually rented a passenger van to do it, because traveling with a baby was a logistical nightmare, requiring almost as much gear as was needed for a seven-man SEAL team.

That gear plus the five traveling humans of varying sizes—Eden, her brother Dan who was also Izzy's SEAL teammate, Dan's wife Jenn and their super-baby Colin, plus Eden and Danny's teenaged brother Ben—wouldn't fit into an everyday, average vehicle. And the van rental was financially cheaper than hiring a car service, and emotionally cheaper—gods forbid—than waking up at zero-dark-thirty to make two separate airport runs.

Also? Since Izzy had the thing for twenty-four hours, it suddenly occurred to him that he could use it to help Grunge at the low, low price of *nearly free*. He could pop on up to Palm Springs, and at least start to move all that stuff out of the storage unit and into the officer's garage.

His plan was to zap Grunge a text—maybe swing past

the man's house and pick up the padlock key—as soon as he got less sad.

I'm sorry you're not coming, too. Danny had actually said that to Izzy, out loud and clearly enunciated, before he'd followed Jenn and the baby into the airport terminal. And yeah, part of Dan's sorrow had to do with the fact that a weeklong visit to Jenn's family back east could be exhausting. But Ben and Eden would be there to help Dan and Jenn—at least they would be when they weren't off visiting colleges.

Missing that was what made Izzy most sad. He'd wanted to go, too—mostly so he could continue to talk up all the great schools in nearby SoCal.

But one of the biggest problems created by being related through marriage to a teammate was that they couldn't always take leave at the same time.

And this time, sadly, Izzy had had to stay behind.

This morning, Eden had lingered, holding Izzy close as Dan and Ben humped their luggage into the terminal. She wasn't fooled by his pretending to not be sad. She'd sweetly kissed him goodbye, and then hugged him again, seductively whispering, "You should stop for pancakes at the Grill on your way home."

Ah, his woman knew him well.

Blueberry pancakes with *real* maple syrup, an order of scrambled eggs and bacon, and the Grill's homemade sourdough toast . . .

Izzy pulled into the Grill's driveway. It was still early enough that there were plenty of spaces in the lot, so he prepared to get slightly—just slightly—less sad.

* * *

"I got an automated phone system. Fiona's aunt Susan works in a law office here in San Diego," Shayla said, her cellphone to her ear as Pete followed her out of the high school and back to his truck. She'd already dialed the woman's work number, even though it was still too early for most offices to be open. "Discount Family Law. They open at nine. I think we should just show up, have a conversation face-to-face. You know, not call first."

"That's smart," Pete agreed. "Although, I'm wondering if I should fly up to Sacramento."

"You might want to wait until after we hear from Lindsey," she reminded him. "If she can give us Dingo's real name, and maybe even his local address—or even Daryl Middleton's address . . . While Fiona's leaving seems to be the likely catalyst to Maddie's current crisis, I'm not sure what this girl could tell us that we can't find out by staying local. I mean, yes, if we come up short with info about Dingo and Daryl . . ."

Pete opened the door for her and as she climbed in, she gave him one of her looks—but this was one he hadn't seen before. It was less attitude and more, well, *vulnerable* for lack of a better word. "You don't have to do that. I'm capable of opening a door for myself."

"I know," he said. "I just, um . . . want to."

She was still embarrassed about the weirdness that had happened in the office—that was what he was seeing in her eyes. So he caught her arm—*nice arms,* oh Jesus, he was an idiot—and even though her skin beneath his fingers was almost unbearably soft and smooth, he made himself hold on until she met his gaze again. At which point, he said, "I'm great at a lot of things—" okay, whoa, back it down there, Bozo "—I'm a SEAL, so I'm highly trained and highly skilled, and frankly I'm even more proud of my chops as a BUD/S instructor, but the truth is, I'm a fuckup when it comes to women, Lisa being Exhibit A. I've never really had a woman as a friend—" he caught himself again "—one who's not married or engaged to a teammate, anyway. And you're really pretty, and you're funny, and Jesus, you're smart, and that's *really* attractive. And every now and then, I slip and run the pattern—the bar hookup pattern—and stupid things come out of my mouth, or I do something disrespectful, like help you down but then not let go. I just wanted to, well . . . I apologize. Your friendship means a lot to me, and I don't want to mess it up."

She was sitting there, gazing up at him, and for a moment he just lost himself in the dark brown warmth of her eyes, in the full curve of her lips. . . .

Which was exactly what he was trying *not* to do. He cleared his throat, and forced himself to take a step back instead of leaning even further in, because yeah, he was doing that, too. *Shit*.

"Well, I happen to be great at a lot of things, too," Shayla said. It was possible she was mocking his rocky start, but then she added, "I am, after all, a mother of teenagers, and that training's pretty intense. Maybe not as physically intense as BUD/S. I was curious so I did a little research on that last night. But *Quitting is not an option*"—she quoted a well-known SEAL motto—"and *The only easy day was yesterday* absolutely apply."

And huh. Last night while Pete had Googled her, she'd also been Googling him. Well, maybe not him per se—unlike her, his work tended to be secret, so he didn't have a website. But she'd clearly been interested enough to seek more info.

"One of the things I'm very good at is being a friend," she told him. "So relax. I appreciate that you caught yourself—what did you call it? Running the pattern. *Nice arms* was good subbing in for whatever your animal-brain was reacting to—I won't bother guessing—because I *do* have nice strong arms, thanks." She held them out and her triceps moved. "Not as strong as yours, but strong enough, and trust me, as a woman, I'll never turn down a compliment about my strength."

"Well, good," he said, except now that he'd said all that, he was oddly discontent. Or maybe that was just his—what did she call it? *Animal-brain.* His animal-brain was stuck on the image of him Googling her while she Googled him. And his animal-brain was fourteen years old and thought that *Googling* sounded more like something one did to another person with mouths, hands, and genitals rather than alone with a computer.

"Yeah," Shayla agreed, "it is good. In fact, it's great. For someone who claims to be communication challenged, you're doing really well. So, where to now? What's next on the *Find Maddie* to-do list? And please say, *Now is when we get coffee.*"

Pete laughed as he closed her door and humped it around the front of the truck. "Coffee sounds lifesaving," he told her as he climbed behind the wheel and started the engine with a roar. "Breakfast sounds even better—if you've got the time. When do I need to get you home?"

"I'm yours for the day—really for the entire weekend—if you want me," Shayla told him. "The boys'll be at Carter's, starting tonight, through Sunday. And I thought while we're waiting—to hear from Lindsey, and for Susan Smith's office to open—maybe we could work on Chapter Two. You know, to send to Maddie? *How Peter Met Lisa.*"

Her generosity made Pete's words catch in his throat. At least he thought that was what made his throat feel tight, but his animal-brain had finally stopped toying with *Google* and was now replaying her words *I'm yours . . . for the weekend . . . if you want me.*

Pete's animal-brain said, *Woof,* but he smacked it down and cleared his throat, and said, "Thank you. So much. That would be unbelievably great."

* * *

"Why are you really here?"

Great-Aunt Hiroko's words made Dingo look up warily from his eggs and toast, but Maddie didn't even pause. She just kept shoveling the food into her mouth.

It tasted good, although Dingo had hoped for more interesting spices than mere salt and pepper. In fact, he'd expected a far more Japanese feel to the entire cottage, but not only had they kept their shoes on as they'd gone through a slider into the house, but the living room had a regular sofa and chairs, and the art on the walls was sharp and bright and very modern. The kitchen they were sitting in now was just a normal kitchen. Old-fashioned, for sure, but there wasn't even so much as a wok in sight. Was that racist? Fack, it was—subtle for sure, but he was guilty of that stupidity. He hated when people looked at *him* and made idiotic assumptions, and here he'd gone and blithely done the same.

Maddie finally swallowed and started in again with her spiel about the school history project, but the old woman cut her off. "No, why are you *really* here?"

There was silence for a moment as the question seemed to hang there in the air.

Maddie surprised the crap out of him when she put down her fork and said, "I miss Lisa and I thought . . ."

Dingo held his breath as Hiroko locked gazes with Maddie. The old woman didn't speak—she just stared, waiting for the girl to finish her sentence. The only sound was that of a clock ticking from its perch above the door that led into the dining room. *Tick, tick, tick.*

Maddie'd hunched so far in on herself that her shoulders were nearly up to her ears, and her eyes had actually filled with tears. Dingo wanted to reach for her, to comfort her by taking her hand, but his new rule was *No touching the fifteen-year-old*. He knew himself well enough not to allow any exceptions. Never, ever.

As he watched, Maddie seemed to shake herself. "But she's gone, and you're not her—you're not even close." She gave a huge *whatever* shrug with a massive eye roll that was supposed to telegraph just how little she cared, but Dingo knew better as she added, "Also? I thought maybe you could lend me some money."

"Ah," the old woman said as Maddie went back to eating.

"No, wait, she meant it—what she said," Dingo spoke up. "Yeah, we're low on funds, but really we're here because she misses her ma."

"Dingo, shut up." Maddie glowered at him.

He spoke over her, leaning across the table toward Hiroko. "And her father just told us the story of how he met Lisa here, that you and him became chums because he stopped to help when you had a flat tire."

"Dingo!" Now Maddie was shooting daggers at him with her eyes. "Just finish your eggs, and we'll go. She doesn't want us here—"

"Did you know that? That he met her—Lisa—right here, in your yard?" Dingo asked the old woman, who'd calmly risen to her feet to carry her plate to the sink. "He was taking a rinse in your outdoor shower-thingy, and there she was."

"I did know, yes." Hiroko turned to face them and her mouth was tight. "I didn't approve of their relationship."

Maddie was intrigued despite her desperate need to look and sound disaffected, so her tone was combative. "Why, because he wasn't Japanese?"

Hiroko made a raspberry sound. "That may have been Kiyo's—your great-grandmother's—thinking, but I couldn't've cared less. I liked the boy." She looked at Maddie. "Peter was different, and Lisa was, well, she wasn't good for him."

Maddie was not in a place where she was willing to hear any negative talk about her mom. She stood up, the chair screeching against the linoleum floor. "Well, screw you! *She* wasn't good enough? Look who's talking. If you're so freaking perfect, you'd visit Gram in Palm Springs, instead of letting her rot all by herself in that stupid nursing home—"

"I visit her every other month," Hiroko said curtly. "I have for years—since she hurt her hip. And if you'd listened, you'd know that I didn't say your mother wasn't good *enough*—"

Maddie was already making a disgusted sound. "Lisa and I *lived* there for nearly a year, so . . ."

Hiroko widened her eyes as if waiting for her to continue.

"*I* never saw you visit," Maddie said.

"Are you calling me a liar?" Hiroko asked.

"Of course she's not," Dingo said hastily.

"I'm just saying, all those months, I never saw you, not even once." Maddie crossed her arms.

"I don't drive at night. I had to leave early enough to get back to San Diego before dark, because your mother made it very clear that I wasn't welcome in her home," Hiroko informed her. She looked from Maddie to Dingo. "How much money do you need?"

"Three hundred dollars'll do it," Dingo said because Maddie had finally been silenced.

"*That* much?" Hiroko said as she took both Maddie's and Dingo's plates and brought them to the sink.

"His car is big and stupid." Maddie finally spoke as Hiroko gestured for them to follow her out into the living room. "The gas mileage is for shit."

"And where, exactly, are you going?" the elderly woman asked.

There was a series of black-and-white pictures on the wall, Dingo now saw, that were obviously that internment camp where Hiroko had spent a chunk of her childhood. Long rows of barracks-type housing stretched out into the distance.

Maddie saw those photos, too, and now pointed to them. "Well, Manzanar," she lied. "Of course. We need to see it. I mean, photos are well and good, but we need to *smell* it. *Feel* it. And since it's four hundred miles there, four hundred back . . ."

Hiroko's eyebrows lifted. "And your car gets . . . three miles to the gallon?"

"We also have access to more primary source materials further north in . . . Reno," Maddie lied.

"Reno," Hiroko repeated as Dingo leaned in to get a closer look at a photo that had to be Hiroko as a child, standing in front of an exquisite garden, barbwire fencing in the background.

"Yes. Reno." Maddie stood there, looking at her great-aunt as if daring her to call out her lie.

There was silence then, as Hiroko just looked out her living room window, unperturbed.

And sure enough, Maddie cracked first. "She was embarrassed," she said. "Lisa. We had this really tiny, shitty studio apartment in a really shitty part of Palm Springs, and she was working as a waitress at this total crap bar, and she hated it, and . . . There was barely enough room for the pullout sofa. I don't know where you would've slept—in the bathtub? And yes, I wish she'd told me, I would've cut school to come to see you at the nursing home when you came to visit Great-Grandma. Because I've always thought of you as a superhero, and I really, really wanted to meet you again, because I was, like, five, that one time we did meet. And I'm sorry that you hate me now, I am."

Maddie started to cry, and Dingo did, too, because God. And he broke his rule and took her hand and she held on to him so tightly even as she pulled them toward the sliding door.

"I don't hate you," Hiroko said, surprising them both into stopping and turning back. "I didn't hate Lisa. She was braver than I ever was. I both resented and admired her . . . and . . . I just knew she and Peter wouldn't . . . fit. That he was too traditional, too . . . *sane* for her." She shook her head. "Neither of them could bear to hear that, so they stayed away from me, which I suppose was just as well, because I couldn't bear to watch her break his heart. I don't carry much cash, but I can write you a check." She paused. "Do you have the ID you need to cash it?"

Her question was aimed more at Dingo than Maddie, and he nodded even as he wiped his eyes.

"Good," she said curtly. "Wait here, I'll get my handbag."

CHAPTER NINE

They did the coffee-and-bagels-to-go thing, at Shay's favorite local mom-and-pop coffee shop. She could tell, without even asking, that Peter wouldn't've been able to bear a sit-down breakfast.

And it was a good thing, too, because when they got back into Peter's truck, Shay realized that Tevin had texted her.

It was a long message—segmented into four, no, five long paragraphs, and she scrolled back to read aloud, "*Fiona's last name is Fiera, and she's def crazy and gone for good. But biggest rumor via Bobbie Ramone*—I'm not sure who that is—*is that Maddie's got a much older BF.* That's boyfriend."

"Tell us something we *don't* know," Peter muttered as he unwrapped his bagel and took a bite.

Shay obliged as she continued reading. "*More than one member of Bobbie's gossip-head gang*—oh, she's *that* Bobbie. Tevin sometimes refers to her as APB because, well, right. Anyway, going on. *More than one member of* the aforementioned gang *saw her with him last Tuesday after school; rumor is he's a SEAL.*" She looked up, filled with pride. "My son is possibly the only teenager in the universe to use a semicolon—correctly—in a text."

Peter, meanwhile, was choking. "A SEAL . . . ? There's no way that that Dingo kid . . . No."

He was right. Not even in Dingo's wildest dreams was anyone going to mistake him for a Navy SEAL. In response, Shay read on. "*He's big and blond and kinda hard to miss. Definitely not Dingo. Ooh, Tevin says, Janet Lundgren took these photos.* I don't know who she is, but thank you, Janet!"

Tevin had forwarded two photos to her. Shayla peered at the first one. It was blurry, but yeah, that was definitely Maddie talking with great intensity to a hulking giant of a crew-cutted blond young man outside of what looked like a convenience store.

"This is definitely not Dingo," she told Peter, who leaned over to look, too, his shoulder pressed against hers. In a friendly manner, because they were friends. *Friends, friends, friends,* she emphasized to herself, because for once Harry wasn't present to argue, thank God.

She forced herself to focus. The young man in the photo was wearing a U.S. Navy SEAL tank top over a well-muscled body, but that didn't mean anything. You didn't need to be a SEAL to wear a shirt advertising the Teams.

And frankly, there was no law against a man of any age talking to a girl on a public sidewalk.

"That's Hans fucking Schlossman," Peter said, his voice tight.

"So you know him," Shayla said as she scrolled to the second photo. Eek.

That one was far more damning.

In the second photo, Maddie was encircled in the big blond man's giant arms. He was holding her tightly, her head tucked under his big Dudley Do-Right chin, and she was clinging to him, too, and yeah. Shay realized that it was entirely possible that she and Peter had gotten it wrong. Maybe Dingo wasn't the girl's inappropriately older boyfriend—and this SEAL was.

They weren't kissing but they were definitely glued tightly together—and the emotion in their body language was off the charts. In fact the SEAL's face—Schlossman's face—was twisted, as if he was trying not to cry.

Peter saw the same whatever-it-was that she was seeing, and he made a sound, low in his throat, that was close to a growl. "I'm gonna fucking kill him."

"He's really one of your SEALs?" she asked. That made him likely even older than Dingo, since these days most SEALs were college graduates.

"No, he's a candidate," Pete said tightly. "He's not a SEAL yet, and now he's never gonna be. Mother*fucker*."

"So he's one of your *students*," she clarified. "Do you think that's how he and Maddie met?"

"I have no idea how they met," he said. "*No* idea. Maddie's never even come to the base with me, so . . . Jesus, he must've gone after her—targeted her. *Son* of a *bitch*."

"That's pretty creepy," Shay said. "Do you really think he's capable of—"

"He went through phase one of BUD/S under me—Hell Week—and I was hard on him." Peter paused. "No, I was *brutal*. I didn't think he'd make it, but he surprised me, and . . . he did. But now he hates me. He's made that pretty clear."

Shayla used her fingers to expand the photo on her phone's screen, enlarging Schlossman's face. His expression was one of anguish. "Whatever this is, whatever's going on, he's not happy about it."

"Is that supposed to make me feel better?"

She looked up and into Peter's eyes. His anger was mixed with frustration and his own darkly private pain.

"How can I help?" she asked him in response. "What do

we do next? Okay, here's an idea. How about if *I* go and talk to this young man?"

He laughed as he jammed his truck into drive, and pulled out of the parking spot and then out of the lot. "Nah, I'm gonna take you home."

She made a high-pitched *hmm* sound. Where was Harry when she needed alpha-male-wrangling backup? But he didn't appear, so she went with, "That's not a very good idea."

Peter pretended his reasons were logistical. "Yeah, actually, he's probably on the base, so it'll be faster and easier just to drop you home, instead of checking you in as a guest."

Shayla took a deep breath and refused to cosign his bullshit. "I'm calling you on that, Lieutenant," she said flatly. "Will you please think with your brain for a second—instead of cavemanning this? I mean, I have kids, so I get it. I do. But there's a reason *good cop, bad cop* is a thing. If you want to get info from this man, it simply makes more sense to bring me along. Of course, if your *real* goal is to just beat the hell out of him . . . or have him beat the hell out of you—" She pointedly looked at the photo again. "This young man is *big,* and maybe deep down you think that his kicking your ass would be well-deserved—"

She'd purposely stomped on his alpha-male button and he responded as expected with a flash of frost in his blue eyes. "Yeah, no way can that idiot kick *my* ass. Just let him try."

"So you *do* want to start a fight," Shay said as he braked to a stop at a traffic light. She sighed, maybe a tad too dramatically. "Well, that's disappointing. I thought you wanted to find your *missing* daughter."

Peter's hands were so tight around his steering wheel, his knuckles were white. As she gazed pointedly at him, he closed his eyes and inhaled a long, slow, deep breath. "I do want to find her," he said on his exhale, opening his eyes to look at her. "But I also really want to punch Schlossman in the face. If he used Maddie to get back at me . . ." He shook his head.

"The key word there, Lieutenant, is *if,*" Shayla pointed out. "And *if* he used Maddie that way, well, he's going to have bigger problems, don't you think? Why muddy it by giving him a reason to play the victim card?" She pretended to be a blubbering Schlossman. "*Yeah, I know she's only fifteen, Detective, but Lieutenant Greene punched me in the face!*"

He actually laughed at that—good that he could still laugh—but then his phone rang. It was connected to the Bluetooth in his truck, and it was up so loud they both jumped. The name *Zanella* appeared on the dash's screen, and Peter said, "I'm gonna take this," even as Shayla told him, "You should answer that."

"Zanella, you're on speaker. I'm in the truck with Shayla," Peter curtly said as a greeting.

"Ah, you're still with Shayla-the-neighbor." Izzy Zanella's voice was loaded with *That's interesting* innuendo.

"Not *still*." Peter didn't try to hide his annoyance. "*Again.*"

"We made a plan to go over to the high school early this morning," Shay explained.

"Any luck?" Izzy asked.

"Not much," Peter said. "A few leads—best is from Shayla's son. We're kind of in the middle of it. What's up?"

"Drove the fam to the airport and on the way home, it occurred to me that I have this spacious rental van for another fifteen hours," Izzy's voice cheerfully said. "I thought I could bop on over to the storage space in Palm Springs, bring all that stuff back and stash it in your garage for you, save you the road trip. I just need the key or the combo to the padlock—oh yeah, and the storage unit number would be helpful, too, so I don't have to wander the place, weeping as I try to open every lock."

"Wow, that would be great," Peter said. "Thanks, man, but . . . you really wanna do that drive all by yourself?"

"Noooo," Izzy said. "No, no, no. I tried Lopez, but he's *busy*—" somehow he managed to make air quotes with only his voice "—but then I remembered da boyz in Boat Squad John have today off, and I figured, hey, they were prolly looking for something to do, am I right? And since those young'uns owe me a giant-ass favor in the vague shape of humping boxes into a van—"

Peter cut him off. "Boat Squad John is going to Palm Springs with you? Today?"

"Well, not *all* of 'em," Izzy said. "Five more guys in the van would take up a lot of space and kinda defeat the purpose. But Seagull volunteered, bless him. The rest of the idiots drew straws and Hans won." He paused. "Or maybe he lost. Nah, I'm gonna go with *won*."

"Hans *Schlossman*?" Shayla asked and Peter looked at her sharply, shaking his head in a very clear *Say nothing more*.

"That's right," Izzy confirmed. "What? Wait, let me guess—Grunge has been regaling you with the timeless tale of the mighty, mighty Boat Squad John. Oh. And no wonder. Those tadpoles did us proud during Phase One, but the biggest surprise of all prolly had to be when Hans—"

Peter cut him off. "Where are they meeting you—or are they already there? Where the fuck are you?"

"Well, *you're* sure interested in the minute details, G. I'm *the fuck* at the Grill—I just had breakfast. Timebomb Jackson's gonna drop off Seagull and Hans in about ten, but we'll need to get that unit number and key from you before we hit the road. Breakfast was delicious: blueberry pancakes with sides of scrambled eggs and—"

Peter did a U-turn right in the middle of the street even as he cut Izzy off again. "I'm five minutes from you, I'm bringing the key, don't go *anywhere*." He punched the end-call button and looked again at Shayla. "*Good cop, bad cop* it is."

* * *

"What, or maybe I should be asking *who*, exactly, is Boat Squad John?"

Pete glanced over at Shayla as he grimly drove toward the Grill and his confrontation with Schlossman. "It's a long story, and we're almost there."

"Give me the log line." At his blank look, she added, "Describe it in a tweet."

He shook his head.

"You're not on Twitter—not a big surprise. Okay, remember back when you were a kid, did your grandma get *TV Guide*?"

"Neither Grandma nor *TV Guide* made it to the island," he told her. "But yeah, pre-island. *TV Guide* was on her coffee table."

"Those little blurbs—a single short sentence—about a show or a movie are called *log lines*," Shayla told him. "*Friendly alien encounter turns ugly when a plan to enslave humanity is revealed. Man discovers his biological father is a notorious serial killer. Quirkily named boat squad of Navy SEAL candidates . . . what?*"

"*Surprise instructors with their grit and determination and unswerving loyalty to their misfit teammates,*" he finished for her. "They started out as total underdogs, and finished up Hell Week at the very top of the class. It was . . . inspiring."

"And Hans Schlossman was one of them?" she asked, but then answered her own question. "*Hans* is German for John. Were they really all named John?"

Pete nodded again. "Or a variation. The squad's de facto

leader was an enlisted kid named John Livingston. His nickname's Seagull, for obvious reasons. His swim buddy was Jon Jackson—nicknamed Timebomb. There's Q—John Pilkington. Doe—John Capano. And finally John Schlossman—his nickname's Hans. He was the squad's great big whining clod of dogshit stuck to their proverbial boots. He learned a lot that week, and, well, certainly impressed *me* the most."

"Ouch," Shayla said, giving him that soft-eyed look of empathy that made his chest feel tight. "So if he *did* mess with Maddie, that's gotta hurt even worse, because you liked him so much. I'm so sorry."

"Yeah, I'm not sure I *liked* him," Pete said. "But I liked that I was wrong about him. Or that I thought I was wrong about him. I don't like that this proves I was right, you know, from the start—and yeah, you're right, I'm lying. I liked the asshole. *Fuck.*" His stomach hurt.

"You're an extremely interesting man," Shay said with a laugh but then asked, "What exactly did he do? Hans."

"He requested to be medically rolled, to keep Boat Squad John intact." Pete knew she had no clue what that meant, so as he braked to a stop at yet another endless red light, he expounded. "One of his squadmates got hurt, so he pretended he was hurt, too. When a SEAL candidate gets injured, he's not kicked out of the program, he's rolled back, into a newer class, so he's allowed to heal before he continues with the training. The catch is that he's got to do Hell Week all over again. So if a man gets rolled on the last day of Hell Week, he's particularly screwed. That's what happened to Timebomb. And the entire rest of Squad John—led by Seagull, but including Hans—they asked to be rolled, too. They were all willing to do Hell Week again, simply to keep Boat Squad John together. That's a pretty huge thing."

Shayla nodded. "I can only imagine."

"It's what we want—what we're looking for during BUD/S," Pete told her as the light finally went green. "Men who understand what it means to be part of a team. That kind of loyalty is . . ." He shook his head. "Hard to find."

"Loyalty's a lot like love," Shay murmured. "And love is . . . crazy. It happens or it doesn't. You can't force it—or control it. Love just *is*. Trust me, I'm a romance writer—I've given this a great deal of thought. People can't make themselves fall in love, and they also can't stop themselves from falling in love. And sometimes it's awkward and inappropriate—like if one person's only fifteen and the other's twentysomething. But that age difference is pretty meaningless if they're twenty-five and thirtysomething."

"So you think it's okay for Maddie to date a grown man?"

"Of course not," she said. "There's a reason we have laws about age of consent. She's a child in the eyes of the law. But truthfully, neither one of us knows her very well. It's possible she's mature beyond her years. It's also possible that she's completely messed up, and using sex for power, or as a way to prove to herself that she's of value. But whatever the case, it's also possible that she truly loves this guy. And if she does, if it's real, then she'll still love him when she's eighteen. And if he's got any kind of moral compass, he'll recognize that and behave accordingly."

As Pete signaled to make the left turn into the parking lot for the Grill—it was nearly full, but there were a few spots near the Dumpster—Shayla continued, "Remember Dingo's reaction to finding out Maddie's only fifteen. If telling people—men—that she's older is part of her MO, it's entirely possible that *she* approached Hans. Which brings us back to your personal experiences as a young man, asking for ID when a pretty girl implied that she wanted to get busy with you in the back of your car."

He smiled grimly as he pulled into the lot and backed into the space. "I've never had sex in the back of anyone's car."

She rolled her eyes, thinking he was being cute with se-mantics. "In the back of your truck, then."

"Car, truck, motor vehicle," he said. "Nope. Well, an RV once, but it had a king-size bed, so I don't think that counts."

"Definitely not," she said. "So, wait. You had a car, but you and Lisa really never . . . ?" She quickly backpedaled. "I don't mean to pry or be creepy. She just seemed like . . ." She started again. "Her character, at least in the way you've been telling the story, with her just showing up in your car—taking what she wants . . . I just thought . . ."

Pete shook his head. "We didn't hook up until we were both in college, and by then, we lived in dorms. And after Lisa, I was . . . well, careful. And older. Sex in cars is a teen-aged thing."

"Yeah, you don't read enough romance novels," Shayla told him. "It's not just a teen thing. It's a symbol of *I want you and I can't wait*. It's hot."

"Yeah, but that's fiction," he argued. "In real life, don't you get, like, a cop shining his flashlight through the car window, which—maybe it's me—feels like a mood killer."

She laughed and her eyes sparkled, and she even blushed a little, and his body shifted—just slightly with a *Hello, I'm alive*—as he realized they were sitting here talking about sex. And he'd forgotten for that brief moment that they'd come to the Grill to find out if Hans fucking Schlossman was sleeping with Maddie.

But then Timebomb Jackson's pale blue late-model sedan—a remarkably sedate method of transport, consid-ering Jackson's love of both state-of-the-art weaponry and technology—pulled into the parking lot and took the spot on the other side of the Dumpster.

And Shayla reached over and grabbed Pete's hand.

Her fingers were cool against his heat, but her grip was

strong. "You know, I could be the bad cop," she said, surprising him. He actually laughed.

"I could," she insisted. "That way, you could just hang back. No risk of accidentally punching him in the face."

"I promise I won't punch him," Pete said, and kissed the back of her hand, which surprised her in turn. He then got out of the truck.

* * *

Boom.

Izzy looked up from signing his credit card receipt as the noise echoed through the Grill. He leaned over to look out the window and into the parking lot. . . .

Boom. When it happened again he saw that it was the sound of SEAL candidate and Petty Officer Third Class Hansie Schlossman getting thrown up against the Dumpster. Hans was a big boy—tall, strapping, square-jawed, blond, like a movie poster for *Das Boot* come to life—and therefore made a loud noise upon impact.

But the shocker wasn't that Hans would piss someone off to the point of them throwing him against a Dumpster—twice. The shocker was that the Hans-toward-the-Dumpster thrower was none other than Grunge, aka Lieutenant Peter Greene. Who was wearing his gleaming dress whites and looking every inch the officer and gentleman. Except for the throwing-Hans-at-the-Dumpster part, which could, in some circles, be construed as rude.

What the *fuck*?

Izzy was on his feet and heading for the door, even before Timebomb Jackson—as tall, strapping, and handsomely square-jawed as Hans, but black, so no room for him on any boat commanded by Nazis—launched himself in full sprint toward the restaurant, presumably to come fetch Izzy to help.

The third currently present member of Boat Squad John

was Seagull—brilliant but height-challenged and usually rendered invisible by his two giant, handsome, muscle-bound besties. Seagull was standing near Hans and Grunge doing what he did best, i.e., talking everyone down. The Gull's body language was pure referee, but he was keeping his distance, smart boy. Grunge was, after all, an officer. And enlisted guys didn't shove back even when hitting a Dumpster was involved.

Grunge's new pretty "friend" Shayla was there, too. Unlike the Gull, she wasn't enlisted so she'd grabbed on to Grunge and was holding him back—not that she had the size or strength to stop him from doing whatever he damned pleased. But she'd wrapped her arms around him and seemed to be speaking directly into his ear. She, too, had cleaned up nicely since last night. She was pretty and shapely, and Izzy made a mental note to text Eden later: *Grunge and the neighbor lady are definitely doing it.*

Meanwhile, Schlossman was right where Grunge had left him, back against the Dumpster, hands up in a pose that was more not-hitting-an-officer-back than surrender, the look on his face not unlike that of a kid caught trying to glue Mom's favorite coffee mug back together. Hans had done something wrong, and he knew it. His shame practically radiated from him.

"What the fuck?" Izzy asked Timebomb as they met on the sidewalk.

"There was some kinda thing, happened this past Tuesday." Timebomb swiftly reversed course so that they were now both running toward the Dumpster. "With Schlossman and Lieutenant Greene's daughter, Maddie."

"What?!" Izzy's voice went into Soprano-Land. "Are you fucking kidding me? And this is the first I'm hearing about this . . . ?"

"Hans just told us, ten minutes ago." Timebomb's voice got higher, too. "After *you* told us that Maddie'd gone missing, he goes, *Fuck, I gotta tell the LT what happened Tuesday.* We went, *You think?* But when we got here, before anyone said anything at all—I mean, no words, none—the LT just went for Hans, like he already knew and was pissed as hell."

"Maddie's *fifteen,*" Izzy pointed out as they skidded to a stop beside Grunge and the others, who were all still frozen as if posing for a tableau entitled *Hans Schlossman Dances with Death.*

"Yo, man, we know," Timebomb said. "That's why Hans stopped her outside the Seven-Eleven. He told us, not only was it obvious she was cutting school, but she was with some stoner who was, like, twenty, who had his hands all over her, right, Hans?" He turned to his friend who nodded emphatically. "Hans was all, *Hey,* and the guy ran away."

Grunge, too, had heard all that, and he now turned to ask Schlossman, "Is that true?"

Relief flashed in Hans's blue eyes. "Yes! Sir! That's what I've been trying to tell you! Maddie was with this guy, and they were having a fight—or at least *she* was really angry, he wasn't saying much of anything. And he finally just grabbed her and held on to her, and at first she looked like she wanted to get away—which was when I went over to them, because shit." He looked at Shayla. "Excuse me, ma'am. Anyway, that's when I realized it was Maddie—*your* Maddie. And I heard the guy saying *It's gonna be all right,* and *We'll fix this,* and he was calling her *love,* and I think maybe he was English, you know, British.

"And I'm all, *Maddie Greene?* And they kind of spring apart, and she's like, *No,* but I know it's her, so I say *Yeah, but your dad's Lieutenant Greene, right? What are you doing here? Does your dad know you're not in school?* And the guy starts backing away, and he's all *Call me, I'll meet you later* and he jumps into some piece of shit—sorry, ma'am—car and drives away."

"Maroon?" Grunge asked as Shayla finally released her hold on him. But he didn't let her go far. He took her hand and held on to it, intertwining their fingers. Izzy made a note to include that in the text to Eden, and he was pretty sure she'd agree. Friends didn't hold hands like *that*.

Hans nodded even as Shayla took out her phone and found a photo to show him. "Is this the man you saw with Maddie?" she asked.

He took a few steps toward them to look and . . . "Yes! That's him," he confirmed.

Shayla used her thumb to find another photo and held that out, too, as she asked, "And what, exactly, is happening here?"

Hans looked at the photo and actually turned a shade whiter. "Oh, God," he said. "Who took that?"

Izzy leaned in to look, too, and yeah, okay, suddenly all the throwing-Schlossman-against-the-Dumpster noise made sense.

Hans immediately recognized his question was irrelevant, because he quickly followed it up with, "Oh, my God, sir, when you saw that you must've thought . . . but no! *No!* God, no! See, Maddie told me that Angus McFeeney—the man in the photo?" He looked from Grunge to Shayla and back. "Okay, yeah, that doesn't sound real, so his name's probably not really Angus McFeeney, but she told me he was from Palm Springs—that he was a really good friend of her mom's."

He stopped, and had to collect himself. "I'm so sorry," he told them. "My mom died when I was around Maddie's age, and I was shipped off to live with my dad, who I barely knew, and it was really hard. And I was trying to tell her that I was here if she needed someone to talk to, and I'm pretty sure I started to get choked up—because *shit*. She hugged me, and really, LT, that was *all* that it was. I was just trying to help, but I fucked it up, because I believed her about Angus McWhatever. And she asked me not to tell you—she begged me not to say anything about her cutting school, too. She said everything sucked because she missed her mom so much, and . . . I gave her my cellphone number, and she promised she'd call if she needed to talk more or . . ." He exhaled hard. "I should've called you, sir. I guess I was hoping that if I didn't, you know, say anything and she didn't get in trouble, then she'd know she could trust me and maybe she'd, I don't know, I don't know. It's stupid when I say it out loud."

"No, it's not," Shayla murmured. Grunge, however, clearly agreed with that *stupid*.

"I should've called you right then, sir," Hans said, "and made her wait with me until you got there, but I didn't. And I'm so, *so* sorry."

CHAPTER TEN

Peter handled John Schlossman's emotional apology with as much grace as he could manage.

Shay alone knew just how badly the encounter had rattled him—from the way he'd reached for her hand and held it so tightly. . . .

She wasn't sure if Peter's sudden need for connection was the result of confirmation that they'd been right all along and *Dingo* was Maddie's inappropriate older boyfriend, or if it came from his relief that SEAL Candidate Schlossman wasn't the evil, revenge-seeking asshole that they'd feared he was.

Either way, she was glad to offer support, but every reason on earth for her to keep her distance from Peter echoed in her head. He could've really hurt John Schlossman. The violence with which he'd grabbed and thrown the younger man had been startling. And really, how well did she know him . . . ?

As introductions were being made and information about the search for Maddie was being shared, Harry popped back in to offer *his* commentary.

What was that supposed to be? That full-body embrace? Was that really your idea of "good cop"?

Yes, it was. She'd been holding Peter back, like the good partner she was pretending to be. Problem was, there was just so . . . much of him. In order to get her arms all the way around the SEAL, she'd *had* to press her entire front against his entire back. It was only after she'd done it that she'd realized how awkward it was to be, essentially, spooning him.

Spooning? You were dry-humping his ass.

She hadn't moved—she'd merely hung on while he'd tried to shake himself free and . . . God, yes, she'd had a bit of an intimate encounter with the man's impossibly lovely, ridiculously firm derrière.

And girrrl, when you licked his ear?

She had *not* licked Peter's ear. She'd merely murmured a few supportive *Don't accidentally kill him*s.

Yeah, your lips touched flesh more than once, and admit it—you wanted to lick his ear and bury your nose in his neck because he smells so damn good.

"Shh!" Whoops, she'd shushed Harry aloud, and Peter heard and glanced at her.

Her friend, Peter. Her neighbor, Peter. Still a stranger to her in so many ways . . .

He stood out in this group of rather remarkably strong-and-handsome men, and not just because he was wearing that bright white uniform in contrast to the others' shorts and jeans and T-shirts.

Right after the confrontation with Schlossman, Peter had received a text from Lindsey with an address in Van Nuys—an LA suburb, about a two-hour drive away—of a James and Mary Dingler, to whom "Dingo's" maroon car was registered. His parents' home address? *Probably.*

Lindsey's police department contact had also pulled up a

more local San Diego address with an apartment number for Dingo's long-haired buddy, Daryl Middleton.

So now, along with the San Diego work address of Maddie's friend Fiona's aunt Susan, they had three potential leads to check out.

Four, including Maddie's great-aunt Hiroko, Harry reminded Shay.

Peter, Izzy, and the two SEAL candidates who'd volunteered to go with him to Palm Springs were organizing and prioritizing who should be visited first. And since Shay was unfamiliar with locations and drive times, she had little to add, aside from "Might make sense to hold off on the trip to Palm Springs," since that was just to pick up a bunch of packed boxes.

"Yeah, but the rental van has to go back by nine tonight," Izzy pointed out.

"I've got the day free," the handsome young man nicknamed Timebomb offered. "I can help. And maybe Q and Doe can—"

"I already called 'em," wiry Seagull announced. "They're in Tucson today—something with Q's sister or cousin. How about Timebomb and I go to Palm Springs—" he turned to Izzy "—if you're okay with handing off the van to us."

"I am," Izzy said.

Seagull continued, "That way you and Schlossman can head out to the Dinglers' in Van Nuys, while the LT and Ms. Whitman stay local."

"If it helps to split up even more," Shayla volunteered, even as Harry sputtered *No, no, no, no, no! What are you doing?* "I could get my car from Tevin—"

Before she could finish, Peter's cellphone rang. He glanced at it—his intention was clearly to let it go to voicemail, but then he did a double-take, and brought it to his ear with an authoritative "Peter Greene."

His eyes narrowed slightly as he listened for several long moments to whoever was on the other end, but then he covered the phone's mic with his other hand as he said, "It's Maddie's aunt Hiroko. Maddie and Dingo were just at her house, asking to borrow money. If we hurry . . ."

"Go," Izzy said. "Fly. We'll figure this out and be in touch."

Peter looked directly at Shayla and gestured for her to follow as he headed quickly for his truck.

Jesus, those blue eyes in that face with that uniform!

"Shh!"

Peter spoke over her, thank God, again into the phone, "I thought the number looked familiar. Thank you so much for tracking me down, because yeah, Maddie's gone AWOL. We're on our way." He hung up as he started his truck with a roar as Shayla, too, fastened her seat belt, and he pulled out of the parking lot.

* * *

"You gave Maddie *three* hundred dollars," Pete heard himself echo Hiroko's words. "In a personal check . . . ?"

In his mind, he time-traveled and was using those moments when Hiroko had first called to organize a hard-and-fast search pattern of the banks immediately surrounding this still sleepy little beach community. With three vehicles—his, Izzy's, and Timebomb's—and with six sets of sharp eyes, they might've actually spotted Maddie in a bank parking lot in Dingo's distinctive maroon car.

But Hiroko hadn't thought to tell him that there was a check to be cashed, and he hadn't thought to interrogate her when she'd reported she'd given Maddie and Dingo some money. But Jesus, he wished that he had.

Shayla now reached between them as they sat on the sofa in Hiroko's tidy little living room and she put her hand on top of his, clearly knowing exactly where his thoughts had gone. But she also knew as well as he did that wallowing in *should've*s wasn't going to help them find Maddie, so even as she gently squeezed and released his hand, she pushed the conversation forward.

"Did she say why she needed it—that much money?" she asked Hiroko as she pushed up the sleeves of her sweater. It was cooler here, near the water, and she'd pulled it out of her bag and put it on, but Hiroko had always kept her house warm.

In truth, the elderly woman had gone above and beyond. She'd managed to get Maddie and Dingo to pose for a photo before they left. She took it with her phone, and even managed to get them to stand directly behind Dingo's car, so the plate number was included. And then she'd tracked down Pete's cellphone number, to get in touch with him.

She had no idea that Pete had already IDed "Dingo" Dingler, formerly of Van Nuys, California, via his car's license plate number. Instead, via her photo, he got confirmation of what they already knew—yup, Maddie was definitely still in the company of the idiot who owned the maroon car.

Now Hiroko sat across from them on the edge of a leather-covered easy chair, her posture impeccable. She'd had coffee ready when they arrived, and had gotten out a plate of cookies—store-bought and stale. She'd never been much of the grandmotherly type, even twenty years ago, and age had not mellowed her.

The art on her walls, however, was still brilliant—vibrant and chaotic. Pete recognized one piece that he'd seen, incomplete, in her studio—which was really the little cottage's tiny second bedroom—back even before he'd met Lisa. The swirl of different shades and hues of blue and green somehow captured the very essence of life itself—but then again, he'd always preferred modern art, wild and unfettered, to the Norman Rockwell school of realism.

"She and the boy gave me some story about a school

project and a road trip up to Manzanar," Hiroko told them with the same matter-of-fact grimness that she'd had when he'd met her, years ago, "but it was clear they were lying. I gave her the check because I thought she needed it to break the cycle."

Shayla nodded, but Pete was lost. "What cycle?" he asked.

Hiroko put it plainly. "Babies having babies."

Babies having . . . oh, shit. Oh, Jesus. "You honestly think . . . ?"

Hiroko shrugged.

"Did Maddie say anything, specifically," Shayla asked, with another squeeze of his hand, "that made you believe . . . ?"

"No, but while she was here, it didn't take much to make her weepy. Hormones."

"It hasn't been that long since her mother passed," Shay pointed out. "Plus she's a teenager, and on top of that, she's probably feeling uncertain about her decision to leave home. I certainly don't think we should jump to conclusions based on her being a little weepy." She leaned forward a bit. "Where's this Manzanar?"

"Head toward Reno on 395, but then stop in the middle of nowhere," Pete told her.

She was perplexed. "Is it . . . like Coachella? Is there some kind of music festival or—"

"Manzanar is one of the prison camps where they kept us—Americans of Japanese descent—during the Second World War," Hiroko told her.

Shayla sat up straight. "Oh dear God," she said. "I'm so sorry I didn't know that. I mean, of course I know that it happened and it was awful. I mean, it must've been . . . I can't imagine . . . ." Now it was Pete's turn to reach over and squeeze her hand as she turned to look at him with eyes that were enormous and filled with horror at her gaffe.

"It's okay," he murmured.

"It *was* awful at Manzanar," Hiroko said. "And it's not a big surprise that you didn't know it by name—it was one of many. We don't talk about it enough. We should. And of course, now the last of us are finally dying off."

Shay pointed over her shoulder at the collection of black-and-white photos on the wall by the front door. "Is that what . . . ? Are those pictures of . . . ?"

"Yes, that's the camp. I was ten years old when I arrived. We were there for three years. Until the war ended, in '45."

Shayla gracefully rose and went to look more closely at the photos that Pete had seen many times when he was a teenager. Rows of long, barracks-style cabins lined the flat valley surrounded by the snow-capped Sierra Nevada in the west and the Inyo Mountains in the east. Families had been in Manzanar long enough to plant gardens and flowers bloomed—and in the photos, Hiroko and her brothers got older. At one point, the U.S. Army even "allowed" the boys who were old enough to enlist, and many—including Hiroko's brother Kaito, resolute and impossibly young in his uniform in a posed portrait—went off to fight and die for a country that considered their families a threat.

Meanwhile, Hiroko corrected herself. "The *prison* at Manzanar. If I call it a camp, it sounds fun. Festive. Macramé. S'mores. Sitting around a fire and singing 'If I Had a Hammer.'" She shook her head. "It wasn't fun. It was an ordeal with the dust and the dirt and the freezing winters and deadly hot summers. But all of that was secondary to the humiliation."

"I'm so sorry," Shayla said.

"*You* have nothing to apologize for," Hiroko said. When Shayla turned and focused on the photos, the old woman silently mouthed to Pete, *I like her.*

Maybe she *had* mellowed a bit with age and time. Back when he was in high school, she'd spoken openly about how miserable Lisa would make him—even as Pete had blushed and insisted that he and Lisa were just friends.

It was funny how people saw a boy hanging out with a girl—or a man with a woman—and assumed that romance and lust were involved.

Pete knew that like Hiroko, Izzy also thought there was something-something going on between him and Shayla. And Shay's playing *good cop* back at the Grill had only added fuel to that imaginary fire.

She'd surprised Pete when she'd grabbed him like that—that full bear hug from behind—although in hindsight, he couldn't come up with another way for her to have "stopped" him from pummeling Schlossman. At least not that would've looked believable.

And despite his anger at Schlossman and his focused need to get to the bottom of those damning photos, part of his brain had been acutely aware of a variety of things. First, that Shayla was stronger—sturdier—than he'd imagined. There was a solidness to her, and at the same time, a softness. It was a good combination, which made him aware of the second thing, which was that it had been too damn long since someone who cared about him—truly, honestly cared—had put their arms around him.

It had shocked him—just how much he'd missed something that he hadn't even really known that he'd been denied.

It was different from sex. He was well aware of just how much he'd missed *that,* but oddly, this hurt worse.

"Maddie told you that she and Dingo were going here—to Manzanar?" Shayla asked as she continued to study the photos.

"For a *school project*." Hiroko was heavy with her ironic emphasis. "The girl's got her mother's ability to lie like a professional card shark, but the boy was one giant, twitchy tell."

"Please forgive me for not knowing, but is the prison still there?" Shay asked as she finally came back and sat down beside Pete.

"It is and it isn't," Hiroko said.

Shay leaned in again. "Didn't anyone, I don't know, preserve it as an historic site?"

"Who would've done that?" Hiroko asked. "The families who'd been imprisoned there? We'd lost everything when we were rounded up—farms, businesses, jobs—all gone. My parents spent the war unemployed—like everyone in the camp—and when it was over, we were tossed back into a society who'd been taught to hate an enemy who looked exactly like us. Creating an historic site was the last thing we were thinking about. As for the government, they wanted Manzanar to disappear since yes, it had been unconstitutional and illegal—our imprisonment. So they tore down the cabins and sold off the wood and the metal from the fencing. But there's really nothing out there—no town needing the site for a shopping mall or a suburban development, so in that sense, it's still there—that great, big, dusty, empty space. And yes, it *is* a national site *now,* all these decades later—with a small monument to mark our national shame—but that happened only after we kicked and screamed to make it so. Now there's an organization trying to preserve it, to rebuild more of the cabins according to the photos, but until they do that, there's not much there to preserve. The high school auditorium that we built. I think that still stands, but other than that, there's just some eroding foundations in a big dusty field, marked with a few little signs—apparently. That's what I've heard. I have *not* been back."

"So it's unlikely Maddie would go there, expecting—I don't know—a place to hide out?" Shayla asked.

"It's unlikely she'd find much of anything to hide in or

behind," Hiroko replied, "if she and the boy with the ridiculous name did go there."

Pete spoke up. "I don't suppose you'd be willing to put a stop payment on the check."

"If I wanted to stop the payment, Peter, I wouldn't have given the check to the girl in the first place" was the curt reply. "And actually, I didn't write it to Maddie. She said she didn't have a bank account and wouldn't be able to cash it. So I wrote it for the boy. Ricky—Richard—Dingler. She calls him *Dingo*. I don't know why, when Ricky is a perfectly fine name. I'm not sure what else I can tell you."

And that was their cue to go. As Pete stood up, he took out his phone and texted Izzy: *FYI, Dingo's name is Ricky, short for Richard, Dingler.* That info could be useful if Izzy encountered Dingo's parents up in Van Nuys. "Please call me if they come back," he told Hiroko.

"They won't." She seemed certain.

"Thank you so much for the coffee," Shayla said, giving Hiroko a hug, which was actually amazing. Pete had never seen the old woman reach out to make any kind of contact with anyone—not even a handshake. In fact, she shrank from it. Because of that, people tended to keep their distance—himself and Lisa included. And even now, as Shayla hugged the old woman, it looked a lot like she was hugging a marble statue. Still, she pulled back to look into Hiroko's eyes and say, "It was so nice to meet you—Peter's told me a lot about you. I hope we'll see you again, soon."

Hiroko's response was a prickly "Well, I don't know about that." But then, after Shay had gone out the door, as Pete was heading out himself and pulling it closed behind him, the old woman said, "I hope you're finally happy, Peter."

He almost stopped and went back inside to confront her, because that was just cruel. She hoped he was *finally* happy?

With Lisa dead, and Maddie run away and possibly pregnant at age fifteen . . . ?

Instead, he closed the door behind him.

Thanks, Hiroko. Jesus. Just . . . *thanks*.

* * *

"Is Maddie a morning person?" Shayla asked as they headed toward the next item on their search list: the San Diego address they'd gotten for Daryl Middleton, Dingo's long-haired friend.

Peter had been silently grim since they left Hiroko's lovely little beach house, lost in thoughts and memories, no doubt, from being back in the very place he'd first met Maddie's mother. Now, as he navigated his way through the morning traffic, he glanced at Shay and the expression on his face was intentionally comical—an over-exaggerated *Seriously?* "She's a teenager," he reminded her. "She'd sleep until noon every day if she could."

"Yeah, that's what I was thinking, too." She smiled at him. "I've got two of my own, and Tevin's currently doing a workout regimen before school. I think his desire to put on some muscle, you know, to stop being the tall, skinny kid currently trumps his need for sleep—but it's a daily battle and sleep sometimes wins. Frank's solidly in the sleep-all-day-if-he-could phase." She paused, then asked, "So what's she doing up this early on a day she has no intention of going to school? Why not sleep in? Instead, she and Dingo must've gotten to Hiroko's before seven. That had to take some serious effort." She could tell he didn't quite understand why this mattered, so she added, "I keep thinking there's a clue in there. Like, whoever they're staying with has to get up and go to work. Or . . . what?"

He nodded. "You're right. Although it's possible their motivation was the money. We told Maddie, in the story we sent, that Hiroko often got up early. Maybe she wanted to get there before we did."

"Or, maybe they're sleeping on the beach or in a park somewhere," Shay said, "or even in that car, and got told to *move it along*, so they were just out, doing what I think of as the early-morning zombie shuffle, except they're in the car. Drove past Hiroko's as recon, stumbled on her up and in her garden."

He nodded again as he threw her another glance. "That writer brain of yours," he said. "It's a good one."

"Well, thanks, but if I were writing this scene, I'd have 'em staying with Dingo's buddy Daryl at—" she checked the address she'd input into her phone's GPS "—the Riverside Arms, unit three-fifty. Does San Diego even have a river?"

"We've got a few. Most of 'em are more like riverbeds—arroyos. So being riverside isn't necessarily high-priced real estate with scenic views. And since it looks like we're heading toward the airport, I think we're doubling down on the potential ugly."

As Shay looked out of the truck's windows, she had to agree. This was the part of town where she and the boys had camped out when they'd first moved to San Diego. The truck carrying their furniture had been delayed by two whole weeks, so they'd gotten a suite at one of those extended-stay hotels. It had been relatively nice, but just a few blocks away were pawnshops, strip clubs, massage parlors—and, apparently, a worn-down, three-story brick box of an apartment complex loftily called "Riverside Arms."

Peter found a parking spot on the street and as they got out of his truck, the roar of an airplane taking off made it impossible to hear. He pointed toward the building's front door, and Shay nodded, and together they went up the pitted concrete path. The door was locked, but there was a panel of a dozen buttons for buzzers near a dented, ancient speaker.

Peter hit the buzzer for 350. There was no name next to it—there was nothing written next to any of the buttons, except for one marked *Manager* in childishly careful block print.

Nothing happened. He hit it again, holding it longer this time.

Shayla pointed to the speaker. "That might not even work," she said—the jet engines now a rumble in the distance.

"Or no one's home," Peter said. He hit the button for the manager, as he glanced at her. "You up for playing private eye? A few white lies for the sake of information gathering?"

She nodded. "Of course. What are you thinking?"

But instead of the speaker squawking on, the manager came out of an apartment that was at the very front of the lobby—they could see a man peering at them through the glass as he came to push the door open.

"You here about the rental?" he asked. It was clear he was wary of Pete's naval uniform, but his semi-unwelcoming demeanor went even farther south when he looked at Shayla. "Sorry to say it, but management just upped the security deposit to three full months."

There was no way that was true for anyone but a family of color—or maybe a white sailor from the Naval Base, who was in an interracial relationship.

As if this man had the right to judge anyone, with his beer belly gaping between the bottom of his stained white sleeveless undershirt and jean cutoffs that were much too short, considering this was not the 1980s. And that wasn't even taking into account his beady little blue eyes, orange-tanner skin tone, and lack of chin. His fleshy face just went straight from his head down to his shoulders, and God, he smelled like a bad combo of locker room and distillery. But he was white and male and presumably hetero, which in his mind gave him the right to assess and find them lacking.

Shayla smiled sweetly at the man, even while inwardly she was performing a *Game of Thrones*–style massacre—and maybe even writing warning messages on the lobby walls with his entrails. White lies? Nope. They were gonna hit this man with a full fictional fucking.

And before Peter could respond—it was clear he was both astonished and outraged—she said brightly, crisply, "Oh, that's well within the studio's budget—I've been authorized to offer in the neighborhood of seventy-five thousand for the month, with the possibility that we'll need to stay for two. Maybe three—four at the most. At the same monthly rental amount, of course."

The manager's jaw had dropped. "I'm sorry, I'm—" he started, but Shayla cut him off.

"Excuse me, *I'm* sorry, I'm so rude! I'm Harriet Parker from Heartbeat Productions, and this is Lieutenant Thomas McGee—the film's official military consultant. We're scouting locations here in San Diego for Mr. Howard's latest film, *SEAL Team Sixteen*—working title, of course. Lieutenant McGee is with me today, since the movie's based on a true story, and he was there. And while apartment three-fifty isn't exactly right, it's very close to what Mr. Howard needs. We've all seen pictures, and we were supposed to meet the leaseholder here this morning—" she took her phone from her handbag and scrolled through her latest texts from Tevin, pretending they contained vital info from *Mr. Howard's studio* "—a Daryl Middleton . . . ?"

The manager was shaking his head, but his eyes had turned into cartoon dollar signs and he pushed the door open wide enough for them to come in. "I'm not sure where you got that info—three-fifty's one of our currently-vacants.

But I'm happy to show it to you, and talk to the owner about working out some kind of short-term deal."

Yeah, Shayla bet he would. But as she and Peter stepped into the lobby—which smelled like locker room, distillery, urinal, *and* sauerkraut or maybe that was rotting cabbage, hard to tell—she said, "Three-fifty's vacant? That's strange. Unless . . . Oh, in his last email, Daryl said something about his father's failing health, so maybe he had to leave town unexpectedly. And then *we* got delayed because of the *thing* with Ryan Gosling. . . . You know, but *shhh,* can't talk about it."

The manager was trying to lead them toward the back of the lobby, to an elevator door that didn't quite close all the way—as if someone had taken a crowbar to it in order to allow someone else to escape. No way was she getting into that, so she planted her feet and took Peter's arm to stop him, too.

He complied and even covered her hand with his and squeezed—it was clear he was trying not to laugh as the manager realized they weren't following and came back.

Shay asked, "Has three-fifty been empty for long?"

"Oh," he said, "um, yeah, actually. I think the tenants moved out in December. Yeah, it was right before Christmas, when the semester ended. They were students."

"Wow," Shay said. "So . . . months ago. That's strange. Are you sure we're talking about the same tenant—Daryl Middleton? Maybe I got the apartment number wrong."

The manager shook his head, absolute. "I've been here ten years. I know everyone. No one named Daryl Middleton in three-fifty or any other apartment. At least not as a leaseholder."

"I'm certain it was three-fifty, *Harriet,*" Peter told Shay before turning to the manager to say, "Daryl's tall, white, long straight hair, beard, early twenties . . . ?"

The manager laughed. "Tenants were co-eds. From

Ohio—nice girls, pretty. Blondes and maybe not the sharpest tools in the shed, if you know what I mean. This Daryl sounds like one of their boyfriends. They had shitty taste in men."

In other words, he'd hit on them and gotten turned down.

"I'm happy to show you the apartment though," the manager continued.

Both Shayla and Peter reached for their phones at the exact same time, feigning an incoming call—because there was no need to go upstairs.

Shay pretended to look at her phone and covered by saying, "Oh my God, Lieutenant McGee, are you getting a call from Ron's office, too? Hang on, I've got to take this."

"I do, too," Peter said, and they both turned away, pretending to listen to someone on their other end.

"We're there right now, sir," Shay said as she heard Peter murmur, "ASAP? Yes, of course. We'll reschedule. Not a problem. I'm sure."

She fought her laughter and instead said, "Certainly, Mr. Howard, I can arrange that." She paused and then said, "Yes, sir, I'll let him know."

She and Peter both "hung up" their phones at the same time and turned back to each other and the manager, who'd been trying to look as if he weren't listening in.

"You get a call about the meeting, too?" she asked Peter.

He nodded, and turned to the manager. "We're going to have to reschedule."

"I'm so sorry," Shay said. "We've got to rush back to LA. But Mr. Howard was hoping to get a look at the place himself, maybe early tomorrow? If it's still available, of course. And please, please, don't hold it for him if someone wants to rent. As much as he likes working on location, having a set built on a soundstage has its benefits, and it's a constant give-and-take with the movie's producers."

"If he can get a real Mark Five he might give in to the

pressure to build the apartment on the soundstage," Peter said.

She had *no* idea what a Mark Five was, and she almost laughed. Instead, she just blinked at Peter and said something ridiculous like, "Yes, of course, he does want a real . . . Mark Five."

Peter opened the door and held it for her. "Shall we?"

The manager was doing at least *some* of the math, and realized he hadn't given them his name or number. "It's Bob Watkins. Eight-one-eight . . ." As he recited his phone number, Shay called out "Thank you!" She pretended to put it into her phone even as she went out the door. Peter was right behind her, and somehow they managed to make it down and across the street to his truck before they started to laugh.

"You're a little too good at that," he told her, his eyes giving off a huge amount of sparkle. "I think I might be scared."

"It's really just writing a scene on the fly," she told him. "And believe me, once he pissed me off . . ."

Peter sobered as they stood on the sidewalk next to his truck. "That was . . . unbelievable. What he did was illegal. And it's pretty damn easy to prove that he was lying. *Three* months' security?"

"But who wants to push to live in a building where *that guy* has a master key to your apartment?" Shayla shook her head. "In a way, it's better to find it out up front. You know, *before* you move in and he ties a rope with a lynching noose on the stair rail for your kid to stumble across?"

"Fuck," he said. And the way he was standing there, legs slightly spread in a stance that was more than a little combative, as if he were ready to slay the dragons of injustice, made her smile.

"Come on," she said. "Susan Smith's law office is surely open by now. Let's visit her, see what she knows about

Fiona and Maddie's friendship, then check in at home, see if Maddie's been there, maybe take a break to have lunch and write that *Peter and Lisa*, Chapter Two. The sooner we have something to send to Maddie, the sooner we'll get another *still safe* text message—or even an invitation to talk. I was thinking, regardless, that it might make sense for Hans to text her, see if she'll talk to *him*—"

Peter lunged at her. He moved so quickly, she honestly didn't see it coming. One second, he was standing there, nodding in agreement, and the next he'd grabbed her, pulling her in hard against his chest as he dragged her with him behind his truck.

There was another truck—big and black—on the street, pulling away with a squeal of tires, a roar of an engine, and the harsh sound of voices shouting—something about *Navy motherfucker*—the other words indiscernible but the rage unmistakable.

Shayla shrieked her surprise as she tripped—over her own feet or maybe Peter's—and this time instead of keeping her from going down, he went to the sidewalk with her, somehow managing to turn with a weird-sounding *clang*, so that she landed on his chest and front instead of on the hard concrete.

And yeah, her knee was lined up pretty perfectly with his crotch, and he made that unmistakable noise, deep in his throat, that she'd heard Carter and her various other exes make when she'd accidentally whacked them in the balls. She had given him, without a doubt, a direct hit.

Carter would tightly shut his eyes and curl into a bit of a ball himself, moaning for ice. But then, when she got it, he'd mutter *Don't touch me* as she apologized.

Peter's eyes, however, were wide open and mere inches from her own as he focused on her. "Are you okay? Did you get hit? Are you hurt?"

Hurt? Hit? "No," she said, still dazed by suddenly being

tackled. This current body-to-body contact wasn't helping to clear her head. He was warm and solid, with those giant arms still wrapped tightly around her. "What . . . ?"

As she pulled back slightly—his face was too close to have any kind of a conversation that didn't include the phrase *Kiss me, fool,* an utterance that would be a *mistake*—she realized that he was covered—*covered*—in some kind of hideously disgusting brown slop.

Had they fallen into horse manure, or God, the place in the neighborhood where the homeless population emptied their bowels, because, yeah, it smelled like that kind of nasty, too. Except she would've made note of it earlier, upon getting out of Peter's truck—they were lying there right beside the very door she'd emerged from.

As she pushed herself even further up and off of him, she saw a metal bucket—that was what she'd heard make that *clang* as it hit the sidewalk. It was lying on its side, and was clearly the source of the nastiness.

"Oh, my God," she said as Peter started to hold out a hand to help her up, but stopped when he realized that doing so would transfer that whatever-it-was onto her. She was miraculously clean, probably because he'd made himself into a rather large shield to protect her. "Did those men in that truck throw that at us? Who *was* that? Oh, my God! Are you all right?"

"I'm fine, I don't know who they were, I didn't really see much," Peter told her. "It was a black truck, large, relatively new, maybe a Ford, but I can't say for sure. At least two occupants in the cab, but whoever threw this was riding in the back."

"Navy motherfucker," Shayla echoed the few words she'd heard.

He nodded as he glanced down the street. "Yeah, I heard that, too. Whoever they are, they're long gone."

The bucket was not a little one—it was floor-mopping

size—and as they both got back onto their feet, Shayla could tell from the way he'd been splattered that it had hit him squarely in the back. God, the shit—literal shit—was in his beautiful hair, and had gone down his collar. But despite that, he was looking at her carefully, as if double-checking that she truly was unharmed.

There was only one *Navy motherfucker* between the two of them, but while they may have been aiming at Peter, they'd missed. Shay realized that if he hadn't gallantly thrown himself between her and the bucket, it would've hit her, right in the head. Even empty, that would've hurt. But *full* . . . ?

Instead, she was almost completely unscathed. Her knee was a little sore—the one that had hit the street instead of Peter's male anatomy. Although, she discovered that she did have quite a bit of dookey on the back of her sweater, which she quickly slipped out of, turned inside out, and then used to wipe off a few stray patches of ick that smudged her pants. "Are you sure you're all right? That must've hit you hard."

"Yeah," he said. "I'm okay. But the smell is kinda . . . I might throw up. I'm gonna apologize for that in advance."

"I kicked you in the gentleman's accessories," she reminded him. "That can't be helping."

"I'll live," he said as he started to undress, right there on the sidewalk. "Reach into my pocket and get my keys—and my phone and wallet while you're at it—I don't want to touch them. I'm riding in the back—you're driving us home."

CHAPTER ELEVEN

Shayla wasn't used to driving a vehicle this enormous, and it was a little scary, but she focused instead on the positives. Being able to look down on all of the other drivers as she pushed past the edge of the speed limit was pretty cool.

The exception to that were the people driving the big rigs. They still looked down on her—and had a clear shot of the nearly naked Navy SEAL lying on his back in the bed of the truck, trying not to puke. He'd kept his underwear on—white boxers, which really, when she thought about it, was the only option under white uniform pants.

He had an angry red mark on his back from where the bucket had made contact, but it hadn't broken the skin.

His right elbow, on the other hand, was shredded. Shay didn't want to think about whatever it was in that bucket making contact with an open scrape, but it had. And the sooner she got him home, the faster they could get him cleaned up.

He'd had a pack of utility-size trash bags—thick black plastic—stashed in one of the locked compartments in the back of the truck, and at his instruction, she'd gotten out a few. One for his clothes and her trashed sweater, and a second to contain the bucket.

So far, Peter had resisted her suggestion that they call the police. She knew he desperately wanted to get home to wash, so she hadn't pushed, but it was possible there were fingerprints on that bucket, so they took it with them.

Traffic was heavier than she liked, especially since she was piloting the *Millennium Falcon,* but she finally pulled onto their street.

And oh, good. Mrs. Quinn was out watering her flowers, and yup, she'd perked up into hyper-nosy mode as she realized that Shay was driving the SEAL's truck.

Harry popped in, already laughing his ass off. *Mrs. Quinn's gonna shit a full flock of Canadian geese when she sees . . .*

Yup, even before Shay had completely braked to a stop in Peter's driveway, he was up and out of the truck, a flash of mostly tanned skin and golden hair, beelining for the backyard.

That, Harry finished with a chortle as yup, in the rearview Shay saw that Mrs. Quinn had dropped her hose. It must've been locked into an *on* position, because it kept spraying and it danced around wildly—causing Mrs. Quinn to shriek and run for cover.

Shayla waved to the woman as casually as she could as she locked Peter's truck with a *beep* from the key fob.

Harry hovered. *Now what? Follow him back there to help? He's no longer* nearly *naked, FYI.*

Shay confirmed the obvious—Peter had, indeed, left his boxers behind in the truck. He probably would've left his poop-matted hair if he could've.

He was probably using his own hose to, literally, hose himself down. Odds were that he didn't need any help.

But you have his keys, Harry pointed out.

She looked down at them—the chain included the keys to his house. She had his phone and wallet, too, pulled from his pockets before the slime had contaminated them. She *had* to go back there to give it all to him. And while she was there, she could offer to get him a towel from inside.

Yeah, Harry said as he followed her down a neatly swept path that led around to the back of Peter's house. *That's why you're going. To get the SEAL a towel.*

And to help him clean out that scraped elbow after he was done with the hose-down. She could hear the sound of water running—Peter had, indeed, turned on his hose.

You want to get a good look at his elbow, because you're the witty neighbor, so you definitely didn't bother checking out his ass as he did his streaker impression.

He *had* been running pretty fast.

Right.

Okay so, naked, the SEAL was an eleven on a scale from one to ten. And yup again, there he was, holding up the hose with one hand as he used the other to attempt to comb the crap out of his hair.

He'd done an all-over rinse, so now his mostly-tan-and-goldenness was covered with shimmering droplets of water.

Harry whistled. *Well, my, my, my, my-my-my my! Isn't he well—*

"Shh." Women didn't focus on superficial things like that. Shayla tried to see if the bucket-impact mark on his back was still as angry looking.

Liar, liar, pants on fire. Oh, wait. Your pants are also on fire for another reason.

Peter straightened up, squeegeeing his hair back as he rinsed his face, and all of his muscles rippled and moved and . . . Oh, my goodness.

"Goodness" is putting it mildly. Lordy, Lordy, woman, I can feel the heat from your pants afire—the non-lying kind—from here.

"Shh!"

That man saved your life back there. I think it's okay to

thank him with a neighborly hug. A special, naked neighborly hug with your vagina around his oh-my-goodness—

"Shh!" Oh, crap, her hushing Harry had gotten so loud that Peter'd heard her even over the sound of the water, and he now turned to see her standing there, practically ogling him.

Practically? Harry drawled.

"How can I help?" she asked the SEAL a tad too briskly, in a voice that was somehow supposed to signify that she hadn't been enjoying the view. "I have your keys. Should I get towels from inside? Soap? Shampoo?" She felt herself slip into the vortex of full-babble. "A scouring brush? Do you have a nail brush? You should really use a nail brush, and we're absolutely going to want to scrub that elbow with some kind of antiseptic, so—"

"A towel would be great," Peter interrupted her. "And maybe you could get me a pair of shorts. Running shorts, please. They're in the top basket in my closet. You can't miss 'em."

"Absolutely," Shayla said, briskly crossing to the back door that led into the laundry room just off his kitchen. She fumbled the keys and dropped them—oh dear God—as Harry continued to just laugh and laugh and laugh.

She finally made it inside. The house was warm—he'd clearly turned off the air-conditioning before leaving this morning. *That* was the kind of thing that made a man more attractive to real-life, nonfictional women like her—the fact that he was both environmentally conscious and economical—not his physical attributes, as nice as they might be.

Shayla set his keys on the kitchen counter with his phone and his wallet, and headed for the hallway that led to the bedrooms. She'd given one bedroom a peek last night—it was the first door on the left, right across from the bathroom. It was small, with a utilitarian, narrow twin-size bed against one wall, and a single chest of drawers. She'd assumed it was the guest bedroom—it certainly didn't belong to any teenaged girl *she'd* ever met—but as she now went farther down the hall, she realized that there was only one other doorway at the very end.

It led to the master, with its own attached bath, and . . . "Holy crap."

Harry said the obvious. *Peter gave the master bedroom to Maddie.*

Teen girls weren't at all different from teen boys when it came to both laundry and life's clutter. The room was a mess, with about a dozen cardboard moving boxes scattered about. Most weren't even close to unpacked but all were definitely rummaged through. Peter had bought his daughter some lovely furniture, including a big, wooden bookshelf that held maybe ten books total on a single shelf, and a dresser that had still-empty drawers.

It was textbook passive-aggressiveness, and Maddie's subtext was clear: *I'll live here, but I'll hate both it and you, so I won't unpack.*

Damn, Harry said as Shayla went back to the smaller bedroom where Peter's running shorts—the lightweight kind with the mesh underwear sewn in—were right where he'd described them. In a white wire slide-out basket that was part of a tiny but carefully organized closet.

She loved her boys like crazy, but no way would she ever, not in a million years, give them the master bedroom in *any* house.

You're not a near-total stranger to them, Harry pointed out as she went into the hall bathroom and found a stack of clean towels in the linen closet. *You're also not a male near-total stranger and your kids aren't female.*

Shay started to take from the bottom, assuming those would be the oldest, but they were all clearly brand-new. She grabbed a washcloth, too, then headed back into the kitchen as Harry continued, *Father-on-daughter sexual abuse is common enough to be a thing. Your SEAL was thoughtful enough to try to make Maddie feel as safe as possible by giving her the privacy that comes with having her own bathroom.*

Harry had a point.

This guy is pretty freaking amazing, he said as he followed her out into the yard, where Peter was still working on his hair.

"Here," Shay said, holding out the shorts. "Put these on, and then I'll work on your hair, make sure you got it all."

"Thanks," he said. He let go of the pressure handle, and the water shut off as he effortlessly caught the shorts that she tossed him.

Shay politely turned her back and pretended to be fascinated by the roofline of the house as he pulled them on.

"But I think I got it all," Peter said. "You don't need to—"

"I'm pretty sure you still have a little in your ear," she said.

"*Fuck.* Really?"

"It's not like you could see it," she said, turning back. "I mean, even with a mirror, it would've been easy to miss." He was clearly feeling discouraged, so she pointed to one of two sling-style lounge chairs that were artfully arranged on the pavers that made up the patio, a little table between them. "Let's move that onto the lawn—well, whatever this is that you Californians think makes a lawn, and may I just say that you are so, *so* wrong—and adjust it so it's more flat. So you can lie back, dangle your head off the edge, and let me get the last of it."

He was not happy. "There's no way you can do that without getting wet."

"That's okay." Shay put the towels down on the second chair as she started to move the first herself.

As expected, Peter came to assist. "No, it's not."

She told him, "If you think for one second that after I help you, I'm not rushing home to bleach the hell out of these clothes and take an extra-exfoliating shower myself . . . ? You are greatly deluded, my friend."

He smiled at that. "Still . . ."

"You have shit in your ears." Shayla went point-blank as she also pointed to the chair. "Sit."

Peter sat.

"Stay upright for a sec," she ordered. "I want to get that last bit out before we do a final pass with the hose."

Shay got the washcloth a little damp while Harry walked in a circle around them.

He likes being ordered around. That's good to know for when you have screaming animal-sex, he commented as she leaned down and gently wiped a clump of god-knows-what from Peter's ear. *It'll make it extra hot.*

"Shh," Shayla hissed at the exact moment that the SEAL looked up at her and their eyes met. "It. Shit. Indeed. In your ears."

Harry laughed, because God, she sounded like an idiot.

"These are skills that I haven't practiced since Frankie grew out of that toddler put-your-dinner-everywhere-but-in-your-mouth phase," she said while she used a different part of the cloth to briskly but thoroughly clean the entire rest of Peter's ear. "But some things a mother just never forgets."

Oh, good. Compare him not just to a two-year-old, but to your own two-year-old, Harry said. *Way to create some real sexual tension, Mom; get it sparking and popping.*

Shay clenched her teeth as she pushed Peter's hair back from his other ear. Creating sexual tension was *not* what she was going for here. God, this man had nice ears, nice hair, nice face, nice neck, nice shoulders and chest . . . *God.*

Peter cleared his throat. "I'm keeping you from your writing."

What? It was such a non sequitur, she laughed her surprise. "Nah, you're really not," she said, stepping back a bit and checking to make sure both of his ears were clean. She tapped his shoulder. "Come on. Lie back and let me do your hair."

Again, he obeyed, but he moved so that his shoulders and head were down at the end where the lounger's feet normally went. "I'm afraid if I go the other way, I'll tip it over," he explained, and yes, he was probably right.

As he let his head hang off the end, he'd pulled his legs up so that his knees were bent.

To hide his boner.

To support his back, she corrected Harry. And of course, Peter didn't let his head actually dangle, he used his incredible eight-pack of abs to hold it up.

He met her eyes again and said, "Please be careful not to hit yourself with any backsplash."

Shayla picked up the hose. "I can see what I'm doing, remember. We're definitely past the backsplash phase." She'd already reset the hose nozzle to a slightly gentler stream in order to wet the washcloth she'd used on his ears. "It's cold," she warned as she squeezed it on and crouched down next to him to run it through his hair.

She used her other hand the same way he'd done, combing her fingers through hair that was both soft and thick. But unlike him, she could see what she was doing.

He'd closed his eyes—he had long, thick dark lashes that had no doubt induced jealousy in every girlfriend he'd ever had, and probably his mother, too. But the muscles in the side of his jaw were jumping, so she asked, "You okay?"

He opened his eyes. Smiled. "My day has included a literal bucket of shit."

Shay laughed—whatever it was she'd expected him to

say, it wasn't that. And it was true. How often could you say that? Not that she'd want to repeat the experience. Ever.

"So compared to that," he added, "I'm very okay. I really appreciate you doing this, and um—bonus. It, uh, feels . . . really nice." He whispered the last words.

Shayla froze, because, yes, he had absolutely just said that. To her. While looking into her eyes.

Kiss him.

She didn't move.

Kiss him!

She found her voice. "Well, that's . . . good, at least," she said as she shut off the hose and stood up.

What are you doing? Are you crazy? Kiss him! Kisshimkisshimkisshim! Ahhhhhhh!

She ignored Harry's total meltdown and backed away instead. Grabbed a towel and got just close enough to hand it to Peter before she backed away again as Harry moaned, *What is* wrong *with you?*

Peter didn't mean what he'd just said. He'd simply slipped back into—what had he called it before? His *bar hookup pattern.*

Peter sat up, rubbing his head with the towel.

Shayla pointed over her shoulder with her thumb. "I'm gonna . . . go shower myself now."

"Right," he said. "Of course."

"It'll take me about forty-five minutes," she said. "To get ready to go to the lawyer's office—Fiona's aunt—Susan Smith?"

"Oh," he said. "No. Don't. You don't have to. I got that. I'll be ready myself in just a few minutes, so I'll just . . . do it. Myself."

Stupid, stupid, stupid, Harry muttered. *You are so stupid, it was contagious and now he's caught your stupidity, so he's being stupid, too.*

"Oh," she said, unable to hide her dismay. "I thought . . . Well, I *could* hurry—"

Peter cut her off. "Really, Shayla, it's okay. I don't expect to get any information from the woman anyway and . . . You should be writing. You've already gone above and beyond."

He didn't want her to go with him.

Yeah, because he wanted *you to kiss him, and you didn't, so now he's all "Let's not spend an awkward hour in the car together, 'kay, thanks, bye."*

"Will you let me know if Izzy and Hans find anything in Van Nuys?" Shay asked.

"Yeah," Peter said. "Sure. I'll, um, text you."

* * *

Jesus, he was stupid.

As Pete stood in his shower and washed his hair with a second handful of shampoo—for the first time in his life, he was following the directions to lather, rinse, and repeat—he marveled that he'd managed to stay alive for closing in on four decades. Someone as stupid as he was should've been eaten by a tiger by now. After stupidly jumping into the tiger's enclosure at the zoo. Because that's what stupid people did. They did a stupid, stupid thing, despite all of the signs that warned them, *Don't Do That Stupid Thing.*

Shayla Whitman wanted to be friends with him. Period. She'd made that very, very, *very* clear.

And just because *he* loved spending time with her, and just because *he* thought she was both cute and hot as hell, and just because the *idea* of her running her fingers through his hair had given him a raging hard-on . . .

She'd posted the sign, he'd seen it, he'd heard it, and he'd jumped in with the tiger anyway. What a fucking stupid idiot.

And his dick was even more stupid than he was. It was still at high alert. Like painfully high. Like *Jesus, I'm gonna come just from her running her fingers through my hair* high alert.

He'd had to close his eyes and clench his teeth, but God, he'd wanted her hands on him, all over him, wrapped around him . . .

As he rinsed his hair again, he looked down, and yeah. His dick was like one of those one-legged, happy air dancers, bobbing in front of the local used-car dealer. If it could talk it would be shouting, *Yo, bro, we had the foreplay, it was awesome, but where's the fucking sex?! Come on, come on, come on!*

Pete closed his eyes and breathed as the water washed over him and made his elbow sting. He'd scrubbed the crap out of it—literally—as Shay had suggested.

Shay. *Sit,* she'd ordered with that commanding conviction that he found so utterly attractive. Ah, Jesus, thinking about her was not helping.

He focused instead on Maddie and Dingo—on his daughter maybe making him a grandfather before he turned forty, and on Hiroko who was still angry about injustices she'd faced when she was a child, on Lisa shouting that he didn't give her what she needed, that it was *his* fault that she was packing up and leaving and taking Maddie with her. . . . His sweet little Maddie, whom he loved more than he'd ever thought he could love anyone . . . It was his fault, his fault, *his fault.* . . .

No wonder Shay had backed away.

And yeah. That did it.

Pete shut off the water and dried himself off, vowing that he would not make that same mistake again, but knowing that he was so stupid that he just might jump back in with the tiger, if he was given half a chance.

* * *

As Izzy approached the house in Van Nuys, he saw that it was locked up tight.

It wasn't just a gone-to-work locked up, but more like gone-to-Spain-for-six-months. Shades were pulled down and dry leaves, dust, and cobwebs adorned the little porch outside the front door. Of course, not everyone used their front entrance, but as Hansie Schlossman followed him around to the back of the house, it was clear that no one had been through the kitchen door in a long time, either. The spider who'd made a web back there was big enough to give them the middle finger.

Hans exhaled something that sounded a lot like a sigh of relief, and Izzy glanced at him.

"I was not looking forward to confronting Maddie," the younger man admitted. "I mean, yeah, she lied to me, but . . ." He shrugged. "I remember how hard it was. Losing *my* mom."

Izzy's bullshit meter trembled. Just a little. "Didn't I meet your parents? At the party after Hell Week?"

"Yeah," Hans said. "My dad came. With my stepmom."

"She seemed nice."

"She is," he said. "She's also not my mom. I mean, I love her, she's great. And she loves the hell out of my dad. He's happy. Maybe even happier than he ever was. I don't know, I don't like to think about it too hard."

"I get it," Izzy said. "Because . . . Whoa. That's . . . deep." Years ago, Eden had lost a baby, extremely late in her pregnancy. Pinkie—his in utero name—had been stillborn, which had been awful. Add postpartum depression into the mix, and . . . Eden had suffered intensely. But lately, Danny and Jenn's procreation had triggered a bit of impatience in Izzy. Baby-fever was highly contagious. But he could tell that Eden still wasn't ready, despite the years that had passed.

Maybe it was because she was afraid that they'd be happier, and that would somehow dishonor Pinkie's memory . . . ?

"It's weird," Hans agreed. "You get kinda crazy when someone dies. I mean, my dad was, like, forty when Mom died. What's he supposed to do, just lock himself away, and be alone forever? I didn't want that for him. But at the same time . . . You know, my stepmom—Doris—she always identified herself as my dad's *second* wife. And she talked about my mom—she didn't try to make her disappear. The first year—and really, all the years—she was like, how did your mom celebrate Chanukah? Which plates did your mom use for Thanksgiving dinner? What was your mom's favorite song?" He smiled. "She didn't try to erase her."

"That's freaking brilliant," Izzy said, as his cellphone rang, and he pulled it out to check. . . .

It was Grunge. Izzy hit *answer* and put the call on speaker. "Greetings from Van Nuys, where Schlossman and I are bonding. I may have to embrace him."

The lieutenant's voice was flat. "Any sign of Maddie?"

"Nope," Izzy said. "And no one's been here for a while. Like weeks at least."

"Fuck. Daryl Middleton's address was a dead end, and the lawyer aunt is gonna be in court all day." Grunge sighed. "I'm thinking about flying up to Sacramento."

"You want company?" Izzy asked. "Or prolly not, 'cause you'll want to go with Shayla. I like her, by the way."

Grunge sighed. "Yeah, I like her, too, but . . . Thanks again for making the trek to Van Nuys."

"De nada," Izzy said.

"Lemme know what I owe you for gas."

As the connection to Grunge was cut, Hans exhaled, and Izzy realized that the younger man had been holding his breath.

"I know we just bonded," Izzy said, "but if you've been

lying, and all this time you've really been fucking around with G's daughter? I *will* kill you. With my bare hands."

"I haven't, I wouldn't, I . . . No," Hans said. "But FYI? Kids whose moms die? They sometimes lie."

"So . . . are you cryptically saying that you have been lying?" Izzy asked.

Hans pointed to himself with both hands. "Not a kid anymore."

"Good point," Izzy said. "I'm hungry—are you hungry? Let's get a pizza for the road."

CHAPTER TWELVE

The sun was starting to set before Shayla finally got another text from Peter.

He'd dashed her a quick one earlier: *Nobody home in Van Nuys, nothing from the aunt, going in to an unscheduled meeting on base, more later.*

She'd texted him back: *I'm here if you need help w anything. Chapt 2??*

She knew that he'd know that stood for the second installment in the *When Peter Met Lisa* story he was writing as part of the let-Maddie-get-to-know-him offensive. But he didn't text back and he didn't text back, and she tried very hard not to keep going into the living room and kitchen, where her windows had a clear shot of his empty driveway.

After school, Tevin had dropped her car off, but that had taken all of forty-five seconds. Carter had been in a hurry as usual—her ex-husband was a gifted musician, but his time management skills were for crap—so she'd gotten little more than a "Keys are on the key hook!" shout, and waves from all three of them, as Carter zoomed off in his sweet little sports car, taking T and Frank to his place. Their shared custody meant that she had the boys every other week—Thursdays were transition days. Although odds were strong that Carter would get an out-of-town gig and drop them off early Saturday morning with an apology and a promise to pick them up again on Monday, but that was okay, because she missed her children when they weren't around, and frankly, she never had plans. Not-writing and more not-writing. Maybe a trip to the gym or a run in the park.

Harry popped in. *Yeah, but this weekend you might have plans of the sexy kind.*

Stop.

He still not home?

Shayla pointedly turned her back on the window where, yes, Peter's truck was still not in his drive.

Ooh, maybe he's made a connection with Fiona's aunt Susan. Maybe they're having a drink together right now— no, maybe he's fucking her in the law office bathroom—

"Stop!" Shit, she'd actually said that out loud. Fictional-characters'-voices-in-one's-head was appropriately, quirkily writer-crazy. But talking back to them, out loud? Nope. That was crazy-crazy, and she was not that.

You shush me all the time. Out loud.

That was different.

No, it's not. And your SEAL has heard you do it, and yet he still wanted you to kiss him—

"If he wanted that so much, why didn't he just kiss me?" Damnit, she was losing it.

It was then that her phone swooshed and she lunged for it to see, yes, Peter had finally texted her. *Sorry about the delay,* he wrote. *Problem on base, solved now. Lots of waiting around though, so I "wrote" chap two. OK if I email to have you read first?*

Of course, she typed back and hit *send.*

Okay, with the speed of your response, you just essentially told him you've been sitting around, waiting for him to text, Harry pointed out.

She had been. But only because she wanted to help him find Maddie.

Riiight. Aren't you gonna ask him if it was good? Harry asked. *Go on and ask him that. You know. His sex with Aunt Susan. Isn't that your job as the quirky neighbor? To make sure he gets a proper romance-hero-worthy fucking? Shouldn't you make sure they hooked up, and encourage him to do so, immediately, if they didn't? "Life is too short," you could tell him that. Or YOLO him. While you bring him a neighborly tuna casserole.*

Whoosh! Email sent, came Peter's texted reply, with another whoosh for his *thank you,* hot on its heels.

Shay's computer was on the kitchen counter, so she opened her email and started to read.

About two weeks into our ride-to-school-based friendship, Lisa called me.

"Has Mr. Jimenez called you yet?" she asked.

"Why would Mr. Jimenez call me?" I asked. He was the drama teacher. He taught English, too, but I wasn't in his class.

"So he hasn't called yet," Lisa said. "Good. When he calls? I need you to tell him that you were part of this big Shakespearean drama program, and that you played Romeo. You know, on your island."

"But that's not true," I pointed out. "I mean, I've read some Shakespeare, but mostly his comedies. I started Romeo and Juliet, but . . ."

"That's close enough," she said. "I'll help you learn the lines. We've got nine whole days before opening night."

"Wait," I said. "What? Whoa . . ."

She hit me with some classic Star Wars. *"Help me, Obi-Wan Kenobi, you're my only hope." And then she told me that the kid who was originally cast as Romeo got suspended for drinking—along with his bestie, who just happened to be his understudy. Mr. Jimenez was going to cancel the performances, because who were they going to find to play Romeo on such short notice . . . ?*

That was when Lisa told him that not only was I an accomplished actor, but that I'd already played Romeo, so I'd just need to brush up on my lines.

Lisa was a really good actress, so of course he believed her.

I told her I wasn't willing to lie, and she said, "It's not lying, it's just bending the truth. Stretching it."

"That I'm qualified because I've read some Shakespeare . . . ?"

"No, because I'm going to meet you over at Hiroko's right now, and we're gonna rehearse the crap out of the audition scene. That way, you won't be home when Mr. Jimenez calls, so when you do talk to him, in school tomorrow, you won't be lying when you say you know the part inside and out."

"Audition scene?" I was not happy about that. "There's an audition?"

"Tomorrow afternoon," she told me. "It's Friday, so that gives us the entire weekend for you to learn the rest of the play."

First it was I'd have nine days to learn lines that were in iambic pentameter, and now it was the weekend? Except, the way she'd said it, we'd be spending that time together. I was slowly warming to the idea.

"The audition scene is Act One, Scene Five," Lisa told me. "Where Romeo and Juliet meet."

"Wherefore art thou Romeo?" I asked. "The scene with the balcony?" I'd seen the Bugs Bunny *version, at least.*

"Nope," she said. "The scene at the party. With the kisses. There are two. Kisses."

She knew damn well what she was doing when she dropped that statement there. I'm pretty sure she was the one who picked that scene as the official audition, because yeah, Shakespeare wrote some kisses into R&J's flirty first encounter.

And since I was already madly in love with Lisa . . .

I met her at Hiroko's and we rehearsed the scene, kisses included. And I auditioned for Mr. Jimenez without actually directly lying to him, which was good, because I'm not sure I could've done it, even with all of those ongoing promised liplocks.

In short, I played Romeo to Lisa's Juliet in high school. And I kissed her about four thousand times which was really nice, but sadly didn't magically turn me into her boyfriend, the way I'd hoped it would.

Throughout the run of the play, she continued to date her douchebag sports hero boyfriend. In fact, she stayed with him—Brad—until graduation, when he broke up with her in a spectacularly douchie way.

That'll be Chapter Three.

Here's a link to that scene from R&J. It's pretty fun. Lisa killed it. I was okay, but only because she was so good.

Please be safe.

* * *

"I love it—it's a poem," Dingo said as Maddie finished reading aloud the scene in question. "A sonnet—it rhymed. Did you notice?"

Maddie looked up from the screen of her phone and over at him. "Yes. Did you not just hear me reading it? And rhyming?"

"Yeah, but some people who shall remain unnamed— Fiona—didn't appreciate literature. Did you know that I ended up writing a paper for her on *Romeo and Juliet,* because she didn't seem to notice or care just how much Shakespeare had it going on."

"*Romeo and Juliet* is massively stupid—they were both idiots. And Fiona's an idiot, too. I read that paper—and I definitely wondered who wrote it because I knew she didn't. I'm impressed, but only because I didn't know you could even read."

"Ha-ha, you're so funny."

"Ha-ha, you're not." Maddie shut off her phone, plunging Dingo's car into semi-darkness in the lot of the truck stop just north of the San Diego city line, where they'd stopped for the night.

It had taken far too long today to cash that check Hiroko had given them, since the bank where Ding had been certain he'd be able to cash it had flatly refused to accept his ID.

They'd wasted a shitload of time arguing about using a payday loan place—which ended up also not cashing it.

Plan C involved them driving around and trying to find Dingo's stupid friend Daryl, so they could ask him to cash the check for them.

They'd finally found Daryl, and then began a search for an ATM, because it was already dark and his bank was closed.

But they'd finally—*finally*—gotten the money, minus five bucks for Daryl's help, and instead of immediately hitting the road, they spent a few dollars on a bag of potatoes, and then had to drive around to find a Whole Foods with a café microwave that actually worked. It was *The Martian* diet—several microwaved potatoes, plus a package of overripe cherry tomatoes that had been marked down to 43 cents. Half were rotten, but the other half were delicious, and with the potatoes, Maddie's stomach finally stopped grumbling and growling.

It was only then, after dinner, that they'd hit the road. Only to have extreme fatigue set in, because they'd been up since dawn.

"Maybe you should drop 'em a quick text," Dingo said quietly now. "Your da and his girlfriend."

"My mother showed me pictures," Maddie told him. "Of *Romeo and Juliet*. From high school. We talked—at length—about the fact that schools never do the *good* Shakespeare plays, they always do the same old stupid ones. And she never told me—*ever*—that the kid in those photos, playing Romeo, was my father."

"That's . . . weird," he said.

She turned to look at the outline of his profile in the dim parking lot light. He'd built another wall with piles of stuff between them, but she still had a clear shot of his face. "What if he's lying?"

Dingo turned to look at her. "Seems unlikely. Especially since GAH can corroborate the story."

"How would I know that *she* wouldn't lie, too. For him." Great-Aunt Hiroko had obviously liked Maddie's father more than she'd liked Lisa.

Dingo sighed. "You know, love, it's all right to be mad at your ma. Not telling you that your father was right there in the pictures she was showing you is pretty mean. Selfish-like. Like, she didn't want to tell you anything good about him at all, so she just didn't tell you anything. That's not fair. I know I'd be mad."

"I always thought that she loved him, but that he didn't love her—us—back," Maddie said. "But what if he was the one who loved her? What if she just kept using him, the way she used him in today's story, so she could do that play? What if *she* was the terrible one?"

"Your dad seems pretty smart," Dingo said. "Self-aware. Like, yeah, okay, he caved to the pressure and played Romeo, but he knew exactly what was going on. And, you know, they say love is blind, but it's hard to imagine someone as smart as him falling in love with someone truly terrible."

Maddie shot him a look. "Like you with Fiona?"

"Me and Fee," Dingo said with another heavy sigh, "was never my proudest moment. A perfect example of the flesh being weak. Thanks ever so much for bringing that up."

Maddie laughed. "You're lucky she didn't kill you—like tear off your head and devour you after sex."

"Well, there's still a chance for her to do that tomorrow—the tearing-my-head-off part. The sex is long over and done. I've decided to embrace a vow of celibacy for a few years."

"A few *years*?" Maddie laughed. "Yeah, that vow's gonna last. Until the next time you go to the beach and meet some pretty blond girl in a bikini and—whoa! What's that? Is that . . . ?"

"Earthquake! Shite! Hold on!" Dingo confirmed, knocking his wall away to reach for her. "It feels like a big one!"

* * *

Pete was in the kitchen when the tremors started.

He'd washed again after returning home late from the base, and he was wearing board shorts and flip-flops and little else, his hair still damp from his shower.

He was gazing into the fridge, as if hoping something more exciting would magically appear when the unmistakable shaking started.

Shayla! Shit! And Maddie! Jesus, did Maddie know what to do in a quake? He had no idea—he also had no idea where she was, but he hoped to hell she was somewhere safe.

He swiftly closed the refrigerator door, making sure it latched, and moved away from the kitchen cabinets and into the doorway that led to the living room. If it was going to be a big one, the cabinet doors would come open and dishes and glasses would turn into missiles. Likewise, keeping his distance from the front windows was smart, and Jesus, the shaking was so intense, the walls seemed to ripple as his furniture jumped and shook. As he figured out his next move, he braced himself against the doorframe—if he hadn't, he might've fallen down.

The power went out, plunging him into darkness—and great, it wasn't just his house, it was the entire street at least.

Throughout the neighborhood, car alarms had triggered and were going off, but they sounded almost faint beneath the quake's roar. Movement of the earth's plates was never a quiet thing. Still, he heard a crash from behind him in the kitchen—and he didn't need light to know that Maddie's new computer had been out on the counter. With his luck, that had been what he'd just heard hitting the floor, probably along with the empty mugs from the coffee that he'd shared with Shayla last night.

He couldn't see Shay's house in the pitch-darkness. He knew it was stupid as fuck to move, but he scrambled across the room on his hands and knees—the shaking immediately pushed him down to the still-moving floor—and out the front door.

The row of shrubs that lined his front path tripped him, and he went down, hard, but used his momentum to roll farther out onto the lawn and away from the windows, as the tremor finally, blessedly stopped. The postquake "silence" was filled with those car alarms and barking dogs—and despite that, it still felt quiet without the low-pitched rumble.

As Pete pushed himself up, his eyes were already adjusting to the blackout—it seemed to be contained to just his neighborhood because he could see the haze from lights just a few streets away, which was good. "Shayla!" He ran across the street to her house. None of her windows seemed to have broken, either—that, too, was good. The entire quake had lasted maybe twenty-five seconds—from experience, he was guessing it was around a five, maybe five-point-two. Not exactly small, but certainly not the *Big One.*

Still, Shayla wouldn't know that, its being her first since she was a kid. *"Shay!"* He banged on her front door, but she didn't open it, didn't answer.

Pete ran around to the back and—

There she was.

Her back door hung open—she'd made it out of the house and was sitting in the middle of her yard, her face lit from the screen of her cellphone.

"Shay! You okay?" he asked.

"Yeah," she said, looking up at him and sounding extremely normal, like riding out a five-point-two was no big thing. "Are you?"

"Yeah."

She held up her phone. "Maddie's okay. The boys and Carter are, too. I tried to call them, but I got one of those weird busy signals, but then I remembered that texts often get through when calls don't, so I texted, and they all just texted me back." Her thumbs moved across her phone. "I'm texting Maddie that you're okay. She was shaken, pun not intended, and worried about you—I mean, she didn't say that, but . . . She was definitely worried. I was just about to go check on you. I texted, but you didn't answer."

"I don't have my phone." Pete sat down next to her. She was sitting, tailor-style, right on the ground, dressed in what must've been her pajamas—a barely there white tank top over boxers that were covered with little flowers, possibly pink ones. Her arms and legs were bare but she didn't seem to notice that the night air was cold.

She'd managed to put on sneakers before leaving her house—no doubt she'd had them right beneath her bed. For such a rule-follower, it was weird that she hadn't stayed put in a doorway, but then he realized that she'd come out here so she could check on her kids, and go rescue them single-handedly, if she'd had to.

Her phone whooshed with the sound of an incoming text that she immediately read. *"What?"* She looked up at Pete with an expression of outrage and disapproval. "Tevin says that was only a four-point-nine on the Richter scale. Seriously?"

He had to smile. "My guess was a little higher," he told her. "But just a little. The amount of shake also depends on depth—how shallow it is. And the location of the epicenter."

"Tevin says it was about a half mile east of us."

"That sounds right."

"So Southern California's still here." She chose to embrace the good news rather than be pissed that the quake wasn't as big as she'd thought. "No need to go into Zombie Apocalypse Prevention Mode."

He smiled again at that. "Nope."

Her phone whooshed, and she looked down at it and laughed. "Earthquake selfie," she said, showing him a photo of her sons, their heads together, making wide-eyed, openmouthed faces into the camera. She used her flash to take a similar photo of herself, smiling as she sent it back.

He wanted that, he realized. That easy, friendly, intensely devoted relationship that Shayla shared with her boys—he wanted that with his daughter. But the odds of ever having it were slim to none. Even if Maddie did a complete about-face and suddenly welcomed a relationship with him . . . He was a lot of things, but unlike Shayla, *funny* and *fun-to-be-with* weren't on the list.

Right now, however, he'd settle for being glad that Shay thought Maddie had been worried for his safety.

Also? "If Maddie felt the quake," Pete said, "that means she's still somewhere local."

"So not in Manzanar," Shayla said. "Or Sacramento."

"I'm betting Los Angeles didn't even feel this one," Pete told her. "Manzanar and Sacramento are both much farther away."

She gave him some serious side eye. "I knew that. I'm not *that* geographically challenged."

He laughed. "My bad. I just thought . . . But you're keeping it together really well." He paused. "Unless you were just kidding about the diving under the table, and the earthquake helmet?"

She shook her head. "Inside, I'm a mess. Outside, I'm Mom. Last thing I ever want to do is scare the boys, or somehow transfer my fears to them. Of course, they're older now. Tevin's definitely aware that earthquakes aren't my favorite thing. That's why he was texting me with all the science."

As she spoke, Pete tried to listen, but that *I'm Mom* reverberated in his head, and all he could think was that the world had changed enormously from the days when moms went to bed with rollers in their hair and mud masks on their faces. And Shayla may have been focused on being Tevin and Frank's mom, but she was also a tremendously beautiful, sensual, incredibly strong, sexy woman, and he wanted to . . .

He wanted . . .

She'd stopped talking and he looked up and into her eyes, suddenly aware that he'd been staring at her mouth. Her mouth, and the soft curves of her body beneath that shirt that was so thin, he could see right through it.

She was aware, too, of the direction his thoughts had

turned, but she didn't back away. She didn't say a word. She just sat there, looking back at him.

She wanted, too.

He waited a moment, just looking into her eyes, because God, he didn't want to get this wrong. But she just held his gaze—until she didn't. Her eyes slipped down—just for a fraction of a second—to his mouth.

So he leaned in, slowly, and even reached to touch her face and gently pull her chin up and . . .

He kissed her.

As far as kisses went, it was G-rated. His lips against the sweet softness of hers. No tongues, no way. He wanted to— Jesus, his heart was pounding—but he didn't.

He just pulled back to look into her eyes again, and time seemed to slow and not-quite stop, but change and expand. He'd experienced something similar a few times, while out on ops with the Teams. There was a name for it, that sense of being present and acutely, intensely aware: *kairos*. The word also meant *opportunity*, and he was not a fool, so he slowly leaned in and when, once more, she didn't pull away, he kissed her again.

This time, she opened her lips to him. This time, she leaned in, too, and he took that as an invitation to put his arms around her, even as she slipped her arms up and around his neck and her tongue into his mouth.

And their G rating was instantly revoked as he tried to devour her in return, because the way she was suddenly hungrily kissing him completely ignited the fire in his veins that he'd been trying to control.

Pete pulled her up and onto his lap even as she tried to move closer, and she straddled him as he wrapped himself more tightly around her. Her arms and shoulders and back were cold, but the softness between her legs was hot against him. Jesus, her fingers were back in his hair as she kissed him and kissed him, and Christ, he was going to come, her breasts soft against his chest, his body straining and sliding against hers through their thin layers of clothes.

He needed to be inside of her. He needed a condom, and he needed it now.

He started to pull back to tell her that—that he was going to pick her up and carry her inside. But as he moved his hands down her back to the incredible softness of her ass, the added pressure pushed her even more tightly against him, and God, God, God, the way that felt both against his dick, and in the palms of his hands . . . So instead he kissed her harder, deeper, longer as she rubbed herself against him, and then his fingers slipped beneath the thin fabric of her shorts, and he found her—hot and soft and wet.

He pushed one finger, and then two, just a little bit inside of her, and she came almost instantly, with a moan, right there in his hands, pressed up against him, and it was such an incredible, mind-blowing, total turn-on that he came, too.

* * *

The earth was shaking again and Shayla lifted her head from Peter's shoulder.

"Aftershock," he murmured. "Just a little one. We're okay."

Aftershock. Was *that* what this was?

Shay was still clinging to him, her legs still tight around his waist, the tips of his fingers still inside of her as he smiled into her eyes.

"That was a first for me," he said.

So okay, they *were* going to have a conversation right now. Like this. Before moving and adjusting and doing all those awkward post-orgasm things. She had to clear her throat to get her voice to work. "Sex in the backyard?" she asked.

"Well, that, too," he said. "Sex—or not quite sex—with our clothes still on."

"It's called *dry humping,* and you've seriously never . . . ?"

"Nope. In high school I was pretty single-mindedly in love with Lisa. And back then, she wasn't having sex with me."

That's right, he'd told her they hadn't hooked up until college, in the relative comfort of their dorm rooms.

"For the record, that name for it is deceptive. I'm pretty sure it can't be called *dry* humping at this point," he said. "At least not on my end."

Shayla laughed—which caused her body to tighten around his fingers and push him a little more deeply inside of her. She drew in a sharp breath, and their gazes met and locked. His eyes were hot.

"Let's go inside," he said. "I have a sudden burning desire for us to achieve a sexual hat trick. I'm thinking, I'll make you come with my mouth while my *gentlemen's accessories* catch up, and then, a little later, we can finish with good old-fashioned full penetration."

Sweet God, yes please. But then Shay said, *"Gentlemen's accessories?"*

"Isn't that what you called it? It's a nice euphemism, although I wasn't in a position to discuss it at the time."

Dear God, this man actually listened to the words that came out of her mouth—even after getting whacked in the balls and hit with a bucket of shit. So she told him, "Tevin and I were out shopping when he was just learning to read, and there was a sign—I think it was in Macy's—and he thought the accessories were specific to the male anatomy, although that puzzled him, because aside from a jockstrap, he wasn't sure what that might be. For a while, we called athletic supporters *gentlemen's accessories,* and somehow it transitioned to become the full euphemism."

He nodded, then leaned in and kissed her, and it was a replay of their first kiss—tender and gentle—and God, his lips were so soft and warm. "Let's go inside," he breathed against her mouth, before kissing her again—really kissing her now.

He tasted as delicious as he smelled—Navy SEAL–flavored, had to be—and she lost herself in the sweetness of his mouth, the feel of his hair between her fingers, the heat of his chest against hers.

But then she felt him start to shift, as if he was going to just stand up and carry her inside, so she made herself stop kissing him. "Wait."

He waited, but the heat in his eyes had ramped up in its intensity.

"God, you're beautiful," she told him, touching the side of his face. "And as good as that . . . hat trick sounds, I'm just . . . Well, can we . . . not?"

She could tell that he didn't fully understand, that he thought she was shutting him down, so she quickly added, "Go inside, I mean. I . . . don't suppose you'd want to help me set up our . . . tent? It's a pop-up. Pretty quick and easy."

He got it—it was the going-inside to which she objected. "Oh, Shay, no. The likelihood of another earthquake—"

"I've read that sometimes the aftershocks come first," she said. "And if that was an aftershock, the real quake's gonna be huge. I mean, yeah, it's rare, and I know I probably sound irrational and crazy, but . . ." Her voice shook and she felt her eyes fill with tears, despite her best intentions. "That scared the *fuck* out of me."

"Fair enough." Peter immediately nodded. "I've got an air mattress and one of those crazy-fast pumps. We're gonna need a blanket or two, tonight's gonna get cold. But other than going inside to grab that—and make sure the gas line's okay—we can stay outside as long as you need to."

Stupidly, his kind response to her crazy made her tears well and overflow. God, she hated crying in front of anyone—in fact, she hated crying when she was locked alone in the privacy of her own bathroom. She hated it, because it never changed anything; it never helped, it only impeded. And on top of that, it made her feel weak and helpless and gave her a congestion headache.

But everything she was feeling—or trying not to feel—was jumbled up inside of her. The residuals of her overwhelming fear—not for herself, but for her precious babies and even for Carter and Tiffany, but then also for herself as the quake had slammed her to the bedroom floor again and again—and the knee-weakening relief of finding out, quickly thank God, that everyone was all right, combined with the crazy whatever-this-was that she was feeling after dry humping her Navy SEAL neighbor in her own backyard . . .

It was all apparently exiting her body through her tear ducts. Damn it.

"Hey," Peter said, pulling her close and wrapping his arms around her even more completely. "Hey, hey. It's okay."

"You're so nice," she told him.

His laughter was a rumble in his chest. "Not really," he said. "But I'm okay with you thinking that I'm being nice when I'm really just trying to shorten the time it'll take before we can, you know."

She did know. She also knew that the responsible adult thing to do would've been to have a conversation in which they discussed the high emotions that had led to that unexpected orgasm, because really, where was this going to go besides a place of hurt or awkwardness? Despite knowing that, she threw caution to the wind as she wiped her eyes and smiled and said, "Hat trick. I'm with you on that. As long as you're in a tent."

"Where's the tent?" he asked in response.

"In the garage. Left side, top shelf. Plastic container. Purple. Airtight. Spider-proof."

His smile broadened. "Of course."

"California has some *very* nasty spiders. Black widows—"

He kissed her as he moved her off his lap. "Your backyard or mine?"

CHAPTER THIRTEEN

Maddie risked a glance at Dingo. He was clinging to his steering wheel with both hands as he drove, his eyes focused fiercely on the freeway ahead of them.

The earthquake had shaken him up and gotten his adrenaline flowing—or so he'd said. So much so that he'd insisted they forget about sleeping and drive through the night, hit Sacramento at just past dawn.

But Maddie knew that it wasn't the earthquake that had shaken him—it was the fact that after he'd grabbed on to her to try to protect her as his car rattled and shook, he'd kissed her.

She'd kissed him back. In fact, they'd made out for a good long time—until he'd jumped away from her as if he'd been bitten by a snake.

"Do you want to talk about it?" she asked him now.

He laughed, but it was a sound of despair, not joy. "Nope."

"Well, *I* wanna talk about it," she said. "I don't know what the big deal is. I like you and you seem to like me—"

"Fiff," he said. "Teen. As in: You. Are. *Fifteen*."

"Drama, drama, drama, drama," Maddie said on an exasperated exhale. "So what?"

"So what?" he said. "*So what?* So I could go to jail. I'd have to register as a sex offender, forever. For*ever*, Mads. It happened to a friend of my cousin."

"What happened to your accent?" she asked.

"It's fake!" he shouted. "I'm fake! Everything's fucking fake, all right? So, see, you don't really like me after all! Say the word, I'll turn around and take you home!"

"Well, that's stupid," she said. "If you take me home, you'd practically be handing me over to Nelson. And until I get the money or the proof that Fiona was the one who stole it, you'd pretty much be sentencing me to death."

"Fuck," he said, because she was right.

"You know, I think maybe I like you more now," she told him. "So, really, all this time, you've been, what? Playing a character?" She imitated his Australian accent. "*I'm Dingo from down under.* That's pretty freaking brilliant, Richard. I bet most girls really go for that."

"See, you are mad. No one calls me Richard unless they're mad at me."

It was weird—that flat California accent coming out of his face, his mouth.

He glanced at her, several times, probably because she was staring at him. "What?"

"You're a good kisser," she said.

"Oh, no," he said. "No, no, no, no, no."

She shrugged expansively. "I'm just saying. Kissing isn't sex."

"Mads," he begged. "Please. Can we just . . . not?"

She sighed heavily. "Can Dingo come back now? Because you're right, I think I like him better than *you*. You're a buzzkill."

"Can't have a buzzkill without a buzz, love," he said in his fake Australian accent.

"Whatever," Maddie said, sinking down in her seat.

"Why should I have anything good or nice or happy in my life?"

"I'm not good *or* nice," he whispered.

Maybe not. But when he'd kissed her, for the first time in a long time, she'd felt happy. Or at least less relentlessly alone.

* * *

Shayla surrendered.

At first, she was a little weirded out—going into that grown-up version of a bouncy tent with the deliberate intention of taking off her clothes and having some happy-fun time with the Navy SEAL. This was a man to whom she'd not so much as spoken two words until last night.

And now she was going to let him plant his face between her legs.

How do *you do?*

He hadn't just brought blankets and pillows into her backyard along with his air mattress. He'd brought a hurricane lamp—an electric one that wouldn't catch fire, but could still be turned down low. He'd also brought condoms and some towels and a bottle of wine. Pinot noir—how did he know? He'd brought a pair of stemless glasses, too, and he poured her one as the romantic light from that lantern played across his handsome face.

"I turned off the gas in both our houses," he told her as he handed her the glass of wine. "Just to be extra safe. Everything looks good in yours—just a few things broken— a couple framed photos. Books fell out of bookshelves. Nothing big fell over."

"There's nothing big to fall over," she pointed out. She'd purposely gotten rid of anything tall before the move to California. Now all of their bookshelves and cabinets were either built-in or low to the ground. "How about your place?" she asked.

"I had a few expensive casualties," he told her. "Maddie's computer was on the kitchen counter. It hit the floor and did not survive."

"Oh, no."

"Better hers than yours," he said.

"I don't know about that," she countered. "I'm militant when it comes to backup. You know, I was thinking. About Maddie? That in the morning, we should push. Just a little. See if she'll take a call—talk to me on the phone."

Peter nodded. "I also want to touch base with that lawyer—Fiona's aunt."

"I thought you did that this afternoon."

"No," he said. "I tried, but she wasn't in—she was at the courthouse. I was going to wait, but then I got the call to go to the base. And then everything took too much time. It's okay—I seriously doubt she's going to tell me anything new."

"I'd like to go with you," Shayla said. No way was she making that *I'll go if you want* mistake twice.

He smiled because, like always, he was paying attention. "That's great," he said, "because I'd like for you to come, too." He lifted his wineglass in a toast. "To good communication."

Shay smiled back at him as they clinked—and the earth shifted again. It was hard to know if that was real or an illusion created from the heat in his eyes. Either way, she felt safe.

He took a sip, so she did, too, and . . . "Wow, that's excellent."

"A reminder that California's got a lot more going for it than earthquakes and black widow spiders."

"And crazy people who ride around in their trucks with a bucket of feces to throw at sailors?"

"That was another first for me," Peter admitted. "My day's been full of them—some significantly better than others." He smiled at her, leaning back on his elbow, but then wincing, because, yeah. That was the elbow he'd scraped, saving her from the flying shit-bucket of doom.

"Let me see that," she said, putting her glass down on the ground beside the air mattress, and he smiled, because yes, again, he knew that she wanted to touch him, and this was an easy way to get that party started. He obediently held out his arm as she scooted closer, letting go of the fleece blanket that he'd draped around her shoulders to keep her warm while the mattress inflated.

Shay took his arm and angled it toward the light. The scrape was still raw, but he'd cleaned it well and although it looked angry, it didn't look infected. He leaned back, in order to set down his own glass beyond the edge of the mattress, and all of his many, many muscles shifted and flexed as he did a halfway, diagonal equivalent of a sit-up, pulling her attention away from his elbow.

When he sat back up, his face was right there, so she took it between her hands, and kissed him.

It was a kiss of the same variety as the one he'd first given to her—sweet, practically chaste. She'd liked it—not just the sensation of only their lips touching, but the very idea of it. It held a subtext—no, actually it held a message that was unmistakable in its inherent respect. *I'd like to kiss you, and I think you'd like to kiss me, too,* it said. *But if I'm wrong about that, please let me know, and I'll back it down a notch.*

And sure enough, as Shayla pulled back to look into those blue, blue eyes, Peter smiled. He leaned in to kiss her again, this time with a gentle mingling of their tongues, and he said, "Mmm. I was right. That wine is good, but it tastes even better on you."

There they sat, then, her fingers back in his hair, just smiling at each other, on a cheap air mattress in the pop-up tent that she'd gotten during Tevin's oh-so-brief camping phase. The boys had slept out in their Massachusetts back-yard maybe half a dozen times—and always with her sleeping between them, right in the middle.

Tonight was going to be an entirely different, completely new experience. "Huh," she said.

Peter nodded as if he could somehow read her mind, as he lightly ran his hand down her arm, from the narrow straps of her top to her wrist and then back. But then, as he used just a few fingers to trace her collar bone—a sensation that made her breathless—he asked, "Have I apologized yet for this afternoon?"

Shay shook her head, no, as he ran his fingers along her tank's neckline, his fingers warm against the tops of her breasts. "You don't have to."

"Yeah, I kind of do. I wanted . . . this. And I was too afraid to just say it." He smiled, but he didn't go any further. He just ran his fingers back the other way. "In my defense, I was, well, it's kind of like, you don't try to kiss the prettiest girl at the party if you've just puked. I was a little too aware of the whole shit-caked-in-my-ears thing."

Shay laughed. What he was doing to her felt so good, she returned the favor, but since he was shirtless, she trailed her fingers across his stomach, along the top of his shorts.

It was his turn to draw in a deep breath as she did go farther, tucking her fingers—just a little, just the tips—into the waistband right below his belly button.

Peter was looking down at her bare legs, touching her with his gaze from the edge of her shorts all the way down to her toes before following with his hand—his full palm this time, and God, that nearly made her eyes roll back in her head, so she touched him the same way, running her hands from his shoulders down his arms, down his chest.

"Babe, your hotness factor has at least seven zeros regardless of what's in your ears," she whispered. "Although,

I have to confess, I *do* like you hosed down and squeaky clean. And lying on your back."

Oh dear God, had she really just said that? It was a line of dialogue one of her extra-feisty heroines might say.

But, damn, it was effective, because he gently pulled himself free from her hands, and lay back on the mattress. On his back.

He was close enough to touch her, and he did—reaching for her, and pulling her toward him. "I'm not sure how I like you yet—I'm reserving that for after I conduct a thorough investigation—but I strongly suspect that you, naked, on top of me, while I'm on my back, is going to vie for *my* favorite."

She resisted—just a bit. "I'm sorry, aren't we skipping ahead in the whole hat-trick thing?"

"Just reversing the order." Peter smiled as he gently tugged the strap of her top down her arm, kissing her shoulder as he finally—finally—moved his hand to her breast. His touch was still gentle so she pressed herself more fully into his palm even as she straddled him, and yeah, God, there he was. Long and hard and already weirdly-but-wonderfully familiar, except this time she wanted all that gentlemanly accessoriness deep inside of her as she came.

Peter obviously wanted that, too. He'd let go of her so he could push down and kick free from his shorts, and she climbed back off of him, both to get out of his way, and to do some clothing removal of her own. Tank up and over her head, and boxers down her legs.

It was a good thing she wasn't a man, because she'd be feeling mightily intimidated by his naked perfection. All those muscles, right where they were supposed to be, every part of his body perfectly proportioned to his extra-large size. She'd felt his penis against her, but seeing him for the first time, erect like this, made her laugh, because *damn*.

But then she flashed both hot and cold because, God, she

was naked, too, and the light was on, but the way he breathed, "Jesus, you're beautiful," helped. That was his opinion, and even though, like most women, she could list her flaws and imperfections on a full page, single-spaced, who was she to say what anyone else should or shouldn't find beautiful?

She had lovely skin—she knew that. It was smooth and soft and a beautiful, rich color. And maybe her stomach was a little too soft and full but it seemed to work nicely with the curves of her hips and breasts. Also? She was forty, and she'd lived well and joyfully—borne two beautiful sons with this body that Peter was now studying with real heat in his eyes.

She laughed again as they both reached for a condom, their hands colliding. She pulled back. "You do it, I'll take too long."

"*Too long* sounds fun, but yeah, another time," he said as he tore open the packet.

She shifted back, just a little, to watch, her hands on the hard muscles in his thighs, his gaze hot as his attention flickered from that task at hand to her body and up into her eyes and back again. He smiled again. "Best earthquake ever."

She had to agree.

As he finished, she reached for him, wanting to touch, wrapping both of her hands around him as she looked into his eyes. He made a noise of pleasure and his hips rose off the mattress, and she knew he had to work it—hard—to form actual words, even as he reached down to take her by the wrists. "That, too, will be fun, but right now, I want . . ."

Yeah, she wanted the same thing.

So Shay didn't wait. She straddled him, reaching down to guide him as she took him deeply inside of her. They both made noise at that—it would've been impossible not to, it felt that incredible.

As she began to move against him—with him—she leaned down to kiss him, and he met her halfway, sitting up and pulling her closer to take her mouth with his. His hands were everywhere, touching, skimming her skin as she did the same to him, wanting to touch and, God, taste every inch of him. It was hard to tell where she ended and he began. Her soft fit against his hard with perfection—and she was not one to throw that word around lightly.

And maybe, just because it had been close to four billion years since she'd last done this, it merely *seemed* so amazing, but she doubted that as she broke their kiss so she could push his shoulders back so he was lying down again. Because she wanted more—and she opened herself wider even as this new position gave her access to that more-of-him that she desperately wanted. They both cried out again, and then both laughed—she in wonder, because they were so in sync.

Peter's hands were on her hips, and he tried to slow her down.

"Nuh-uh," she told him, their gazes locked.

"I'm gonna—" he breathed. He was close—she could see it in his eyes, but he didn't want to go first.

"I know. Me, too," she gasped. "Tell me when."

"Ah, Jesus!"

She took that for the *now* that it was, and immediately shifted gears, slamming them both to a stop, and then lifting herself up off of him and languorously pushing him home. Again. And again. And again. And again.

She came in slow motion, for damn near forever, and she wasn't sure but she thought maybe he did, too, because he kept saying, "Jesus, Jesus, Jesus . . ."

And when she couldn't hold herself up anymore and collapsed forward onto him, he put his arms around her and kissed the side of her head. She could feel his heart beating—

pounding as hard as her own—and she felt him laugh a little even as he, too, struggled to catch his breath.

But then he started moving again—or at least she thought it was him—but he tightened his arms around her, and said, "Another aftershock."

Sure enough, it didn't last long. She lifted her head to look down at him and smile. "You *know* the sex is crazy great when it creates an aftershock."

He smiled, too. "For the record, I'm pretty sure that, by the end there, I was tasting words."

Shayla laughed in surprise, because again, he'd been listening.

She had to climb off of him then, and she muttered something about avoiding the human error factor when it came to the efficiency rate of condoms. But really, she settled onto the mattress beside him so that he wouldn't have such an unfettered view of her face. This man was so damn good at reading her, and she didn't think she could hide how much she liked him.

Like him? Pfft. Get real. You love him.

And no, that wasn't Harry. He was too polite to show up at an intimate moment like this one.

No, that was all her.

She didn't do casual sex, never had, never would—and to think that she could was sheer idiocy. Oh, God, what had she gone and done?

"You okay?" Peter asked, picking up on her silent freak-out—maybe because for the first time, she wasn't babbling about something like the ability to taste words. He'd taken care of the condom, and was using one of the towels he'd brought out there to clean himself up.

"Yeah," Shay said, trying to sound normal, like someone who really was okay about having just had incredibly hot sex with the neighborhood Navy SEAL. "Just . . . starting to feel the chill, and way too tired to do anything about it."

"Here." He put one of the blankets over them both, making sure her feet were covered, even as he wrapped himself around her, spooning her back against his front. She was instantly warmer.

Oh, good. Now the man that she'd already fallen for ridiculously too soon was taking care of her. *That* would bring her to her senses. That—and the way he kissed her neck, right below her ear, after he'd doused the light . . .

He sighed a sigh of perfect contentment, and even murmured a sincerely appreciative "Man," before he instantly fell asleep.

Man, she was screwed.

Harry, where were you? Why didn't you stop me?

Harry popped in. *Oh, please. Like I could've. And besides, good for you! You needed that. A little hot sex to wash away the last memories of Carter.*

She hadn't thought of her ex-husband at all. Not even once.

Doubly good for you.

And it wasn't *a little* sex. It was gargantuanly, enormously *great* sex—no, it wasn't just great sex, it was *the greatest* sex. Ever.

It's been a while. Your ability to judge is probably at least a little *impaired.*

Okay, that was probably true. She might have to recheck that. Maybe first thing, when they woke up . . .

Good plan.

He was just so great. It was hard not to . . .

Don't say the L-word again. Don't make that mistake! L-l-l-lust. Call it lust. *Because that's what it is. LUST. Yay, lust!*

Yay. Lust.

Oh, come on. Peter is a lovely distraction, a nice little stop on the train ride of life. A Navy SEAL. Hoo-yah! Just keep reminding yourself that this is not your forever home.

Shayla was *not* a shelter dog, thanks. Also? Kind of obvious, considering they were in a tent.

You know what I mean. Love him hard, have some fun, but when it's over, it's over. Just be ready to let him go.

Yeah, and how had it worked out for Harry, when *he'd* done that?

Badly, because I'm a character in a romance novel. You, however, live in the real world, with its shades of gray. With that, he was gone.

Shayla sighed and muttered, "Man."

Peter's arms tightened slightly around her as he roused himself. "Y'okay? Was there another aftershock?"

"No," she said. "It's all right."

He lifted his head. "You sure?"

She turned to see that he was looking down at her, suddenly fully awake.

"We didn't get a chance to do, you know, a debrief of the earthquake. Sometimes, talking about it can really help," he said, then asked, "You want to talk?"

Shay shook her head, filled with more of that feeling that she shouldn't be feeling, damnit. "Just . . . kiss me," she said.

And he smiled, and did.

* * *

Someone was following him.

Daryl had had that feeling all night, and it was annoying as hell. More so, now that it was three o'clock in the morning and he was heading home on foot.

Fucking Dingo with his fucking jonesing for jailbait Maddie Nakamura. Normally, when Daryl worked this late, he'd call up the Ding-man and toss him a few bucks for gas, get a ride back to Sheryl-Ann's apartment, where he was crashing on the couch.

But tonight, Dingo had been piloting his boat-on-wheels

northward up the Five. Heading for Van Nuys, no doubt, where if he cried loud enough and long enough, Mummy would donate to the Support Dingo Super PAC.

As he crossed the street, there was no traffic moving in any direction, red lights stretching into the distance as far as the eye could see. So that someone's-following-me feeling must've been a figment of his imagination, triggered by that encounter with Maddie's Navy SEAL father in the mall parking garage.

"Hey, Daryl."

Daryl jumped and screamed as a shadowy shape emerged from a storefront. It was Cody O'Keefe—not quite a friend of Dingo's, but more of a work associate. Assuming Dingo's on-again-off-again consignment-style drug sales for that moron Bob Nelson could be considered a job. "Shit, man, you scared me! What the fuck?"

This was a weird coincidence—except, fuhhhhck, it was probably not any kind of coincidence, considering the whole matter of Fiona stealing ten thousand dollars and trying to pin it on Maddie.

"Sorry, bro," O'Keefe said without an ounce of sincerity behind his apology. He wasn't quite as tall as Daryl, but he weighed twice as much, which was intimidating, especially since he had that schoolyard bully attitude.

"A little late to be doing business," Daryl said, hoping against hope that he was wrong, and that O'Keefe's being here was a coincidence.

But "No such thing as too late," said another shadow who'd appeared behind Cody.

Shit, it was Eddie Facciolo, a fucking skinhead, along with his creepy twin brother, Stank Stedman. They weren't really related, but the shaved heads made them look it. Eddie had a nose ring, and Stank had a neck tattoo. Or maybe it was the other way around . . . ?

"You out here making a delivery for Nelson?" Daryl

asked, but his heart sank as Eddie and Stank moved back behind Daryl, so that between the two of them and O'Keefe, there was nowhere for him to run.

"Information gathering," O'Keefe said with that smile that didn't touch his eerie pale blue eyes. Reptilian, Dingo had called it. Dingo could be an idiot, but in this case, Dingo was right.

"Maybe I can help you out," Daryl said quickly.

"I know you can," O'Keefe said. "That's why you been hiding from us, bitch."

"What?" Daryl said. "Hiding? No, man, I haven't been hiding from anyone."

"We've been looking for you," Eddie said, "and you've been fucking hard to find."

"Full transparency, Ed," Daryl said. "I've been working the kitchen for Yuri, you know, like I have for, fuck, five whole weeks now? He runs that high-end card game over by the Hyatt and the Hilton? You know, where the Richie Riches stay when they come to town?"

"I thought you worked at the Irish," O'Keefe said.

"Nah, brah," Daryl said. "That didn't last. And this is way better. It's all under the table. The walking home is for shit, but I'll get my license back in another four months." He cleared his throat. "So how can I help you? And I do want to help you. Let me guess, this is about Fiona's friend Maddie, and some missing money?"

O'Keefe crossed his ginormous arms. It was meant to intimidate, and yes, it did.

"If I had to guess," Daryl said, "Fee took that money. She hated Maddie because Dingo has a thing for her."

"We're not looking for your guesses," O'Keefe said. "We're looking for the girl."

"Well, okay," Daryl said. "That simplifies things, because I don't know much about her. Her last name's Nakamura. Her father's in the Navy." He almost said SEAL, but he suspected that wouldn't be well received, so he didn't. "Let's see, *his* last name's Greene, they live over on, um, Janson Street, yeah. I was with Ding and Fee, and we dropped off Maddie, once."

"What's the number?" O'Keefe asked.

"Dude," Daryl said. "I don't know. I wasn't in remembering-numbers mode at the time, if you feel me. It's kinda yellow stucco, Spanish style, with pink and orange what-cha-call-it—barrel tile roof. Her dad has a truck, it was in the drive. I think it's blue . . . ?"

"What else?" O'Keefe asked.

"Uhhhh, Maddie used to live in Palm Springs?"

"Are you telling me that or asking me?" O'Keefe said.

"A little of both?" Daryl shrugged, and gave him the smile that had won him friends and influenced people—particularly enemies—through the years. People liked him for a reason. "I don't really know her—Maddie."

"But she's fucking Dingo?" O'Keefe asked.

"I didn't say that," Daryl backpedaled. "Dingo likes her. He's probably, yeah. He says he's not, but . . . Come on. Right?"

"So where's Dingo?" O'Keefe asked.

Okay. Okay. Daryl's mouth was dry and he wet his lips. "To be honest, that's the question of the evening. He usually picks me up from work and drives me home. Well, not home. I'm staying with these girls and, um . . . whatever. But when I called him tonight, he told me he was heading north on the Five."

"Was he with the girl?"

"Yeah, I, um . . . He didn't say. I didn't ask. Didn't want to know. Maddie's father, you know? He was a little scary."

"North on the Five to where?" O'Keefe asked.

Daryl was a lousy liar. "Fuck," he said. "Man, I'm only guessing, and you said you didn't want me to—"

"Guess," O'Keefe ordered.

"Dingo's parents live in Van Nuys. If I had to guess, he's heading there."

"Address?"

Daryl hated himself as he recited it. He and Ding had been friends since seventh grade. But if he knew Dingo, and he did, Dingo would understand.

Stank wrote the address down in his phone.

"Anything else I can help you gentlemen out with?" Daryl asked.

"Yeah," O'Keefe said. And punched him in the face.

Daryl felt his nose break as both Eddie and Stank began to pummel him, too.

"No fair, brahs, I *helped* you," he tried to say, but something heavy hit him in the back of the head and the world went black.

CHAPTER FOURTEEN

Friday

Fiona's mother had her eyes—blue and annoyed. In fact, the woman might've been Fee's older clone, they looked that much alike—a fact that Dingo knew must've royally chapped Fee's ass.

One of her fav topics of discussion had been how much she hated her mom.

"She's not here," the woman said flatly in response to Maddie's politely asked, "Excuse me, ma'am, is Fiona home?"

She started to close the heavy wooden front door in their faces, but Dingo asked, "Is she at her da's, then?" He leaned on his accent because Fee had loved thinking that he was Australian, and maybe she didn't just look like her mother—maybe they shared some similar personality traits or at least a few major likes and dislikes, too.

And sure enough, the woman stopped and looked at him. "You must be Dingo," she said. "Fiona warned me that you might come looking for her." She looked at Maddie. "That makes you Maddie. The thief. At least that's what she said. I've learned to take the things she says with a very large grain of salt."

Dingo often went with his gut, and right now, his gut was telling him to be as honest as possible. "Fiona stole ten thousand dollars from a drug dealer in San Diego and framed Mads here."

Fee's mother laughed. "And I'm supposed to just give it to you, right? Is ten thousand dollars the going price for bribing the security guards at Longfield Academy? I'll pass, thanks." She started to close the door again.

This time Maddie reached out to lean against it, to keep it from shutting. "Wait," she said. "We're not here for money. I didn't even think that was a possibility—"

"But as long as you mention it," Dingo started, even as Fee's mother said, "Step back from the door! Don't make me call nine-one-one!"

"Dingo, shush." Maddie stepped back, intentionally bumping into Dingo, no doubt because she knew that would make him immediately leap back toward the edge of the front stoop. *No touching, no kissing*—sweet Christ, he'd gone and kissed her last night, and now he was struggling to think about anything else.

Maddie was focused, though, and she begged the woman. "Please, Mrs. Clark—" that was her remarried name "—we just want to talk to Fiona. That's all."

"Well, you can't," the woman said. "Her father sent her to a *boarding school*." She made exaggerated air quotes. "The kind with locks on the doors."

"Longfield Academy?" Maddie asked. "Is that here in Sacramento?"

"Honey, it's out near Roanoke, Virginia."

Virginia? As Maddie looked at Dingo in obvious dismay, he immediately found himself thinking maybe it would be okay if all they did was kiss and—*Shit!* Inwardly, he slapped himself. *Snap out of it!*

Meanwhile, he could tell from Maddie's face that she was checking a mental map of the United States and trying to figure out how much money they'd need to drive to freaking Virginia. Shite, the idea of Fee living anywhere with the word *virgin* in the name was like a bad joke. Also? It was hard to imagine her going into lockup without kicking and screaming. In fact . . . "She didn't try to run away? You know, when Daddy said *boarding school*?"

"The decision was sudden," Fee's mother said. "And unannounced. The school came out here to pick her up."

He exchanged another look with Maddie, managing this time not to think about kissing her—except, shit, now he was thinking about it. *Focus.* What Fee's mother had just told them sounded a bit like kidnapping. Violent, like. Hard to imagine Fiona hadn't fought back—literally kicking and screaming. That must've been awful to witness.

Mrs. Clark must've known what he was thinking, because she added, "This particular school provides psychological and psychiatric support. They'll get her off the drugs and back on the meds she needs to—hopefully—achieve some sort of balance, and, well, they started with that immediately."

So . . . Fiona had been both surprised and then instantly sedated. That explained how they got her onto a plane—unless the "school" had its own private jet, which was entirely possible. As for the meds, was there truly a pill that would counteract sheer evil?

"Her father went with her," the woman continued, and to Dingo's surprise, her eyes filled with tears. "To get her . . . settled in. We both thought it was best if I stayed home. I seem to . . . set her off more easily."

So yeah, everything nasty that Fee had said about her mother was probably as much of a lie as her telling Auntie Susan that the camera in the bathroom was his, and her telling Nelson that Maddie'd stolen his ten grand.

"But she was staying here," Maddie confirmed, "with you. Right up until she . . . left for this school?"

Left was a good choice of verb. It was nicely neutral. Sans any screaming.

"Yes. Her father wouldn't let her stay with him. He and wife-number-three have two-year-old twins. We didn't have a lot of options." She shook her head. "Look, I already know what you're going to ask, and no, you cannot come in. We've already searched the house and found the drugs. They're gone. We destroyed them."

Maddie shook her head. "That's not why we're here."

"What, then?" Mrs. Clark said. "You think she's hidden ten thousand dollars somewhere in her bedroom? Honey, it was gone—probably already up her nose—long before she left San Diego." She looked from Maddie to Dingo and back. "Go home. I'm sure your parents are worried about you."

And with that she closed and locked the door with a very firm *click*.

* * *

According to the law office receptionist, Susan Smith, Esquire—also known as Fiona's aunt, she of the burned-down condo—would not be in until later this afternoon.

Pete squinted in the morning sun as he followed Shayla out of the building and into the parking lot, checking the time—it was a little after 0900. "When do you think we should text Maddie, see if she's open to talking? I don't want to piss her off by waking her up."

"I was thinking ten," Shay said. "It's respectful but not overly indulgent."

He nodded.

She met his eyes and smiled, and it zinged right through him, confirming that he was hard. Again. Already. Hell, he'd been ready for more while they were walking around outside of her house, checking for cracks and structural damage—that was how bad he had it for this woman.

Because just a few minutes before *that*, shortly after they'd woken up, they'd had yet another round of heart-stopping high-octane sex. And that was on top of last night's hat trick.

And . . . thinking about that wasn't helping him right now. Pete cleared his throat. "I'm not sure what to do next."

"Write Chapter Three?" Shay suggested. "We could do it, you know, rough and fast, and yeah, I just heard that come out of my mouth, but that's actually writer talk, not me suggesting you pin me against the wall in your entryway, although as *those* words come out of my mouth, I'm finding that I like that idea, a lot."

He laughed and grabbed her, pulling her in for an embrace, burying his nose in the curls of her fresh-smelling hair, and loving the softness of her body against his. He'd left off his uniform today but wore what he thought of as his *nice* shorts. No cargo pockets. A short-sleeved button-down shirt instead of a T. Shay was dressed a lot like she'd been yesterday, in a brightly printed sleeveless shirt and khaki pants that didn't quite reach her ankles. She had some kind of sweater or jacket—in a vibrant shade of red—tucked over her handbag.

"Let's go back, and see what happens," she said. "You can tell me Chapter Three in the car, we can figure out whether we want to get it onto paper before or after, dot dot dot."

Pete kissed her, and she kissed him back, her arms up around his neck, fingers in his hair. She seemed to melt against him and . . . He suddenly realized they were standing in the middle of a public parking lot, which was strange.

He didn't do PDAs—public displays of affection. Well, Lisa hadn't liked them, and . . . it was crazy. They'd broken up fourteen years ago, and apparently he was still living his life by her rules.

So he kissed Shay again. And yeah, you know what? Turned out he fucking *liked* PDAs. He liked them a *lot*.

As they finally got back into his truck, Shayla had clearly made note of his change of mood. He was trying to figure out how to tell her he'd been thinking about Lisa while he was kissing her without having it sound completely wrong, when she spoke.

"Hey, can I just say something?" she asked as he pulled out of the lawyer's lot.

"Of course." He laughed. Since when was she shy about anything?

She hesitated. "Something potentially awkward and blunt?"

Uh-oh. "Go."

"The sex is great."

That was blunt, but not what he'd call awkward. "I'm not sure *great* is a good enough word," he said. "I mean, you're the writer."

She smiled. "The sex is transcendent."

"Much better. And I agree."

"But I know it's not real," she said.

He could go light. Funny. *Wait, are you a witch? If it's not real, does that mean it's magic? Because I wholeheartedly agree about that, too.* Instead, he went for a simple questioning echo. "Not real."

"Neither one of us is looking for anything heavy," she said. "I mean, you've got more than enough on your plate, with Maddie. Once she's home . . ."

Pete nodded, but he wasn't quite sure what she was saying.

"I mean, talk about complications," Shayla continued. "Right? I know you're going to need to focus on her, and that's going to take up a lot of your time, and that's okay."

Time management was something he was very good at. But her *I know you're busy* message combined with *not real* and *not looking for anything heavy* meant that management of time was secondary to the main issue.

"I just wanted you to know that we're on the same page," she continued. "We're having fun—I mean, you know, when we're together *transcendently*—and that's good. It's nice, it's light, it's easy. It's right now, you know? No expectations, no pressure."

He didn't think he was letting anything show on his face—disappointment or dismay or whatever the hell this sinking feeling was that he was experiencing—but she took it upon herself to further expound.

"I'm saying that it's okay with me if we, um, label this thing—this ridiculous heat between us—as *friends with benefits*. God, that's such a terrible, trite expression, but it kind of . . . fits. Right?"

And there it was, fully blunt and awkward.

She smiled and tried to make a joke. "Although, *friends with transcendental benefits* does sound a *little* better. . . ."

"Is that what *you* want?" he asked, because yeah he'd only met her a few days ago, but that just did not fit with what he knew—thought he knew—about her. No, fuck that. He knew. She was the most WYSIWYG—what-you-see-is-what-you-get—woman he'd ever met in his entire life. And this did *not* compute.

But she was already nodding emphatically. "Yes. Like I said, I'm on the same page."

So opposed to being potential soul mates . . . "You wanna be fuck buddies," he said, because he had to confirm it.

Shayla winced. "That might be my *least* favorite name for it," she admitted.

"Transcendental sex buddies."

She laughed a little too loudly. "*Much* better."

Why didn't he believe her?

But then, as he replayed this conversation, he knew. *It's nice, it's light, it's easy. It's right now . . .* And there it was. *Right now.*

It wasn't her. It was him. He was her *Mr. Right Now.* She'd talked about this concept more than once in the many online interviews that he'd read. The romance novels that Shay wrote were focused on her characters finding their Mr. or Ms. Right. But along the way, as she wrote her ongoing series of connected books, her characters sometimes shared an interlude with a *Mr. Right Now.* Imperfect to the point of being unacceptable—at least in terms of finding lasting happiness—and sometimes destined to be killed off, Mr. Right Now provided a sexual escape valve and/or the fodder for a rebound relationship.

When exactly had Shayla split with her ex? Pete thought it had been years, but maybe that made him even more of a Right Now, depending on how long it had been since . . .

"Can I ask you something," he said, "that's also potentially awkward?"

"Uh-oh," Shay said. "Um, yes . . . ?"

He went for it. "Am I the first? Since . . ." What was her ex-husband's name? "Carter?"

Shayla looked surprised and then embarrassed. She laughed as she made a face. "Yeah. Is it obvious?"

"No," he said. "I was just curious."

And there it was. All along, she'd been dead serious about not wanting to be more than friends with him, but then that earthquake had happened, and sheer physical attraction had taken control. She liked him, but not enough to want any kind of future with him. And he really couldn't blame her. Especially since she knew most of the story of how he'd fucked things up with Lisa, and with Maddie, too.

Hey look, here's a man who really *sucks at relationships of all kinds. Maybe if I'm lucky, he'll be my boyfriend.*

Shayla was right to keep her distance and to establish clear boundaries like this, right up front. In fact, Pete respected her—and liked her—even more for it.

The heroine's relationship with a Mr. Right Now, Shayla had explained in one of those interviews, also provided her with a learning experience. She'd laughed and added, "*and pages and pages of molten-hot sex.*"

So okay. All right. He, too, could keep this thing light and easy. He'd done it plenty of times before in the years post-Lisa.

But bottom line, if having Shayla Whitman as a fuck buddy or friend with benefits was his only option?

He'd take her however he could get her.

Shay cleared her throat. "So," she said. "Chapter Three . . . ? It would be great if we had something to send, before I text Maddie."

Right. Yeah. Rough and fast. Pete remembered. He, too, cleared his throat as he took the ramp onto the freeway that took them home. "Chapter Three. The Graduation Party Fucking—no, better make that *Fiasco.*"

It was like something out of a bad '80s movie.

A high school graduation party on the beach. A junior boy, crazy in love with the senior girl who was his best friend.

I knew Lisa was going to the party with Brad, her boyfriend, but I'd heard rumblings of rumors that he was going to dump her that night. People were talking about it, because, well, she was a drama student. Whatever happened was going to be dramatic.

I never went to those things. Why torture myself, watching her with him?

But that night . . . I think Lisa must've been aware of the rumors, too, because she started drinking early. I bumped into her in the parking lot of the local ice cream place a few hours before the sun even set—kids went there to use the bathroom and/or get a raspberry swirl cone. That was why I was there. I still won't say no to a good raspberry swirl.

She hugged me. "Peter Greene!" I could smell the alcohol on her—she was already trashed. She made me promise that I'd go to the beach, and that we'd dance together to "Let's Go Crazy," since that was "our song." Whatever that meant, since there was no "our" anything.

So yeah, I went, and I witnessed the dumping, which was about as horrific as it could be, considering Lisa was so drunk that she had no clue what was happening. It was a cross between a breakup and a key party—and if you don't know what a key party is, Google it. But brace yourself first.

In short, Brad—football hero that he was—was "setting Lisa free" as they went off to different colleges on different coasts. He was Notre Dame–bound, she was going to some little two-year performing arts school in LA. But to celebrate their new "freedom," he was going to go fuck Karen Possingham, while Lisa was handed off to whichever one of Brad's football buddies "won" her. Seriously, Brad was actually holding a raffle, and the winner got to drive her home, stopping in some dark cul-de-sac along the way.

I wanted to kill them all.

So I just went over to her, and picked her up. Brad was shouting something at me, but I ignored him. I carried her out of there and put her into my car.

And here's where it got super-'80s-movie. Because yeah. I took her to Hiroko's. She was so drunk, I didn't want to take her home; get her into trouble with her parents. Hiroko already disapproved, but I trusted her, and she and I took turns with Lisa as she puked her guts up all night long.

Fast forward to the next day. Lisa finally woke up, and pieced together the horror show of the night.

I remember we were out in Hiroko's garden, and she said, "You saved me from that douchebag. Thank you."

I said, "You're welcome." I didn't say "You'd do the same for me," because I knew she wouldn't've. But that was okay, because she was Lisa.

She hugged me, and when she didn't let go, I asked, "Are you okay?"

That was when she kissed me.

And I'm human, so I kissed her back. And Jesus, it was nice. It was perfect. It was everything. Everything.

Except it wasn't.

She put her hand on my thigh and started heading north, up the leg of my shorts, and I wanted—so badly—both for her to touch me and for this to be real. For her to have finally recognized that she loved me, too.

But I stopped her, because I didn't want to be her fuck you *message to Brad. And I sure as hell didn't want to be her Karen Possingham.*

Apparently, I was the first boy in the history of Lisa to say no.

And I kept saying no, *because I wanted her to love me. I had to be the guy who didn't sleep with her. So that's what I did. In August, she went to LA. I visited her on weekends during my senior year, and I'd bring a bedroll and sleep on the floor of her dorm.*

I hated acting—I liked the backstage stuff—but even though I hated performing, I auditioned for the same school, and got in. In hindsight, it wasn't as boneheaded a decision as it looks. Even though my test scores were high, my grades were shitty because I just didn't care, so the alternative was community college or the armed services. I was good at stage managing, and you could argue that learning how to act would help me deal with actors. But bottom line, I was majoring in Lisa.

So, in the longest '80s movie plotline ever, in August

after I graduated from high school, I moved to LA, too. I didn't have the money for a dorm room, but that was okay, because I just moved into Lisa's room, where I slept on the floor—assuming she didn't have an overnight guest.

Seventeen months after I first turned Lisa down, she told me that she didn't think she could live without me. And she asked me to be her boyfriend instead of just her friend. And then, for a while, I had everything I'd ever wanted, because Lisa loved me, too.

Shayla looked up from her computer. "Let's delete *assuming she didn't have an overnight guest*. Maddie doesn't need to know that her mother did that to you."

"Trust me," Peter said, as he cut open the tape that sealed another box. "Lisa wasn't doing it *to* me—she wasn't thinking about me. At all."

"Still." Shay kept it to herself, but she was pretty damn certain that Lisa had hoped Peter was listening at the door.

"That change is fine with me," he said, so she made the deletion and hit *send*.

"Okay, Maddie," she murmured as she also sent Maddie a text: *Just sent another email.* "Send me something back."

She and Peter were in his garage, where yesterday afternoon the SEAL candidates nicknamed Seagull and Timebomb had neatly stacked all of the boxes of Lisa and Maddie's belongings that had previously been in the Palm Springs storage unit.

They'd made the decision to multi-task and have Shay type Peter's Chapter Three while he opened and searched through boxes. Neither of them knew what he was hoping to find, but they both agreed that doing something was better than nothing.

Whoever had done the actual packing of those boxes hadn't taken the time to label any of them. They'd also packed weirdly random things together, like piles of junk mail in with the coffee mugs. A small garbage pail filled with dryer lint had actually been packed in with a mound of unfolded laundry.

Maddie's computer was indeed deceased—a casualty of the quake. So after Shay had changed into garage-rummaging clothes—an old pair of shorts and a tank top that clearly dated from 2008—she'd brought over her own laptop. She sat with it now, in a folding lawn chair, in the shade at the open door of the garage.

"What happened to make Lisa change her mind? Seventeen months after graduation," she asked. Something *must* have happened.

"Her mom died," Peter told her.

"Oh, no."

"Yeah, it was rough. Not completely out of the blue, because she'd been ill, but . . . I went back to San Diego with Lisa. There were so many of her relatives in town, we ended up staying at *my* mother's house. She assumed we were together, so she put us in my old room. It wasn't a big deal, we were sharing a much smaller space in LA and I was fine with sleeping on the floor. But Lisa was really upset, and . . ." He cleared his throat. "We ended up sharing more than a bed—whoa! Hey! Look at this."

He held up a book, and whoa indeed, it was *Harry's War.* The familiar red, white, and blue cover was from the first hardcover edition that had come out four, no, *five* years ago.

But Shay was too freaked out by what Peter had just told her to really comprehend. Lisa had been upset—the way Shay had been upset after the earthquake. And sex had happened in both instances, because he was too kind and well-mannered to say no.

It was stupid of her to be freaked out—it was exactly what she already knew. She'd been in need of his comfort and pity, and she was clearly female enough so that he'd run his bar hookup pattern and—

Wait. Which was it? Pity fuck or bar hookup? Or maybe, in her case, a weird mashup of both?

"Lisa was a Shayla Whitman fan," Peter said, pulling more of her books out of the box. His ex had what looked like ten of them, most in paperback. "I'm reading this one—" he held up *Outside of the Lines* "—right now."

"What . . . ?" Shay said.

He stacked the books in a neat pile. "Yeah, didn't I tell you?"

"Noooo."

"I'm pretty sure I did. I downloaded it the night we met."

"You definitely didn't tell me that." Oh, my God.

"I really like it," he said.

Oh, shit. "You don't have to say that."

"Well, yeah, I know," he said. "But I mean it. It's well written, the characters are great—I could swear that I know them, that I've worked with them. You got that FBI team dynamic really right. But I think what I like the best is that it's fun. It's wildly entertaining—every time I pick it up, I can't put it down. It's like reading a really good action movie, with porn thrown in."

Whoa! Wait! "Romance is *not* porn," she told him. "Porn is sex without an emotional connection. Romance is all about the emotions. I mean, yeah, insert tab A into slot B, but the end result isn't just a balloon-drop with confetti. There are massive feelings happening, too."

Peter nodded. "Fair enough. But it's also true that the feelings ping-pong everywhere. They aren't quite *You complete me.*"

"Well, *yeah,*" Shay said. "Because that's bullshit. People—particularly women—don't need someone else to be whole. They need someone else to stand beside them and help them be the best person that they can be. To support—and enhance who they are. Not to fill in some mythical missing piece." She made a raspberry sound, muttering, "*You complete me.*"

He was laughing at her. "I suspect I hit a hot button. I apologize."

"Believe me, I'm very familiar with the disrespect this genre gets."

"So why not write something different?"

"Why are you a SEAL?" she countered.

Peter smiled. "Got it."

"So, what part are you up to?" She couldn't keep herself from asking.

"The scene in the utility closet," he said. "During the gala at the marina?"

Oh dear.

"Your characters have a lot of sex. Not that I'm complaining. Just observing."

"People, in general, have a lot of sex," she pointed out.

He opened another box. "I'm not sure about that," he said. "I've had more sex in the past twenty-four hours than I've had in the past . . . hell, I-don't-know-how-many years. And your characters are even busier than we've been."

Wait, what? Really? Was he saying . . . ? Back in the truck, after that awkward friends-with-bennies conversation, he'd asked her about Carter. Was he now telling her . . . No, that was ridiculous. This man had definitely had sex—and a lot of it—post-Lisa. *Bar hookup pattern,* he'd called it. But bar hookups, by nature, were one-and-done—which made for generally shitty sex. Okay, maybe not *shitty* precisely, but certainly not transcendent.

"This guy Jack," he continued.

"The book's hero," she said. "Romances have two main characters—the two people who fall in love and win their HEA—actually, I prefer to say *earn*. They earn their happily-ever-after."

He lifted the box, which made the muscles in his arm do

amazing things, and set it into the *I have no clue if the contents are Lisa's or Maddie's* pile before turning back to her. "Right, but Jack's got this penchant for tossing Loretta up against whatever wall is nearby, and he's always got a handy condom in his pocket."

"Safe sex," Shay said as Peter moved toward her. His worn-out T-shirt fit him just fine, as did his ripped and faded cargo shorts. She cleared her throat and checked her phone. Still nothing from Maddie. "A lot of my readers are young women. Girls, really. Some are younger than Maddie. The message I want to send is that strong, smart women *always* have protected sex. And that one of the things that makes hot guys extra hot is their respect for the safety of their partner."

"But the wall-tossing part," Peter said, reaching down to take the computer off of her lap. "That's where I'm feeling the pressure to suspend a *little* too much disbelief." He closed it and put it onto the concrete floor, on the far side of the boxes. "Sex like that can't be comfortable for anyone, especially Loretta."

"It's not about comfort," she said. "It's hot. It's *I need you now, and I can't wait.* Don't get me wrong. Beds are great. They're lovely, and yes, you're right, most people make love in the glorious comfort of a bed, but I write those non-bed scenes to show the height and the power of the characters' need and emotion."

He came over to her and held both of his hands out. "Come here."

She put her hands into his. He had very nice hands—big hands—with long, broad fingers. He had even nicer eyes, and she met his gaze as he pulled her out of the chair so that she was standing in front of him.

He gently tugged her over to the stacked wall of unsorted boxes, and turned her so that her back was to them. But then he backed them both up about four steps as he said,

"Okay, so when they're in the utility closet, Loretta's here." He let go of her hand and took another few steps backward, putting a few feet of space between them. "And Jack's here. And they're talking, yada yada . . ."

Shayla laughed. "You're not seriously going to try to *mythbust* a scene from a romance novel . . . ?"

"I am, yes, so *shh*. You're telling the story at this point through Jack, right?" Peter said.

"It's called POV—point of view," she said. "And yes, that scene's in Jack's, but seriously, Peter . . ."

"So we know what Jack's thinking, and he's mad at Loretta for taking that risk out on the balcony with the killer, what's-his-name—"

"Alfred Sinclair," Shay said. "And he's the *suspected* killer. They don't know for sure yet that he's—"

"Right. But *we* know he is. And Jack's a smart man, and in that moment when he was watching her with Sinclair on that balcony, he was terrified and now his fear has turned to anger, but he's also relieved as fuck that she's all right. And that's brilliant, by the way, because relief can really bring you to your knees after a high-stress situation. Plus since we're seeing her through his eyes, and she's wearing that dress, and we know just how much she turns him on, so when she says *Shut up and kiss me*—or whatever it was she said, I'm paraphrasing—it makes total sense that he'd be, *Game over.*"

"Thank you." She was delighted. "That was exactly what I was attempting to communicate with that scene."

"What was it that she said to him . . . ?" he asked.

"Oh, God, I don't know," Shay admitted. "I wrote that book a long time ago. But the subtext was definitely *Shut up and kiss me.*"

Peter smiled as the words left her lips, and she realized she'd played right into his ridiculous mythbusting hand. He moved toward her—fast—and kissed her, exactly as Jack had kissed Loretta in that fiery scene from *Outside of the Lines*.

He wrapped his arms around her, which was a good thing, because the way he was all but inhaling her—his mouth hard against hers, his tongue damn near down her throat—made her weak in the knees. He lifted her up and wrapped her legs around his waist, and God, he smelled so good and she'd been sitting there all that time, watching the play of muscles in his back and arms and dying to touch him. So now as she kissed him, she did just that, and she felt him push her back so that she bumped up against that wall and—

Whoa!

The stacked cardboard boxes shifted and moved beneath their combined weight, and Peter quickly regained his balance, stepping away, and setting her back on her feet.

"Sorry," he said. "I thought I could prove my point without any risk of hurting you. I thought the boxes would provide a little give—just not that much."

Shayla was standing there, out of breath, with her heart practically pounding out of her chest. She could still barely stand by herself, and all she could think was that this must be what it felt like to get hit by lightning. How could he kiss her like that, and then . . . just . . . talk like normal?

"We need a real wall," she somehow managed to say. "So I can prove *my* point." She made her legs walk and she forced herself not to stagger or weave as she went toward the back of the garage, looking for . . . "There." She pointed.

Hidden back behind the towering cube of unsorted boxes was a flat metal door that led to the backyard. Seagull and Timebomb had obviously taken care not to block it, instead creating a corridor with the boxes on one side, a real wall with utility shelving on the other, and the door down at the end. She put herself a few steps in front of it. "Let's try that again."

Peter shook his head. "Sorry, I'm not going to slam you against that."

"You don't slam. You connect. You use it to brace yourself, and me. Loretta. Jack does, I mean." Oh God, she was getting a little too into this.

"You used the word *slam*," he said.

"But before I did, I switched point of views," she told him. "Right at Loretta's line of dialogue. *Kiss me*—boom. New scene. For the actual sex, we're now inside Loretta's head. You were reading the ebook, right? Sometimes scene changes aren't clearly marked in the e-format. I hate when that happens. Trust me, Jack doesn't slam her. He kisses the shit out of her, yeah, but he's always careful—in fact, he's too careful for Loretta. She feels like he's always holding something back. Still, when he grabs her and kisses her in this scene, it feels to Loretta like a slam. For her, that's a *really* good thing, because not only does she like sex a little rough, she desperately wants this man to lose his mind over her."

Peter was paying attention—doing that thing where he really listened—and now he moved toward her. But slowly, unlike before. He leaned in, gently touching her chin and lifting her face up toward him, but then just barely brushing his lips against hers as he said, "So he kisses her, and she kisses him back." He moved her arms up around his neck then put his own arms around her. "And he does this—" he lifted her up, his hands supporting her derrière, same as he did before, only slowly this time as he talked them through it "—so she does *this*—" her legs went around him "—as meanwhile, he's doing *this*." He carried her forward—his forward—until her back gently bumped up against the metal of the door.

It was surprisingly warm. She'd expected coolness, but then realized that the midmorning sun was beating down on it, on its other side.

And there they stood—not just nose to nose, but body to body. Shay could feel him hard against her and had to work to keep from melting into a little pile of begging protoplasm.

"Okay," he said. "It makes sense that as long as he doesn't drive toward her like a linebacker, she won't get hurt when she hits the wall. And I see how these mechanics work." He shifted against her. "But he's also gotta not drop her while they're having sex."

"I think that's what makes it extra hot," she said. Compared to him, she sounded embarrassingly out of breath, considering she was the one being held, not doing the holding. "The idea that he's giving her this—" she now moved against him "—while he's doing this . . ." She ran her hands down his shoulders and arms and chest, where he was very definitely getting a workout.

"This is extra hot?" Peter asked.

"Oh, yeah."

He smiled and shifted all of her weight into one arm— *what* . . . ? That was *crazy* that he could do that. But then he used his free hand to pull a condom from his pocket. "And I hear on good authority that *this* makes it even hotter."

Oh, thank God. Shay laughed. "My panties just burst into flame."

Peter laughed, too, but then he frowned. "Maybe this is where we bust the myth, because if I'm supposed to put this on with one hand, *while* kissing you . . . ?"

"Of course not," she said. "You put me down—just for a few seconds, while we . . ."

He did and she shucked off her shorts and her panties while he unfastened his shorts and tore open the condom wrapper. As he covered himself, Shay glanced toward the open garage bay door, but the pile of boxes shielded them completely from the street. In fact, someone could stand right in the driveway, and not know they were back here. It was really not *that* different from having sex in a tent.

Peter was as perceptive as always. "Want me to close that?"

"No." What was her line? She smiled and said, "Shut up and kiss me."

* * *

Shay was right.

This was fucking hot.

Pete held her, her back against that door as he pushed himself inside of her.

They both had their shirts on and she was still wearing her sneakers, but even that was weirdly hot, too. And the garage door being open added something dangerously sexy as well.

This kind of sex not only put Shayla completely into Pete's hands, but also completely at his mercy. He alone controlled how slow or fast they moved—she had little to no traction, save for her ability to pull him more deeply inside of her by applying pressure around his butt with her legs. But even then, it took almost no effort for him to resist her.

Unlike Jack from her book, Pete took his time. Maybe he was showing off—*look at how long I can hold you like this.* But Jesus, he loved the way it felt to surround himself completely with her softness and heat, and then to pull himself almost entirely free and then do it again and again and *again,* while he gazed into her eyes.

The look on her face . . . it was killing him. Both her smile and her eyes were dreamy and satisfied—as if he didn't even need to make her come to bring her unbelievable pleasure. And yeah, that was one page they absolutely were both on together. If he could just spend the entire rest of his life right here, doing this, *feeling* this . . . It would be more than enough.

But then she came—and proved him wrong yet again, because Jesus, making Shayla come like this was his new favorite thing in the world. And for those endlessly long seconds, as she unraveled in front of him and around him, it didn't matter what they called their relationship. This connection, these feelings, this moment they were sharing—it was real. It was truth.

It was there, solid, beneath whatever name they gave it.

And Pete came, too.

CHAPTER FIFTEEN

Fiona hadn't lied about where she'd hidden the key to her mother's house. It was exactly where she'd told Maddie she'd left it—buried in a bright blue flowerpot that sat out on the back patio, by the pool.

After their conversation with Mrs. Clark, Maddie and Dingo had sat in his car, parked just down the street, prepared to wait for however many hours it took for her to leave her house.

They hadn't been there long when Maddie's phone vibrated and she saw that she'd gotten a text from "Dad's" girlfriend, Shayla. She'd sent another email with another attached installment of the story about Lisa and Peter.

Maddie had just finished reading it aloud—the graduation party and her dad being the first boy ever to say *no*, which must've freaked Lisa out—when the garage door opened, and Mrs. Clark pulled out and drove away.

Since they had no idea how long Fiona's mother would be gone, Maddie had put her phone back in her pocket as she followed Dingo around to the back of the house. She didn't even attempt to discuss it with Dingo, or even reply in any way to Shayla's text as he dug through the dirt for the key. There'd be time for that later. Assuming Nelson's men didn't catch them and kill them first.

Maddie watched as Dingo used the pool water to rinse off both the key and his hands, and then unlocked that back door.

It led into a mudroom that was nearly as big as the studio apartment she'd shared with Lisa in Palm Springs. That opened into a kitchen the size of a ballroom. God, Lisa would've loved cooking in here.

"Found the stairs going up," Dingo called—he hadn't stopped to gape at the granite countertops and real wood cabinets and center island with its own little sink.

Maddie followed the sound of his voice over to a set of plushly carpeted stairs. Together, they went up.

"Find the master, then look for the bedroom farthest from it," Ding said, and sure enough, there was Fiona's bedroom at the end of the hall.

"Holy shite," he said, echoing what Maddie was thinking.

The room was decorated in girly hues of pink and lacy whites—not only the curtains and bedspread, but the furniture was painted in those colors, too. It was a generic decor that held not an ounce of Fee's own personality. It was like someone had come in and vacuumed every little last ounce of the girl out of the pink carpeting. It made Maddie appreciate the neutral tones of the bedroom furniture that "Dad" had gotten for her, instead of pretending that he magically knew what she liked and . . .

Huh.

The bookshelf beneath the window was Maddie's destination, and that was pure Fee. It was filled mainly with DVDs instead of books—mostly horror movies and inane romcoms with an entire shelf dedicated to ancient TV shows. *Mr. Magoo* and *Mr. Ed. My Favorite Martian* and *Petticoat Junction. Gilligan's Island* and *Lost in Space.*

In the midst of it all, there were only two books. *Anne of Green Gables* and *Little Women*. Neither of which Fiona had probably ever read.

Maddie reached for *Anne* because it was hardcover, and flipped it open.

Nothing. She turned it upside down and shook, but nothing fluttered from its pages.

She tossed it onto the floor and pulled out *Little Women*.

And there it was. The pages had been carefully cut out from the center, leaving a storage area in which Fiona had put the roll of bills.

Maddie's heart leapt, but her elation didn't last long, because there was no way that this was ten thousand dollars. At the most, it was half. Probably less.

Dingo was thinking the same thing. "Better'n nothing," he said. "Take it, and let's go."

Whrrrrrrrr!

Shit, that was the sound of the garage door going up.

"Run!" Dingo said. "Go!"

Whrrrrrrrr! Now, it was going back down.

Together they galloped down the stairs and through that palatial kitchen to that giant mudroom, where—God, there was a door leading into the house from the garage.

Dingo was first out the door to the back patio, and Maddie was right behind him. She made the mistake, though, of turning to close that door behind her.

And as she did, Fee's mother came in through the garage.

Her surprise was all over her Fee-like face as she saw Maddie and gasped.

Maddie opened her mouth, and instead of *Tell Fee to go fuck herself,* she said, "I'm *so* sorry, Mrs. Clark," before she slammed the door closed behind her.

And, as she ran like hell toward Dingo's car, she realized it was true.

She *was* incredibly sorry. For herself, for Fiona's mother, for Dingo, and even for her dad.

But most of all, she felt sorry for the Fees and the Lisas, who crashed through life, probably through no real fault of their own, fucking it up royally for everyone around them.

* * *

"Any word from Maddie?"

Shayla checked her phone. "Nothing yet."

Post-sex dishevelment repair was even more awkward in a garage, she had just discovered.

Fortunately, Peter had been dealing with his own shorts-around-his-ankles awkwardness and hopefully hadn't paid too much attention to her tank-top-and-sneakers-only fashion statement. *Temporary* fashion statement. She'd pulled her shorts on over her bare ass as quickly as humanly possible.

"You hungry?" Peter asked as he finished zipping up his own shorts.

"I would not say no to your scrambled eggs," she admitted. When he'd cooked them the other night, they'd smelled impossibly good.

"I can do more than eggs," he told her with a smile. "Believe it or not, I'm a pretty good cook."

"I believe it," she said, reaching up to pull his mouth down for a quick kiss.

He caught her, holding on to both of her arms, so that he could kiss her again. Longer this time. "That was amazing." He smiled into her eyes. "Let's do it again. But unlike Jack-of-the-magic-penis, I'll need a few hours to get mine ready to go again."

Shayla laughed. "Jack does not have a magic penis."

"I think he might. Either that, or you left out the part where he takes a shit-ton of Viagra."

"How about if we don't attempt to schedule a replay,"

she told him. "Instead, let's have a signal that says *Meet me in the back of the garage, ASAP.*"

He nuzzled her neck. "Like, if we run into each other out by our mailboxes, and one of us says, *Hello*."

She cracked up. "You want *hello* to be our *Let's go have sex* signal?"

He kissed her lips. "I very much do," he said.

And for a moment, Shayla lost herself as she let him kiss her and kiss her and kiss her. She might've kissed him forever if he hadn't suddenly lifted his head.

"Did you hear that?" he asked.

"You mean, the sound of my vagina applauding?" she asked.

Peter laughed. "Jesus, I love . . . your sense of humor. But no, that's not what I meant."

Okay. Had she just imagined that hesitation after *love*? She must've. Although, God, the idea that she was breathlessly analyzing his language usage in hopes of a clue or a sign that he wanted to, what? Marry her? Harry was right. She sucked at casual sex. Sometimes *I love your sense of humor* meant exactly and only that. She made the man laugh.

"There," he said, but she shook her head.

There were lots of different sounds and noises in their neighborhood. Traffic from the main road, a few streets over. Airplanes regularly passing overhead. Mrs. Quinn's hose as she watered her garden.

"As long as it's not another earthquake," she started to say, following him out of the garage and onto the driveway. Where, most definitely, they now both heard a crashing sound coming from inside Peter's house.

"What the fuck?" he said. "Maddie? *Maddie!*"

He charged toward his kitchen door, with Shayla right behind him.

* * *

Izzy was on the phone with Eden when Lindsey Jenkins called.

His amazing, beautiful, incredible wife was telling him all about Ben's tour of Boston College, which the kid apparently *loved*. "Bonus is it's not that far from Jenn's brother—the one who lives in Needham."

"That's great, sweetheart," he said, glancing at his phone as Lindsey gave up. "I just . . ."

"You just want him to go to UCLA," she finished for him. "So he won't be far away from home. That's definitely still in the running. But seeing all of these other schools is important."

"I know," he said as Lindsey's name popped up again on his screen. "Fuck, Eed, Lindsey's calling me—that's twice in a row."

"Take it, take it!" Eden rarely used exclamation points. "Izzy, come on! What if she's having the baby and needs you? Go! Go!"

"Right! Shit! Love you!" He switched over. "Yo, Linds! You giving birth on the freeway, or what?"

"Yeah, that's the super-fun part of being ten months pregnant," she said dryly. "Every time I call anyone, the assumption is I'm popping out a baby in the middle of some arroyo."

"I believe I said *freeway*."

"*Or what* means arroyo, and you know it," she countered. "And no. Mark's ridiculously large spawn isn't going anywhere anytime soon."

"Famous last words," Izzy warned her.

"Yes," she said. "I know. I am absolutely and intentionally tempting fate. Please, sweet God, create some crazy hijinks by sending me into immediate labor." She paused, waiting, but then sighed heavily. "No, apparently it's not going to happen yet."

"Well, since you don't need me to deliver the baby," Izzy said, "how else can I help you?"

"You wouldn't happen to be over at Grunge's right now, are you?"

"I am not," Izzy said. "Why?"

"I've tried calling him, and he's not picking up."

"Aha!" Izzy said.

"Aha?"

"Proof that he's gettin' it on with the pretty neighbor lady." Izzy was delighted. "What else would he be doing at eleven hundred in the morning?" As he said the words he realized that 11 A.M. was probably the *least* likely time for the LT to be doing the dance of love with his new "friend" Shayla.

"I could think of about a dozen different things." Lindsey further shot him down. "He could be in the shower, or maybe his phone got set to silent and he doesn't know it . . . ?"

"La la la," Izzy said loudly over her. "I prefer to live in a super-happy world where all of my friends get laid regularly. Hey, can I ask you something?"

"With that lead-in, I'm not sure."

"Different subject. Way less happy," Izzy said. "Does Eden ever talk to you about . . . losing the baby?" Lindsey, too, had had a relatively late pregnancy miscarriage. It made sense that she and Eden might've discussed it, having the tragedy of that loss in common.

"Yeah," Lindsey said. "We talk all the time. I still get scared, like if I don't feel the baby move, and I know Eden gets that in a way that most other people just can't. Everyone else tells me to relax or lighten up or take advantage of the fact that the baby's sleeping instead of doing his/her usual gymnastics, and that's maddening. But I know if I call Eden, she'll drop everything and just come sit with me—or even take me to the ER, if I get too freaked out. And likewise, she knows I've got Pinkie's birth-and-death-day permanently blocked off on my calendar. You know, in case you're wheels up with the Team."

As Izzy drew in a deep and shaky breath, he realized he'd stopped breathing as she'd told him that, and yeah, now he had tears in his eyes, too.

"Thanks," he whispered. "And you know I'm here, too, while Eed's out of town."

"I do know that," she said. "Oh, my God, these hormones! Please forgive me if I start to sob."

"Yeah," Izzy said. "Those pregnant lady hormones are so strong, they came through the phone and zapped me, too."

Lindsey laughed. "You're an idiot."

"You know it."

"If you see or talk to the lieutenant, tell him I'm trying to reach him. That name he gave us—Daryl Middleton, the friend of Maddie's friend Dingo? I just got a call from my friend in the PD. She told me that a Daryl Middleton popped up as a possible assault victim in the hospital ER."

"Possible?" Izzy asked. "Like, he's not sure he was assaulted?"

"Like he's still unconscious, in ICU. Serious head injury. Beat cop found him bleeding on the sidewalk, with the shit kicked out of him. It was a stretch of road without any traffic cams so we can't look back and see what happened—I'm betting that's not an accident. Whoever did this to Daryl is not your run-of-the-mill jealous ex-boyfriend, that's for damn sure."

"Fuck," Izzy said. "Grunge is gonna hate this news."

"Yup."

"I'll swing past his place," Izzy told her. "Give it to him face-to-face."

"Thanks," Lindsey said. "If I get more info, like if Daryl wakes up? I'll pass it along to both of you."

"Roger that."

"Hey, Iz?"

"Yeah?"

"Eden wants to try again," Lindsey told him. "She's scared, but I think she's ready. Just FYI. If you can, be super-low-key when she tells you. You know, don't go rushing out to buy everything in the zero-to-three-months toy aisle at Babies 'R' Us, because that'll scare the crap out of her."

"Super-low-key is my new middle name," Izzy said as he silently high-kicked with joy around the living room.

Lindsey snorted. "Yeah, that'll be the day. Just do your dancing and hoo-yahing in private until the baby's born."

Until the baby's born. As Izzy ended the call, he realized that Lindsey had just zapped him with more of her pregnant lady hormones. Yeah, that must've been why he was misty-eyed.

* * *

The moment that Pete stepped into the kitchen, he knew something was seriously wrong.

His house was in the middle of being robbed.

Drawers and cabinet doors hung open, and it was only because he hadn't yet accumulated a lot of crap that it hadn't been tossed out onto the floor.

He kept his voice low as he told Shayla, "It's not Maddie who's in here, get outside and stay outside, call nine-one-one." She, too, apparently recognized the signs of a burglary-in-progress from her writing research, because she nodded, her phone already out.

But then she caught his arm. "Do you have a handgun in the house?" she whispered.

He nodded *yes,* but then shook his head *no.* "It's locked

up, in the bedroom closet. I seriously doubt I can get to it before they see me."

"I'm not saying that you should. . . . No, I'm asking if it's securely locked," she said. "Don't you dare go back there and get killed with your own weapon. Also? If there's even a chance that whoever's in there is armed, I'm thinking this might best be handled like coming home to find a squirrel in the kitchen. You open all the doors and windows so it's got an easy escape route, and then make a lot of noise."

"But I don't want to let whoever's in there escape," Pete told her. "Go outside, call nine-one-one—"

"Holy fuck!"

While they were arguing, the burglar had come back down the hall and had been startled when he saw them standing in the kitchen. Pete leapt in front of Shay, pushing her back from the man, who was dressed in all black—including black gloves on his hands. His face, however, was white, but Pete only caught a glimpse of a stubble-covered chin as the man fumbled to pull a ski-cap down over it.

The man bolted for the front door, shouting, "Go, go, go!"

"Stay here," Pete ordered Shay, and took off after him.

* * *

Shayla put her phone to her ear—it was ringing; the emergency dispatcher had not yet picked up—as she hurried over to the living room door to watch as Peter tackled the man in black, bringing him down to the lawn.

She heard a bump and a ragged breath behind her, and she turned—too late—to see that there was another man, also dressed all in black, still inside the house.

She was between him and the exit, so he went directly through her, aiming low and hitting her hard in the solar plexus with his shoulder, pushing her with him out the screen door. She heard herself squeaking—he'd knocked the air clear out of her and she could not get enough of a breath to full-on scream—and her phone went flying, a little voice on the other end saying, "What is your emergency?" as it tumbled through the air.

Shay went flying, too, as the man grabbed her and took her with him. He launched himself off the stoop and over the bushes to the front lawn, where they landed in a tangle of arms and legs. Shay kicked and hit and slapped and thrashed, trying to get free as she struggled to suck in oxygen. But then the man moved so that most of his body weight was on top of her—it was a ploy, she realized, to force Peter to let go of the first man.

"Shay!" Peter shouted.

"I bet you'd be fun to tie up and fuck," her burglar breathed into her ear, and it pissed her off so much that instead of screaming, she used what little breath she'd collected to gasp, "I'm FBI, asshole, and you are under arrest!"

Her goal was to get him off of her while Peter was still detaining the first man, but alas, the SEAL had already abandoned his burglar so he could race over to rescue her. And of course, as soon as he let go, that first man scrambled out of the yard and was already halfway down the street.

As for Mr. Tie-Her-Up-and-Fuck-Her, he quickly rolled off of Shayla. Peter was pounding toward them, his teeth practically bared. If she were an asshole-bad-guy, and saw *that* coming at her, she would've run like hell, too. The man bolted in the opposite direction that his co-burglar had gone, which was smart, since Peter now would have to choose whom to chase.

Not that he was about to go after either of them while she was lying there, still unable to fully catch her breath, with bits of his lawn in her hair and probably even in her teeth. Shay struggled to sit up as Peter skidded to his knees next to her. "Don't move, baby," he told her. "Just stay right there."

That *baby* aside, his concern for her was actually quite lovely to see as he ran his hands gently around the back of her head, and then down her entire body, arms and legs included.

"I'm okay," she told him, still unable to do more than whisper as he helped her sit up.

"Did he hit you in the throat?" he asked, his hands now warm on her neck.

"No. Here." She pointed to her center.

"Good," he said. "I mean, not *good*. But better than . . ." He held her face between his hands. "Jesus, Shay, I'm so sorry."

"How was this your fault?" she whispered.

"I should've checked that the house was clear before I left you in there with a fucking intruder." Peter helped her to her feet as the first emergency vehicle arrived—sirens screaming. It was, of course, a fire truck.

He looked at her. "You called the fire department?"

Shay looked at him. But he was a smart man, and he figured it out even as she pointed at her phone, which was still lying on the lawn.

"They said, *nine-one-one,* you said *Ugh* or a variation, so the dispatcher made his best guess," Peter said as a police cruiser also pulled up.

And, of course, since the police had no idea why the emergency call had been placed and all they saw was a large man with his hands on a woman who looked like she'd just been tackled and thrown onto the front lawn, they exited their vehicle with a lot of noise and hostility.

"Sir, step away from the woman! Ma'am, are you all right?"

Peter put his hands up, and Shay did, too, because yeah, those guns were drawn.

"I'm all right," she called out in as clear a voice as possible—glad she had back at least this much ability to talk. "I'm Shayla Whitman, I live across the street. This is Navy SEAL Lieutenant Peter Greene. He lives here. We went inside his house and interrupted either a burglary or a home invasion in progress. Two men, both dressed in black, ski masks, gloves. One of them assaulted me in his haste to get away."

Crap, even though she'd played the Navy SEAL card, the two officers didn't lose their expressions of grim suspicion, and those weapons didn't get lowered.

But then a thin voice piped up. "I saw the whole thing from my window. It's true." It was Mrs. Quinn. "I even saw the two men when they first arrived. Someone dropped them off and drove away. They were riding in the back of a big black truck. They knocked on the front door, but then they went around to the back." She looked at Shayla. "You and the SEAL must've been in the garage, doing God knows what."

But Shayla ignored the elderly woman's obvious judgment and focused on the most important thing that she'd said. "A big black truck?" She looked at Peter. "Wasn't the truck, you know, with the bucket . . . ? Wasn't that also big and black?"

CHAPTER SIXTEEN

$12K NOW

The large block letters were written on the wall of Maddie's bedroom in red spray paint. The police had taken away the paint canister, but since the intruders had been wearing gloves, no one expected them to find any fingerprints.

"This can't be good," Shayla said, taking Peter's hand because if this message had shown up on Tevin's or Frank's wall, she would've wanted someone holding *her* hand.

He was silent, just looking at it.

It's very, very not good.

For the first time in a while, Harry was back.

Peter's SEAL friend Izzy was standing silently beside them. He'd shown up as the fire truck was pulling away, as Peter, Shay, and Mrs. Quinn were all giving their statements to the police.

It takes a lot to silence that one, Harry commented as he glanced at Izzy, and Shay nodded. Yeah.

Of course Izzy's current silence might've been due to the awkward fact that he'd walked right into Shayla earnestly telling both the police and Peter that she wanted to be completely honest about why they hadn't heard the two men approaching the house while they were in the garage "sorting through boxes," as Peter had reported. She appreciated his attempt to be discreet, but she was a grown woman, and there was absolutely nothing wrong with what they'd done. They weren't in public, they were in the back of the garage in essentially a separate room created by the stack of boxes and, yes, they'd been having an "intimate relationship moment."

At the time, Izzy had coughed, probably to cover a laugh, but Shay hadn't needed to look at the man to know he'd been thinking, *I knew it!*

He thought you guys were gettin' it on before you were getting it on, Harry pointed out now. *Kind of like life imitating art.*

"Not even close." And yup, she'd just said that aloud. Thanks, Hare.

"What does it mean?" Peter asked. "I mean, what *could* it mean, besides the obvious?"

"I'm not sure I know what the obvious is." Izzy finally spoke. "Aside from *prank,* which nah, I'm not buying."

The police had suggested that the entire incident was little more than a high school prank run amok. Maddie was obviously dealing with some personal issues, and had "no doubt" run into trouble at her new school.

"Those weren't kids breaking in to prank her," Peter said again. He'd said it a lot while the police were still there. "Those were men."

"Big men." Shay glanced at him. "I, um, didn't tell the police this, because it didn't seem all that relevant, but after my personal creepy assailant threatened me, I told him I was, um, an FBI agent, and that he was under arrest. Sadly, he did not comply."

Peter managed a wry smile as he looked down at her.

"Still. Nice try." He looped his arm around her shoulder to pull her in even closer.

You didn't tell the po-po because you thought maybe impersonating a federal agent might be a crime, Harry pointed out. *For the record, if you're flinging handfuls of bullshit around in order to defend yourself from physical harm, as you were in this case, it's not an issue. But say you go around telling old Mrs. What's-Her-Name that you work for the FBI, that's when your problems get real.*

Izzy was laughing, too. "Grunge, my man, your woman is a keeper."

Awkward.

"That one man," Shay said, bringing the conversation back on topic. "The first man. We saw him without his ski mask. He was not a teenager. In fact, I would bet my life on the fact that he had gray in his stubble."

But she'd made the mistake of reporting, with perhaps too much detail, that the man who'd assaulted her had lowered his body mass to hit her where it would be most effective—very much like a football linebacker. Whoever he was, he'd played football, probably in his high school glory days. But the police had taken that and gone with the theory that he played high school football *now.*

It was easy, while under stress, they'd said, to get a lot of details wrong. A flash of a face before a mask got pulled down could be deceptive. Most of the time, witness reporting was inaccurate.

"I'm a Navy SEAL," Peter had said flatly. "I'm trained to get the details right."

At that point the two police officers had exchanged a knowing glance, and Shay knew they were thinking, *But dude, you'd just had sex* in your garage *with the cougar-next-door. It was likely your brains were still scrambled.*

Damn it. She should've kept her mouth shut.

"The *obvious* is that it's an invoice," Shay said now,

pointing back to the writing on the wall. "Or more accurately, a payment due notice. And whatever it was before, it's *twelve* thousand dollars now."

"What costs twelve thousand dollars in high school?" Izzy asked. "When I was a kid, those fancy Trapper Keeper notebooks—even the *Star Wars* ones—were only twelve ninety-nine."

"Drugs," Peter said tightly.

"I don't know, man," Izzy said. "That's a lot of weed. Twelve K is more the price tag of a mafia-style hit."

Peter turned to him. "Z. Please."

"Sorry."

Unless it's not just weed, and Maddie's actually dealing, Harry said. *Cocaine, meth, ecstasy . . . These days, biggest money's in oxy.*

"The drugs thing would be easier to believe if Maddie was twenty instead of fifteen," Shayla pointed out.

"Her boyfriend is twenty," Peter said.

Oh. Yeah. Yikes.

But then Shay brightened. "And *there's* a possibility," she said. "What if this message isn't for Maddie? What if it's for Dingo? If whoever he owes this money to is having as much trouble tracking him down as we are . . . ? It makes sense that they'd reach out to him however they could—like, via his girlfriend . . . ? That fits with my black truck theory, too."

Peter hadn't thought there was any kind of a connection between the black truck that Mrs. Quinn had seen in front of his house and the black truck from whence yesterday's shit bucket had been thrown.

He still didn't buy it. "I don't know, Shay, there's a lotta black trucks in San Diego," he said. "I mean, were they following us all day yesterday? I would've seen them. No way *those* guys could suddenly be that stealthy."

Unless the shit bucket hadn't been intended—created, shall we say?—for you, Harry said. *Think about where you were.*

"We were trying to track down Dingo's friend," Shay said. "What's his name. Daryl Middleton. Hoping Daryl would lead us to Dingo. What if they were doing the exact same thing? What if that bucket was really for Daryl? Like, *Tell us where Dingo is, or next time you'll get far worse than a bucket of shit in your face!*"

"Oh," Izzy exclaimed. "Fuck!"

Shay was warming to the idea. "Because what if Dingo and Daryl are in business together? Selling weed, selling meth, selling whatever the market demands. It helps to have a girlfriend who's in high school, right? There's a big potential client base there."

"Whoa," Peter said, but she could tell from his eyes that he both liked and hated the idea.

"You guys, you guys, you guys!" Izzy was practically jumping up and down. "I came over, specifically to tell you—but it blew right out of my head with all the drama in the garage—"

"The drama was in the house," Peter corrected him in his naval officer voice.

Yeah, but the house drama's not what blew Izzy's mind, Harry noted dryly.

"Sir," Izzy responded. "Yes. Right. Sorry. But Lindsey Jenkins called. She must've called you right when, *ahem.*" He cleared his throat. "Anyway, she called me and asked me to tell you, specifically, about Dingo's friend, Daryl Middleton. He was brought into the hospital ER last night—severely beaten. He's still in ICU—unconscious, with a head injury."

"Jesus," Peter breathed.

"Lindsey said she'd call if he wakes up," Izzy added.

"When," Shayla corrected him. "*When* he wakes up."

"Right," Izzy said. "That's what I meant. I'm sure he'll be fine . . . ?"

Peter's not an idiot, Harry said. *His daughter's in serious danger. She's no longer just some troubled kid who ran away because she maybe got knocked up by her inappropriately older boyfriend. This is a whole new level of pain. It's not just a bucket of shit; it's a raging river.*

Shayla dug for her phone. "I'm texting Maddie. This has gone too far."

* * *

"Block," Maddie said as she did just that. She'd started to get a string of obnoxious texts from "Dad's" girlfriend. The woman had started with a photo—clearly some of Nelson's boys had broken in and tossed Maddie's room, and when they hadn't found the money, they'd written "$12K NOW" on her wall.

Her father must've been freaking out, but she so didn't want to hear about it, so—expecting a flood of texts from his friends—she shut her entire phone off as Dingo drove them both south and east.

Not toward Virginia, although they might as well go there as anywhere. She'd counted the money they'd taken from Fiona's room. It was just shy of four thousand, which was not enough.

"Maybe I should call him," Dingo said now, glancing over at her. "Bob Nelson. Maybe if I explained—"

"What, he's suddenly going to listen to you now?" Maddie scoffed. "Seriously, Ding, what's he gonna say? He's gonna say, *Yes, absolutely, I'll take the four thousand dollars and we'll call it even. Come on over to the garage, I'll order you a pizza and we'll all have a good laugh.* Except when we show, he'll kill us both. Bullets to the head, buried in the desert. No, thanks. Let's just get to Manzanar, so we can get some sleep before we figure out what to do next."

* * *

"She must've turned off her phone." Pete was filled with frustration as Maddie failed to respond to any of their texts. "God damn it."

"She'll turn it back on eventually," Shay told him. "She's a teenaged girl. And when she does, the first thing we want her to see is a photo of Daryl in that hospital bed. Any ideas how we can—"

Izzy stood up. "I'll go."

"Oh." Shayla looked over at Lindsey Jenkins, who was sitting on Pete's sofa rubbing her beachball of a belly, her feet up. Concerned, as always, with the details, Shay asked the former police detective, "Except . . . doesn't the hospital have rules about visitors to the ICU? Don't they have to be family members?"

"Trust in the Zanella," Lindsey said with a smile and a shrug, even as Izzy said, "I'm pretty sure he's my nephew. My sister-in-law just called, she's *so* distraught. . . ."

"Good," Pete said. "See if you can manage to still be there when he wakes up. We have a lot of questions for him."

"Aye, aye, sir."

Lindsey wasn't the only one who'd come running when Izzy had sent out a distress signal. Adam, too, was back, ready to help however he could, as were Seagull, Timebomb, and Hans from Boat Squad John. Normally, Pete would've been unhappy at the idea of welcoming SEAL candidates into the privacy of his home, but right now he was just grateful for the extra bodies and sets of eyes.

"How about I go with?" Adam said to Izzy. "Because isn't it likely that Daryl's real parents are already at the hospital? And you're good, but I don't think even *you* can sell being a surprise uncle, but—" he pointed to himself, then did jazz hands "—a surprise boyfriend? At least until Daryl wakes up."

"Oh, man," Izzy said, "if this was one of Eden's romance novels, Daryl would be gay and Tony would be in serious trouble."

"Tony's my fiancé," Adam told Shayla. "My Navy SEAL fiancé. Trust me, Tony's in no trouble at all."

But Shay had turned to Pete, a quizzical look on her face. "Does . . . Eden write romance, too?"

Izzy answered. "Write? No. Read."

"Too?" Lindsey asked Shay.

"Shayla writes romance novels," Pete told his friends.

"*What?*" Izzy said. "Really?"

Lindsey sat up. "Wait . . . you're *that* Shayla Whitman? No fucking way! I love your shit!" She winced. "Sorry, I've been hanging with SEALs for too long—that's the SpecOps version of fangrrling."

"That's okay," Shay said, laughing. "And thanks."

"When's your next book out?" Lindsey asked. "I can't wait—I'm so ready. It's been, like, more than a year!"

"Um . . ." Shayla's smile changed—very subtly. Anyone who didn't know her the way Pete did wouldn't have seen it. But she was suddenly enormously uncomfortable. Even more uncomfortable than she'd been when she'd realized that Izzy had overheard her telling the police that she and Pete had been in the garage, having sex,* when the men broke in to his house.

"Can we please get back on track?" he said, partly to save her, but mostly because Maddie was still out there. Somewhere. With her phone turned off.

"Yes, please, let's focus." Shay jumped all over his request, tossing a quick "I don't have a release date yet, sorry" to Lindsey. "We still need to contact Fiona's aunt—and her parents, too." But then she jumped literally—her phone had buzzed. She pulled it out to look at the screen, but then shook her head *no* at Pete, letting him know that it wasn't Maddie, even as she moved into the kitchen to take the call.

"How about if I reach out to Fiona's parents," Lindsey volunteered as Izzy and Adam left for the hospital. She pulled her laptop out of her bag and rested it on the arm of the sofa. "I have that list you emailed, with their phone numbers and addresses in Sacramento." He'd sent the info to her, on the off chance she'd uncover something—anything—useful. But nothing had pinged for either of Fiona's parents, or their new spouses. "I'll take the *Your daughter is probably in danger, too* approach."

"Do it," Pete said. If Fiona's parents didn't talk to Lindsey, he was flying up there and pounding on their front doors.

"Me and the guys could drive back to Van Nuys, sir," Hans Schlossman volunteered. "See if anyone's shown up at Dingler's parents' house—and stake it out, if not. I mean, *you* got hold of the address, isn't it likely that who-ever's searching for them will find it, too? And they'll go there, looking for Dingler? It's an obvious place to start."

"That's a good idea," Pete said. But. "When are you guys due back on base?"

All three of them answered in unison. "Oh-four-hundred."

Seagull added, "Tomorrow."

"So, no. Driving through LA traffic and back isn't the best use of your limited time," Pete told them. "Also, I'm gonna need some help back here. Until this is over, I want someone with Shayla twenty-four/seven."

Lindsey looked up from her computer. "Shouldn't that be your job?" She grinned at him and lowered her voice to add, "I can't believe you're dating Shayla Whitman! Her books are *hot*. Also? She's so funny and smart! Go, Grunge!"

He ignored her. "Maddie's got an elderly aunt. Hiroko. I want to bring her back here, create a safe space. Guards inside and out." He looked around. "Maybe we don't do that here—two of 'em've already been inside—whoever the fuck they are." Should the intruders return, he didn't want to give them any kind of advantage, like knowing the floor plan. "We'll set this up over at Shay's," he decided.

"Set what up?" Shay came back into the room.

"A safe space," Pete told her. "For you and Hiroko. And fuck. I'm sorry, but we should contact your ex, about Tevin and Frank. I want to make sure they're safe, too—until we find out what's going on, and who put Daryl Middleton in the hospital, and just how crazy they are."

She held up her phone. "Welp, Carter just called. He just got a gig, subbing for a player out in Phoenix, or maybe it's Tucson? Arizona, anyway. His flight leaves, like, now. Friday's a half-day, so I've got to go and pick up the boys at his place."

"Not by yourself, you're not." Pete heard the words come out of his mouth, and just as he expected, Shay gave him her WTF face. "Sorry," he added. "I meant, please let me come with you. Please."

She smiled at that extra *please* as he knew she would, but then she said, "Are you sure that's necessary?"

"Very," he said. "Also, if you're all right with it, we can swing past Hiroko's and pick her up, too."

"Hiroko," Shay said, with a laugh. "You really think you can convince her to just . . . pack a bag and come hang out with a bunch of strangers?"

"I dunno," Pete said, "maybe not, but I don't want her to get hurt, so I intend to try."

CHAPTER SEVENTEEN

Shayla drove. Her car was small, but three passengers would fit in the little backseat, as opposed to Peter's truck. Tevin's long legs would be crunched and he'd probably make some noise about that, but they wouldn't be in the car for long.

"So. This is a little awkward," she began, glancing over at Peter.

"Yeah," he said.

"Your friends think we're dating," Shay said. "But my boys haven't even met you, and I really don't want them to get the news that I'm your *girlfriend*—" she made air quotes over the top of the steering wheel "—from something someone says in passing."

He took a deep breath. "Well, we could let everyone know that we're keeping it on the down-low. . . . No . . . ?" He trailed off as she shot him a heavy *Oh, really?* look.

"Two operators outside, at least one in," she recited what she'd heard him tell Seagull, Timebomb, and Hans as she'd unlocked her house and gotten the AC running and Lindsey comfortably situated inside. "And since those three boys with the ridiculous nicknames have to report back onto the base at *oh-four-hundred*—" She heard her stress leaking out in her voice, and took a deep breath instead of asking why they couldn't just say *four A.M.* like normal people, because really, that wasn't even close to the real issue here.

Peter took her rebalancing pause as an opportunity to speak. "Those three boys are named John, Jon, and John."

Shayla nodded. "I know." She'd talked to them while Peter had been giving more last-minute instructions to Lindsey. She'd brought them into the kitchen, showed them where she kept the snacks and told them to help themselves. "But they told me you have a lot of friends who were SEALs, and no one would mind helping out by rotating in for a *watch*—I think that's what they called it. So *letting everyone know* feels like a recipe for disaster. I don't want Tevin and Frank to be hurt, or confused, or . . ."

Peter nodded. "So, we tell the boys we're dating."

"And then what?" Shay said. She also didn't want to lie to them. But what was she supposed to say? *Hey, come meet this guy I'm sleeping with that I met two days ago. It's just sex. But don't you dare do what I do. Great talk. K, thanx, bye.* "In a week or two from now, after Maddie's safely home, and they start to wonder why we don't actually go out on any dates—" She broke off. "I'm sorry. You know what? At that point, I'll just tell them we went out a few times, and then decided to just be friends." Which was the truth, if by *we went out a few times,* she meant driving to the mall searching for Maddie, and that visit to the high school office.

Peter cleared his throat. "Or . . . we could go out to dinner every now and then," he said. "In addition to our daily meetings in my garage."

Shayla laughed to cover the twisting feeling in her stomach. Dinner would mean that they'd actually be dating. She focused on the least frightening part of what he'd just said. "Oh, so we're meeting *daily* now?"

"At least," he said. "Except, I usually only go out to check the mail once a day. I suppose, in order to drop that *hello* code word more frequently, we could both develop an intense interest in yardwork."

"You, me, and Mrs. Quinn. We could start a neighborhood club."

Peter laughed as she braked to a stop at a red light. "Not *quite* what I had in mind."

She smiled at him, and he smiled back, but she could see his intense worry for Maddie in his eyes.

"I'm so sorry to be focusing on this right now," she told him softly. "I've just always tried to be honest with my children."

He reached over and took her hand. "Shayla Whitman, will you date me? Please?"

And now her heart joined her stomach in its twisty, jumping dance as she nodded her answer. She couldn't risk speaking, because she knew her voice would break.

"Good," he said, kissing her hand before he let her go. "See, easy fix."

Easy?

Not even close. Shay smiled grimly as the light turned green and she hit the gas. She'd written this storyline before. It was the same trope that Izzy and Lindsey referenced when teasing Adam about going to the hospital to pretend to be poor, beaten Daryl's significant other. It even had a name—*marriage of convenience*—despite the fact that, in these modern times, marriage usually wasn't involved.

But two characters were forced to pretend they were in a romantic relationship, and in the course of doing so, they fell hopelessly in undying love, and happy endings of all kinds—literal and euphemistic—ensued.

Except, in real life, it was likely that only *one* of them—in this case Shayla, because she was already more than half-way there—would fall hopelessly in love, and *heartache* would ensue.

And okay, that was overly dramatic and in need of revision. She might instead fall—happily—in undying lust, and mild disappointment might ensue. Yes, that was better. Also, who said *dating* had to be serious? Dating could absolutely be casual.

So stop whining, and worry instead about Maddie, Harry helpfully popped in to admonish her.

He was right. The most important thing was finding Maddie and bringing that girl safely home.

* * *

"Where is it?" Maddie looked at Dingo as he pulled off Old U.S. Highway 395. A sign announced they had reached the Manzanar National Historic Site, but . . .

"Maybe we have to drive further in," Dingo suggested.

Maddie just shook her head. The mountains in the distance looked like the photos she'd seen on Great-Aunt Hiroko's wall. But that was where the similarities ended.

Where were the rows upon rows of cabins, stretching out as far as the eye could see? There was a fence and a guard tower and signs pointing the way to the "Auditorium Interpretive Center," and "Block 14," the "Children's Village," and the "Hospital Site." Aside from that, this was just a great big scrub-filled dusty field.

The speed limit was fifteen mph, and a woman in a volunteer shirt picking up trash along the side of the road gave them the stink eye and a *slow down, you asshole* gesture, because they were apparently going too fast. Dingo not only slowed, but he stopped and even backed up, rolling down his window.

" 'Scuse me, miss," he said in his best fake Aussie. "How far is it to Manzanar?"

"You're here," she said.

"No, no," he said. "I mean, to the part with all the cabins?"

"That's just around to the right," she said, pointing. "Just past the auditorium, at Block Fourteen. We've reconstructed two of the barracks, and moved one of the original mess halls back into the camp."

"Reconstructed," Dingo echoed. "D'ya mean the rest of 'em are gone?"

"They were torn down or moved, immediately after the war," the woman said. "All that information is in the Center—in the auditorium. There's a great film, we run it every half hour. It shows what it looked like back when—"

Maddie burst into tears. She'd been holding it in ever since she'd counted the money they'd taken from Fiona's room, ever since she'd seen the picture of Nelson's spray-painted message, *$12K NOW.* And now that she was thinking about it, she realized how stupid she'd been, not only to assume that all those cabins would still be here, but that they'd be a place where she and Dingo could hide and get some desperately needed rest.

What had she expected? That they'd just drive up, and it would be deserted but preserved, like time had stood still? God, she *was* stupid, but it had just seemed so perfect, her seeking sanctuary in this place where Hiroko and her great-grandparents had been harmed.

"Her great-grandparents spent the war here," Dingo told the woman as Maddie continued to sob. "It's an emotional experience."

"Oh my God, honey, of course!"

"Is there possibly a place, maybe somewhere in the shade, where we can rest for a bit?" Dingo asked. "Maybe a . . . covered picnic area?"

"I'm afraid there's not. We've got picnic tables near the

main parking lot, but they're out in the open," the woman told him.

Dingo nodded. "Thanks so much, that'll do. Excuse us, please."

"Of course! Oh my God! Let me know if you need anything!"

He put the car back into drive and rolled his window back up.

"I'm sorry," Maddie said. "I fucking hate it when I cry." But she still couldn't stop.

"Well, love, it's not like we're both not exhausted," he pointed out.

"We can't stay here," Maddie said. "What if my father calls, *Hello have you seen a really stupid half-Japanese girl and her douchebag fake Australian boyfriend?*" She answered her own question, *"Why yes, as a matter of fact, they completely caught our attention when the really stupid girl burst into tears."*

"A) I'm not your boyfriend," Dingo said as he pulled into the nearly empty lot, and parked over by a set of very sad-looking picnic tables. "And B) even if he calls, he's in San Diego, which is like, a million hours away from here. So I think we have time to stop for a bit and figure out *what the fuck.*"

She looked at him. "But that's just it. I keep thinking, *What are we gonna do now?* and I come up completely blank. Because we die, Ding. That's what we do. Nelson catches up to us, and we die."

Dingo broke his stupid rule and pulled her in for a hug.

Maddie closed her eyes, because even this—his arms around her—didn't make it better.

"I don't want to die," she whispered.

"Well, good," he said, kissing the top of her head. "That's an excellent place to start when figuring out our Plan B."

* * *

Shayla's ex lived in a neighborhood similar to hers and Pete's, but on the other side of town. This street was slightly busier, though, with a heavier flow of regularly passing traffic.

Still, the first thing Pete saw when Shayla pulled up in front of her ex-husband's house was a little car in the driveway with *$12K* spray-painted in red on the back window.

"Oh, my God! That's Tiffany's Honda!" Shay said.

Pete was out of the car and running toward the house before she'd finished parking.

She was right behind him, though, running up the lawn as he hammered on the front door.

A tall, skinny, teenaged kid—had to be Tevin, he looked a lot like Shay—opened it, his brown eyes wide behind a pair of yellow plastic-framed glasses. He was dressed like he'd stepped from the pages of a magazine. Everything about him from his closely cropped haircut to his sneakers to those glasses screamed high fashion.

"Tevin, thank God!" Shay called as she saw him.

"Is everyone all right in there?" Pete asked.

"Yes . . . ? Hi . . . ?"

The kid might've just been reacting in surprise to their urgency, but Pete needed to be sure his questioning tone was meant to be irony instead of some kind of code. "Are you alone in the house—you and Frank?"

"Tevin, where's Frankie?" Shay breathlessly asked as she joined Pete on the stoop.

The kid pointed over his shoulder with his thumb. "He's doing his homework in the dining room." He looked back at Pete. "Are we alone? No, Tiff's still home. She was going to some meeting in San Jose, but it got canceled, whoa, hey!" He laughed as Shayla hugged him, but then released him to go into the house.

"Tiff!" she called. "Tiffany?"

"Hey, Shay! I'm in the kitchen!" a female voice sang out as Tevin stepped back to let Pete in, too.

"I'm Tevin," the boy said, holding out his hand in greeting as Shay disappeared into the back of the house. "You're the SEAL from across the street. I mean, not this street, but . . ."

"Yeah. I'm Pete. Nice to meet you."

They shook hands—Tevin had long, strong fingers and a very solid grip. He also met Pete's gaze unabashedly, which was something that many SEAL candidates had trouble doing, and most of them were in their twenties.

"So, *that* was kinda weird," Tevin remarked with a smile.

"Yeah," Pete said as Shay and a young woman came toward them from the kitchen, with Frank—smaller and far less fashion-conscious, with those same big brown eyes—trailing behind them. "Brace yourself. It's about to get a whole lot weirder."

* * *

Tiffany had been home all day.

The boys had taken the bus from school. Fridays were half-days this session, and classes ended around noon. But they'd stopped for ice cream on their way back to Carter's. Neither one of them had noticed the vandalized car when they'd arrived around 1:00 P.M.

And while it was entirely possibly for Frank to walk right past something shocking without noticing it, Shay knew there was no way Tevin would've *not* seen this.

So whoever had spray-painted that message onto Tiffany's back windshield—*Two men dressed in black with ski masks and gloves for $500, Alex*—had done it some time between 1:00 and 2:30, when Shayla and Pete arrived.

They all stood out on Carter's front lawn, just gazing at

the car. Tiff was *pissed*. As always, her weave was perfect and her makeup was meticulously done. She was dressed in her trademark skintight pants, heels, and mega-cleavage. It really didn't matter what color or style her top was—Tiff's outfits always featured the copious square feet of satiny smooth brown skin from her graceful neck and throat to the tops of her perfect double-D breasts. If Shayla tried to wear a shirt that low cut, she'd live in constant fear of costume malfunction, yet she'd been with Tiffany while the woman danced and jumped and even lugged groceries in from the car, and not once had she witnessed a nip slip.

"This car is six months old," Tiffany said. "Six! Months!"

"I'm so sorry," Peter said, not for the first time.

Tiff turned her annoyance toward him. "Did you do it, Lieutenant? No, you did not. So stop apologizing!"

Shayla turned to Pete, too, and found him watching her, which was nice because most men tended to be unable to look away from Tiffany. "We might've just missed them. Do you want to take my car and drive around the neighborhood, see if they're still in the area—maybe in a big black truck?"

Peter shook his head. "I'm not leaving you here without protection." He reached out to pull something from her hair—yup, it was a piece of mulch from his front flower bed.

Point taken. She turned back to Tiffany. "Come with us. It scares me that they knew this address. That they knew you and Carter are connected to me, and that I'm connected to Peter and . . . We're going to have round-the-clock guards back at my house—Navy SEALs. So please, stay with us, at least until Carter gets home."

Tiffany looked at her car, and then back at Shayla, her brown eyes narrowing. "Navy SEALs?"

Shay nodded. And Tiff went inside to pack a bag.

* * *

Tevin was friendly despite their weird introduction, but Shay's youngest son, Frank, was not happy at the news that, over the course of just a few days, his mother had started dating Pete.

"So, Pete, your daughter's a hot mess," the kid said as Pete unlocked the trunk of Shay's car, so the two boys could load in their backpacks.

Shay was standing a few yards away, still waiting for Tiffany to come out of the house and exchanging texts with Izzy. He'd sent a couple of really awful photos of Daryl Middleton—his face bruised and stitched and swollen as he lay, still unconscious, in that hospital bed. She'd already emailed them to Maddie, and gotten Lindsey to text them, too, in hopes that the girl would turn her phone back on sooner rather than later.

"Well, I think it's fair to be a mess when your mother dies in a car accident," Pete told Frank.

"Yeah, well, if my mom died, I sure as shit wouldn't start selling drugs."

"Language." Tevin policed his little brother.

"We don't know that Maddie's the one selling the drugs," Pete said evenly.

"Well, I wouldn't have a boyfriend or a girlfriend or even just a friend who sells drugs," Frank insisted.

"You have no idea what you would or wouldn't do if Mom died," Tevin chastised his brother. "Don't be so judgmental."

"We don't even know that it's drugs that's behind these threats," Pete said. "We're making an assumption."

Frank veered into new hostile territory. "So when did you and Maddie's mom get divorced?" he asked.

"We split when Maddie was a baby. Her mom and I

weren't married," Pete said. "I asked, but . . . She didn't want to marry me."

"Why, because you're, like, a serial killer?"

"Frank," Tevin said. He rolled his eyes at Pete. "Sorry. Frankie's in a douchey mood. He had a hot date with Dad's flatscreen TV. Tiffany lets him watch *Game of Thrones,* and Mom doesn't."

Boom.

Fuck, was that a gunshot?

Peter sharply looked up and a truck—black, big—was at the end of the street, moving in their direction at much too fast a clip.

"Get down!" he shouted and the two boys, no doubt well trained by life in this sorry world of potential school shooters—immediately sheltered behind their mother's car.

But Shay was still standing in the middle of the yard, her phone in her hands. She was caught up in her task and oblivious, and Pete ran toward her—it was possible he'd never moved faster in his entire life. He threw himself forward just as the vehicle went past, putting his body between her and whoever was in that truck, as he grabbed her and shielded her, and took her with him down to the ground.

Boom.

And this time, he heard it for what it was—an engine backfire. And as he turned to look, he saw that yeah, the truck that had passed *was* big and black, but it was far older, with sharper angles and an ancient, obviously shittier engine, than the truck he'd seen, and the truck Mrs. Quinn had described to the police.

"Oh, my God, Peter!" For the second time in just a few hours—the third time in two days—Shay'd been knocked off her feet.

This time, though, Pete hadn't tried to do what he'd done on that sidewalk outside Daryl Middleton's old apartment, and land between her and the ground. This time he'd landed on top of her, intentionally, to protect her from an active shooter.

She still hadn't realized that the noises they'd heard were from a malfunctioning engine, and now she feared he'd been hit and wounded. Probably because he was lying there motionless, like a fool. She scrambled out from beneath him—it was possible he was more stunned than she was—checking for blood even as she called out to her sons. "Tevin, Frank, are you okay?"

"Yeah, we're good, are you?" Tevin asked as Frank squeaked, "Mommy!"

"I'm okay, baby," she called back.

Frank's fear turned to anger. "What the hell was that?"

"Don't be dead," Shay muttered as she tried to roll Pete over. "Please, please, please, don't be dead."

"I'm not, I'm not." Pete sat up and caught her hands, "I'm okay. Jesus, I'm so sorry." He called to the boys, "Sorry, guys, false alarm. I'm a little on edge. The men we've been dealing with have a black truck. I saw that one, it backfired, and I should've known what the noise was, but I just re-acted. Overreacted."

"You scared me to death!" Shayla kissed him, and as he kissed her back, he heard Tevin say, "Whoa!"

Frank started to say something, but it was possible Tevin had clapped a hand over the younger boy's mouth.

But right now was definitely not the right time for Pete to kiss Shayla the way he really wanted to, so instead he pulled back and looked into her eyes. "I'm okay," he confirmed. "You okay?"

Shay nodded and exhaled hard. "It's been a really intense few days," she told her sons as Pete helped her back to her feet. "Which is why we're going to do this whole safe house thing. Spend the weekend with our heads down, just watch-ing movies, all right?"

"Yes, ma'am," Tevin said. He gave her a hug.

Meanwhile, Frank was still looking hard at Pete. "You thought that whoever was in that truck was gonna shoot Mom."

"I did," he admitted. "I got scared. I should've known that sound was just a backfire, but—"

"If they *had* been shooting, you'd be dead," Frank pointed out. "Doing what you did? Running toward her like that?"

"Maybe, but your mother would be alive."

"So, you're saying you'd die for her? I mean, you're not saying it—you *did* it, and everyone's always telling me that actions speak louder than words. It was like you're her secret service agent, or her bodyguard. You were ready to die for her."

"Frank," Shay said.

"No, it's okay," Pete said. He looked at Frank. "You got a problem with that?"

"Shit, no!" Frank said.

"Language," Shay said on a sigh.

He glanced at her. "Sorry, ma'am." Back to Pete: "I'm just trying to figure it out. You're ready to die for her, and you're all kissing-her-on-the-front-lawn, but you just met her."

"Yeah," Pete said. "But, look at her. She's pretty fucking great." He glanced at Shayla. "Sorry, ma'am." Back to Frank: "I mean, you and Tevin both know that."

Frank was finally smiling and he now held out his hand. "Pete," he said. "I do believe this is the start of a beautiful friendship."

As they shook hands, Shayla said, "Pete? I think you might want to call him *Lieutenant Greene*."

Frank turned his smile onto his mother and shrugged expansively. "He told us to call him *Pete*. I gotta do what the man says."

"Someone please help me with this bag." Tiffany had finally emerged from the house, oblivious to the drama as she locked the door behind her. Tevin leapt to get her luggage and wrestle it to the car. "It's all files from work plus my laptop. Project's due on Monday." She smiled at Shay. "I can borrow clothes, if I need 'em, right?"

"Frankie's more your size," Shay said diplomatically, "but sure. Clothes yes, computer *never*."

"See, I knew that," Tiffany said.

Meanwhile, Frank had turned back to Pete. "So what was it? Like, love at first sight?"

"Oh, my God, *Frankie*," Shayla said. She actually clapped her hands at her son, as if he were a misbehaving puppy. Pete tried not to laugh. "Just get in the car! *Everyone* into the car! Now!"

"It's really okay," Pete told her as they all climbed in. He turned to look back at Frank. "More like at first conversation. Don't get me wrong. Your mother's beautiful, but . . . That brain, that amazing mind inside of her brilliant head . . . *That's* what you look for in a woman." He glanced at Tevin. "In a person."

"That is *so* sweet!" Tiffany enthused as Shayla pulled out into the traffic. "You are so sweet!"

"Nope," he said. "Just observant. And very lucky."

"Can we focus here, *Pete*?" Shayla shot him a hard look, clearly uncomfortable with this conversation, her fingers tight on her steering wheel. "Since Izzy got those photos— the money shots of Daryl—that we sent to Maddie, he figured it was okay to leave Adam alone at the hospital. He thought it was a waste of person-power to have them both sitting there, waiting for Daryl to wake up. He wanted to know what was next on your to-do list, so I asked him— Izzy—to pick up Hiroko. Will you please give her a call to tell her he's coming?"

Pete nodded as he got out his phone. "Thank you, that's . . . You'd make a great senior chief."

"I don't know what that means," Shay said, "but I'm going to pretend it's a good thing."

"Trust me, it is," he said, and dialed Hiroko.

* * *

Hiroko Nakamura lived in the home of Izzy's dreams.

The house itself was nothing special, but location, location, location! The ocean was *right* there.

Eden sometimes claimed that Izzy would live in an underwater house if he could, and maybe that was true, but if he did, he'd miss the beauty of the above-water environs. The sea and the sky, and the sound of the constantly moving surf . . . Underwater, everything was muted and in slow motion. Most of the time. Sometimes, the Pacific could be a deadly monster, and that underwater house would have to be built pretty deep beneath the surface to avoid the churning and turmoil.

Izzy went up the front path, but he didn't need to ring the doorbell. The door opened before he hit the front stoop.

Ms. Nakamura was diminutive in size, but the glare she gave him was gigantic.

He deflected it with a smile. "I'm Izzy Zanella," he said.

"I know who you are," she said. "You wasted a trip. I'm not going with you." And she shut the door in his face.

Ho-kay. He knocked—ringing a bell just wasn't his thing—and he kept knocking until she opened the door again.

"What?"

"Grunge—Peter—said you have some really rockin' pictures from Manzanar," Izzy told her. "Won't be a wasted trip if you'll let me take a look."

"You just want to get inside, so you can talk me into coming with you."

Izzy nodded. "Yup. But I'd rather do it while looking at

photos of something I'm deeply interested in, instead of shouting through a closed door."

She *hmph*ed at him, but she didn't shut the door.

He waited.

She did, too. She just stood there with that glare on heavy stun, trying to psych him out—make him speak or turn away.

But he had older brothers. There was no psych-out game on this planet that Izzy could not win. So he settled in for the duration, pasting his blandest smile on his face.

And sure enough, she cracked. "Why are *you* interested in Manzanar?"

"Well, there's a lot of reasons, maybe the top one is *Because I'm an American . . . ?*" He thought about it. "Yeah. That's right. The forced internment of American citizens during World War Two is a stinking stain of dog crap on our history as a nation, and it's important that we don't erase it. I was eleven when I first found out about it, and I read everything I could get my hands on—even talked my brother and his wife into going on a roadtrip to Manzanar and Tule Lake, too. They had one of those pop-up campers."

Hiroko did her silent stare-down thing again, and again, Izzy just waited.

She finally opened the door wider, and gestured for him to come in.

Twenty minutes later, he was carrying her bag as he walked her out to his truck. Because after he'd looked at her photos, he'd shown her his.

And that close-up of Daryl Middleton in his ICU hospital bed did the trick.

"I'm going to hate this," Hiroko told him, as he pulled away from her house.

"Probably," he agreed. "But maybe not. Shayla's got it going on."

"Hmph," she said, but the tone was slightly different, so he decided to interpret it as *Hmph, I agree.*

The drive to Shay's was going to take about twenty minutes, and he resisted the urge to suggest they sing their favorite show tunes, and instead opted to ride in what he chose to believe was a mutually respectful silence.

CHAPTER EIGHTEEN

As Shayla stood in the middle of her kitchen with activity swirling around her, she realized that she was never going to be alone with Peter again.

Well, at least not until they found Maddie, and whatever danger the girl was in was finally over.

Hugely pregnant Lindsey Jenkins was parked on Shay's sofa in the living room, trying to track down a cop friend who had a lawyer friend who knew Fiona's aunt Susan. Apparently, Fiona's parents weren't picking up, and hadn't returned the messages that Lindsey'd left. And Susan still wasn't in her law office. Lindsey was hoping her friend of a friend might help.

Peter was "walking the perimeter" with Timebomb and Hans, while the young man named Seagull was at the kitchen table, attempting to create a schedule for guard duty from a long list of volunteers, taking into account the various times each person was available.

Tiffany, Frank, and Tevin were attempting to help, but probably making life significantly harder for the SEAL candidate. Particularly Tiff, who was leaning over from across the table to check the list of names every chance she got.

Poor Seagull was going to have an aneurysm from all that boobage in his face.

Hiroko sat at the other end of the table, her own laptop open in front of her, arms crossed, earbuds in. Shay had no idea what the elderly woman was watching, but she didn't want to get too close and find out for sure. This way, Shay could at least conjure up a small smile as she pretended that it was porn.

Izzy had dropped Hiroko and dashed back to Van Nuys—if one could call a two-and-a-half-hour drive a *dash,* especially since he was heading directly into the Los Angeles Hellmouth of terrible afternoon traffic. But he'd gone willingly and cheerfully to stake out the Dinglers' house, in case Dingo and Maddie—or the bad men chasing them—showed up.

Izzy was, without a doubt, one of Peter's very best friends.

Although, glancing at that long list of SEALs and former military personnel willing to volunteer their time to help keep them safe . . .

Peter had a lot of very good friends.

He came into the house through the kitchen door, filling up the room as only he could. It was funny how that happened. Izzy was taller and broader than Peter. Both Hans and Timebomb were, too. But when Peter walked in . . .

He smiled at her, and the room got even smaller.

"Hello." Shay put almost no voice to the word, but he heard her.

The flare of heat in his eyes was proof of that, but it was accompanied by disbelief as he glanced over at the crowded kitchen table before giving her a *Seriously?* look. She also could see that he was actually doing the math equation in his head. If they snuck out now to rendezvous in his garage, could they be back inside before anyone even knew they were missing . . . ?

But then, as he realized she had been only kidding, Shay could see his amusement and chagrin, along with that ever-present slow burn.

"Sorry," she murmured, at a level for his ears only. "I couldn't resist. We'll have to somehow stay strong."

Peter laughed as he moved in to put his arms around her, and everyone at the table looked up and over. At them.

So he backed up and pointed to the door instead. "I have, um, a, uh . . . question about the fence," he said loudly. "If you don't mind stepping outside . . . ?"

Shay followed him out into the backyard. "You know, that fooled no one."

"Yeah," he said, finally pulling her in for that embrace. She wrapped her arms around his waist and enjoyed the feel of him, solid against her. "I'm sorry about before."

"That's okay," she said. *Was it love at first sight?* "You kind of had to, you know, say what you said. I mean, Frankie was in your face."

Peter pulled back to look down at her. "I was talking about tackling you."

"Oh," she said. Oops. "Well, I'd tell you that you can make it up to me by kissing my scrapes and bruises, but that's not going to happen with our current cast of thousands."

Peter smiled. "Safety over sex."

"Is that, like, another Navy SEAL slogan?" she asked.

He laughed and then kissed her. Briefly. Sweetly. "You know, sadly, it might be."

And now they were both smiling at each other.

He came back to earth first. "Any word from Adam?" he asked.

Shayla checked her phone, pulling it from her pocket. Adam was still at the hospital, with Daryl. "Just that *No change* text that I told you about. It's only been ten minutes."

Peter sighed. "Sorry. Still nothing from Maddie?"

"Not yet. She'll contact us. I know it. Just give her time."

He nodded.

"You know, your friends are amazing," Shayla told him.

"Teammates," he corrected her.

Did he honestly think . . . ? "Lindsey's not a teammate."

"She's a teammate by marriage," Peter said. "And yeah, everyone's really stepping up. They *are* great. And speaking of the Team, I'm sorry, but I have to go over to the base. I won't be long, but I really need to do a face-to-face with my CO. Are you gonna be okay here?"

"You know it," she said. "If trouble shows up, Hiroko will kick everyone's ass."

He laughed and kissed her again. "With her sidekick, Tiffany."

Shayla laughed, too. "We're good here. We're safe. We're in extra-safety mode. You know how I know?"

"Oh, yeah." He nodded, his eyes doing that sparkling thing she'd loved right from the start. "Because no one's getting any."

"That's right. Safety over sex. Hoo-yah! Isn't that also what you SEALs say?"

"Hoo-yah," he agreed as he followed Shay back inside. "Yeah. But generally not about . . . that."

* * *

Dingo had put his foam mattress under the picnic table so that Maddie could curl up there, in the improvised shade, in the otherwise relentlessly barren Manzanar National Historic Site parking lot—and she'd fallen fast asleep.

He sat in the passenger seat of his car with all the doors opened wide, and he watched her for a while. People generally looked younger while they slept, and she was not an exception to that rule.

She looked maybe twelve.

Which wasn't that much younger than the fifteen that she really was. And yeah, yeah, Juliet was fourteen or whatever, but back in Shakespeare's day, thirty was considered old age. Also, Romeo wasn't twenty.

Or a loser whose parents had kicked him out.

He reached for her phone—she'd shut it off and stashed it in the cupholder—and as he watched her gently breathing, he turned it on.

He knew her screen lock code—4242—not that she'd shared it, but she certainly hadn't tried to hide it from him, either. And as the phone powered up, he both silenced it and covered it. He had no intention of looking through her personal messages—she'd gotten about a billion texts since she'd shut the thing off. He had one goal here: open up a line of communication to Maddie's dad.

He sent a text. Not to her father, but to her father's girlfriend. Shayla. *Can we set up a time and place to meet and talk? Not just dad, but you, too?*

He didn't know Maddie's dad aside from that one encounter in the mall garage, but his own father was way less of a douche when his mother was around. Having Shayla present could well make it easier for Maddie. At least he hoped so. He pushed *send,* and the text whooshed away.

The response came back almost immediately.

Yes! Say when and where, and we'll be there!

Dingo looked at Maddie, still sound asleep beneath that table, and he almost typed *Now, in Manzanar,* but he wasn't quite ready to betray her that absolutely. And she *would* see this as a betrayal.

So instead he input both the number for *Shayla* and the number for *"Dad"* into his own phone. Just in case, after getting some rest, Maddie failed to recognize that the time had come for a full surrender.

And then he typed, *Too tired to talk right now. Will text tomorrow w location. Still safe.*

After he hit *send*, he turned Maddie's phone off and put it back into the cupholder. Then he, too, closed his eyes and fell asleep.

* * *

Pete's meeting at the base went about as well as could be expected, considering he'd been informing his CO that he was considering resigning his commission. Maddie needed her father, and this temporary leave he'd arranged was almost up.

Commander Koehl had immediately offered to extend it. The Navy didn't want to lose Pete.

Likewise, Pete didn't want to lose the Navy. But if he *was* going to quit, he didn't want it to be a surprise to anyone on the Teams.

For now, he gratefully took the extension, but he also took an envelope of paperwork—forms to fill out—should he need to resign, God help him.

He pulled his truck into his own driveway, tucked the envelope into the pocket on the door, gathered up his cover and—clicking his truck locked—headed across the street to Shayla's house.

The windows were open—it was a beautiful afternoon. Pete stopped for a moment, just absorbing the sounds of life—music and laughter—spilling out of Shay's little house. Food was cooking. Whatever it was, it smelled delicious.

Someone was singing some top-forty pop song. Had to be Frank, and maybe Tevin, and . . . Hiroko?

Holy shit, Hiroko was singing a Katy Perry song, along with . . . Wait. Was that Mrs. Quinn . . . ?

But before Pete could laugh at the absurdity, the thought popped into his head: *Maybe she was lonely, too.*

Lonely. Too. As in, *also* lonely. As in, how absolutely different would it be for him to come home to *this* every day, instead of a cold, empty room in the officers' barracks?

A cheer went up from inside, along with whooping and scattered applause. And yes, that was definitely Mrs. Quinn saying, "More turmeric, dear! I can barely taste it."

And then he thought, how abso-fucking-lutely different would it feel to *Maddie* to come home to this every day, instead of a cold, empty house with a still-angry, too-lonely man sitting grimly in the silent kitchen?

"Jesus," he said.

"You okay there, sir?"

Pete looked up to see Hans Schlossman up on the roof, standing guard near the fireplace chimney, where he could see both the front yard and the back.

"Yeah," he told the kid, forcing a smile. "It's just been a long coupla days. I appreciate your willingness to spend your downtime here, Schlossman. Especially since I know that *you* know it's not going to get you any kind of preferential treatment. In fact, I'm gonna have to tell Lieutenant MacInnough to challenge Boat Squad John extra aggressively in the next phase, to make sure there's no appearance of impropriety."

"Sir, yes, sir," Schlossman said dryly. "Can't wait, sir." But then he realized what Pete had said. "Lieutenant MacInnough? Wait, where are *you* gonna be?" He quickly added, "Sir?"

But Pete's cellphone was buzzing in the pocket of his uniform pants, and he held up a finger to Schlossman as he pulled it out. It was Shayla. "Hey," he said.

"Hey!" she said.

And for a second, with his eyes closed, he was buried deep inside of her as she shattered around him, and Jesus, in just a few short days he'd become completely addicted.

"Where are you?" she asked, excitement in her voice, bringing him back to here and now. "Are you still at the Navy Base? Are you in your truck? Are you—"

"I'm back. I'm actually standing in your front yard."

Shay's needs took priority over breaking the news to Schlossman that Pete would probably not be further involved in the rest of Boat Squad John's BUD/S training, so he headed for the front door.

But she beat him to it, bursting her way outside, the screen door slapping closed behind her, before she even hung up her phone.

"She texted!" Shayla told him as she danced down the front steps. "Peter, Maddie texted me! She wants to meet; she wants to talk!"

"Oh, thank God!"

"But not until tomorrow," Shay said, "except Lindsey made contact with Fiona's mother, and well, I'm pretty sure I know where they are. Maddie and Dingo. And I think we should go there. I don't think we should wait until morning."

Pete looked over at the house—the windows were filled with watching faces. Tevin. Frank. Hiroko. Tiffany. Seagull and Timebomb. And yeah, even Mrs. Quinn. The only one missing was Lindsey, who probably hadn't been able to push herself up and off of the couch.

"Where are they?" he asked Shay, but it was the crowd in the house who answered in unison.

"Manzanar!"

* * *

Shay brought Peter into her bedroom.

Oh, honey, if only . . .

"Shh."

"Hey, good, you're back!" Lindsey was sitting up, supported by pillows, on Shay's bed. Shay had moved her in here after it got too noisy in the living room. She'd needed a door that closed as she'd talked on the phone, and a seat more comfortable than the desk chair in Shay's home office. So the bedroom it was.

He likes it in here.

And yeah, Shay was hyper-aware that Peter was in her room for the first time, and as she looked around she saw it as he did—with its bright white-painted furniture and soothing blue walls. Mexican tile floor. King-sized bed. Private bath. Super comfy reading chair that was big enough for two. Provided the two liked each other significantly.

"Fiona's mother finally called you?" Peter asked.

"I called her," Lindsey said. "After I saw the police report." At Peter's obvious confusion, she looked at Shay.

"He just got here," Shayla told the woman. "All he knows is that I think Maddie's at Manzanar."

"Okay, Lieutenant," Lindsey said as she looked up at Peter. "Full sit-rep. Right after you left for your meeting in Coronado, I ran another search through the system and discovered that the police in Sacramento just posted a B&E report for Fiona's mother's address. It happened this morning. The two perps: one male and one female. The homeowner—Maisy Clark, aka Fiona's mom—described the intruders as a scruffy man, thin, average height, white, in his early twenties, and a teenage girl, petite, of Asian descent. So definitely Maddie and Dingo. They also knocked on the mother's door this morning, looking for Fiona, who apparently has been—and I quote—*sent away to boarding school.* Later, the mom went out, but came home to find the same two had gained entry via a house key and were fleeing the premises."

"Was anything stolen?" Peter asked.

"Not that the mother knows of, no," Lindsey said. "But several books had been moved in Fiona's room, and one of them had the inside pages cut out. You know, a stash-hole."

"Fuck," Peter said.

"So, I called the mom again, and left a message telling her I was a private investigator working on a runaway teen case, which is not untrue, and that her description of the girl who broke and entered was similar to the girl I was looking for, and could we please talk?" Lindsey nodded at Pete. "She finally called me back. She's actually really nice, but definitely exhausted both by her bullshit ex-husband and her drug-addicted—her words—daughter. I sent her a photo of both Maddie and Ricky Dingler—aka Dingo—and she gave me a positive ID. Maddie and Dingo were in Sacramento this morning."

"They must've driven all night," Shay murmured to Peter. "After the earthquake."

Lindsey nodded. "Shay told me that you guys got a text from Maddie right after last night's quake—which means they had to be close enough to San Diego to have felt it. But they were definitely in Sacramento at ten A.M." She smiled at Peter. "Ten hundred hours for the SEALs in the room."

Peter was already processing the information he'd received. "So Fiona's already off at some boarding school. Do we know where? And isn't it likely Maddie and Dingo would go there, to get whatever it is that they think she has?"

"Longfield Academy in Roanoke, Virginia," Shayla told him. "It's a lockdown facility—really more of a rehab center than a school."

"It's for rich kids with addictions." Lindsey put it more bluntly. "I called their head of security and asked them to watch for Maddie and Dingo. She promised to give me a call if they show."

"But we don't think they're going to Virginia," Shay said. "We think they know that they've gotten everything they're going to from Fiona."

"Her mom told me that she and her husband found drugs in their house. She believes Fiona brought them with her, from San Diego," Lindsey reported. "The mom wasn't helpful when it came to what kind of drugs, or quantity. She was really freaked out when she found them, and she just flushed them all. So it's hard to say if there were twelve thousand dollars' worth. Or eleven or ten or whatever the value was before the interest rate went up."

"What do we think was in the cut-out pages of the book?" Peter asked.

"Not drugs," Lindsey said. "Mrs. Clark told me that her husband—not her ex, her current husband—was so freaked out by Fiona that he hired a drug-sniffing dog. That's how they found the drugs. They were hidden in his den. The dog was completely uninterested in Fiona's bedroom."

"So, money?" Peter asked.

"Or an address book with the names and numbers of high-level U.S. Navy admirals who regularly hired Fiona as a hooker," Shayla suggested.

Lindsey looked at her. "Your brain is a wonderfully dark and scary place."

Peter turned to her, too. "So why, exactly, do you think they're in Manzanar?"

Shayla shrugged. "To start with, it's not *that* far from Sacramento—I mean, considering the size of California— and . . . well . . . bottom line, Maddie told Hiroko that she wanted to go there. It's possible that some of what she's said is the truth. I've seen the pictures, and *I'm* fascinated— and horrified and intrigued. If I were Maddie, I'd want to see it and . . . smell it, you know? Feel it. Really know where I came from—or maybe more important, where Maddie's mother came from, since she was raised by people who'd been unjustly imprisoned there. Lisa's gone, but there's still a little piece of her—an echo of a moan, a wisp of a lingering sigh—in the dust of Manzanar."

"Does she talk this way all the time?" Lindsey asked Peter. "God, I love writers."

Peter glanced at his watch, and Shay knew he was calculating the time it would take them to get to Manzanar. Three-hundred-ish miles, should take five and a half hours, plus traffic. . . . If they left immediately, with a little luck, they'd arrive well before midnight. He nodded. "All right. You sold me. I'm going up there."

"I'm going, too," Shayla said.

"Not a chance," Peter said. "You're safest right here."

Her response was to hold out her phone and show him the text that Maddie had sent. *Can we set up a time and place to meet and talk? Not just dad, but you, too?*

"She wants me there. I'll be perfectly safe," Shayla said. "I'll be with you."

Peter looked into her eyes and whatever he saw there made him nod. "Let's do it," he said. "Let's go."

"Don't go into labor while we're gone," Shayla ordered Lindsey, who laughed.

"Okay, you just pretty much guaranteed that I'm having this baby tonight," Lindsey called after her. "Thank you!"

But Shay was already out of the room, quickly packing her laptop and her power cord in her computer case. "Boys!" she called to Tevin and Frank. "Pete and I are heading to Manzanar. Tiffany and Lindsey and Hiroko are in charge! Do not leave this house! Be good; I love you!"

They sang their response in their trademark tight harmony, "Love you, love you, love you, too!"

Everyone laughed, but both boys hugged her extra tightly, and Frank looked hard at Peter, saying, "You promise she'll be safe . . . ?"

"I do," Peter said solemnly as he took Shayla by the hand and pulled her out the door.

CHAPTER NINETEEN

Shayla opened her computer as the freeway whizzed beneath the wheels of Pete's truck. "Let's send Maddie Chapter Four."

"Um," he said. "Don't we have to write it first?"

"Write, then send," she agreed. "We're gonna be in this truck for hours, and we don't have anything else to do, unless we can figure out a way to have sex while you drive—"

"I could definitely do that."

"—without getting arrested," she pointed out.

"*That's* a little more difficult."

"Right. So. Chapter Four."

Pete sighed. "There's really not a Chapter Four. I mean, not that I necessarily want to share with Maddie. Life with Lisa was a roller coaster. She struggled with fidelity and a need for immediate gratification. I'm also pretty sure she used sex with strangers as a way to measure her self-worth."

"They want me, therefore I have value," Shay murmured. "I'm so sorry."

"It was what it was. And I'm the fool who kept taking her back. I should've walked away the first time it happened."

Shayla's eyes were soft. "You loved her—enough to forgive her. That doesn't make you a fool."

"Doesn't it?" He focused on the road, stretching out ahead of them. "It happened a lot. I'm not talking twice or three times. I'm talking fingers on both hands."

She winced. "Ouch."

"She was always sorry," Pete said. "Except for the last time. It was after Maddie. And man, that year—when Lisa was pregnant, and right after Maddie was born—it was the best, and the worst. I was scared to death. We were both so young—how were we going to take care of a baby? But then, Jesus, Maddie was this tiny little thing, and we both fell completely in love with her, and for a while it was better than it ever was. Except for the part where the only work I could find was part-time and minimum wage. I had three different jobs, I worked all the time, and I still couldn't pay the bills.

"So I told Lisa I was thinking about enlisting in the Navy—not just for the paycheck, but for the health insurance. I tried to talk about it, but she said, *Do what you have to do,* which turned out to be code for *Don't you dare join the Navy,* but I was too stupid to recognize it. In the end, she accused me of running away when, Jesus, that was the last thing I wanted. I thought I was making this huge sacrifice to feed them and put a roof over their heads.

"It was when I was gone—at sea—that she replaced me. I think I probably knew. . . . My seabag got drenched right after I showed up for duty, and my photos of Lisa and Maddie were destroyed. This was before digital photos. I didn't even have a cellphone back then. I emailed her and asked her to send me hard-copy replacements, but she never did. I just kept waiting, but . . .

"All those other guys had been collisions. One and done. This was different, his name was George, and even though she didn't leave me for him—they'd already split by the time I came back home—I think it made her realize just how much she didn't need me. Or want me.

"That day she left? It's burned into my brain. We were shouting at each other, and Maddie was crying. And Lisa just kept saying it was my fault, that not only was I terrible at communicating, but that I obviously didn't want a family—if I did, I wouldn't've joined the Navy, and I'd be better off without them, and they'd be better off without me. I remember she called me hard, *cold,* because I didn't seem to care who she slept with—was she fucking kidding me? But she was serious. She called me *heartless.* And all I could think was *heartless, yes,* because she took my heart with her when she walked out that door."

Shay's fingers had been moving across her computer keyboard while he'd been talking, and as he fell silent, that was the only sound in the truck's cab.

Miles passed beneath the wheels as she clicked and tapped and backspaced and rearranged.

Finally, she glanced up. "First off, Lisa was crazy. And probably seriously clinically mentally ill, along with being full-on stupid. I don't know *what* she was talking about because you're an expert-level communicator. You know that, right? That she was flat-out making shit up, probably to make herself feel better about leaving . . . ? Also, you have the biggest, warmest, *kindest* heart of any man I've ever met."

Then why don't you want to be more than fuck buddies with me? Things not to say at the one-hour mark of a five-plus-hour drive.

Shay took his silence as the expert-level evasion of honest communication that it was, saying, "Okay, sorry, let's focus on this. I pretty much took what you told me and made it Maddie-friendly." She read aloud.

Life with Lisa was a roller coaster. When she loved me, she loved me, and it was amazing. But when someone else caught her eye—and it happened more than once—I was brokenhearted.

We danced that dance—on again, off again; euphoria and heartache—for years. I always forgave her—how could I not? She was Lisa, and I loved her. I knew I'd never change her, although I always hoped that someday she'd surrender.

And that was my mistake, because I know you know your mother. Better than I ever did. And surrender was the last thing she'd ever do.

But man, that year—when Lisa was pregnant, and right after you were born—it was the best, and the worst. I was scared to death. We were both so young—how were we going to take care of a baby? But then, Jesus, you were this tiny little thing, and we both fell completely in love with you and for a while it was better than it ever was, because you were in my life.

Shay covered it all—Pete's lack of a job, his joining the Navy, his days away at sea, his heartache when Lisa took Maddie and left.

"But really, my biggest mistake," Pete said, when she'd reached the end. "Write that. Please."

Shay nodded and her fingers flew across her keyboard.

"My biggest mistake was letting you go," he dictated.

My biggest mistake was letting you go. After your mother took you away, I told myself that it was better not to push to see you. I convinced myself that your life would be better without my grief and anger. Jesus, I was so angry. I let myself become as cold and as hard as Lisa claimed I was. I didn't just lose you, Maddie; I lost myself because I didn't fight to find you—I didn't even try to get you back. I was wrong, and you have every right to be angry at me for abandoning you. I will regret my inaction for the rest of my life.

I hope someday you'll be able to forgive me. Hell, I hope someday I'll be able to forgive myself. In the meantime, I hope you'll take a chance and get to know me. We have a lot in common. We both really loved your amazing, imperfect, irreplaceable mother.

* * *

Maddie sat on the crumbling stoop of the foundation of a disappeared cabin that had once been part of Manzanar's Block Twenty-Four, gazing out at the distant mountains as Dingo finished reading the latest email that her stupid father's stupid girlfriend had sent.

Ding was trying to wipe his eyes surreptitiously. God, he was stupid, too. Didn't he know that girls liked boys who were sensitive enough to cry?

Of course, he'd made it clear that he didn't want Maddie to like him.

After she'd woken up from her nap beneath the picnic table, after she'd discovered that he'd used her phone to text Shayla with a *We'll meet you tomorrow* message, Maddie'd had a major WTF attack. She'd stomped her way through the site's museum-y parts with Dingo trailing after her.

She'd sat in stony silence as they'd taken the drive around the camp—there was a road around the entire thing, with another parking lot here, on the far end, near the cemetery. At which point, they'd gotten out. She'd given Dingo her phone with an order to text Shayla back and cancel all plans, but instead he'd found and read her *The Story of Peter and Lisa*, Chapter Four.

"Imagine having to bury your baby here," Maddie said now. Some of the markers on the graves in the cemetery were for young children, because face it, back in the 1940s, children died. They still sometimes died. "First you're rounded up, despite living in America for your entire life, and then you're locked in here, in the middle of nowhere. And then your three-year-old gets the flu and dies. And she's in the ground, right there, but then, whoops, war's over. *Everyone go home—sorry about the whole violating-your-constitutional-rights thing! Our bad! You have until Tuesday to pack up and leave, good luck!* So you're just supposed to trot on back to San Diego, and every time you want to tend your baby's grave, it's an eleven-hour round trip. Longer, because cars didn't drive as fast back then."

Dingo sat down next to her. "I can't imagine that."

"My grandfather's sister—Hiroko's sister, too," Maddie said, gesturing with her chin. "She's buried right there. Lisa told me about her. She was three, she was fine, and then, boom, she was dead. Her name was Shinju, but I can't read Japanese, so I don't know which grave is hers."

Dingo took her hand. "I'm so sorry," he said in his regular, non-Aussie voice.

"I hate you," she told him.

"I know."

"I'm not meeting my father and Shayla. Not tomorrow, not ever. You can just text them back and tell them that."

"Okay," he said. "But I'll wait until tomorrow. They're probably happy right now. Let's at least let them sleep tonight."

"Fuck you," she said. "I don't want to feel sorry for them."

"How about Daryl?" Dingo asked. "Should we also not feel sorry for him?"

"Double fuck you." That photo of Daryl, taken in the hospital, was terrifying. Obviously Nelson's men had found him and beaten him up.

"I just don't think we have a lot of options," Dingo pointed out.

Maddie stood up. He was probably right, but she wasn't

ready to admit that. "I'm starving," she said. "Let's go find a nice restaurant and blow some of stupid Nelson's stupid money on something good to eat."

* * *

Izzy called Grunge from the street outside of the Dingler house in Van Nuys.

"Greene. You're on speaker. I'm in the truck with Shayla."

"Yo, Grunge," Izzy said. "Last night's quake was nothing compared to the shaking going on today in the SpecOps world with the news that you're—"

"You're on speaker," Grunge repeated, louder this time, interrupting him.

"And with *that*, you're implying Shayla doesn't know," Izzy said.

"Doesn't know what?" he heard Shay say. Her voice was thin because she wasn't in front of the Bluetooth mic.

"Zanella," Grunge warned. He came in plenty loud. Probably because he was on the verge of shouting.

"Feel free to go all officer on my ass, *sir*, but you just might want to talk your potential resignation through with your girlfriend. I'm just saying."

"Resignation?" Shay said. "Oh, my God, is *that* why you went to the Navy Base today?"

"I went to float the idea," Grunge admitted. "Nothing's been decided. Zanella, are you calling for a reason other than you simply wanted to fuck up my day worse than it was already fucked up?"

"Sir, yes, sir," Izzy said. "When I arrived at the Dingler house in Van Nuys, the owners were home, much to my great surprise. Hey, it's both a report *and* a poem. Huh. I wonder if I can work in *can't believe my eyes* and/or *I donned my disguise*."

"The owners are home?" Grunge demanded.

"Mr. and Mrs. James and Mary Dingler," Izzy said. "We had a little tête-à-tête, and it's been a full year since they've seen their wayward son, Richard. Judging from Jim Dingler's heavy scowls and mumbling growls—ooh, I did it again!—it's unlikely our boy Dingo's going to be bringing his seriously underage girlfriend around for a visit with Mummy and Daddy any time soon."

"Did you warn them about—"

"I did," Izzy said. "Mr. D seemed positively psyched at the idea he might have to fight off a home invasion. I think he was hoping to rack up a body count. Mrs. D was significantly less thrilled."

"I bet," Shay said.

"I also asked them to call you if their son—or anyone who might want to murder their son—did appear."

"Good," Grunge said. "Thanks."

"So, whaddaya want me to do now, G?" Izzy asked. "I'm parked on the street and I can sit here, watching the house, for as long as you need me to. I just think it's a waste of time."

"I agree," Grunge said. "Get back to San Diego."

"Aye, aye, sir."

"And Z?"

"Ooh! Ooh! Let me guess! Let me guess!" Izzy said. *"Fuck you?"*

"Sideways," Grunge agreed.

"Awesome! Thanks, and you're welcome, sir!" Izzy sang cheerfully as the lieutenant cut the call. He got into his truck and headed south to San Diego.

* * *

"Grunge," Shayla said as Pete ended the call with Izzy Zanella.

He glanced at her as they drove relentlessly north, with

the sun starting to set out the left window of his truck. "Yeah."

"It's your nickname," Shay said. "Like Seagull or Time-bomb."

"It is."

"Or *Dingo*."

Ouch. He winced at the idea of being in the same Venn diagram circle—grown-ass men who have dumb nicknames—with Dingo. "Yep."

Shayla took out and opened her laptop. "Let's have it. The story. I'm sure Maddie would love to know."

"It's not all that exciting," he said. "The official story is that there was an incident with a Dumpster, shortly after I joined the Teams."

"*With* a Dumpster?"

"Inside of a Dumpster. The tango—terrorist—we were pursuing thought he'd try to hide, and I said nope and went in after him. When it was over, no one wanted to get too close to me. I'm lucky I didn't get called *Stinky*."

"So what's the unofficial story?" she asked.

He glanced at her, and she was looking steadily back at him.

"You said that was the *official* story, which means there's an unofficial, i.e., *real* story." She smiled. "So spill."

Pete sighed. "I heard that coming out of my mouth and I knew you'd catch it." He shook his head. "You know how Lisa used to call me Goldilocks?"

"Uh-oh," Shay said.

"Yeah, a nickname like that would've clung worse than Stinky." He laughed. "Okay, it's stupid but . . . I got, I don't know, maybe *one* email from Lisa the entire time I was doing a six-month WestPac cruise, right after I enlisted, and in it she called me G. Someone saw it and wanted to know what that G stood for, and I mumbled something like

It's a nickname. They pushed to know what my nickname was, so I said the first word I could think of that started with G that wasn't *giraffe* or *grapefruit*—or freaking *Goldilocks.*"

"Not G for Greene?" Shayla suggested, her eyes dancing with amusement.

"I panicked," he admitted. "There was music playing, so I just said *Grunge.*" He smiled ruefully. "The Dumpster happened, but it was long after the fact. It definitely helped cement the *Grunge* thing, though. Which was fine with me. Way better than carrying *Goldilocks* until the end of time."

Shayla laughed as she finished typing and finally closed her computer. "You've probably got more in common with Dingo than you think. I'd bet he made up his nickname, too, to steer people away from calling him Dingle or, God, Dingleberry."

"Yeah," Pete said dryly. "Me and Dingo. Two peas in a pod."

She laughed, and then fell silent for . . .

Three . . .

Two . . .

One.

"So what's up with the resignation?" Shayla asked him, right on cue. The question about *Grunge* had been just a warm-up. "I thought you loved being a SEAL."

"I do," he said. "I just . . . I see it getting more complicated, not less."

"With Maddie," she said.

"What else is there?" he said, but then realized how callous that was.

But she didn't flinch or even blink. "Of course," she said.

"You and me," he tried to explain. "I see that as extremely simple. I mean, it's sex." Okay, that didn't come out right, either.

This time she shook her head slightly as she said, "Can

we please focus on the Navy and your plans to leave it because . . . ? Why exactly . . . ?"

"I intend to tell Maddie that I'm willing to move to Palm Springs," Pete explained, "if she wants to finish high school there. And in order to do that, I've got to leave the Navy. I mean, I can't be a SEAL and live in the desert."

"She's a child," Shayla pointed out. "She'll live where you need to live."

"Said the woman who's terrified of earthquakes who moved to California so her kids would be closer to their dad."

"That's different," she insisted.

"Not really."

"Yes, it is. You're comparing my overcoming one little fear to you blowing up your entire career."

"And how does your fear fit with *your* career?" Pete asked.

Her reply was glib. "Quite nicely, actually. A rampant imagination works well for a novelist."

"So why aren't you writing?"

Shayla looked at him hard. "I'm sorry," she said sharply. "Are you really that insecure that we can't have a conversation about something that's of vital importance to you, without you lashing out and attacking me?"

* * *

"Whoa," Peter said. "I was asking a simple question—" he exhaled hard "—that, yeah, I'd already figured out was a hot button for you. You're right. I'm sorry."

Shayla looked at him.

He was wearing his uniform—clearly he had more than one pair of working whites hanging in his closet, because the last one had gone head to head with that bucket of shit. That he'd taken, square in the back as he'd kept her from getting slimed. Or worse.

She sighed. It was very clear that he was trying. "I'm

sorry, too," she said. "And you're also right. It *is* a hot button. I'm not writing, and it's scaring the hell out of me, because I've never not-written before. It's never been easy, but I used to do ten, maybe even fifteen pages a day. Now I'm lucky if I can get a half a paragraph down. Normally, writing feels like pulling a grand piano—on those little teeny, tiny, creaky wheels—up a very steep hill with a rope. But for the past two years, I feel like I'm doing it with my hands cuffed behind my back, with that rope now clenched between my teeth, as that hill keeps getting steeper and the road keeps getting longer."

Peter smiled at that. "See, that's a really good image. If you can describe things like that . . ."

"Why can't I write?" she asked. "I don't know. I've always taken the judgmental *Writer's block is bullshit* approach, but here I am, fully blocked." She laughed in exasperation. "You don't want to talk about this. You've got enough on your plate."

"Now, see, *that* was a cliché," he said.

"Clichés are cliché because they're so commonly true," Shayla defended herself, and yes, her tone came out a touch self-righteous.

"A cliché, *and* a conversation ender. *You don't want to talk about this* is code for *I don't want to talk about this,*" Peter pointed out. "Which is baffling. You never speak in code. That's one of the things I like most about you." He glanced at her. "Which means this really does scare the living holy fuck out of you, doesn't it? Kinda like me being terrified at the thought of leaving the Teams, but knowing it's the right thing to do. Who am I, if I'm not a SEAL? Who are you, if you don't write?"

Shayla stared at him. "Okay, I *do* want to talk about this," she said. "You asked for it. Last chance to back away and keep it safe, like, we could talk about the weather. . . ."

He smiled. "Nope. Go for it."

She took a deep breath. "I'm dealing with this . . . *horrible thing* that I didn't ask for. I used to love to write. It brought me incredible joy—being able to make a living and support my children doing something that I not only loved but I was damn good at doing. I woke up every day, filled with excitement and an urge to rush to my computer so I could continue to tell whatever story I was currently writing. It was never easy, but it was always fun, and somewhere down the line, it stopped being fun. And then, I stopped wanting to do it. Instead, I've been waking up every morning filled with dread. So now it's hard and painful and literally dreadful—and I feel like it's draining the very life out me. It's like the book that I'm writing—that I'm trying to write—is a vampire and it's sucking me dry, so by writing it I'm cutting my life expectancy by ten years, and it doesn't seem worth it. Not anymore. So I'm in free fall, because you're right. I don't know who I am, or what I'll be if I just stop writing. Except I've already stopped, and not-writing sucks worse than writing, because the not-writing is sucking me dry at an even faster rate. So I guess I'm wondering why you would even *think* about quitting something you love before you actively stop loving it."

Peter nodded. "That was impressive. Particularly the re-direct, away from you—"

"Answer the damn question."

"Because I desperately want to be Maddie's father," he told her quietly. "More even than I want to be a SEAL."

Shay felt her heart go into her throat. She'd written that line countless times, but she'd never actually felt as if it—her emotion—was on the verge of choking her. Not until now.

So. Now I'm completely in love with you. Things not to say aloud.

Instead, she cleared her throat. "Okay, that's valid. And *deeply* appreciated. But step outside of the, uh, gooey bubble of parental love for just a sec and look hard at the logistics. Maddie's fifteen. In three years, she'll be graduating high school and going off to college. I'm facing that next year with Tevin, and Frankie's right behind him. And that scares me even more, because even though right now I'm a not-writer, I'm also still something important: I'm Tevin and Frank's mom. And I love that job, but it's got an end date. And yeah, yeah, I'm going to be their mother forever, and I know they're going to need me—at times—when they're twenty and even when they're fifty and seventy, and I *will* be there for them. Shit, even after I'm dead, I'm gonna be there for them. I know that. I do. But the job gets a whole hell of a lot less work-intensive when they no longer live in your home. And when I look three years into my future, I see myself dropping Frank off at college and coming home to an empty, lonely, too-quiet house where I will wake up filled with dread until I finally just don't get out of bed, unless it's Parents' Weekend or Thanksgiving."

Nothing sexier than announcing to the man you're having crazy hot sex with that you anticipate sliding into debilitating depression in the relatively near future. *Run, run, as fast as you can. . . .*

But Peter couldn't run, because he was trapped in his truck with her. So she kept going, bringing this discussion back to him. "Best-case scenario, you have three years to be Maddie's father twenty-four/seven, and frankly? There's not a fifteen-year-old girl alive who wants her father helicoptering around her every damn minute of the day. You're going to have a lot of free time on your hands out there in Palm Springs. And in three years . . . ? That's gonna increase. I know exactly nothing about the U.S. Navy's hiring practices, but . . . if you resign now, can you un-resign in three years?"

Peter cleared his throat. "Usually not. But it depends on how many wars we're fighting," he told her. "And how badly they need men with my particular skills. I do see your point, though. I also have to face harsh reality. And mine is that as much as I want to be Maddie's dad, and as glad as I am that she finally seems ready to talk, that she reached out to you in that text—she still might never fully accept me. And I might have to face the fact that living with me might be too upsetting—too toxic—for her." He exhaled hard. "And I know that sounds a lot like what I did before—just letting her go. But she needs to feel safe in her own home, and if I can't give that to her . . . we'll have to find an alternative. Maybe boarding school—someplace great, though. And this time I *will* insist on weekly visits. And every other weekend. So I'm going to want to live relatively close to wherever *she* lives, and if that's Palm Springs, then yes, I'll have a lot of free time." He shrugged as he glanced at her again. "So that's my worst-case scenario plan. What's yours?"

"Well, it *was* alleviate the current torture that is the writing of this latest book by daily conjugal visits in the back of your garage, while hoping like hell that this is just a phase, and someday, soon, please God, I'll wake up to find that I *want* to write again," she admitted. "But if your garage is suddenly in Palm Springs, the frequency of those visits will have to change."

"*Hoping things will change* is not a plan," Peter chided her. "Don't writers need inspiration and, I don't know, periods of renewal? Maybe you shouldn't write. And I don't mean the not-writing that you're doing where you, what? Sit there and try to write and don't?"

She nodded.

"That's gotta suck. Maybe your plan should be to lock up your computer for a month, or six months, or a year," he said. "In the meantime, you can go on a vision quest to rediscover your muse."

"Yeah, right, my muse." She laughed. "Sorry, but that's

not a real thing. If I waited to be inspired by some kind of muse, I would simply never write."

"So a muse is not a real thing like the way you thought writers' block wasn't a real thing?"

Shayla looked at him. "You're, like, the world's best listener," she said. "I never actually realized there might be a downside to that."

He ignored her. "You write love stories, right?" he asked.

"Romances," she corrected him. "Love stories are diff—"

"Okay, yes, sorry, you write *romances*. Two people meet and earn their happy ending. *And they lived happily ever after.* How do you write stories like that when your heart's been vaporized? How did you describe it? A complete Alderaan."

"And you know what?" Shayla told him. "Here's what I *should* be thinking. *Wow, Lisa's an idiot, because this man would win the Olympic gold medal in relationship communication.* Instead, I think *What kind of freak remembers that kind of detail? Why is he paying such close attention to the things I say? When is he going to turn into a monster?*"

And there it was.

Peter glanced at her again, his eyes narrowing. "Did Carter . . . ? Nah, there's no way you'd let Tevin and Frank near him if he—"

"Beat the shit out of me?" Shay asked. "Damn right, I wouldn't. No, it was Kate, my best friend—former best friend—who kept needing to go to the emergency room. But she wouldn't leave him—her husband. She kept coming to me for help, and I kept thinking, *This time she's finally going to leave and be safe,* but she always went back, and I couldn't take it—having my hopes dashed like that. And I knew I had to put distance between us, because I wanted to save her even though she didn't want to be saved, but I couldn't. I couldn't stay away, and I pushed too hard, and he finally managed to turn her against me. She cut ties with me, completely. She changed her phone number and . . . I know they moved about a year ago, but I don't know where. Every now and then I email her, hoping . . . But she never responds. And all I can do is force myself not to think about it. About her. But it's always back there—my dread of what's coming. Because someday he'll kill her, he will— that's how it works—and all of his friends and co-workers will finally go *Oh, my God, he seemed like such a nice guy, maybe that crazy lady who sent us those emails saying he was a monster wasn't lying after all*. But Kate'll be dead and I'll hate myself even more than I do right now. And until then, and maybe for the rest of my life, as a bonus, I'll look hard at every man I meet, thinking, *Is there a monster hiding under that good-natured smile?* And *How do you abuse your wife or girlfriend, when no one's around to see?* And when I'm in a *really* dark place, I'll think, *Well, maybe you're one of the 'good' ones, and you'll only lie and cheat, the way Carter did—the way I'm pretty sure he does to Tiffany right now*." She forced herself to laugh. "And please don't panic. I know this all is extremely heavy. And see, this is why it's a really good thing that you and I are just friends—who occasionally go out on dinner-dates so that I don't disappoint my boys, thank you very much."

"No expectations, no strings, no chance of getting hurt," Peter said. "I get it now. I do. I'm glad you finally told me that. And you're right—you can't save someone who doesn't want to be saved. You just can't. But, Jesus, I'm so sorry . . ." He glanced at her again. "For the record, I would never . . . I'm not . . ."

"I know," Shay said. Or, in truth, she *thought* she knew—and as he glanced at her again, she knew that *he* knew what she was thinking.

"Time heals all wounds," he said, then smiled. "Since I'm not a writer, I'm allowed to use clichés. But it's true.

Time is really the only thing that can counter broken trust. I've experienced that, from both ends. My heart was also vaporized," he reminded her. "But I've recently discovered—to my surprise—that it grew back. Yours will, too." He glanced at her. "And maybe, when it finally does, you'll be able to write again."

CHAPTER TWENTY

Dingo came out of the motel office and got back into his car. "It's eighty-nine dollars, plus taxes and something called a resort fee, which is insane. This place should have a shithole fee, instead."

"That's too much," Maddie said.

"I know, but I think we should stay here anyway. Well, you should. I'm going to sleep in the car."

She was incredulous. "Then, what's even the point?"

"Mads, I'm not sleeping in a motel room with you. In the morning, I'll come in to take a shower. And *that's* the point."

"Not really," she argued. "We might be clean, but we'll still stink because we're wearing these shitty, dirty clothes. We're not far enough from Manzanar, anyway. Just, *drive.*"

He sighed as he pulled out of the motel parking lot and onto Route 395, and tried his accent. "Lookit, love, I'm exhausted."

"So then let's find a side street," Maddie said. "Here. Turn left—East Inyo Street—it looks like it goes back behind the high school."

He took the left, shaking his head at his own lack of backbone as she continued, "Let's just drive until we don't see any more houses, and then pull off and sleep. I really don't want to spend any more money—all dinner did was make me tired again."

They'd had some pretty decent BBQ for a relatively low price—the early-bird special—but she was right. Dingo's full stomach was making it even harder to keep his eyes open.

"I'll do this," he told her, "but we'll just take a nap. I'll set my phone alarm for a few hours, okay? And when we wake up, we're finally going to talk. About keeping that meeting tomorrow with Shayla and your father."

She sighed, an exaggerated exhale of exasperation. "God, Dingo."

"Not God, *yes*," he pushed. "Yes, Dingo, we'll talk."

"All right," she said.

"Say it."

She rolled her eyes, and her tone was mocking. "Yes, Dingo, we'll talk."

"Good," he said. "You can have the back, I'll take the front."

She was disgusted again. "Well, that's stupid. You can't sleep in the front. You're too tall. At least *I* fit up here. No deal, unless *you* take the back."

"Fine." He figured he could at least give her that.

"There!" Maddie pointed to a long-abandoned service station off to the right. It had burned, but enough of the garage remained so that he could tuck his car behind it and not be seen by anyone passing by.

Gravel crunched beneath his tires as he parked his car and turned it off, and then just sat there as the engine ticked.

The sun was low enough in the sky so that the day's heat was already transforming into the night's desert chill. He left the keys in the ignition and the windows open a crack, set the timer on his phone, and crawled into the back, where he caught a whiff of himself.

"Christ, I smell disgusting," he mumbled, thinking, good, that would keep Maddie away, as he closed his eyes and fell instantly asleep.

* * *

At 5:15, as Pete drove north on U.S. Route 395, a staff member from the Manzanar National Historic Site finally called back.

When they'd first gotten into Pete's truck, before they'd even left San Diego, Shayla had had the idea to call the former prison camp—to find out if anyone had seen Maddie and Dingo. She'd even emailed photos of the pair to the person who'd answered the phone—who'd promised to check with the rest of the staff and give them a call back.

Pete punched the phone on. "Lieutenant Greene."

"Hi, ooh, sorry," a female voice said through the truck's speakers. "My name is Melinda Anders and I might have the wrong number, I'm looking for a . . . well, I think it's Peter Nakamura?"

"No, you've got the right number," Pete said. "I'm Peter. I called earlier, because my daughter, Maddie Nakamura, is missing and we think she might've gone up there with her . . . boyfriend." The word stuck in his throat, but he choked it out.

Shay reached over and took his hand.

"Yes!" the woman said. "Oh, good, because yes, I saw them. They were here today."

"Oh, thank God," Shayla said.

"Are you sure?" Pete asked.

"The boy and the girl from the photos you sent? Absolutely. In fact, they were in the same car that was in one of the pictures, too."

"The maroon sedan?" Pete asked.

"Older model, not in great shape, yes."

"Thank God," Shayla breathed again.

"I remembered seeing them, because they stopped me to ask where Manzanar was, even though they were already in the park. They seemed a little confused, and then the girl—Maddie—started to cry. The boy told me her family had been interned here. It *can* be a very emotional experience, seeing the camp for the first time. They were looking for some shade so they could rest, but I had to tell them that there's not any shade here. Purposely, because there wasn't any back in the 1940s, either. This was *not* a comfortable place, by any means. Anyway, a few hours later, I saw them going through the exhibits near the visitor center, and then they drove out toward the cemetery."

"They left the park?" Pete asked.

"No, sorry, I mean, yes, they *did* leave the park, but only a few hours ago. Before that, well, there's a driving tour—a road that goes through the site. The cemetery is on the far end, inside of the reconstructed security fence. One of our other volunteers saw them parked at the lot out there—they were there for quite a while. The view *is* beautiful."

"Thank you so much for calling us," Shayla said.

"If you were heading south from Manzanar, toward San Diego, and you were hungry," Pete asked, "where's the first place you'd stop?"

"Lone Pine," the woman said, with no hesitation. "It's a few miles south of the site. It's a pretty big town. Everything from fast food to barbecue."

"Thanks," Pete said.

"I hope you find her. She seemed like a really sweet kid."

"She is," Pete said.

"And her boyfriend was especially caring and considerate," she said.

Yeah, great. "Thanks again," Pete said. He cut the connection and looked at Shay. They hadn't said all that much to each other since their incredibly deep conversation about . . . Jesus. People were complicated, and she'd given him a crapload to think about. And he'd like to think he'd done the same for her. He hoped so. He smiled at her now. "You were right."

She nodded. "Eyes open. Maroon sedan, heading south."

But they didn't have a lot of daylight left. When it got dark, the best they could do was drive through restaurant and motel parking lots, searching for Dingo's one-of-a-kind car.

"They're tired and hungry," Pete said. "They drove all night, last night, and they've had maybe a nap, at best. It's hard to believe they're gonna get very far."

* * *

Dingo was dreaming about Maddie.

She was kissing him, and his dream must've been set in the future, because in it, he was kissing her back. Ah, God, she was on top of him, and his hands skimmed across the softness of the bare skin that was between her T-shirt and her jeans and—

Dingo screamed. "What the *fuck*!"

This wasn't a dream, it was real—she was here in the moonlit darkness in the back of his car, with him. He tried to scramble away and out from under her, but all that did was make him hit his head not once, not twice, but three times.

"Stop," she said as she untangled herself from him and backed away. "Stop. *Stop!*"

But he was already grabbing his blanket and his pillow and even his really nasty, muddy hiking boots that he always kept tucked along the side of the trunk and he used them to build a wall between them. But then he grabbed the blanket back so he could hide his giant boner.

God help him. "What the fuck?" he said again. "You

can't just go and kiss people who are sleeping! Sleeping people can't give consent!"

"I didn't kiss you!" she shouted. "You kissed me! I just kissed you back!"

"I was asleep," he shouted. "And I'm pretty sure that—while I was asleep—I didn't pull you from the front seat here into the back! I'm pretty sure you're the one who climbed back here—again, without my consent!"

"I didn't know I needed permission to get warm!" Her mouth trembled and her eyes filled with tears, and Dingo had to close his own eyes.

In fact, he put his hands up over his face. "No, no, no, no, no," he said. "No, no. Don't you dare!"

"I didn't know I needed permission to get just a *little* bit of comfort and . . . and . . . *contact* on the night before I die!"

"You did too know that," he spoke loudly, over her and through his hands. "You knew goddamn well why you were up front and I was back here! Because my fucking wall doesn't work anymore! Because I can't keep my fucking hands off of you! You came back here, intentionally. You knew, absolutely, that this would happen! And you did it anyway!"

Maddie started to cry in earnest.

"Nice to see exactly what you think about me and *my* feelings!" He kept going. "Oh, look, Dingo's struggling. Let's make it even harder for him. Thanks a fucking million!"

"I'm sorry," she sobbed.

"Good! You should be!" he shouted, finally pulling his hands away from his face to glare at her. And . . . that was a mistake, because even though she was ugly-crying, her beautiful brown eyes were filled with pain and remorse and grief—and he found himself melting.

And then, as she tried to stop her tears and wipe her face, she whispered, "I love you."

Oh, *fuck.*

"And I know you love me," she continued. "And I just wanted . . . well, I wanted to have sex at least once, before I die."

Well, that sounded *entirely* reasonable—

"No!" Dingo shouted, mostly at himself. "I mean, yes, of course, you will. Maddie, come on. Really. You're definitely going to have sex before you die. But not right now, not like this. Not . . . with me. Because, see, you're *not* going to die anytime soon. You're just not, Mads. I'm not going to let you." He took a deep breath. "I know you don't want to ask your dad for help, and I get that—I do. I've been trying to figure out what other options we've got—and running away is not one of them. I mean, we wouldn't get far and then we'd be right back where we started.

"So what I'm thinking is this: I call Nelson, and I set up a meeting. By myself. I bring him the money and I take the blame. I admit that I stole it from Fee, that I was mad at her and wanted to get back at her—and that *you* had nothing to do with it. I grovel and beg and tell him that I'm sorry and I want to work to pay him back."

Maddie was horrified. "But then he'll just kill *you!*"

"Maybe," Dingo said. "But maybe not. Maybe he'll just make me his personal slave. God, I hope I won't have to degrade myself too badly. Like perform weird sex acts with his dog, for his amusement. Although that would be better than having to kill someone for him. That would be even more of a challenge. But I'd do it if it meant keeping you safe."

A fresh wave of tears welled in her eyes. "You're just trying to force me to ask my father for help."

Dingo didn't deny it. He just looked at her and shrugged.

"I love you enough to do this, if you want me to. So now the question is: How much do *you* love *me*?"

Her tears escaped. "Right now I hate you."

He nodded. "I know."

"Let me sleep back here with you," she said, "and I'll do it. I'll meet with my father and stupid Shayla in the morning."

Dingo sighed and looked at his barrier, wondering how to make it taller.

But she knew what he was thinking. "No wall," she demanded. "I want your arms around me."

"Clothes stay on," he countered. "In fact, we both take a blanket and wrap it tightly around ourselves." Like giant body condoms. With that, he could do this. He could survive the night.

Maybe.

Maddie rolled her eyes, which was her way of giving in.

So Dingo pushed for even more. "But before we do *that*, you need to send your father a text. A real one, with a real apology, confirming that we'll meet them tomorrow. And considering that you're about to ask him to borrow eight thousand dollars . . . ? Try to say *something* nice."

* * *

It was nearly 2200—ten P.M.—when the text came in on Pete's phone.

"*I'm so sorry. I know you've been worried.*" Shayla read it aloud as they drove slowly through the open-all-night McDonald's parking lot, still searching for Dingo's maroon sedan. "*But I'm safe. Dingo is honorable. None of this is his fault. We will meet you and Shayla tomorrow.*"

He looked at her face, lit by his phone's screen. "Text her back. Please. Tell her *I'm glad you're safe. Let's meet now. We'll come to you.*"

Her fingers moved as he spoke, and his phone whooshed as she hit *send*.

"What does she mean—*Dingo is honorable*?" he wondered. "That he's going to marry her and help raise my grandchild?"

"I'm picking up more of a *The drugs aren't his* vibe," Shay said. "Along with *Please don't kill him on sight when we meet tomorrow*."

"So she's trying to protect him," Pete concluded as he left the McD's. Just across the street was a Carl's Jr. He pulled into that parking lot. "Any response?"

"Not yet."

He was tired of waiting, and since Maddie had finally unblocked him to send that text, he used his truck's Bluetooth to call her phone.

But it went right to voicemail. *"You've reached Maddie. Leave a message. Or not."*

"Maddie, it's your dad. Call me. Please. We've tracked you to both Sacramento and Manzanar, and I'm worried that if we could find you, the men who hurt Dingo's friend Daryl might be able to find you, too. We're nearby. Please call. I just want to help. I love you." His voice fucking cracked, and as he punched the connection, he shook his head in disgust.

Shay, however, was doing her warm-eyes thing. "We should add one more thing," she said. "Maybe in a text? I know we don't know how far their reach is—the *$12K NOW* people who put Daryl into the hospital . . . ? But if this *is* drug-related, well, I've done research and that type of criminal activity tends to be territorial, so . . . Maddie's *definitely* safer out here."

He glanced at her. "Writing research?"

She nodded. "Yeah, so it is what it is. Although, despite what you told Maddie, I'm pretty sure that you, me, and maybe Hiroko are the only people on the planet who might've guessed she would go to Manzanar from Sacramento. I seriously doubt she's in immediate danger."

"I agree." He paused. "Well, she *is* with Dingo. And he's an idiot."

"But in Maddie's eyes, he's an honorable one. *P.S.*," she recited the words as she typed the text. *"Please stay put. Do NOT go to San Diego. It's not safe. Please let us come directly to you ASAP so we can help."* She looked up. "I'll leave out *Dingo sounds swell, can't wait to meet him again,* and just say, *Love, Dad."*

Pete laughed. "Thanks."

She hit *send*.

Pete cleared his throat. "If you were Maddie and Dingo, where would you really be?" he asked. "Right now?"

She took a deep breath and narrowed her eyes. "After an overnight drive from San Diego to Sacramento, a little morning B&E at my old friend Fiona's, and then another long drive, with an emotional afternoon at the windswept, sun-baked historic site of a national embarrassment? I'd be sleeping. In the car. Regardless of whether I'd taken a wad of cash from Fiona's room. Because I wouldn't want Dingo's car sitting in a motel parking lot, like a giant, flashing MADDIE IS HERE sign, within view of the highway. Likewise, I wouldn't be sleeping while parked at the Desert Flower All-Nite Diner." She gestured at the restaurant whose lot they were driving through. "I'd find some dark, deserted backstreet, in one of these little towns along 395, and even then I'd sleep very lightly, and plan to wake up early, get moving at dawn. Hopefully checking my phone when I wake up, for a message from my father."

Pete nodded. "That's what I thought, too," he said, as he pulled next door, into the parking lot for the Desert Flower Motel, where a neon vacancy sign was lit. "So how about we call it a night, and get, um, a couple of rooms."

CHAPTER TWENTY-ONE

"Do we need more than one?" Shayla asked, but then immediately backpedaled. "I mean, it's okay if we do. You know, need more than one room. It's been a long day. I'm tired of me, too."

Peter laughed. "I'm not tired of you."

Yeah, but what was he supposed to say? And God, there was a huge difference between the kind of sex they'd been having—caused by earthquakes and various other aftershocks—and the kind of sex in which they checked into a motel, first, and then slept all night in the same bed, after.

And true, they'd slept all night in what Shay would forever after think of as the Hot Sex Tent, but this was definitely different. This time, they'd get washed up, and brush their teeth, and turn down the bed, and then even actually say good night and fall asleep afterward.

This was relationship sex, and it was *not* going to help her remember that this thing they shared was not a real relationship.

"And no, I mean, I thought," Peter was saying, "that you'd prefer two. Rooms. So that it wouldn't be awkward when you told everyone back at the house that we were staying in a motel."

"Ah." Shayla understood.

"Yeah," he said, "believe me, we are not sleeping in separate rooms. I mean, unless . . . *you're* tired of *me*."

She leaned over and kissed him. "One room," she confirmed. "Because here's the text I'm going to send." She recited as she typed. "*Contact from Maddie! Plans to meet her tomorrow! Hooray! Staying at Desert Flower Motel, Route 395, just south of Lone Pine. Cellphones on all night, call if you need ANYthing! Love you!*" She hit *send*. "Now imagine if I'd said, *Staying at Desert Flower Motel in rooms 214 and 216.* The subtext is *Note that we are staying in TWO ROOMS, that's T-W-O, as in two separate rooms, one for each of us,* and everyone would immediately know, absolutely, without a doubt, that we're really sharing a room and having incredibly hot sex, because that was too much information for a text, and clearly I was attempting to misdirect."

Peter was laughing. "The crazy thing is, you're right." He looked out of the truck's windshield at the motel office, but he didn't move.

"You know, it's okay with me if we just keep looking for her," Shayla said quietly.

He looked at her. "And do what? Drive down every road in every town along 395?"

"Well, we won't hit them all, but we can make a dent," she said.

Peter shook his head. "It's an impossible task. And futile."

"We might get lucky."

"The only way we find them is if we get phenomenally lucky. To be effective, we'd need to search on foot. Maddie's been with Dingo for days now. Even if he's stupid enough to park where his car can be spotted from the street, *she's* not.

No, I'm going to use this time to rest, and wake up early enough to get a good meal, so I don't walk into that meeting tomorrow exhausted and hangry, because that won't be good."

But he still didn't get out of the truck.

So Shay said, "It's okay with me if we just rest. We don't have to, you know, have, um, sex."

He turned sharply to look at her as he laughed. "When do I ever not want to have sex with you?"

"Well, you just seem so worried—"

"I *am* worried."

"Sometimes sex and worry don't go together all that well."

"In what universe?" he asked, then said, "Oh, is it possible that when I finally have time to finish reading *Outside of the Lines,* I'm going to find out that Jack's magic penis doesn't work when he's worried?"

Shay laughed despite herself. "Jack doesn't have a magic penis," she reminded him.

"I'm pretty sure it's *extra* magic if he can't get it up when he's worried," Peter said.

"It's not that he *can't* get it up," she said.

"What, then? He doesn't *want* to? That's worse. We've got about seven and a half hours before dawn, which is when we think Maddie and Dingo are going to wake up and get moving. I can spend that time worried and wandering the streets, running my batteries even lower and becoming stupid and useless, or I can recharge. I'm going to pick *recharge*—which includes fucking both of us into a very deep REM sleep. In full disclosure, a shower before we do that would be really nice, too."

"So why are you hesitating?" she asked.

"I'm not hesitating."

"Do you need . . . help, paying for the room?" she asked.

"Jesus, no! Why would you think that?"

"Sorry! I'm trying to figure out why you're . . . kind of just sitting there . . . ?"

"I'm moving very slowly," Peter said. "I got a little side-tracked before, trying to imagine exactly what that meeting's going to be like tomorrow. *Dad, I need to borrow twelve thousand dollars to pay off the loan shark I used to support my drug habit. Oh, by the way, in Sacramento, I accidentally-on-purpose killed a man for his mocha latte. Have fun raising my meth-addicted baby with your new roommate, Dingo, while I spend the rest of my life in jail!*"

Shayla laughed. "Peter, my God, that is some *serious*, professional-grade worrying."

"And yet . . ." He smiled at her. "I need a shower," he said. He leaned in and kissed her. "And maybe this means I'll never be a hero in a romance novel, but I desperately need you."

* * *

Smash cut to love scene.

If Shayla were writing this story, after a line like *I desperately need you,* she would've cut immediately to them having literally steamy sex in the shower, skipping over the humorously awkward reality of the too-lengthy check-in that included a key card that didn't work. Twice.

Yeah, that third trip to the motel office was a hoot.

Harry popped into her head as they finally got the motel room door unlocked and . . .

Oh, dear, he said, as Peter muttered, "Ah, Jesus."

"It's not that bad," Shay said. But it was. The room was decorated in Quiet Desperation, circa 1972, complete with cheap paneling on the walls, dark green indoor-outdoor carpeting, and a worn-out bedspread that was no longer quite as emphatically flower-power since its yellows and oranges had faded about two decades ago. The "art" on the walls consisted of pictures of owls with big eyes.

Peter went up to one to look more closely. "This is what the desk clerk meant by *the Owl Room*."

Harry laughed. *I don't want to know what the other choices were.*

"At least it's clean," Shay said, attempting to bright-side it as she pulled back that spread to reveal bright white sheets.

"These are paint by numbers," Peter pointed out.

"That makes it sweet," Shay said. "Like, someone's kid or elderly parent painted them."

"Hmm," Peter said, as he headed for the bathroom at the back of the room.

A kid with a devil-mutant, crazy-eyed owl fetish at age twelve, who is now in his forties and regularly murders the guests at the motel he inherited after pushing his grand-mother down the stairs?

"Shh," Shay said. Those owls used up the full crazy allot-ment for this room. Because of them, there was space in here *only* for even reason and carefully considered sanity.

Like, at least we're on the ground floor in case there's another earthquake?

Yes.

But not: we're doomed if there's a tidal wave.

Right.

But definitely check to make sure the security lock is on that door.

She did. It was.

The toilet flushed, and Peter came back out of the bath-room and washed his hands in the sink that was out in the main part of the room.

"I've been nurturing a fantasy about making love to you in a real bed," he said, looking at Shayla in the mirror as he dried his hands. "But I don't think that one counts." He unbuttoned his white uniform shirt and hung it on one of the bent hangers that dangled from the sad-looking metal rack bolted to the wall next to the sink. He pulled off his T-shirt and hung that, too. "I mean, yeah, it's slightly more real than an air mattress, but not by much."

The room looked significantly nicer and way less depressing with the muscles in his arms, chest, and abs rippling—in duplicate, thanks to that mirror. And then it was nicer still as he kicked off his shoes, and stepped out of his pants and hung them up beside his shirt.

Harry didn't comment—he was just instantly gone.

"So maybe we can plan to extend our little . . . whatever this is," Peter continued, slipping out of his socks as he glanced at her again in the mirror. "Friendship, plus. At least until I can take you someplace with room service. Is that okay with you?"

There were two cheerfully decorated Desert Flower Motel Traveler's Packs on the worn gold-and-yellow-speckled linoleum sink counter, and he pulled out a toothbrush and small tube of paste and, while continuing to watch her in the mirror, he brushed his teeth.

Shay looked at him standing there in his white boxers, and she found herself blurting, "You're a really good communicator. I mean, really good. You just demonstrated . . ."

He spit and rinsed and dropped the toothbrush into a glass with a plastic clatter as he turned back to face her.

Her Navy SEAL.

Harry's words—but Harry had vanished. Those were *her* words now, God help her. Her Navy SEAL—wearing only white boxers, leaning back against the sink in the motel room where in just a few minutes, they were going to make love.

Shay's brain stuttered and she started over. "What I mean to say is that some people play games, but you don't. You ask for what you want. You're direct, you're tactful, and you're honest. I've said this before: I don't know what Lisa's problem was, but you did everything right—and you still do. You're funny, you're smart, you're kind, and you obviously care. You listen, you pay attention, *and* you remember details."

And oh, my God, look at him—although that was just icing on the cake.

"So . . . is that a *yes*?"

"Yes," she said. "Of course. What other answer would there be?"

He smiled, and dropped his boxers on the floor. "Get naked. I'll be out in about thirty seconds."

Good communicator. *Good* communicator.

As the shower went on, Shayla hung up her clothes, too.

* * *

Maddie woke up from a nightmare—her father was screaming at her, like a drill sergeant at boot camp, but then he surprised her completely by bursting into tears—to find herself alone in the back of Dingo's car.

"Ding?" She sat up, careful not to hit her head, but he wasn't in the front seat, either. "Dingo!"

"I'm out here," he called. He was sitting out on the hood of the trunk, leaning up against the back window.

She pushed her way out through the door that didn't stick, but then reached back in to grab a blanket and wrap it around her. "It's cold."

"Yeah, but look at these stars. They're bright enough to keep me warm."

The sky *was* pretty amazing, away from the city's lights, but still. "Are you high?"

"Only on life, love."

"What time is it?"

He checked his phone. "Around two thirty." No, wait, that was *her* phone.

"Are you pretending to be me again?" she asked.

"No, I was just checking messages," he said. "You got a

bunch of texts. Your dad and Shayla tracked you out here, which is a little alarming. They said we shouldn't go back to San Diego because *danger, danger.* And although I mock, I wholeheartedly agree. We could call them right now and they'd come meet us, and . . . I think we should."

Oh, God. "I'm not ready," she said.

"There's really no *ready*," he pointed out. "This is just something we've gotta do. Band-Aid pull."

"I can't," she said. "Not like this. I changed my mind about spending money. I want to get a motel room so we can take showers. I need to take a shower and wash my hair before we . . . I have to . . . I don't care if our clothes smell. We can get some of that stupid freshener spray and—"

"All right," Dingo said.

She looked at him. "You're not going to argue?"

"Nope. But after we check in, before you shower, even, you have to call him. We'll pick a place to meet for breakfast, and we'll set the time to meet, right then."

"You really want to get rid of me, don't you?" Maddie asked.

Dingo slid down off the trunk. "Not taking that bait, love. Not gonna dignify that shite with any kind of response."

"I'm so sorry," she said.

"I love you," he told her. "Get in the car."

* * *

The bed was in better shape than Pete first thought.

Of course, the fact that Shayla was in it—with him, beneath him, tightly clenched around him—sure as hell didn't hurt.

Her fingers were in his hair as her gorgeous body strained up to meet him, and her tongue was in his mouth, entangled with his.

He was glad they'd driven out here—and obviously not

just because it meant they'd be meeting Maddie far earlier in the morning than they otherwise might've. He couldn't imagine the sheer frustration of being in Shay's house right now, surrounded by a crowd, and wanting her with no hope of doing . . .

Exactly . . .

This.

"Oh, Peter," she breathed as she came beneath him, around him, and he came, too, in a rush of heat.

"Jesus, we're a good fit," he said when he could finally speak, and she laughed.

"We are very, *very* good at this," she agreed, smiling up into his eyes.

Ask for what you want. . . .

"Can we talk—seriously?" Pete asked. "About what really happens to us—to our friendship—if Maddie takes me up on my offer to move to Palm Springs?" Just say it. "Because I feel like we're just getting started here, and . . . I don't want this to end."

She didn't answer right away, which wasn't all that good of a sign. She was choosing her words again, but she was still running her fingers through his hair, so it wasn't all bad. "I've done long-distance," she finally told him. "Carter traveled a lot, as a musician. That's partly what split us up. It's not easy."

"The only easy day was yesterday."

She smiled at him. "Hoo-yah!"

He nodded. "Hoo-yah."

"You SEALs can be pretty freaking pompous."

"Maybe," he said, laughing, "but we've earned it. You should come see what BUD/S training looks like, up close."

She looked startled. "Are you inviting me to visit you at work?"

Pete nodded, but then shrugged. "Assuming I'm not in Palm Springs."

"Yes, that," she said. "How does *one day at a time* sound?"

Pete nodded. "It sounds good," he said, shifting off of her and carefully pulling himself free.

She made a little noise—a little murmur of dismay—and he had to smile as he quickly disposed of the condom he'd been wearing. "And *that* sounds even better," he said as he came back to her and kissed her. Her lips, her throat, her breasts—he got distracted, but only temporarily, because he was a man on a mission.

Shayla shivered as he kept going, all the way to the soft insides of her thighs. He stopped there to say, "You know, the woman in your book—Loretta—she's missing out. Jack's magic penis means that he never has to go down on her."

She laughed and propped herself up on her elbows. "*Has to go down on her,*" she repeated. "Not the best collection of words in the Giant Lexicon of Romantic Words. *I have to go down on you,* Jack told Loretta as he checked his to-do list of weekend chores. *But first I have to clean the refrigerator, pick up the dry cleaning, and wash the dog.*"

Pete smiled as she laughed. "You're just saying it wrong," he told her, and lifted his head. He met her gaze and just held it and held it and held it until she finally stopped laughing. And when he spoke, he didn't have to work very hard to make his voice low and rough. "*I have to go down on you. I* have *to.* See?"

Shay's laughter was now breathless. "I was definitely saying it wrong," she agreed, and then sighed when he lowered his head and kissed her. "As far as the book goes . . . Jack and Loretta get there. Keep reading."

"I will," he murmured. "But I'm a little busy right now."

One day at a time meant not worrying about tomorrow—about what the future might bring.

So Pete surrendered to *right now*—which was pretty fucking great.

* * *

Dingo picked a national chain over one of the more quirkily named mom-and-pop-type motels. The Ride On Inn. The Desert Flower. Nope. Not going to stop there. But the chain with its bored-to-death, minimum-wage-earning night clerk behind the front desk . . . ?

"I'll be right out," he told Maddie as he parked by the doors. As he got out of his car, he patted his pocket to make sure he was still carrying the wad of bills they'd taken from Fiona's room. He was holding it for Maddie, for safety's sake. Right.

He had to hit a buzzer—and really lean on it—to get into the motel office due to the "night lock."

A man finally appeared behind the desk—middle-aged, balding, puffy-faced—and looked hard through the glass at Dingo and then over at Maddie, who was visible in the car. Whoops, maybe it was a mistake parking there.

She was his adopted sister; they were traveling together to meet their dad. Yeah, that would work.

The lock finally clicked open, and Dingo went inside. The scent of industrial-strength insecticide didn't quite cover the musty blend of ancient mildew and dust. God, working here would be a living hell.

He cleared his throat and prepared his smile. If the clerk had been a woman, he would've automatically gone Australian. But the accent didn't always work with men— sometimes it did, but sometimes it really backfired. So Dingo stayed silent as he approached the desk, looking at the obviously cranky man with his swollen eyes, sagging jowls, and disheveled, barely there graying hair.

"How can I help you, mate?" The man's voice was thick with a Down-Under accent that had to be real.

Didn't it? Or . . . ? Wait . . .

Dingo's first coherent thought was that he was encountering himself, from some terrible and depressing future. Oh, God, he looked awful.

"Well, speak up! You woke me—best make it worth it. Come on!"

"Yes," Dingo said, in standard Southern Californian. "Sorry, dude, it's late, and you . . . remind me of someone. Is your name Rick, by any chance?" Okay, that was stupid, as Maddie would say. This man was definitely *not* him, from the future. That kind of technology didn't exist. Still, morbidly curious, part of him wanted to know. "Or Richard . . . ?"

The man sighed heavily. "You want a room, but you don't have a credit card. Well, it's your lucky day, we take debit cards, here at Bedbugs R Us."

Okay, *that* wasn't good. But since they only wanted to use the shower . . . "I have cash."

"That we also take," the man said. "With two forms of ID."

"*Two* forms?" Dingo said. "I have a driver's license, but . . ." Nothing else.

"Credit or debit card'll do it."

"Well, that's stupid. If I had those I'd use them to pay, and I wouldn't need a second ID," Dingo pointed out.

"No, you'd still need your driver's license," the man said. "Can't have criminals and ne'er-do-wells checking in."

"Do I look like a criminal or a . . . ?" Dingo stopped himself. Okay, stupid question, particularly smelling the way he did.

Future Dingo looked at him hard, then pointedly turned to look at Maddie, waiting out in the car. "How old's your lovely little morsel out there, twelve or maybe thirteen?" He laughed. "Oh, I know, I know, she just *looks* young, right? Or wait, she's your sister."

Sis-tah. His accent was awesome, but then again, with another few decades of practice, Dingo's would be, too.

He tried straight-up bribery. There was little *he* wouldn't do for a quick fifty bucks. "Look, I'm sorry. Can we bend the rules? We're not going to stay long—an hour, at most—"

"Hourly rental, eh? Fuck her and run?"

"Nope," Dingo said. "Don't want bedbugs, aren't gonna—nope. We just want to use the shower."

"Off-the-books hourly rate is five hundred, cash, the timer starts now."

Dingo choked. "*Five* hundred . . . ? An hour?"

"Take it or leave it."

"Dude, come on. We just want to get cleaned up. We've been living in the car, and we're meeting her father for breakfast—"

"God, you're a terrible liar."

"It's the truth!"

The man smiled. "Clock's ticking."

"Five hundred dollars is insane," Dingo said. "I'll give you a hundred, and we'll be done in a full hour, with the clock starting only when we walk into the room."

The man laughed in his face. "Price just went up to six hundred, mate, with fifty-seven minutes left on the clock."

"Fuck you!"

"Seven hundred."

"God, you're a douchebag!"

"I'm the douchebag?" The man suddenly seemed to expand and get taller and broader. "*I'm* the douchebag? Said the pathetic little man-boy who messes with children?" He reached for the phone. "Deal's off, I'm calling the police."

Fuck! Dingo ran for the door.

"Yeah, run, run, as fast as you can, pathetic little man-boy!" his future self called mockingly after him. "But you can't run fast enough, because wherever you go, there you are! Give my love to your sister!"

Dingo jumped into the car, turned it on with a roar.

Maddie was startled. "What happened?" she asked as he pulled out of the parking lot with a spray of gravel.

"They don't take cash," he said flatly.

"What? Who doesn't take cash? Wait, we should try someplace else—maybe one of the smaller motels . . . Where are you going?" she asked as he blew past both the Desert Flower and the Ride On Inn, heading south on 395. "Dingo!"

"It's you, all right?" he said. "The guy took one look at you, and said he was calling the police. He looked at you, and then he looked at me, and just like the entire rest of the motherfucking world, he thinks I'm a loser and a creep. So, no, I'm not going to try someplace else, thanks."

"I want a shower!" Maddie said.

"I fucking know that you fucking want a fucking shower!" he shouted back at her. "I'm gonna get you your fucking shower at a place where I won't be arrested, and then I'm going to bring you to your father and be done with you! For once and for all!"

"You said you love me," she whispered, and when he glanced over, her eyes were filled with tears, her face aghast in the dim glow from the dashboard's light.

Dingo hardened his heart as he blasted toward his parents' house in Van Nuys—the one place he knew he could get her cleaned up without having to run a gauntlet of shame, derision, or scorn. His folks were out of town—his mother had emailed to let him know.

"There are limits, love," he told Maddie quietly. "To everything. And I think I've finally hit mine."

CHAPTER TWENTY-TWO

Saturday

"Can you imagine it?" Shayla murmured.

"No," Peter said. "I can't."

They'd woken up before dawn, showered, had breakfast, and then climbed into Peter's truck—but there was still no word from Maddie.

A brief text to the girl—*We're awake*—also got no reply.

So, as the sun rose, they'd driven the last few miles north to Manzanar, and just as it was promised on the former internment camp's website, the gates were wide open. Admission was free—as it rightfully should be for a National Historic place of shame.

They'd driven through—the visitor center and barracks wouldn't open until later—to the cemetery where they'd been told that Maddie had been, just a day earlier.

The mountains in the distance were beautiful but starkly forbidding. Shay and Peter stood there, in the middle of that flat desert plain, with the mostly barren earth stretching as far as the eye could see.

Shayla looked around them, doing a full 360. She was

going to come back here, with the boys. Rent a van, bring as many of their friends as they could fit and . . .

Her phone buzzed. Yes!

"It's Maddie!" she told Peter. "She texted, *We won't go to San Diego. In LA.* Oh, my God, they're in Los Angeles? That's *hours* from here!" They both started to run toward his truck, as she finished reading, *"Will text soon with place to meet."*

As they climbed in and Peter started the engine with a roar, he said, "Text her back and tell her *not* to go to Dingo's parents' house in Van Nuys!"

"Oh, I'm on it," Shay said, doing just that.

"Why would they go all the way back to LA?" he muttered as he tried to call Maddie's cellphone directly, even as he broke the speed limit leaving the compound.

But the girl didn't pick up. There was no response to Shay's text, either, so Peter punched in Izzy Zanella's phone number.

"Good morning, Away Team." The big SEAL's cheerful voice filled the truck cab. "Did you have a pleasant stay at the lovely sounding Desert Flower Mo—"

Peter cut him off. "Where are you?"

"In Shay's kitchen, with Hiroko. Uh-oh. With the frying pan. That sounds disturbingly Clue-like. I hope I'm not the murder vic—"

"Who else is over there?" Peter demanded.

"Lopez and Jenkins. All three of us are here for the day. Assuming Lindsey's baby behaves. If she pops, Jenk's going with her, of course, but that's okay because Boat Squad John just called in. Their dive was canceled, so they're on their way. I plied them with the promise of pancakes."

"I need you to go to Van Nuys, to the Dinglers', ASAP. Take Seagull, Hans, and Timebomb, if they get there in time, if not, just get up there."

"Lieutenant, it's your lucky day. They just pulled up."

"Go," Peter ordered. "Now. Call me when you're on the road. Oh, and Z? Cowboy up."

"Aye, aye, sir."

Peter punched off the connection.

"We should call Dingo's parents," Shayla said. "I've got the number. It's early, but . . ." She input it into the dashboard's Bluetooth screen.

Peter nodded, so she pushed the button that would dial the call, and as it rang, she said, "Maddie said *LA,* not *Van Nuys.* It's possible that Dingo has friends in the city. His parents' house, in the suburbs, is probably his last choice in terms of places to go."

"Unless she said *LA* because she didn't know how to spell *Van Nuys,*" Peter countered as the line continued to ring.

"And then there's that," Shay had to agree.

* * *

The landline was ringing and ringing and ringing. Who even had a landline anymore? And wasn't it overkill to put an extension—fully corded—in the bathroom?

Maddie stood naked in front of the mirror in the shitty bathroom of Dingo's parents' shitty little house, using a hair dryer to attempt to dry the underwear she'd rinsed out in the sink while she was in the shower.

She'd made the mistake of hooking her cellphone into Dingo's parents' wi-fi shortly after they'd arrived, and it had instantly begun to install an update to her operating system, which had rendered it useless. To make things worse, the wi-fi was sketchy so the upload was taking forever. For the past twenty minutes, it had been promising her it would be done in eight.

Maybe she'd been sucked into a different dimension.

It had certainly felt that way during the endless drive to Los Angeles.

Well, they weren't in LA, they were in the Valley—the burbs, north of the city. Dingo wasn't even close to Australian. He was a Valley boy. Although boys and men probably didn't get labeled like that. It was probably just the women and girls who were given that meant-to-be-insulting name.

But Dingo hadn't uttered the classic Valley girl *Oh my God* as they'd approached his parents' house. In fact, over the entire course of the drive, mired in this new, awful dimension that Maddie was currently trapped in, neither of them had said much of anything.

I'm going to get you your fucking shower . . . and then I'm going to bring you to your father and be done with you. For once and for all.

They'd driven past the house, and everything was still and dark even though the sun was starting to rise.

"We're good, they're gone." Dingo had finally spoken.

At Maddie's questioning look, he'd grudgingly explained. "My mother sends me emails, so I know where they are, partly in case they die in a fiery ten-car pile-up. They have an RV and they travel a lot. They just got home from a long trip east—my sister had a baby—but then my dad wanted to go to some asshole festival in Arizona, so . . . She said she wasn't sure if they were leaving last night or this morning, but the RV's gone. She hides bags of food for me in the spare room, and sometimes money, too. We'll have to be careful not to move anything or leave anything out of place, because I'm sure my dad checks. So we'll want to wash and fold the towels after we shower."

He'd gone around the block, and parked on the next street over. "Just in case Dad forgot something—like his official *I'm an Asshole* hat—and they come back. That's happened before. If they do, we'll have to hide. And maybe pray."

Once inside, Dingo had raided some boxes that were neatly stacked in the corner of that spare room he'd mentioned. They were all marked *Throw Away,* but they held what had to be his belongings. "This used to be my room before my father attempted to erase me," he'd told her as he handed her a pair of shorts and a T-shirt. "You can wear this until your clothes dry."

With the exception of her underwear, Maddie had put her dirty clothes outside of the bathroom door, and Dingo had immediately started a load in the washing machine—she heard it thumping and swishing from what must've been a laundry room on the other side of the shower wall. It was clear that he'd come here often when his parents were away, and he'd learned to be efficient with his time.

The phone finally stopped ringing, but only a few seconds passed before it started up again.

"Don't answer that!" Dingo shouted through the door. "It's probably my father. I think he suspects that Mom helps me out, because whenever I'm here, the phone rings off the hook, like he's trying to catch me or something. So just . . . don't."

"Don't worry, I won't," Maddie shouted back.

* * *

Dingo was in the living room when the black truck pulled up in front of the house. It was Nelson's man Cody—with the pale eyes and total lack of soul. He didn't even try to approach with stealth. He just parked and started up the front path.

The hair dryer was still buzzing in the bathroom—Maddie wasn't even close to being able to run. Still, Dingo went into the kitchen where—fuck!—the skinhead twins, Stank and Eddie, had just dropped over the back fence, into the dust bowl that was his parents' backyard.

He ducked down behind the counter, so that they couldn't see him through the windows.

Running was not an option. That left hiding, or fighting. . . . He quickly opened the junk drawer, rummaging for something, anything. . . . A jackknife . . . But all he found was a fold-up corkscrew that had a little knife on the end. Better than nothing, except, really? It was sharp as shit, but only three quarters of an inch long. Fighting wasn't much of an option either.

Still, he pocketed it, but then pulled out his phone. With shaking hands he went to his list of texts and found . . . Yes. Nelson had texted him just last night. *Where you at?*

Fist time in days that M hasn't been watching me, Dingo typed. *Recovered some $$$, but now at end of rode. Will bring her to you ASAP.*

He hit *send,* pocketed his phone, and took a deep, steadying breath as he heard the glass break in the back door.

The hair dryer went off, and Maddie called from the bathroom, "Dingo? What was that?"

* * *

Dingo didn't answer her.

Maddie hurriedly put her still-damp underwear back on, along with the much-too-big shorts and T-shirt, then went to the door and opened it a crack. "Ding?"

Had he dropped a glass in the kitchen? God, that would be a mess. She only hoped it wasn't his father's favorite, or even just something that would be easily missed.

But then she heard voices. Dingo saying, "Whoa, whoa, whoa, *whoa.* Mate! Mate! Take a breath! Take a breath!" He was using his fake accent, so he probably wasn't talking to his father. "I *just* sent him a text—this is the first time in days that she hasn't been completely on top of me—lookit, lookit, just check my phone. See? Right?"

"*First* has an *r* in it, you fucking idiot."

Maddie stood there, frozen in disbelief as Dingo said, "But, see? I sent that text to Mr. Nelson. I was playing her, mate, 'cuz I thought, you know, if I was her boyfriend, she'd tell me where the money was, but she honestly didn't have it. We found this, in Fiona's ma's house in Sacramento— they've shipped Fee off to some kind of juvie looney bin. . . ."

He'd sent a text to *Nelson*.

Dingo kept talking, but Maddie closed the door. Locked it. Looked around. There was no window in there—she hadn't noticed until now. No window, but a phone. She picked it up. Dialed 9-1-1.

Her heart was pounding, which was weird, because it shouldn't even be able to beat let alone pound since it had just broken into a million pieces.

Dingo had been playing her. All this time.

"Nelson's garage was our next stop," she heard him saying from the other side of the door as the emergency number rang once and then twice, "but I had to shower. She's in the bathroom—I put her in the one without the window. I even screwed with the wi-fi, to take out her cell. But—fuck! There's a phone in there!"

The doorknob rattled and the entire door shook as Maddie took the phone's handset with her into the shower. "Pick up pick up pick up pick up." But it just kept ringing.

She shrieked as the door splintered—as a giant booted foot came through, and then was pulled free before a hand— also big—reached in and turned the knob.

The door opened with a crash, and two large men— Nelson's skinheads—grabbed Maddie. As she dropped the phone into the tub, the call was finally connected, and a little voice echoed against the porcelain. "Nine-one-one, what's your emergency?"

Maddie kicked and screamed, but her arms were pinned, and her legs flailed as they contacted nothing. One of the men clamped a gloved hand over her mouth.

A third man grabbed the phone and pulled the cord right out of the wall. "Mother*fucker!* Move! Go, we gotta go. The bitch called nine-one-one!"

One of the skinheads laughed as they carried her out of the bathroom. "Dude, we're in Van Nuys. We could have her make us lunch and give us all blow jobs and we'd still be outta here before the police showed."

"Oh, no, no, I wouldn't . . . do that." Dingo was in the kitchen. He'd changed into a pair of black cargo pants and a Superman T-shirt, his hair slicked back—still wet from his own shower. He was holding on to his cellphone, as if the door-kicking-in had bored him so much that he'd spent the time scrolling through his Twitter feed. If Maddie could've, she would've incinerated him with her eyes. "Keep your distance, mates. I'm peeing knives. I'm pretty sure she gave me gonorrhea."

Maddie bit the man through the glove.

"Fuck!" He yanked his hand away, but then smacked her in the face.

Her ears rang, but her mouth was free. "I hate you, Dingo! You're a liar! He's lying!"

He was lying.

He was *lying*.

Oh, my God, Dingo was lying!

Time froze and the world seemed to move in slow-mo as she looked directly into Dingo's eyes, and he widened them slightly—just a little—just enough, even as "I did *not* give him gonorrhea" came shrieking out of her mouth. And she instantly realized why he'd said that—so that they'd think twice about touching her—so she screamed, "*He* gave gonorrhea to *me*," before the third man—the guy with the dead eyes who drove the black truck—slapped a piece of duct tape over her mouth.

"Punch her lights out if she keeps fighting," he said, and she forced herself to calm down and stop resisting, although God, that was hard to do. Still, she knew that if they hit her hard enough to knock her out, she'd have an even smaller chance of surviving this.

"Tie her up," Dead-Eyes ordered, and one of the men who was holding her must've been carrying a rope, because her arms were forced behind her, and she felt it going around her hands and cutting into her wrists.

Dingo cleared his throat. "We should go," he said. "I'm sure Mr. Nelson's waiting."

Dead-Eyes peeled a few bills off of the wad of cash that Dingo had obviously given him—from Fiona's room. He held it out to Dingo. "Dude, your job is done. You've gone way above and beyond."

Dingo looked affronted. "You're kidding, right? That won't even cover the costs of the walk-in clinic. I spent money on gas and food and . . . No, *dude,* I'm going with you. I'm pretty sure there's a real reward coming, and I'mma make sure Mr. Nelson gives it to *me.*"

And with that, Maddie was sure. Or at least mostly sure. There was no way Dingo would willingly do a face-to-face with Nelson, was there? He was coming along so that he could try to save her, wasn't he?

But when the skinhead pushed her to get her to move faster and she tripped and fell onto her knees, they all laughed, and Dingo laughed, too.

CHAPTER TWENTY-THREE

"Sir, it's not good," Izzy's voice came over the truck's Bluetooth. He, Seagull, Timebomb, and Hans had arrived at the house in Van Nuys.

Pete didn't expect it to be good.

In fact, the news just kept getting worse.

He and Shay had been driving for an hour when Lindsey first phoned to tell them that a 9-1-1 call had come in from the Dingler residence, and that the Van Nuys police had arrived to find the place deserted. There were, however, both signs of a break-in and of some kind of struggle inside of the house.

No one had been able to give them more details—like, was there blood? Had someone been killed, and the body removed? Or had Dingo and Maddie merely broken in themselves, and then had a food fight?

Lindsey tried to make a human connection, but the Van Nuys Police Department was still recovering from a very busy night, and she kept getting put on hold.

Another hour had passed as Pete pushed further west. He was still a good hour away from Van Nuys, but Izzy'd apparently made the trip up from San Diego in record time.

"Izzy, be specific," Shayla said now. "Is there blood or any other evidence that Maddie's been badly hurt?"

"No blood at all," Izzy reported, and Pete breathed for the first time in an hour. "But the bathroom door was kicked in. It's splintered. There was a phone—a landline—in there. I'd bet my retirement fund that's where the nine-one-one call originated. Other than the bathroom door, only thing broken's a pane of glass in the back door—it opens into this little mudroom-slash-laundry-room."

"Is that how Dingo and Maddie got into the house, or . . . ?"

"I'm betting that was our bad guys. I think Team Dingo had a key. We found two big boxes of food in one of the bedrooms with a note—just a simple *I love you*. Looks like a care package for our man Dingo, from his mommy. I'd bet your retirement fund that he uses the house at his mom's invitation, when she and Mean Daddy are away."

"Wait, they're away?" Pete asked. "I thought they were home."

"RV's gone," Izzy said. "So unless the bad guys took it along with both parents, too . . . ? Yeah, I'm not feeling that."

Shayla spoke up again. "Did you find any proof that Maddie was actually there?" she asked. "I mean, we don't know for sure—we're assuming it."

Pete knew she was still hoping that this was a bad coincidence, that LA was a big place, and that they were going to get a text from Maddie asking them to meet at a Starbucks in Hollywood.

"Yeah," Izzy said. "That's the really not-good part of what we found here. There were clothes in the washing machine. And Schlossman is dead certain that the girl-sized jeans and shirt that we found in there are what Maddie was wearing when he talked to her outside of the Seven-Eleven on Tuesday afternoon. And . . ."

"There's an *and*?" Pete asked.

"Seagull and Timebomb searched the immediate area and found this car, next street over. Texting the photo to you, Shay."

Her phone whooshed, and she opened the photo, expanding it to reveal . . .

Pete glanced over.

"That's definitely Dingo's car," Shay told Izzy. "Well, okay, then."

"There's one more thing, sir," Izzy told them, and his voice was unusually somber, "and I'm sorry to have to tell you this, but Lindsey called me and I said I'd pass the bad news along."

"Oh, no," Shay murmured. Somehow she knew—or guessed—what was coming, but Pete had no clue.

"What?" he said. "Jesus, just tell me."

"Daryl Middleton didn't make it," Izzy said. "His head trauma was too severe and, well, he died about a half hour ago."

* * *

Peter's response to the enormous pile of bad news was to drive even faster.

Shayla wasn't sure exactly what he was rushing toward, since they had no idea where Maddie and Dingo had been taken. Their hope of getting information from Daryl had also tragically died with the young man.

And then there was the fact that Maddie had been grabbed by killers. It was bad enough when the bad guys had only been drug dealers and thieves.

"We need to speak to both Dingo's parents and Fiona's mother." Shay had her computer out and open as she attempted to figure out some kind of plan. "Also, let's check to see if any of them—Dingo, Fiona, or Daryl—had police records, see if we can find a connection to anyone in San Diego's underworld."

Pete glanced at her, and she nodded. "I know," she continued, "that sounds so *Batman,* but I'm not sure what else to call it."

"Make a note that we should ask to talk to Fiona directly," he said.

"Yes," she agreed. "I also already sent a text to Tevin and Frank, to put out feelers among their friends. I'm making a list of *anyone* who was seen talking to either Fiona or Maddie. I've also asked Tevin to see what he can find out about where, locally, kids buy drugs. And I've asked Lindsey to check with her contact at the San Diego Police, see if she can get us a list of usual suspects when it comes to drug deals, see if we can find Maddie that way." She squinted at her list. "Oh, and I was also thinking that, when we get to Van Nuys? Maybe I could pull Dingo's mother aside while you're talking to the father?"

The latest plan was to meet Izzy and his "tadpoles" in Van Nuys. A neighbor had had the Dinglers' cellphone number, and while they hadn't been willing to share it, they *had* called about the break-in, and Dingo's parents were heading back home.

Peter glanced at her again. "Yeah, I think I'd rather just get you safely home."

"What? Wait, we're not going to Van Nuys?"

"No, we're going there. But you're going directly home. I'll let Izzy and Seagull take you. Hans and Timebomb'll stay with me, wait for the parents."

"Peter. I'm certain I'll be safe enough in Van Nuys for the duration of a conversation with Dingo's—"

"No," Peter said.

"Excuse me?" she countered.

He looked at her and said it again. "No. And no, I'm not going to pretty it up with a *please, baby.*"

He's completely, totally freaked out that Daryl died.

Shayla took a deep breath and exhaled it slowly. She didn't need Harry's voice in her head to know that.

"Okay," she said.

Peter glanced at her again—clearly she'd surprised him.

"If it makes you feel better, I'll pretend you said *please,* and I'll go with Izzy. But if you want me to be honest, I'd feel safer waiting for you. I mean, isn't it likely that you'll be heading down to San Diego after you talk to the Dinglers? And I have faith in Izzy's abilities—he *is* a Navy SEAL—but . . . I'm not sure he'd, for example, take a bucket of shit for me."

He smiled—but briefly—at that. "Yeah, he would. Because he'd take one for me, and he knows how important you are to me."

"He *thinks* he knows," Shayla corrected him.

"Nope, he knows." He kept his eyes on the road. "As long as I'm laying down orders and ultimatums, I might as well tell you that I'm coming for you. And as long as you're pretending things, you can keep on pretending it's only about the sex in the garage, or in the tent, or in the cheap motel room, or wherever it happens next. Because it's gonna happen again. And again. And again. And it's just gonna keep on being fucking great."

I'm not sure what the right response to that is, Harry said. *Maybe "Thank you"?*

But Peter kept going before she could speak. "But it's not just the sex that's great. It's all of it. All of you. We fit—not just when we're making love. We're fitting right now. This fits. So I'm gonna just keep showing up. I got Lisa to admit that I was an important—and real—part of her life by *not* having sex with her. I'm gonna do the opposite with you. Partly because I think it'll work—if I just keep showing up—but mostly because I can't keep my hands off you. And eventually the pretend-dating thing will turn real, and we'll go places together and sometimes even have sex in our beds. Jesus, that's gonna be good. And I recognize that it might sound crazy for me to say that I'm going to marry you, four days after we met, but I *am* gonna marry you."

Fuuuuuuck, Harry said.

But Peter wasn't done. "Maybe not right away, because our kids might not want to get all Brady Bunched. But I'm okay with long-term plans, and I'm thinking in three years, after we get Frank and Maddie safely off to college, we'll do it, and then go on a honeymoon. So yes, I want you safe while I find Maddie. I'd love for you to help—you've already helped so much with this latest goatfuck, helping me figure out what to do next, and I know you'll continue to be brilliant—but I want you to do that from the safety of your well-guarded home. Your skill sets and mine are *very* different, so . . . I think that's everything I wanted to say—oh, except, I always thought I was broken. I believed Lisa when she said it was all my fault and . . . having you help me write the story, you know, of what happened with her . . . It makes me see it differently, and that's why I think, you know, that I actually might deserve someone as great as you in my life." He nodded. "That's what I wanted to say."

As Shay was sitting there, trying to figure out what to say—*Okay. Please keep showing up?* Or *Yeah, it's definitely batshit crazy to talk about getting married mere days after you meet someone,* or *Are you sure there's not like, three more little words that you might want to add to that whole long speech?*—her phone buzzed with an incoming text.

It was from an unidentified number, sent to both her and Peter's phones, and it was . . . She clicked on the message and looked more closely. "Peter, we just got what looks like a screenshot from an LA area code. It's some kind of GPS tracking app—something called MapMyRun. Oh, my God! I think this is from Dingo." She looked up at Peter. "It starts at the Dingler address in Van Nuys, and it ends at what looks like some kind of industrial complex, in a town called Clarence, just south of Pearblossom, on this side of the mountains. We passed the exit for it, about four miles back!"

* * *

Maddie was terrified.

She was going to die here, in this run-down garage in the middle of nowhere.

She knew that her captors—Dead-Eyes and the skinhead clones—were going to kill her because no one had bothered to cover her head or her eyes during the drive.

At first, she'd thought they were stupid. She was just sitting in the truck's backseat, between the clones, where anyone traveling past them on the freeway could see that her arms were awkwardly positioned behind her back, and that her mouth was covered by a piece of duct tape.

But then she realized the windows were so darkly tinted, and she was so far back from them, that no one could see in.

Instead of heading south to San Diego, they'd gone north, along the same route that she and Dingo had taken from Manzanar. But they didn't go that far—only about an hour, although it seemed like forever.

During the trip, the skinheads and Dead-Eyes had told Dingo that Nelson had another garage out here—and that he was on his way up from San Diego to "deal with the girl." It was only slightly more remote than his garage in San Diego, but there were far fewer problems with noises that might be overheard by neighbors—because there currently weren't any neighbors. The recession had left this garage surrounded by empty buildings, on a dead end that didn't get much traffic.

Dingo had then changed the subject, prattling on about handguns. He was thinking about using his reward money to get himself one. What kind did they have? Did they like it? Could he see?

He sounded like a fanboy, trying to suck up to his personal heroes, and they brushed him off and even mocked him, just like the mean kids in high school.

Maddie had gone back and forth, several thousand times. If he was Good Dingo, he was attempting to get one of them to hand him their gun. At which point he'd use it to free Maddie, steal the truck, and drive to safety.

Or he was Bad Dingo and just another ass-kissing idiot. . . .

They'd pulled up to the garage, and it was as deserted as they'd described.

It was also a piece of shit—it looked as if it was on the verge of falling down. Although the giant garage bay door was working just fine. It went up so Dead-Eyes could pull his truck inside. And it went back down, too.

But as the skinheads pulled her roughly from the truck, she could see bits of blue sky through holes in the roof.

"Over there." Dead-Eyes pointed to a support pillar, and Nelson's minions forced Maddie to sit on the cold floor as they tied her to it.

"Please," she tried to say through the duct tape, "I'm thirsty." But it came out just a series of weird-sounding whimpers, and it made them laugh.

Dingo laughed with them, but he was looking around, scoping out the place with its dirty and cracked concrete floor, and windows that were up along the roofline. There was some kind of partitioned-off area up in the front corner—maybe an office or a waiting room—with a door that hung ajar.

The walls looked like concrete block and they were far more solid-looking up close.

"Where's the loo at?" Dingo asked. "I gotta go piss out

more fahking knives, before Mr. Nelson arrives. It takes me a good ten minutes to stop weeping after the pain."

He was still pushing the gonorrhea story. Only Good Dingo had a reason for doing that. . . .

One of the skinheads pointed toward the back, and Dingo swaggered off in that direction, taking a detour that brought him closer to Maddie. He suddenly lunged at her, feinting a punch to her head.

She recoiled and squeaked in surprise and fear as he laughed and stomped his feet in amusement—but then she realized that he'd dropped something next to her. He now kicked her in the butt—or at least it looked that way. But in reality he was pushing it behind her, so that her hands could close around it—

It was a . . . corkscrew . . . ? Ow! Yes, it was one of the cheap folding kinds. They'd had one in their kitchen, back in Palm Springs. Lisa had loved a glass of red wine after work each night, and nearly always had an open bottle on the counter. The screw itself was pointy, but it was— yes!—the sharp little serrated knife that opened up to help remove the seal and expose the cork that made this a valuable tool for rope removal.

Dingo—Good, *good* Dingo—must've grabbed it from his parents' kitchen on his way out the door.

As he meandered toward the bathroom—still laughing about "frightening" and then "kicking" her, Maddie pretended to cry as she opened up the little blade and got to work, sawing at her bindings.

* * *

According to their GPS, Izzy and his three tadpoles were an hour away.

"More like forty-five minutes," Izzy's voice rumbled through Pete's speakers. "My GPS doesn't drive like a Navy SEAL."

"Just get here as fast as you can," Pete told him, and cut the call. He looked at Shayla. "I hate that you're here. I need to put you someplace safe."

"Hot tip," she told him. "Authoritarian language is *not* a turn-on. I will *go* somewhere safe, you will *not put* me there."

Fuck. "Sorry," he said. "The Navy isn't a democracy, and I'm an officer—"

"And I'm not in the Navy," she said. "I will never be in the Navy, so you will never be in command of me." She paused. "Even after I marry you."

Pete's world shifted as he met Shay's eyes, and he exhaled, hard. He'd been starting to wonder if she'd heard any of what he'd said. And yeah, the timing had been dead wrong. They'd been navigating and surveilling furiously, as well as arranging for backup, ever since Dingo's—had to be Dingo's—text came in.

"Although, hot tip number two, I *do* like to pretend," she added, "so we could—at times—*pretend* that I'm in the Navy. That could really work for me—particularly if I get to be, oh, I don't know, maybe an admiral . . . ? You know, after the garage-sex gets boring."

Pete laughed. "Trust me, the garage-sex will not get boring." Wasn't the inherent nature of garage-sex extremely *not* boring?

"Turn right, here," Shayla ordered, and he took the right. They were attempting to circumnavigate the building where Dingo's "run" had ended, and they'd yet to see what was directly behind it. The cell service was weak out here, and neither one of them was able to access a map with a satellite view of the area, so they were surveilling the old-fashioned way.

According to the info that Dingo had sent, he and Maddie were being held in an old mechanic's garage—a stand-alone concrete block structure with three giant bay doors and a rotting roof. The doors were metal—no windows to look through. In fact, the only windows—at least on the front of the building—were just below the line of the roof. The garage had an ancient gutter system that didn't look very sturdy. If Pete was going to climb up to get a look inside, he'd have to use a different route—clamber up to the roof, and then lean over to look through the windows.

Unless the back of the structure was more accommodating.

But this turn didn't help as they bumped into another dead end. "Fuck!"

"Sorry," Shay said. "The map on the GPS makes it look like the road goes through. Try the next street north."

Pete swiftly turned around—the road, with its odd mix of warehouses and boarded-up shops, wasn't wide enough for a U-ie. He headed back the way they'd come, banged a right, and then another right. And yes, this road went through.

But the back of the garage didn't extend all the way out to this street.

Shayla's phone whooshed and she grabbed for it. "Another text from Dingo," she told Pete. "Whoa, it's a long one."

She read it aloud: *"In danger need help.*

"3 men, at least 3 guns, with their boss, Bob Nelson, on his way w his posse. No idea how many men will be arriving.

"NOW IS TIME.

"If something goes wrong, please tell Maddie I loved her.

"Dear Maddie's father, she read me your story about how you met her mom, and I'm sorry your heart was broke by Lisa, but know this: You and Lisa made someone special. Maddie is everything. She's perfect. Good job. And no, don't be angry, because I know I'm to old, so I said

no. It was hard, but I stood strong. Right now I wish I didn't, because I think I'm gonna die so you can't kill me twice. Ha ha, but no. I love her, so I protected her even from me. Please love her twice as much if I die.

"She acts like she doesn't care but she does. Lisa not perfect, you know this. Life was hard but Maddie love her mom so much and still so sad, missing her. Give her time. Be gentle and kind.

"I know best case means I probably go to jail. That's ok.

"I love her.

"Please come now to help me save her."

"Text him back," Pete said. *"Hang on, on my way."*

"No! It didn't go through," Shay reported. "He blocked you." She tried with her phone. "Me, too. Damnit!" She looked up. "Although it makes sense. He's in there with them—three armed men—probably doesn't want an *On our way* text message to pop up and give him away."

Pete nodded. Dingo had risked a lot just to send those texts. "I'm going in from this end," he said. He pulled off the street into a pitted gravel lot in front of a boarded-up gas station, so he could quickly change out of his bright white uniform while Shay drove.

She was not happy. "I thought the plan was to wait for Izzy and the nicknamed Johns. Who, by the way, are all *cowboyed up*, as per your command. That means they have weapons, right?"

"Yes. And I do, too," he told her. "A Glock, nine millimeter. It's in a lockbox under . . . well, here. Switch seats with me." He got out and went around to the passenger side as she slid behind the wheel. "Drive," he ordered as he closed the door. "Please. Head back to the main road—to that gas station with the convenience store. I want you to wait there. Please."

She shook her head and didn't put the truck into gear. "Are you going to drop me there?"

His lockbox was under his seat, and he quickly keyed in the combination and pulled out the Glock. "No, I want you to have the truck. I'll run back here."

She made a vaguely laughter-like noise as they still sat there. "That's a mile away. At least. Also? You're not exactly dressed for running."

"I'm changing," he said.

"Into what?"

"I keep BDUs and a pair of boots in a go-bag, so I'm always ready, you know, to go."

"It still looks military. You're going to catch attention. Maybe not as much as *me* running, but . . ."

He inserted the magazine, and set the spare in the cupholder. "You ever use one of these?" he asked.

"I'm a writer," she said.

"Yeah, but you write about men—and women—who carry, usually concealed. Everything I've read—so far, at least—is correct, so I'd hoped—"

"Research," Shay admitted. "And fact-checking via experts. I went to a gun range with a group of writers, so yes, I've fired one. Once. I know the basics. Point and squeeze; never point the barrel at anything you don't want to accidentally kill."

He smiled. "Those *are* the basics. I'm putting it into your handbag; it'll be right here on the floor."

"Wait," she said as he began to unbutton his shirt. "What? You're not taking it with you?"

"I'm just going for a quick sneak-and-peek." Pete stripped off his shirt and reached for his go-bag. He pulled on an olive drab T-shirt and then unfastened and pulled off his white uniform pants as he told her, "That's SEAL for surveillance—looking in the windows, seeing what's up. I'm going to trust you to drive over to that convenience store after I get out. Wait there for me to call. Do you understand?"

Her beautiful brown eyes were wide in her expressive face as she nodded. He fastened his cargo pants and reached for his boots, stashing his white shoes in the back.

"I'm trusting you," he said again as he tied his boot laces. "Please note, I am not *putting* you anywhere. But I *am* trusting you to keep to your skill set, okay? If something goes wrong, if you don't hear from me in, say, twenty minutes, call the police. When they arrive, put the weapon back in the lockbox and make sure the latch clicks."

She nodded, but then asked, "And we're not calling the police right now, because . . . ?"

"Because my daughter is in there with three armed men who have killed before," he told her, covering his head with a boonie. The hat would both shade his eyes and keep his fair hair from reflecting the bright sun. "Because I know, absolutely, when Izzy and his guys show up, the five of us will get both Maddie and Dingo safely out of there—after which we'll call the police."

She drew in a deep, shaky breath. "I'm trusting you, too," she told him as he put on his sunglasses and silenced his cellphone, securing it in the front right pocket of his pants.

He got out of the truck and patted his other pockets—he kept them loaded with bungie cords and duct tape, his Ka-Bar dive knife . . . He went into the back of the truck and got a length of blue rope from one of the side pockets of his truck bed—useful to have when climbing, especially for getting back to the ground. He kept it coiled to fit around his neck and one arm, slanting across his chest. He slipped it on and was good to go.

He leaned in to the cab and kissed Shay. "To quote my future son-in-law, Dingo," he said. "Who is less of an idiot than I thought: *You're everything*. And I've had a few more years of experience under my belt, so I know you're not perfect, but you're pretty damn perfect for me. Drive to the convenience store and stay there. Please."

She caught his arm. "Be careful."

He nodded. "I got this."

This time she pulled him in for another kiss—sweet, hot, and over far too soon. But he had to move.

Pete quietly closed the door behind him—but stood there, waiting. Yes, that's right, Shayla. He *was* going to watch her drive away. Stick to your skill set, thank you very much.

The taillights of his truck vanished around the corner, and Pete started across the dusty ground between the former gas station and the warehouse that neighbored it, staying close to the crumbling building as he moved toward the back of the garage where his daughter was being held.

* * *

"What the *fuck*?" Izzy said as they rounded a curve—and hit a wall of red taillights. He jammed on the brakes. "Isn't your GPS app supposed to warn us about shit like this?"

"Major accident ahead," Seagull reported as Izzy swiftly worked his way over to the far right through a chorus of bleating horns. He made it to the shoulder, where he braked to a stop. "Whoa, it's a bad one. It must've *just* happened."

All three of their heads were down as they locked eyes with their phones, searching for an alternate route.

"Schlossman! I need your head up, looking out the back," Izzy ordered as he put the car in reverse. "Eyes on the road! You know those assholes who back up all the way to the last exit? We are now co-presidents of that exclusive club, only we're gonna do it as fast as we fucking can." He stomped on the gas. "Seagull, find us another way there; 'Bomb, I need both hands on the wheel. Use my phone and dial Grunge and Shayla. I need to let them know we're gonna be late, then grab the California map book from the pocket behind my seat, and find out where the fuck we are and how to get to where we want to go, the old-fashioned paper way. Because if our electronics fail us, I do *not* want to be the one to have to tell Grunge that as we sit here with our dicks in our hands!"

* * *

"Be careful"? You had a chance to go big and you chose "Be careful"?

"Shut up, Harry. You're not helping." Shay didn't even try not to say it out loud. With Peter out of the truck, she connected her cell to his truck's Bluetooth, so that she'd be ready and waiting, hands free, when he called.

But as she was driving to the convenience store parking lot, it was Izzy's cell number that suddenly popped onto the screen. She pushed the button and connected the call.

"Are you here?" she asked. "Please say you're at the garage!"

"No, sorry," Izzy shouted over the weirdest whining sound.

"What is that noise?"

"We hit traffic—a bad accident on the freeway. We're rerouting. Best guess is we'll be there in—" he paused "—Fuck. An hour."

"Shit!" But okay, okay. "At least that means this Nelson guy's gonna be slowed down, too."

"Not if he's coming from San Diego," Izzy shouted. "It's a different route."

"Shit!"

"Yeah. Very very big and smelly shit. Is Grunge with you? His phone went right to voicemail."

"No, he's . . . sneaking and peeking."

"Ohhhh."

"What does *that* mean?" Shayla asked.

"Nothing," Izzy said a little too fast. "Just, *Oh*. Like *Oh, okay*."

It means Peter's going to look in those windows and see his daughter tied up and possibly beaten and bloody, Harry said, *and it's going to be hard for him to not take action.*

"Hurry," Shay ordered Izzy.

"Aye, aye, Commander." The call ended.

She was at the traffic light for the main road. The convenience store where Peter wanted her to wait for him was to the left, down about a half mile. The garage where he was doing his sneak-and-peek was around the block to the right.

Shayla took a deep breath, and made the left as she used her phone to call Peter. He needed to know that Izzy and his men were delayed. But just as it had done for Izzy, the call went right to voicemail. She tried again. Same thing. When she pulled into the convenience store lot and parked, she sent Peter a text. *Izzy delayed. Call me. Please.*

It took forever to send, and when she received the *not delivered* message on her phone, she realized that this part of town was in a cellular dead zone. She didn't even have a single bar showing to be able to make a call or send a text.

So she put the truck back in gear and headed toward the garage. Her phone had worked over there.

She'd make contact with Peter and then find another safe place to wait—one *with* cell service.

* * *

The little knife was sharp, but Maddie had to wait for the stupidity trio to not be staring at her in order to saw away at the ropes.

Dingo must've known that, because he kept trying to pull their attention away from her.

"Does this thing work?" he asked as he pushed the button to one of the car lifts, and yes, it worked, and everyone ran over to get him to turn it off.

But now, Dead-Eyes's cellphone rang and he rapidly went from jocular—*Hey, bro, y'almost here?*—to a more subdued *No, sir. No, Mr. Nelson, we didn't. . . . No, sir.* He moved to the back of the room, and as Maddie watched, the skinhead clones exchanged a *Do you know what's up* glance, and then both shook their bald heads before they trailed after Dead-Eyes, trying to listen in.

Go, go, go! Maddie widened her eyes at Dingo, and moved her head in a gesture that she hoped said, *Watch them for me!*

He nodded almost imperceptibly, his eyes narrowing as he looked toward where Dead-Eyes and the clones were now in a huddle after what was apparently a sobering phone call from their fugly asshole boss.

"What the *fuck*!" exclaimed the skinhead with the neck tattoo—he was named Stank. It was definitely Stank—his voice was higher pitched than Eddie-with-the-nose-ring or Dead-Eyes. "He's dead? He's fucking dead? We didn't hit him *that* hard!"

A murmur of lowered voices as Dead-Eyes tried to calm him, then Stank again: "I'm not going to jail for-fucking-ever! No fucking way! Or . . . worse! Yeah, dudes, you know what's going to happen? It's going to be seriously worse!"

More murmurs.

"You just said he's going to be here in thirty fucking minutes! What do you think Nelson's going to do when he arrives, huh? He's going to come in here and he's going to fucking pop us! He's not even going to say hello, just, bang, bullets in our heads. We are so fucking dead!"

More murmurs.

"Yes, he *will*. Because we fucking connect him to the dead guy—Darron or Daryl or whatever the fuck that fuckwad's name was!"

Oh, dear God. Maddie looked up at Dingo, who was frozen there, across the room. "Ding!" she said, but of course it came out "Mmph!"

Still, it was enough to get his attention, and his gaze moved jerkily over to her, and she knew that she'd heard right. Daryl Middleton—Dingo's best friend since seventh grade—had died from his injuries, which meant that these three men had killed him.

That bad news was even worse news for Maddie and Dingo. Because if Stank was right, and Nelson was going to kill him, Eddie, and Dead-Eyes? Nelson was definitely going to kill Maddie and Dingo, too.

CHAPTER TWENTY-FOUR

As Shayla pulled into the same gravel area where Peter had exited the truck, her phone whooshed, rapid-fire, with incoming texts, five times in a row.

She parked, grabbed, and looked—it was Peter. *Trouble connecting with Z,* his text read. *Forward to him.*

He'd sent a series of photos that she immediately messaged on to Izzy Z-for-Zanella. They were of the back of the building—concrete block, nondescript, single window with security bars covering it, single metal door—plus three shots of the interior, taken through one of the windows.

She could see Maddie, duct tape over her mouth, tied to some kind of support pillar.

She could see Dingo, his body language radiating his anxiety.

And the final picture was of the three men that Dingo had told them about in his text, as they huddled together in the back of the room. The body language there was crazy, too. They were definitely freaked out about something.

She texted Peter: *Izzy hit traffic. New ETA about 55 mins.*

The texts went out more quickly if she kept them short,

so she hit *send* and then wrote: *No cell service at convenience store.* Send.

I'm where you dropped me. Send.

Please come back so we can figure out a plan B. Send.

Shayla's phone rang.

"Get out of there." Peter spoke softly and didn't say hello.

"No. I have cell service here. Those photos for Izzy? They're still sending."

"*Fuck.*"

"Peter, we need to figure out—"

"Something's up," he said. "I'm hearing only bits of it, but our three bad guys are worried as fuck about something. I do know their boss—Nelson—will be here in about twenty-five minutes. Figure twenty. We are out of time. Wait, shh! One of them is saying something—I need to listen. . . ."

* * *

As Maddie turned to watch, Stank broke away from Eddie and Dead-Eyes, moving toward her and Dingo. "Our best shot at surviving this is to kill these motherfuckers, right now! He's going to kill them anyway—and if we do it for him—if he gets here, finds them dead, and us gone? He's gonna let us go. It's called détente. He'll know that we won't ever come back, and he won't come looking for us!"

"That's bullshit," Dead-Eyes countered, following him. "He *will* come after us. If we're out there, floating free? He's going to know that the second we hit trouble, the minute we catch a case, we're going to be looking to make a deal."

"*You're* bullshit!" Stank exclaimed. "You're a fucking idiot, Cody! No way are we going to cop to three murders just to make a deal—because that's what we'd have to do. We'd just be screwing ourselves."

"I'm just saying it's fucking idiotic if we kill them and leave," Dead-Eyes—Cody—said. "And do what, then? Go where? I say we kill them—and stay. We show Nelson that we're loyal—and move up in his organization."

"How about if I make a deal?" Dingo called out, his voice thin and reedy in the sudden stillness. "Right now. I'll confess—to the police—to killing Daryl, if you let Maddie go. Right now! Just let her walk out the door!"

"Dingo! No!" Maddie said, but it came out "Mmph! Mmph!"

* * *

Pete could hear Shayla breathing on the other end of the call as he watched through the hole in the roof, as Dingo offered to sacrifice himself for Maddie.

When he'd first climbed up here, he'd secured his length of rope on an ancient antenna that had held his body weight. He'd tested it. And he'd coiled it there, ready to grab-and-go when it was time to slide back down to the ground.

"Hey," he told Shay, as he picked up that rope now, as in the garage below he could see that the three armed bad guys had rejected Dingo's offer. *No deal! No deal!* There was a fuckload of shouting. And when armed idiots got into a raging disagreement, it never ended well. "I think out of everything I told you, I left out the most important part, and that's *I love you*. I didn't want it to go unsaid."

"Peter." Her voice was thick with emotion because, as always, she knew what he was about to say.

"Call nine-one-one, Shay, and then get yourself to safety. Please. I can't wait any longer. I'm going in."

* * *

He cut the connection. Peter had cut the connection!

Shayla sat in his truck, stunned for one second, then two—but then *Do it!*

She didn't need Harry's voice in her head to know that she had to move. Now. Fast.

Instead of hitting the emergency number on her phone, she dialed Lindsey Jenkins's number, even as she put the truck into gear and peeled out of the lot, heading for the road that led to the front of the garage.

* * *

Maddie sawed frantically through the piece of rope that bound her wrists together. She'd made a stupid mistake, and cut through the rope that tied her to the pole, but if she'd done this one first, she would've already been free. Live and learn. Please, God, she wanted to live. . . .

"We're running out of time!" Stank shouted as Dead-Eyes and Eddie argued over whether or not it would work—Dingo confessing to killing his friend Daryl in a crazy drunken fight over some girl. Fiona. Fiona would like that. Fiona was going to love hearing that Maddie and Dingo were dead. Maddie sawed even faster.

"It could work," Eddie said.

"Nelson'll never go for it," Dead-Eyes insisted. "You're deluded if you think he would."

"And you're deluded if you think he's going to walk in here and give you a *good job* sticker for killing the girl. He's going to kill! Us! All!" Stank had reached his limit, and he likewise reached into his jacket and pulled out his gun. With a roar, he turned and aimed it at Maddie.

And she kept sawing at that rope, even though she knew these were her last few moments on earth. Her last effort, her last breath, her last heartbeat.

She wished she'd never sat with Fiona in the stupid cafeteria.

She wished she'd asked her dad for help.

She wished she'd texted him and Shayla back at Manzanar—OK, *yeah, let's meet right now, but hey, heads up, I haven't showered in days, and both Dingo and I smell a little ripe.*

Her father wouldn't have cared.

She wished Lisa had married him, although she knew why her mother hadn't. He'd loved her too much, and that had scared her. He'd been too honest and honorable.

Too much like Dingo, who dove—*"No!"*—to put himself between Maddie and Stank's gun.

The sound of the gunshot was deafening, so much so that she didn't hear the force of the roof being kicked in as a man—holy shit, that was her *father!*—came fast-roping down into the garage like some kind of Marvel superhero.

"Everyone, freeze!" he shouted as he dropped the last few feet onto the concrete floor, and rolled back behind a stack of crates.

Dingo had pushed Stank's gun aside, and the sheer violence of his attack had knocked both of them over and they were tangled together on the floor.

Dead-Eyes and Eddie had both leapt for cover behind Dead-Eyes's truck as Stank scrambled out from beneath Dingo, who was motionless on the floor.

"Dingo!" Maddie tried to say. "Ding!" But he didn't move, and no, no, no, blood was starting to pool beneath him.

"Don't do it! Don't move! Don't make me shoot you!" her dad warned from behind the crates as Stank looked wildly around, from those crates, to the truck that Dead-Eyes and Eddie were crouched behind, to his gun, presumably still beneath Dingo on the floor, to Maddie.

He dove toward Maddie, which meant, of course, her father didn't shoot as Stank put himself behind her as much as he could. He was sweating as he pressed himself against her, and his breath was foul in her face.

"I'm going to kill you," she told him, but of course he

didn't understand because her mouth was still covered with that tape.

"Who the fuck are *you*?" Dead-Eyes shouted as someone pounded on the door at the front of the garage.

"FBI!" a voice shouted. "Open this door! We have the place surrounded! Come out with your hands up!"

* * *

Jesus, that was Shayla at the door!

With the thug named Stank using Maddie as a human shield, and with Dingo possibly bleeding out, Pete knew that shouting "Get back in the truck!" was not going to help the situation. So instead of gnashing his teeth in frustration and fear for Shay's safety, he used the reckless, foolish, selfless gift she'd just handed to him.

"FBI!" he shouted, too. "Weapons on the floor! Back away from the girl! Now!"

* * *

Peter was alive!

Shay had heard that terrifying gunshot, but he was in there, still able to shout, so if he'd been hit at least he wasn't dead.

Yet.

Her heart pounded as she stood outside the door to the garage.

Up against the frame, in case they start shooting and try to blast you straight through the thing. Harry's voice in her head was matter-of-fact. Calm. *It's metal, but who knows if it's reinforced.*

The metal door she was banging on was way off to the right side of the bay doors, in the front of the building, and it had a little window that she'd peeked into when she'd approached, first with a quick bob of her head, and then a longer look. It opened into a small, dark waiting area that was cluttered with boxes and awkwardly stacked furniture, with a cracked-open door that seemed to lead into the main garage.

Peter continued to shout. "You have exactly two minutes before the rest of our team kicks in the door!"

Except there was no team. There was only her. She'd called Lindsey, who'd called the police and the real FBI, and God only knew who-all else, but with Shay's luck, they'd show up, see her holding that gun, and shoot *her*. She should've insisted Peter take his gun, instead of leaving it with her.

Focus on right now. Double-handed grip on that weapon, that's right, be ready for the recoil in case you need to pull the trigger. Just a gentle squeeze. Eyes open, brain on, don't accidentally shoot Peter or Maddie or Dingo. You got this.

No, she didn't.

Stick to your skill set, Peter had said. Rushing in, gun blazing? *Definitely* not her skill set. She had to get this gun to him—somehow.

"I'm the FBI negotiator!" she shouted as she tucked the thing back into her handbag. New plan: Talk her way inside and then throw Peter her bag. "I'm unarmed! Let me in so we can talk!"

Do you know for a fact that this door is locked?

Good question. But surely Peter would've gone in this way, if it was.

Maybe he didn't want to risk being seen by coming around the front. He approached the building from the back, remember? He may not have checked it.

She nodded, and reached to try the knob.

And the unlocked door clicked open.

* * *

Pete heard a clatter from behind the truck. Holy shit, had he—with Shayla's help—actually called their bluff?

And yes, the two men behind the truck were arguing. They were trying to keep their voices down, but he could hear them. So could Stank.

"What the fuck you doing, man?"

"He said to put it down." That was the one called Eddie.

"Don't you fucking dare!" Stank called.

"Kick the weapon over to me!" Pete ordered.

"Kick it over to *me*!" Stank demanded.

"Nobody move! FBI Agent Harriet Parker, Counter-terrorism! You have exactly five seconds to surrender your weapons and agree to a deal, or we will lock you in Guantánamo and you will never get out."

Holy fuck, Shayla had somehow gotten inside. She was standing there, across the room—just inside the shadow-filled doorway of some kind of front office as she continued to talk.

"Kick me your fucking gun!" Stank shouted at the idiots cowering behind the truck.

"The girl you have kidnapped is the daughter of U.S. Navy Admiral Lisa Nakamura," Shayla said, as cool as if she were a real FBI negotiator, "who is connected to the arm of the military that runs Black Ops. She's recently been the target of a terrorist cell, and unless you cooperate immediately, we will assume you are in league with ISIS—"

"Fucking shoot her!" Stank shouted. "Shoot them both! Don't you know they don't have any guns? They're fucking unarmed and you're gonna surrender to *them*?"

Pete stood, too, hoping those idiots would see him as the greatest threat and aim for him instead of Shay. He held his hands positioned as if he had a weapon, because this goatfuck hadn't gotten bad enough—he apparently had to bring pantomime into it, too. "Drop your weapons!" he roared. "*Now!* Shayla, get down!"

But the moment that he stood and she saw him, she

stepped further into the room and flung something at him, hard—her handbag. It came sailing directly at his head.

* * *

As Pete caught Shay's bag, he realized why it was so heavy.

She'd thrown him his handgun.

As he reached into the bag, one of the men behind the truck gave in to Stank's demands, and his weapon came skittering out from under the truck, directly toward Stank. And Maddie.

Who surprised the hell out of him by pulling her hands free from where they'd been tied behind her back.

* * *

Maddie cut through the rope, and her world went into slow-mo.

She pulled her hands free, still clenching Dingo's little corkscrew knife. But as much as she wanted to drive the blade into Stank's throat, she knew it was dull now, so instead she used her elbow to slam him, hard, in the side of his head.

It didn't stop him for long—just long enough for her to kick that weapon out into the middle of the room before he slammed her in the face and she went down in a burst of pain and flashing lights.

* * *

Stank dove for that handgun, so Pete dispatched him with a quick double-pop to the head, right through the bottom of Shayla's handbag.

"Any further questions about whether or not we're armed?" he called to the men behind the truck, as he scooped up that stray weapon and Maddie crawled over to Dingo. It was a rhetorical question, so he didn't wait for a response as in the distance—finally—sirens wailed. "Slide your remaining weapons over here, then get down! On the floor, hands on your head, roll into the middle of the room, where I can see you. Do it! *Now!*"

* * *

The two surviving kidnappers did as Peter said.

"Shay, you okay?" he called, as Shayla emerged from the office, where she'd thrown herself after throwing him her handbag.

"I am. Are you?"

"Yeah. Maddie?"

Shay tried not to look at Stank's very dead body, and instead focus on . . .

Maddie had pulled the duct tape off her mouth, and as she turned Dingo over, her voice shook. "Dad, help me! Please! Dingo's still alive!"

"Shay!" Peter held out one of the guns, gesturing for her to take it. "If they move—at all—shoot them. Kill shots. Double-pops."

That was not even close to her skill set, but it was important that the men she was guarding not know it. So she answered in "Harriet" Parker's cool voice. "With pleasure," she said, then told Maddie as those distant sirens got louder, "An ambulance is on its way."

It was then, as Pete knelt beside Dingo and administered first aid, that Shay's phone rang. She pulled it out of her pocket with her left hand—gun held in her right—to see that it was Izzy.

"We found a shorter route, and we're out front," he said. "I see Grunge's truck, parked kinda willy-nilly, but other than that, the place looks quiet. What do you need us to do?"

"Izzy's here," Shay called to Peter.

"Tell him to come in," he called back.

"Please come in. The door to the right is unlocked. We've secured this part of the garage," she reported, "but we've got a man—Dingo—down, and two prisoners I could use some help guarding. Oh, and I think Nelson—the bad-guy boss—is going to show up in a few minutes."

Izzy had already come inside. "I was gonna say, *What'd we miss,* but this story tells itself."

"Z, help me carry Dingo outside," Pete ordered. "Hans, take over for Shayla. Heads up, we have not yet searched those men for additional weapons. If they move, kill them."

"Aye, aye, sir." With a nod at Shay, the SEAL candidate named Hans took over for her.

She moved toward Maddie, who'd stepped back to let Izzy lift Dingo.

"Timebomb, make sure no one's hiding in any of the back rooms." Peter continued issuing commands as he and Izzy carried Dingo toward the front of the garage—it was clear this was not the first time they'd moved a badly wounded man together. "Seagull, stay close to Maddie and Shay."

But despite the fact that her nose was still bleeding, Maddie strode to the bay door and pushed the button that opened it, so that Izzy and Peter could carry Dingo out more easily.

"Ambulance is here!" Izzy announced.

"Back rooms are clear. The garage is secure!" Timebomb called.

It didn't take the paramedics long to get Dingo onto a stretcher and into the ambulance.

Maddie wanted to ride with him, but there wasn't room. The paramedics were going to need all of the space possible to try to stabilize him—and the girl instinctively knew that wasn't good news.

"We'll follow in the truck, right behind them," Peter promised her.

Shay handed him his keys. "I can stay here, wait for the police."

But Peter shook his head. "Not a chance," he said. "You're coming with Maddie and me. Get into the truck. Z, tell the police we'll talk to them at the hospital."

Shayla didn't argue or even ask for a *please*. She climbed in next to Maddie, who looked at her and said, "You risked your life for me."

Hi, I'm Shayla seemed an inappropriate response, so Shay said, "It seemed like a no-brainer."

Peter glanced at her.

"I had to do what I did," she told him. "When you went to Plan B, I had to improvise." She looked at Maddie. "I love your dad. And since he loves *you* . . ." She shrugged. "Dingo loves you, too. And he's strong."

Peter cleared his throat. "Shay's right. I've seen men survive far worse injuries. Yeah, he's lost a lot of blood, but . . . Dingo's going to be okay."

"You don't really know that," Maddie whispered.

"No, you're right, I don't," he admitted. "But I hope that he'll be okay. And I know for a fact that he's gonna fight hard to stay alive. He's got a lot to live for."

"Sometimes that's not enough," Maddie whispered, and Shayla knew she was thinking about her mother.

"You're right about that, too," Peter agreed quietly. "Sometimes, it's not enough. But loving someone—" he met Shayla's eyes "—and being loved in return is always a good place to start."

As the ambulance pulled away, they were right behind it, just as Peter had promised, all the way to the ER.

CHAPTER TWENTY-FIVE

Pete didn't get a chance to put his arms around Shayla for any length of time until Maddie went into the ladies' room.

"I still can't believe you did that," he said as they stood there in the hospital hallway. "I guess I should've clarified that waiting in the truck applied to Plans A through Double-Z."

"I had to bring you the gun—that you should've taken in there with you in the first place," she told him. "And slinging bullshit? Making stuff up? That *is* my skill set."

"Admiral Lisa Nakamura?" he asked, laughing despite himself. "In charge of Black Ops?"

"I had to say that—in case they decided to Google her and came up blank. I had a whole long backstory," she explained. "You weren't really Maddie's father, you were her secret service protection, code name *Dad*." She kissed him, her eyes soft, adding, "You okay?"

Pete knew that she was thinking about the man he'd shot and killed. "I am," he said. "That probably seems strange to you. But he was a threat, and . . . I won't lose sleep over him. I'm happy to talk about it, later, if you want."

"I might want to," she said.

He nodded. "Okay." He glanced at the bathroom door. "We have maybe two minutes before Maddie comes back out, and I just wanted to say . . . Well, you scared the living fuck out of me, but I know why you did it, and . . . I love you, but Jesus, please, let's never do that again."

She nodded, too. "I definitely prefer limiting our hands-on action-adventure to our attempts to mythbust my love scenes."

Pete smiled and pulled her close.

The bathroom door opened, and they sprang apart as Maddie came out, grim-faced and eager for news about Dingo. "Anything?" she asked.

"Not yet," Shayla answered.

Maddie's face tightened, but she didn't cry. "How long does emergency surgery take? Is this normal? Why am I asking? You don't know. I'm sorry. I'm . . ." She stomped away, but then turned back to glare at Pete. "You know, you *can* kiss her in front of me. She's pretty freaking badass, and you might want to make sure she feels appreciated."

As Maddie stomped back to the waiting area, Pete kissed Shay, as ordered.

"Come on." She tugged him back toward the waiting room. "Maddie needs her dad."

* * *

"Dark blue sedan—doing a pretty panicked U-turn at the sight of all those emergency vehicles and police cruisers." Hans Schlossman's voice came in over the speaker on Izzy's phone. The tadpole was up on the roof of a building not far from the dilapidated garage where Maddie'd been held captive. "They're heading to you."

The police were still busy collecting evidence and locking down the crime scene, so Izzy had gotten permission—well, in truth it had been permission-ish—from one of the detectives to put Boat Squad John to work, watching and waiting for Bob Nelson, the scumbag druglord responsible for most of the pain of the past few days.

Grunge had reported that the man plus an unknown number of minions were on their way.

In the spirit of making sure that trouble wasn't about to follow Maddie and Dingo back home to San Diego, Izzy and the boyz decided to put their talents to use to tie up that particular loose end.

"You copy that, Gull?" Izzy asked Seagull. In lieu of headsets, they'd tied their cellphones together via conference call. Whatever worked. "Seatbelt on."

"I'm ready," the kid said from behind the wheel of Izzy's car.

"D'ja get a head count in the sedan, Schloss?" Timebomb asked Hans from his position across the street.

"Two," Hans reported. "Both in the front of the vehicle. Plus, the plates match the info Lindsey gave us. It's definitely Bob Nelson. Or at least his car. I'm coming down."

"Excellent, and here we go," Izzy said as the blue sedan in question appeared, coming around the corner and moving much too fast considering the size of the street and the industrial neighborhood. Fortunately, there was no other traffic.

Except for Seagull, who pulled Izzy's car directly in front of the sedan in an impromptu roadblock.

Brakes squealed and the sedan skidded to a near-violent stop, but before the driver could throw the car into reverse, Izzy was at the driver's side window, tap-tap-tapping on it with the barrel of his handgun.

Timebomb was on the other side, weapon up and aimed, as Seagull similarly advanced from the front. They were both young, but their war faces were impressively fierce.

"Bob Nelson?" Izzy asked, first of the driver—another skinhead like the guys back at the garage—and then of the passenger, older and puffy and wild-eyed, and ordering the driver to *move, move!* He was definitely Nelson.

But the driver, wisely, had his hands up in clear view as Hans Schlossman came running toward them, followed by a group of detectives and uniformed police officers.

"Go to jail," Izzy told Nelson. "Go directly to jail. Do not pass go, do not collect two hundred dollars."

The detective who'd granted him that permission-ish-ness was incredulous as she approached. "I said you could *watch* for him," she said. "What the hell is this?"

"This *is* watching," Izzy said, stepping back to give the uni-ed officers access. One of them immediately began to Miranda the pair. *You have the right to remain silent. . . .* "We found him, and now we're watching him. You're welcome."

"They're Navy SEALs," one of the other detectives said, as if that explained everything.

"Let's go, guys," Izzy told Boat Squad John. "I promised you pancakes, and I *will* now deliver."

* * *

Dingo was going to make it.

Maddie hadn't let herself cry—not in the garage when she'd been certain she was going to die. Not when Dingo had gotten himself shot to save her. Not when Stank had broken her nose. Not even when the doctor had examined her here in the hospital, even though that had hurt worse than getting punched.

But after hours of sitting and waiting for Dingo to come out of surgery, after talking, endlessly, to the police and telling them the same story over and over and over—both the story of Fiona framing Maddie for the money she'd stolen from Nelson, *and* what had gone down today in Nelson's garage—when the good news finally came, Maddie dissolved into tears of relief.

Dingo was still in intensive care, and would be for a while, but the bullet had missed his spine, and the doctors expected him to make a full recovery.

And then, when Shayla showed her that text that Dingo had sent to her and Dad, in case he died . . .

Maddie didn't think she'd ever stop crying again.

It was then, while she was sobbing uncontrollably, that she had a number of awkward conversations.

One started with her telling her father, "I'm so sorry that I didn't come to you for help. . . ." She was sincere while she groveled about that, but she *might've* been a *touch* calculating when she then segued into "I know he's too old for me, but after he's out of the hospital, can Dingo come over for dinner, so you could maybe get to know him, and so that both of us can get to know you—and Shayla, too?"

Not much he could say to that, besides *Yes.*

Although, he also wasn't fooled. He knew exactly what she was up to. But that was okay. She knew what he was up to with Shayla. Maddie could tell, just from the way they smiled when they were together, and the intensity with which they hugged each other, that they were in love. And that was good. She'd wished Lisa had found someone worthy, but her mom had been terminally attracted to assholes— which was probably proof that Dad wasn't one.

It was during that weepy period that he apologized again for not being around for her when she was growing up. He got a little teary-eyed about that himself, which got her weeping again. But then he suggested moving back to Palm Springs so she could finish up high school there, and Maddie was so aghast that she stopped crying and just stared at him.

"I hated Palm Springs," she said. "Why would I want to go back? I mean, yeah, I want to visit Grandma every few weeks, and you know, maybe we can give Aunt Hiroko a ride, too? It's hard for her to get there, because she doesn't like to drive at night."

That conversation moved on to a different topic pretty quickly, and it wasn't until later that Maddie realized exactly what her father had offered her. If they moved to Palm Springs, he would have to leave the Navy and stop being a SEAL. Not only that, he'd have to move away from Shayla, whose sons went to high school in San Diego.

That was crazy.

But he was ready to do that.

For her.

Shortly after that, Dingo's mom and dad arrived at the hospital. And because they were his parents, they were allowed to go into the ICU to see him. It was clear that Dingo's mom loved him—she called him Ricky—and she insisted that Maddie be allowed in to see him, too.

And as they walked down the hall to Dingo's room, his asshole dad cleared his throat and said, "Pretty girl like you could do better than Richard."

Maddie looked at him. He didn't scare her. "When's the last time *you* took a bullet for someone? Or fast-roped or even just walked into a room of angry gunmen?" she added, thinking not just of Dingo, but also of Dad and Shayla.

He didn't answer. Because, yeah, his silent *never* was *exactly* what she'd thought.

And then nothing else mattered, because she got to sit and hold Dingo's hand while machines beeped and whirred around them.

Maddie had no idea what the future would bring—only that Dingo was alive, and she was, too, and they were going to be okay.

What was it her father had said, back in the truck?

Loving someone, and being loved in return, was a *very* good place to start.

EPILOGUE

One year later

Shayla was writing again.

In fact, she was on fire.

Peter had tried to take credit, and yeah, having him in her life was a very, very, *very* good thing. In so many ways.

She'd also been inspired by talking to Hiroko and visiting Manzanar. There were important stories yet to tell.

But really, if Shay had to point to just one thing that had, as Peter suggested, "made her heart grow back," that thing was probably Dingo, and the way he'd been willing to sacrifice everything—including his life—for Maddie. And yes, he was still too old for the girl, but that wouldn't last forever. In a few years—which would pass even more quickly now that he'd enlisted in the Marines—the age difference would be no big deal. Until then, promises had been made, and threats had been issued, and chaperones were permanently on standby for his rare visits home.

Bottom line, it was one thing for a Navy SEAL to be a hero. It was, as Peter would say, part of his *skill set*. But it was another thing completely when someone who had been somewhat morally challenged stepped up and went above and beyond.

Shayla had taken a screenshot of Dingo's epic text, printed it out, and pinned it to her office bulletin board, typos and all.

She couldn't read his words without getting misty-eyed and feeling her heart—still—growing bigger and stronger.

She was close to the end of writing her second book since "the garage."

That's what they called it.

"The garage."

And while Maddie and Tevin and Frank, along with the many, many SEALs and friends who knew what had happened, believed that "the garage" referred to a local former—now incarcerated—druglord's property in the little town of Clarence, California, Shayla and Peter both knew otherwise.

And yeah, okay, Izzy probably knew what they really meant when they talked about "the garage," especially when they smiled at each other. But Izzy would never tell. He was a good friend, and doubly delirious these days because his wife Eden was happily pregnant and about to—his word—pop.

Life was good—even with Tevin off at college. His father's son, he'd gotten into Berklee College of Music in Boston. It was far away, but it was where he belonged.

Tiffany had finally left Carter and was now dating a SEAL—smart young woman that she was. And, no, Shay's old friend Kate still hadn't left her douchebag husband, but maybe someday she would.

Anything was possible.

Shay's phone whooshed as a text came in. She normally silenced it completely when she was writing, but Peter had been away with SEAL Team Sixteen for the past few weeks, and . . .

She looked, and yes, the text was from him.

Hello.

Shayla laughed and saved her document, then went to meet her Navy SEAL and properly welcome him home.

Dear Reader,

Thank you so much for spending your precious reading time with Shayla, Pete, and me. In our amazing, busy, connected lives, there are endless options for entertainment, and I appreciate that you chose *Some Kind of Hero*.

If you enjoyed this story, please do me a huge-large (as Izzy would say!) and take a few moments to post some stars or a brief review at your favorite online bookseller's website. In this noisy, crazy, static-filled world, authors need public feedback from readers more than ever. I appreciate it, too, when you share, post, tweet, and talk about this book and the entire Troubleshooters series! (Thank you!)

In case you missed it, the legend of Boat Squad John is told—partly via Izzy Zanella's irreverent point of view—in my Troubleshooters novella *Ready to Roll*. Pete (or Lieutenant Greene, as he's known by his SEAL candidates) is also introduced in that story, which is set in San Diego just a few months before *Some Kind of Hero*.

Ready to Roll is the third in a trilogy of connected Troubleshooters stories that starts with *Free Fall* and continues in *Home Fire Inferno*. Find out more at SuzanneBrockmann .com or sign up for my e-newsletter at tinyletter.com/Suzanne Brockmann to get the latest news about releases and appearances!

Thank you again!

Yours in love, laughter, peace, and hope,

Suz Brockmann

ACKNOWLEDGMENTS

As always, I must thank my brilliant editor at Random House, Shauna Summers. Shauna has been by my side for almost every single Troubleshooters book, starting way back at the beginning of the series with *The Unsung Hero*. She was particularly patient with *Some Kind of Hero,* since although it didn't take me very long to write this book, it took me several years to discover that Pete's and Shayla's was the story that I needed to tell.

Thanks, too, to the entire team at Random House and to the team at Blackstone Audio.

My deepest appreciation goes out to my family, particularly to my husband, Ed; my parents, Fred and Lee Brockmann; my daughter, Melanie, and my grandson, Aidan; and my son, Jason, and his new husband, Matt. (Jason got married to the most wonderful guy! Pictures are on my Facebook page!) Thanks, also, to Bill, Jodie, and Elizabeth. I love you guys!

Special thanks to Katherine Clements, Naomi Litrownik, and Dr. Isabel Legarda. Without your support, wisdom, and kindness, this book would not have been written.